The Desperate Bride's Diet Club

Sherlock enjoyed reading and writing stories
n early age. However, she assumed that being
hor didn't count as a proper job so when Alison
up, she worked as a secretary, training admin-
r and answered an IT hotline. Once older and
wiser, she realised that she really had to write
ovel. So she gave up office life to sit at home and
at what she had done. To fund her dream, Alison
me a cleaner, the experience of which she has used
t er second novel. A chance meeting with a liter-
gent at Winchester Writers' Conference set her on
oad to publication. Alison lives in Surrey with her
and Dave and Harry, their daft golden retriever.
— is her first book.

can follow her on twitter – @alisonsherlock – and
ok.

The Desperate Bride's Diet Club

ALISON SHERLOCK

arrow books

Published by Arrow 2012

10 9 8 7 6 5 4 3 2

Copyright © Alison Sherlock 2012

First published in Great Britain in 2011 by Arrow
20 Vauxhall Bridge Road
London, SW1V 2SA

An imprint of The Random House Group Limited

www.randomhouse.co.uk
www.prefacepublishing.co.uk

Addresses for companies within The Random House Group
Limited can be found at www.randomhouse.co.uk

The Random House Group Limited Reg. No. 954009

A CIP catalogue record for this book is available from
the British Library

ISBN 978 0 09956 2368

The Random House Group Limited supports The Forest
Stewardship Council (FSC), the leading international forest
certification organisation. Our books carrying the FSC label are printed
on FSC® certified paper. FSC is the only forest certification scheme
endorsed by the leading environmental organisations, including
Greenpeace. Our paper procurement policy can be found at
www.randomhouse.co.uk/environment

	Peterborough City Council	
60000 0000 61841		
Askews & Holts	Apr-2012
		£6.99

Typeset in Palatino by Palimpsest Book Production Limited,
Falkirk, Stirlingshire

Printed and bound by CPI Group
(UK) Ltd, Croydon, CR0 4YY

This book is dedicated to my wonderful mum,
Jean Sherlock.
Forever missed, never forgotten.

Acknowledgements

Special thanks must go to my fantastic agent Judith Murdoch whose support and belief in my work has been invaluable. I couldn't have got this far without her.

A huge thank you to my wonderful editor Rosie de Courcy whose enthusiasm and vision was so important to this book. Thank you to all at Random House who have contributed to this book, especially Nicola Taplin for guiding me through the first book process with such patience!

Thanks to everyone at the Romantic Novelists Association for their advice and wisdom – and for throwing wonderful parties!

Thanks to all my friends, both old and new, for their endless support. Special thanks to Jo Botelle for bravely reading every story I have ever written and for two decades of friendship and cakes.

Thanks to my lovely family for their encouragement over the long years to publication, especially my beloved Aunty Vera and my lovely sister Gill Collins for their constant strength and support.

Thanks to my father Ray Sherlock for not trying to change my mind when I said I wanted to write a novel. Your encouragement has brought me to this amazing place in my life.

Thanks to Ross, Lee and Cara Maidens for letting me into your lives and bringing me so much happiness. I hope you all know how much you mean to me. And for Kelly and Sian Maidens for their friendship.

Finally, thanks to my husband Dave for encouraging me to keep writing, even when times were tough. For believing in me. For everything, including bringing Harry into our lives!

Chapter One

Hell hath no fury like a woman without chocolate cake.

And not just any cake. Marks & Spencer's Double Chocolate Gateau. Chocolate sponge filled with chocolate cream, topped with soft chocolate icing and smothered in chocolate shavings. That would stem the tears and stop the pain. It would help. It had always helped.

And Violet Saunders had to have it. Right now.

She rushed through the aisles, the tears beginning to crust on her cheeks from the cold air in the food hall. She cannoned into people, stepping on their feet, and elbowed them out of the way. Violet didn't care. She just wanted her cake.

She crashed to a halt in the bakery aisle. Standing in front of her was one of the most handsome men that Violet had ever seen.

But it wasn't his rugged face that made her pulse race as she stared up at him. Nor the broad shoulders, tapering down to long legs. Even his wavy black hair didn't make her fingers itch to run through it.

Violet wasn't interested in the handsome man at all. She was only concerned about his hands, which were holding the boxed double chocolate gateau. She glanced away to the empty shelf and then back to the stranger's hands. There were no double chocolate cakes left. None except the one in the hands of the man in front of her.

They looked at each other for a moment.

'That's mine,' Violet blurted out, ignoring the inner mortification at her words.

He shrugged his shoulders. 'Finders keepers.'

Then he broke into a smile. And the edge of sanity that she had been teetering on gave way.

'Mine!' Violet wailed into his face, before snatching the cake box out of his hands and running off to the far end of the shop without looking back. She threw her money at the cashier and rushed out.

She kept going, not caring about the spring rain that soaked her as she ran. It was a dark, dismal day and suited her mood perfectly. Finally she reached the car park and rushed blindly across, not caring about the cars that had to brake hard to miss her.

She found her car, slid behind the wheel and put the keys in the ignition. The car started with a vroom but Violet wasn't going anywhere. She needed her fix.

Violet tore open the box and grabbed a lump of chocolate cake with her hands before cramming it into her mouth. Sweet, wonderful, comforting chocolate. The tears had begun again. But the salty taste didn't diminish the chocolate. In a funny way, it made the cake taste even better.

She snatched at another piece of cake and then another. Shoving it into her mouth, she could feel her pulse starting to slow, the hurt beginning to heal.

Two-thirds of the way through the cake, she became

aware that someone was standing next to the car. A traffic warden was staring in at Violet through the windscreen, his mouth wide open. If that was an invitation to share the cake with him, he was going to be unlucky.

Violet quickly threw the car into gear and sped out of the car park. At every red traffic light and roundabout, she stuffed more cake into her mouth. Every last crumb, every glorious piece of icing. More and more until there was no cake left.

She parked the car outside her house and stumbled up the front path, clutching the empty cake box in her hands. Once through the door, she shut it behind her and slid down the wall in the hallway. Sitting on the floor, she realised her whole body was shaking. With a sob, Violet remembered the traffic warden's horrified face. And the man in the food hall whose cake she had stolen. Violet began to cry again.

The phone rang on the little table nearby, making her jump. But she didn't move. She stayed on the floor, the despair welling inside.

The phone rang six times before the answerphone clicked on. She knew it would be Sebastian. 'Violet? Are you there? Pick up if you are.' A little sigh whilst he paused. 'Look, I told you that girl didn't mean anything. I was drunk and so was she. I'm not proud of myself. You've got to believe me. She's an idiot. She's nothing. Call me, OK?'

The phone clicked off, leaving only silence. Violet's sugar rush quickly turned to nausea and she realised she was going to be sick. She grabbed the radiator and hauled herself to a standing position.

She was about to stagger upstairs to the bathroom when she caught her reflection in the small hallway

3

mirror. The nausea died in her throat as she watched herself take a deep breath.

Violet looked a mess. She had smears of chocolate across her face and down her shirt. The shirt was missing a button, having given way against the strain of cleavage. She was already a size twenty. Was she now going up to a size twenty-two? Her blue eyes were red and wild-looking. Her long, black hair was lank and greasy, flopping against her fat cheeks and thankfully covering up the rest of her pale face.

She was disgusting. Ugly. Fat. Horrible. She watched her reflection as a new tear trickled down her cheek. It was her fault that Sebastian had slept with someone else. Why wouldn't he? Just look at her.

Violet shook her head at her twin in the mirror. Did she really want to go through life feeling like this? She'd had twenty-nine years so far but enough was enough. She knew she was lucky Sebastian still wanted her. That anyone wanted her. She had to lose weight. Otherwise she would lose Sebastian for good.

She loved him so much. Her life was empty without him. She had nothing else to love, nothing but him. When he took her in his arms, she was safe. Whatever he had done, whatever he was, she was his girl and that was all she had to hold on to.

Violet hung her head in misery. The abandoned cake box caught her eye. Serves twelve, it said on the cover. Twelve normal people or one fat porker like me, she thought.

She leant down and picked up the box, as well as the post that lay on the doormat. It was all junk including a flimsy bit of pink paper. But she stared at it and let everything else fall back to the floor.

'A New You!' screamed the words on the leaflet.

4

'Join Us! Lose Weight! Get Fit!' It was an advert for some kind of diet club, which would be held the following Tuesday at a nearby church hall.

A New You! That was exactly what Violet needed. A brand-new me, she thought.

Because the old one was dying inside.

Chapter Two

Maggie Walsh put the plate and knife in the dishwasher. Then she shoved the five empty crisp packets as far down the kitchen bin as possible so that they were hidden under more healthy debris. Like the melon that had gone off. Ditto the shrivelled grapes.

She rubbed her back as she straightened up, feeling older than her fifty-one years. A quick glance at her reflection in the back door told her that she looked older too. That new haircut hadn't helped. Her blond shoulder-length hair had been cut way too short and her waves had sprung into tight curls around her ears.

Maggie turned towards the kitchen counter to switch off the radio but her hand hovered over the switch as a new song came on. It was an old favourite, Tavares singing 'Heaven Must Be Missing an Angel'.

Maggie allowed herself a little giggle and kicked off her slippers. She began to shuffle around the kitchen floor, her pop socks slipping on the laminated wood. She huffed and puffed as she tried to keep her samba dancing in time to the beat. But it was no good. After

6

only half a minute, she came to an abrupt halt, holding on to the side of the sink as she fought for breath.

'Heaven's missing a bloody lard arse,' she panted, feeling her pulse racing.

She staggered into the lounge to find her slippers. She was retrieving one from next to the sideboard when a photograph caught her eye. It was Maggie and Gordon, her husband, quickstepping around the dance floor.

Maggie picked up the frame and peered at the faded photograph. When had it been taken? Sometime in the early eighties? They looked to be in their early twenties, sparkling under the lights in the dancing outfits that his mother had made for them. That red dress was one of her favourites.

Maggie looked closer. Had she ever really been that slim? It was hard to imagine now, especially wearing a dress with only thin straps over the shoulders. She needed a bra made out of scaffolding these days to hold up her heavy chest. She was wearing heels too, something that Maggie hadn't done in many years. Maintaining the heavy load on spindly heels put just too much pressure on her knees and ankles.

She and Gordon must have been so fit as well, dancing twice a week. No wonder they looked happy. Of course, this was before marriage, mortgage and a daughter. It all seemed a very long time ago.

She trudged up the stairs to fetch a pile of ironing and had a sudden thought. She went into the spare bedroom and rummaged around in the suitcases that were hidden in the wardrobe. A couple were empty, well used on many sunny holidays. But it was the old battered brown case at the back that she was interested in.

She finally found the handle and pulled hard. The case came free and she dumped it on the bed, out of breath from the exertion. Then she opened up the case. There were pamphlets from various dance competitions. Gordon's velvet jacket and frilly shirt. A lace shawl. Gordon's trousers. A net underskirt . . .

At the very bottom lay her red dress. As she pulled it out, she caught a faint trace of perfume mixed with cigarette smoke. The embroidered crystals sparkled in the morning light against the deep red of the silk skirt. It was as beautiful as she remembered.

The rest of her dresses were up in the loft, buried under the Christmas decorations and boxes of old toys and rubbish. But she hadn't had the heart to send her favourite dancing dress into the oblivion of the attic.

Maggie held it up against her in front of the full-length mirror. For a second, she allowed herself to be back on the dance floor, Gordon leading her round and around. She clutched hold of the dress, swaying from side to side.

Then reality came into focus. She looked more like an aged Shirley Temple with those curls. And as for the rest of her – she was enormous. At some point her boobs and stomach had merged into one big, jellified mass. She couldn't possibly get the dress on now. It was about a third of the size she was these days. It probably wouldn't get past her knees.

Maggie shook her head as she put the dress back in the case, firmly closing the lid and shutting both it and the memories deep at the back of the wardrobe. She knew it was her own fault. She'd gained weight with her pregnancy and had never lost it. In fact, the weight had increased year by year. Each new season, she found her clothes from the year before were a little tighter, not quite so comfortable to wear. But instead of doing something about her growing weight, Maggie just bought new clothes instead.

She picked up the ironing and went back downstairs. She knew Gordon didn't realise how she felt about her middle-aged spread. He had always maintained that she was gorgeous. And after twenty-five years of marriage, she believed him. Sort of.

'I like my woman to have a bit of meat on her bones,' was Gordon's favourite saying. Trouble was, she had a sackload of potatoes and Yorkshire puddings to go with all that meat.

Maggie hadn't felt gorgeous for a very long time. She was fat and bored, with herself and with her life. It really wasn't fair. Gordon's belly was busting out of his trousers yet he seemed to be convinced that he was fine.

Maggie trudged into the lounge and stood next to the ironing board, sighing at the huge mound of clothes next to her. Most of them were Lucy's. She didn't know how long her daughter wore them for. Was it possible that she changed her outfits between meals?

Maggie sighed and picked up yet another Primark top. She caught sight of the label and felt sad. 'Size 16–18', she read. Lucy had inherited her parents' fat genes. But at least Maggie knew that her daughter was happy with her size.

Maggie was miserable and didn't have a clue what to do about it.

Lucy Walsh panicked when she saw the group of girls at the end of the street. It would be too obvious to cross to the other side of the road so she had to carry on along the same pavement.

She wished it had carried on raining, then she could have hidden underneath her umbrella. But the sun had come out from behind the clouds. Besides, she knew no umbrella would cover her enormous stomach and bottom.

She tried to maintain a sense of fashion, despite her size, which was currently a generous size sixteen – or a size eighteen if nobody was looking. A long black jumper, which she had modified with shoulder pads and fake rhinestones, hung down beyond her thighs, which were encased in black leggings. She hated her Ugg boots but couldn't get any knee-length boots to fit over her calves. An oversized black Puffa jacket completed the look.

Lucy knew it would have looked great on Kate Moss but felt as if she was wearing a duvet and hence seemed even bigger.

Everything was black. Lucy's clothes were always black. She knew it made her look like a Goth but she hoped they might make her disappear altogether – because then nobody would see the size she really was. And if she couldn't be seen, then they couldn't say anything about her, to her. She never wanted to draw attention to herself.

She was getting closer to the group. Lucy tried not to panic when she realised that Nicola Bowles was with the other girls. Nicola had made Lucy's life a misery at school with the taunts, the sneers and the laughter.

Lucy had been fine until she'd reached thirteen and then her body had just expanded overnight. It hadn't stopped until she was the heaviest in her class. And that included the boys. PE was the worst. How did they expect her to climb ropes or bounce on a trampoline? She could hear the laughter now.

It was the same laughter greeting her on the street corner right now.

'Oy! Fatty!' called Nicola.

Lucy put her head down and kept walking. But she came to an abrupt halt when the girls stood in her way.

'I'm speaking to you,' sneered Nicola. 'Don't you recognise your name, Fatty?'

Lucy moved to go around her, having to walk on the road to do so.

'No boyfriend, Fatty?' called Nicola from behind her. 'Never been laid?'

The girls were all giggling.

'Who'd sleep with that?' someone said.

Lucy kept on walking, striding out until she was around the corner and far down the road. She hated that her eyes were stinging with tears. She hated that she could feel her fat arse wobbling as she tried to walk quickly.

Most of all, she hated that Nicola could still taunt her, even though they hadn't been at school for two years. Lucy had gone to college and was loving her fashion-design class. Nicola had gone straight to benefits and standing around doing nothing all day on street corners. But Nicola was still superior, still had the upper edge.

What Lucy hated most of all was the fact that she secretly admired Nicola for being so slim. If they could just invent a body swap then Lucy would be overjoyed. With Nicola's body and Lucy's personality, she could go places, have a future. But all the time she was fat, she was nothing. Would continue to be nothing.

Feeling miserable, Lucy stomped through the front door to her home and up the stairs.

'You all right, love?' asked her mum, who was stationed in front of the ironing board with *Midsomer Murders* on the TV.

'I'm fine,' said Lucy through clenched teeth before slamming the door to her bedroom shut and bouncing on to the bed.

It didn't matter. Nicola Bowles was a nobody. A thickie with no future. Lucy was going to be a fashion designer. A famous, fabulous fashion designer. Preferably a thin one, as well.

She lay back on her bed, thinking about what one of the girls had said about nobody wanting to sleep with her. Actually, they were wrong. She had lost her virginity the previous summer.

A guy from college called Robert had taken her to see *Eclipse* at the cinema. Lucy had watched the movie and hoped for a big romance. What she got in return was a quick fumble on the back seat of her dad's Nissan when she drove Robert home and a lot of unanswered texts.

Lucy knew what his problem was. She was the classic fat, easy lay.

She sat up and glanced at herself in the mirror. It was a good thing she had some clue about fashion. It meant she could disguise her large body with trendy clothes. Trouble was, as soon as she stripped off, all the rolls of fat would appear.

Her brown hair was all right. At the minute it had been straightened but Lucy thought it made her round face look huge. She had a few spots from her poor diet but at least she didn't have as many as Nicola Bowles, who had loads across her forehead and chin.

With a sigh, she reached into her handbag and drew

out the Mars bar. She scowled at it, the enemy. But she savoured every last, glorious mouthful.

Then she felt miserable once more.

Edward Conley shuffled in his seat. You would have thought that they would make the chairs in a doctor's waiting room more comfortable. And bigger. At 6 feet 3 inches, it was like sitting on a child's seat. And at twenty stone, he was oozing off the sides as well.

He rubbed his chest. He'd been practising in the cricket nets at the weekend so perhaps he'd pulled something. Whatever it was, the pain was keeping him awake at night and his work was suffering during the day. He'd nearly fallen asleep in a meeting that afternoon.

He caught the eye of a pretty woman sitting opposite him. She gave him a brief smile and then looked away. Edward knew he wasn't bad-looking. OK, so he was a bit overweight, but he still had all his own hair, unlike Tom from the cricket club, who was in his mid-twenties and already very thin on top. Edward ran his hand through his short brown hair, grateful that he was thirty but not bald.

Edward's name was called over the tannoy. As he got up, he attempted to catch the woman's eye once more but she was deeply engrossed in her magazine. Maybe he could strike up a conversation if she was there when he left.

'Hello, Edward,' said Dr Gillespie, smiling at him as he went through the door. 'What can I do for you today?'

She was gorgeous but completely out of his league. Not that Edward was unlucky with women. It was just that as he headed towards thirty, what he really wanted to find was 'the one'. She hadn't turned up yet.

'I think I've pulled something in my chest,' he told her as he sat down. 'The pain comes and goes but it's mostly at night. I played cricket at the weekend so maybe it was something I did then.'

She nodded before getting him to reach across his back with his arms.

'Any pain now?' she asked.

'Not at the minute.'

'Let's do a few other checks, shall we?'

She took his blood pressure before asking him to stand on the scales. Edward waited for the inevitable prescription for anti-inflammatory pills and two weeks' rest from the cricket nets.

'I'm afraid it's not a muscle pull,' the doctor told him. 'Your blood pressure is dangerously high. You're twenty-one stone, Edward. That's morbidly obese.'

Edward sank back in his chair. He was shocked. His weight had crept up by another stone.

'But I play cricket,' he spluttered. 'I'm not a couch potato.'

Edward didn't add that he was normally stuck out on the boundary because he wasn't up to leaping around the wicket. He couldn't run or leap at all these days.

'Do you run? Work out?' she asked.

Edward shook his head.

'The additional weight is far too much for your body to cope with. Your pulse is racing to keep up and it's causing your chest pains.'

Edward was speechless. He ought to have known this. He should have realised. It wasn't as if he was stupid.

'Do you have a healthy diet?'

'I try,' he replied.

He blushed at the lie. He hadn't eaten well since moving out of home four years previously. Away from his mother's large but relatively healthy meals, as a bachelor his diet consisted of vast amounts of toast, pot noodles and takeaways. The weight had piled on in the years since.'You must lose weight,' the doctor told him.

'And if I don't?' he asked. He had to know.

She shrugged her shoulders. 'Tablets for high blood pressure. And for what I'm presuming will be a high cholesterol count. Maybe treatment for diabetes as well. If all that doesn't help, perhaps a small stroke will follow. Do you want to guess the rest?'

A sharp intake of breath was his only reply.

'At six foot three, you should weigh around thirteen stone. If you need help, there's a number of weight-loss classes in the area. Try one of those.' She gave him a sympathetic smile. 'I really don't want to have to give you one of my frequent-visitor passes.'

Edward staggered out of the doctor's surgery in a daze, the attractive woman in the waiting room all but forgotten. This was the last thing he needed. He had a stressful job and a busy social life. He didn't have time to be healthy as well.

As usual for a Thursday night, he bought himself takeaway fish and chips on the way home. But this time, he only had regular chips instead of his normal large portion and he chose a Diet Coke. That was a start, wasn't it?

Kathy Baker hated blind dates. Worse still, it was an internet set-up so she was expecting the worst. Somewhere between psychopath and nerd, she was betting. Maybe she shouldn't have bothered. But when you're thirty and single, you have to keep trying. Or so she had been told.

Kathy worked in a charity shop during the day and normally dressed in jeans and a jumper. She knew she should make the effort, in case a George Clooney look-alike came through the front door one day. But chances were it would just be another pensioner looking for a bargain blouse. So it had been nice to dress up tonight, for the first time in a very long time.

Kathy was quite pleased with her outfit. Her full black skirt had come from the shop, a bargain at two pounds. She was trying not to think about the size-eighteen label inside and the fact that the elasticated waistband was at full stretch and digging into her. The pink, low V-neck top was an old favourite but must have shrunk from frequent use. She tried to sit up straight so that the tight material didn't highlight the rolls of fat around her middle. She knew it was good to have a bit of cleavage to attract the men but was trying to ignore how tight the top felt across the bust. She was worried that any quick movement would result in a Barbara Windsor in *Carry on Camping* tribute.

Kathy knew she had to get out and meet people. Having just moved to the area, she knew nobody except the elderly ladies who worked in the shop with her, and whose idea of a hectic social life was a daytime whirl of bridge, bingo and bowls. But Kathy needed company; she craved it. She was no good on her own.

So Kathy had decided to venture into the world of internet dating. After all, there were some success stories she had read about. And perhaps 'Mike' would be the one, if that was his real name. Maybe Mike would be someone to talk to, to share life with, a hardy soul who could support her no matter what.

His photo had looked nice so here she was, perched on a stool in a wine bar. It was Thursday night and the place was packed with young and good-looking office staff, all loosening their ties and flinging off their jackets. Kathy shuffled on her stool, trying to appear relaxed but in reality she was silently praying that her arse didn't look too big spilling over the sides.

'You're not Kathy, are you?' said a voice behind her.

Kathy turned round and nearly fell off her stool. The man was six feet tall but only about a foot wide. He was the thinnest person she had ever seen.

'I'm afraid so,' she said, giving him her widest beam, even though she was dying inside.

He wasn't exactly a looker but then she remembered his photo being quite dark. Maybe there was a reason for that.

Kathy hadn't supplied a photo, but she knew she was reasonably good-looking. Her cheeks were always too red, her face too shiny and her shoulder-length brown hair could do with a decent cut to give it a bit of body, but her brown eyes were nice and her skin wasn't spotty. She wasn't exactly a fright. Or at least, she hadn't thought so until now.

'You said you looked like Elizabeth Hurley,' he said, with a whine in his voice.

'From a hundred yards,' replied Kathy, still smiling.

'More like Hurley from *Lost*,' he muttered, looking over his shoulder.

She scowled at him. 'Why do you keep glancing around? Are you looking to see if there's someone else here that you know?'

'I hope not,' he said softly.

But she caught it, all the same.

'Just go, would you?' she told him. 'Crawl back under that rock you've been hiding under.'

'Least I could find one big enough,' he snapped back before leaving.

Kathy tried to pull herself together. It was fine. He was an idiot. He was the one with the problem, not her. All she had wanted was someone to talk to, to help stem the loneliness and the grief. But she wasn't that desperate.

She finished her drink and pushed her way through the crowd to the street. Only then did she let her mouth tremble with the emotion hidden deep inside. But she pushed her shoulders back and strode off down the street. There was a lovely, comforting cheesy pasta waiting for her at home. That would take away the pain and make her feel better.

But Kathy knew it was only temporary. The loneliness would soon seep back, suffocating her.

This was why Kathy hated blind dates.

Chapter Three

On Friday, Violet was sprawled on the sofa as usual. She was sliding the crumbs from the bottom of a tube of Pringles into her mouth when the front doorbell rang.

She shuffled into the hallway, regretting that she was still in her grubby dressing gown and slippers at one o'clock in the afternoon. God, she hoped it wasn't Sebastian. She never wanted him to see her like this.

She opened the door and peered around it.

'Hello!' said a cheery woman. 'Are you Violet Saunders?'

'Yes.'

'Then I have this lovely bouquet for you.' She held out a huge bunch of flowers in varying shades of pink. 'Could you just sign this for me?'

She held out a delivery sheet so Violet had no option but to open up the front door. She quickly signed her name.

'Get well soon!' said the florist, before heading back down the front path.

Violet shut the door, trying not to mind that the florist thought she was unwell. She glanced in the mirror before quickly looking away. Perhaps the florist was right.

She put the bouquet on the coffee table in the lounge and opened the card.

'Dinner tonight. 7 p.m. Wear something nice. Sebastian.'

He had rung every day since Monday but she hadn't picked up the phone. She was too busy working her way through the Easter leftovers. Food was the only thing that made her feel better. The only thing that blocked out the pain.

The news had come on to the television in the corner. Lots of headlines about unemployment figures being high. Violet had been made redundant just before Easter. She was a secretary in a small office of account-ants. The directors had told her that they needed to reduce costs and were going to integrate two of the secretarial positions.

So why did they choose Andrea over me? wondered Violet for the hundredth time. Andrea had only been with the firm for six months. Violet had been there since she left school. But Violet knew why. Andrea was slim and pretty.

Violet sighed. She had registered with a couple of agencies but they didn't hold out much luck. Jobs were scarce, they said. And she knew that she hardly gave a great first impression.

Violet knew she would have to face Sebastian tonight. Wear something nice, he had said. Knowing the trauma that lay ahead, she lay down on the sofa, grabbing an Easter egg box from the top of a nearby pile. She had bought a few in the post-holiday sales.

Plus she needed something sweet after all those crisps.

She broke off a piece of chocolate with one hand, using the other to flick between channels. Bored senseless by daytime television, she briefly contemplated doing some housework, but what was the point?

Her mobile suddenly rang. But this time it wasn't Sebastian. It was an unknown number.

'Hello?'

'Violet? It's Patricia from Job Searchers.'

She remembered. A patronising cow who couldn't disguise the horror in her eyes as she beheld Violet's appearance.

'Great news. We've got an interview for you.'

Violet sat bolt upright, scattering chocolate everywhere.

'Really?'

'We've had a bit of bother with this particular chap,' she carried on. 'He doesn't seem to like any of our girls. So we thought we'd try you out. See how you get on. I think you'll be perfect.'

To her horror, the interview had been arranged for the following Wednesday. Only four days to prepare herself for the hideous trauma of meeting new people. Violet began to panic.

She was still pacing the lounge nervously when the doorbell rang at seven o'clock that evening. But this time she knew who was outside. She took a deep breath and opened the front door.

'Hello,' said Sebastian, with a soft smile.

'Hello,' Violet stammered back, her heart leaping as it always had, right from the first time they met.

Two years earlier, Violet had been standing at the counter at a popular wine bar in the centre of town, trying to catch the bartender's eye. The office Christmas party was in full swing back at the table. Violet allowed herself a small shudder. Whilst she had been merely enduring the innuendo and continuous laughter, her colleagues were letting their hair down and having the most marvellous time.

Especially the new girl in human resources, just returned from a lengthy absence with one of the directors, now surreptitiously doing up his flies as he drunkenly lurched back towards the table.

Violet sighed.

'A pretty face like yours shouldn't be so sad,' said a male voice next to her.

Violet glanced over her shoulder, knowing that the man couldn't possibly be speaking about her. But she was nosy enough to want to see whom he was talking to.

To her amazement, she saw a blond man smiling at her. She glanced around but it was just the two of them.

'How about I buy you a drink to cheer you up?'

Without waiting for a reply, he ordered two champagnes from the barman, who had suddenly materialised in front of them. Violet watched him order their drinks. He was slim with spiky, fair hair and had an air of self-confidence, as if he could take on the world and win.

The man handed Violet a glass of champagne and clinked her glass with his.

'Cheers,' he said. 'Here's to my idiot friend who stood me up. And thank God, otherwise I wouldn't have had the chance to meet you.'

Violet stared in wonder as he carried on smiling at her.

'The name's Sebastian,' he told her.

'I'm Violet,' she stammered, before sneaking a quick glance at her colleagues.

'They're too drunk to notice you're missing,' said Sebastian, following her gaze. 'Besides, they don't deserve you. And I want you all to myself.'

Later, he had kissed her under the mistletoe as they left the bar. Violet couldn't believe that someone was interested in her, could even want to be seen in public with her.

She still felt that way after two years of dating.

And here he was, the love of her life, standing in front of her.

'Forgive me,' he asked. 'I beg of you.'

Violet stepped forward into the rain and let him sweep her into his arms.

'I'm an idiot,' he muttered into her hair. He was an inch shorter than Violet but she was able to snuffle into his shoulder if she stooped a little.

'That's OK,' she said, inhaling the expensive scent on his neck.

And perhaps it was, in a way. Had she forgiven him? She didn't care. She just wanted to be with him. Nothing else mattered.

He drew away and held her shoulders. 'It will never happen again,' he said.

And she believed him. She had to. He was all she had. She would do anything to keep him. Even forgive him for sleeping with another woman.

'I'm sorry too,' she told him as he finally drew away. 'I'll behave better. I won't whinge as much. And I'm going to lose some weight.'

He smiled. 'Violet, darling. You're my girl and I love you.'

'I love you too,' she replied.

'But perhaps you should try not to nag me so much,' Sebastian added. 'It does upset me, you know.'

Violet nodded. That was the answer. They would both try their best and everything would be OK.

'Now, what about dinner? You must be starving.'

Sebastian had booked a table for two at the Rajdoot. The Rajdoot produced the most wonderful Indian food imaginable. It was a trendy restaurant, frequented by smart go-getters like Sebastian who worked in the finance sector.

Violet knew she wasn't in his class. She would have loved to have worn a pretty dress like some of the other women but had stuck to black trousers, a bat-wing black top and a few bits of jewellery.

They ordered their food and as the waiter went away, Sebastian raised his glass.

'Here's to us,' he said, clinking the glasses together.

Violet smiled back. He was at his most charming tonight. He was trying desperately to make amends, she knew.

She was stuffing a poppadom into her mouth when she caught Sebastian looking at her and smiling. She quickly swallowed and tried to slow down her eating. She must have looked like a total pig, jumping on the food as soon as it arrived.

But it was after the main course that she became certain Sebastian was acting strangely. He kept staring at her, with that odd grin on his face. Normally he chatted away about his work or the football matches he had seen. His life was always fascinating to her. But tonight he was silent, just watching her.

She began to fret. Something was different. Something was wrong.

After the waiter had taken the plates away, Sebastian cleared his throat. 'I need to talk to you about something,' he said.

Violet felt sick. He was going to dump her. He was way out of her league. It was hopeless thinking that he would want to be with her. After all, that other girl must have been much better in bed than she could ever be.

'Darling Violet,' he said, his voice a little husky. 'There's something I want to ask you.'

When he dropped to the floor, she thought he'd dropped his napkin. 'Are you all right?' she asked.

He took her hand and smiled. It was then that she realised he was on one knee.

'Will you do me the honour of becoming my wife?' asked Sebastian.

Violet gaped at him. Was this a joke? No, he was actually serious. He wanted them to be together. As man and wife. For ever.

She glanced around and realised the whole restaurant was watching them. She looked down at Sebastian whose smile was beginning to fade.

She realised she hadn't given him a reply. 'Yes!' she said, trying not to cry. 'Of course, yes!'

Sebastian's smile clicked back into place and the whole restaurant erupted into clapping and cheering. Violet's cheeks burned with the attention, especially when he kissed her on the mouth in front of everyone.

As the waiter brought out the puddings and two glasses of champagne, everyone was still chattering around them. But Violet was so happy, she didn't even want the pudding.

Back home and snuggled up on the sofa, she told him about the New You! leaflet.

'You sure you want to pay out a load of money for some hippy spin?' he said, popping a small chocolate egg into her mouth.

'I really want to lose weight this time,' she told him, between mouthfuls.

'Of course you will, pumpkin. But you don't have to, you know. You know how much I love your curves.'

But her curves were increasing on a daily basis. She had risen from a size sixteen to almost size twenty-two since they had been together. If she became any larger, she knew he would stray again.

Then he leaned forward and gave her a long, lingering kiss. The desperation was starting to recede. Once she got thin, he wouldn't look at another woman. Once she was thin, she would be happy.

'Let's go to bed,' he said in a husky voice.

Violet nodded and followed him upstairs.

But even after two years together, she was still embarrassed to be seen naked. So as he brushed his teeth in the bathroom, she quickly took off her clothes. Slipping between the covers, she tried to cover up the red welts from where her bra and waistband had been digging into the flesh.

Sebastian came to stand by the bed and smiled at her.

Violet smiled back and leaned over to switch off the bedside light.

Chapter Four

I hate fat people, thought Trudie Connolly. Why are they so lazy? Why don't they just stop eating once they're full? Perhaps all that flab affects their brain cells.

She fixed on a smile. 'Welcome to a New You!' she said so loudly that her voice echoed around the church hall. 'The weight-loss programme that can change your life! Have you got your form?'

The paper was duly handed over. She quickly scanned the page. No health problems. No aches and pains. Yet. Just wait until they'd been through Trudie's gruelling aerobics workout. Then they'd know pain.

Her eyes sought out the name box on the form before she looked up.

'Thank you, Violet. Now, for the first two weeks you get a nutritious shake for breakfast and lunch. It's also interchangeable with a cereal bar for when you want something solid to eat. Follow the guidelines regarding dinner choices. You have to sign up for a year to make sure that you're serious about losing weight. Do you want to pay by debit or credit card?'

The payment duly handed over, Trudie smiled at Violet. 'Why don't you pop yourself up on the scales?'

Then you'll see how much damage has been done by those Krispy Kreme doughnuts you've been scoffing all day, thought Trudie.

She glanced down at the scales. 'You're fifteen stone.'

She gave the girl her best pity smile. Not that she deserved any pity, the great porker.

Trudie knew the type. No self-esteem, eats her way through the kitchen most nights in total misery. Never gonna get a man. Ever. Hates looking at herself in the mirror. Probably spends all her time playing games on the computer.

But a flash of something on Violet's left hand caught Trudie by surprise. She was engaged? Who the hell was gonna marry this big lump?

'I see someone's getting married,' said Trudie, in her smoothest voice.

Violet nodded, her face blushing.

Shame really, thought Trudie. She could be quite pretty if you took all that flab away. Maybe if she got herself a decent haircut rather than that dark curtain flopping around her fat cheeks.

'When's the big day?'

'Don't know yet,' came the mumbled reply.

'Well, don't worry. There's plenty of time for you to slim down and fit into the most fabulous wedding dress you can find.'

Shame they won't do any in your size. It would create a world shortage in ivory silk.

'Your target weight for your height is around ten stone. That's five stone to lose. That shouldn't be any problem.'

28

The expression on the woman's face begged to differ.

'Anyway, have a look through your welcome pack. It has all the details of the weight-loss programme in there. Please don't hesitate to ask me if you have any questions. Good luck and welcome to a New You!'

Trudie gave the girl her most brilliant smile as she shuffled away to plonk herself down on a nearby chair. Why bother with marriage when the groom is sure to run off with the prettier and thinner bridesmaid anyway?

Lord, here comes another one. More smiling. 'Welcome to a New You! Have you got your form?'

'Here you go,' came the cheerful reply.

A woman in her early thirties was grinning at her. She had a jolly, round face with red cheeks and bright red lipstick. The face was shiny with exertion, no doubt from having to heave that enormous body around the hall. Her brown hair was scraped back into a ponytail, making the round face seem even larger.

Trudie knew this type as well. Good-time girl, always up for a laugh. Probably smokes, definitely drinks too much. Loves her puddings and big roast dinners. Been around the block a couple of times.

'Kathy, is it? Do you want to pay by credit or debit card?'

'Do you run a trial? You know, where I could pay for a fortnight to see how I get on?'

Trudie ground her teeth as she shook her head. 'Sorry. It's the whole year or not at all. You can pay by direct debit if you prefer.'

I'm not running a bloody charity.

'Step up on the scales for me, please.'

Kathy gave a guffaw. 'Knew I shouldn't have had that third piece of cake this afternoon.'

Trudie gave her a polite smile before gesturing for her to step down. 'I make that seventeen stone exactly.'

Kathy rolled her eyes and gave a snort of derision. 'All bought and paid for!'

'By my calculations, you should be around eleven stone for your height. How do you feel about that?'

'I've about as much chance of hitting eleven stone as Brad Pitt declaring undying love for me.' Another hearty guffaw.

Trudie tried not to roll her eyes.

'Let's just aim for half a stone in the beginning and see how you get on, shall we? Here's your welcome pack. It has all the details of the diet in there. Please don't hesitate to ask me if you have any questions. Good luck and welcome to a New You!'

You'll go straight to the pub after this meeting and never return, I'll bet.

And here's the next loser. Of the male variety this time. Still, no one ever said the fat curse was limited to women.

'Welcome to a New You! Have you got your form?'

'Yes,' came the curt reply.

The name on the form was Edward. Trudie had his number down, as well. Embarrassed to be here. His attendance at this meeting wasn't going to come up next time he was down the pub with his mates, that's for sure. And that was where he spent too much time before heading on to the kebab shop afterwards. He'll enjoy watching every sport. But playing sport? With that beer belly? And those man boobs? Not a chance.

So why was he here? Spotted a girl, probably. Some librarian who might give him a second look. After all, he was only in his early thirties, despite the bloated face and heavy jowls. Still time to spawn some fat kids and get a cholesterol problem.

'Gosh, you're twenty-one stone and three pounds,' said Trudie. 'You're looking to lose at least eight stone to lose to achieve a healthy weight.'

'Fine,' came the short reply.

This one wasn't going to be a laugh a minute. But he might last a couple of meetings before giving up.

'This is your welcome pack. It has all the details of the diet in there. Please don't hesitate to ask me if you have any questions. Good luck and welcome to a New You!'

Edward snatched the pack out of her hands and strode away.

Whatever, mate. Enjoy a life alone.

Sometimes it was an effort to get through a class, especially a new and untried one like this. It wasn't as if the area was flourishing. But head office had told Trudie to give it a go.

'Hello,' said Trudie to the next person. 'Do you have your form?'

'Yes. Sorry.' The woman was extremely flustered. 'Put it in my handbag. Wasn't thinking. Sorry. Here it is.'

Welcome, Mrs Menopause, thought Trudie. No one ever warned you, did they? They told you about the mood swings and hot flushes. But the steady advance in weight? What was that all about? Your metabolism is grinding to a halt yet you're still downing half a bottle of red wine a night and the same foods you've always eaten and bingo! Suddenly you're twice the size you were five years ago.

Yes, the country walks help but not if you go for a pub lunch afterwards. You hanker after your daughter's miniskirts yet have to resort to elasticated waists and those big knickers to hold it in. No big knickers were large enough for this one.

'Step on the scales for me, Maggie.'

Maggie had an air of gloom about her. And that wasn't going to improve once she faced up to her actual weight.

'Sixteen stone and thirteen pounds. Nearly seventeen stone.'

'What? It can't be.'

'I'm afraid so.'

Maggie blew out a long sigh. 'My scales back at home say sixteen and a half stone.'

Trudie tried not to snap back at her. 'Ours are the correct weight. I know it's sometimes a bit of a shock but let's take this negative and spin it into a positive, shall we?'

'I didn't think I was that heavy. I've never been that big before.'

Wake up and smell your beloved sherry bottle, love. You're overweight. Deal with it.

'We'll aim for eleven stone. This is your welcome pack. It has all the details of the diet in there. Please don't hesitate to ask me if you have any questions. Good luck and welcome to a New You!'

'This is Lucy,' said Maggie, still sounding fed-up. 'My daughter.'

And now the fatties are coming by the household. Lucy was a mini-Maggie, but the attitude was all teen angst rather than menopausal hormones.

'Hello, Lucy,' said Trudie, grinning at her.

Lucy's blue eyes scowled back from under her brown fringe. She looked to be in her late teens and was reasonably fashionable. It was a shame that everything looked too tight, too stretched across her wobbly belly and large thighs.

Trudie knew the form for this one, as well. A sedentary life growing up. Not much sport played or encouraged within the family. Too much time spent texting and on the computer. Wants to wear clothes from Top Shop but they don't do size eighteen.

'Up on the scales, Lucy.'

Lucy darted her a look of pure evil. She was definitely only here because she'd been dragged along by her fat mother.

'That's twelve stone and two pounds.'

Lucy bit her lip and said nothing.

'Not to worry.' Trudie put on her brightest smile. 'We'll get you looking great again in no time, especially once you hit your target of nine stone. This is your welcome pack. It has all the details of the diet in there. Please don't hesitate to ask me if you have any questions. Good luck and welcome to a New You!'

Lucy lumbered away with her mother following behind.

If I was the father, I'd be keeping my head down tonight, thought Trudie. The forecast is for humming hormones and sulks a-plenty.

Was that it? Was no one else coming tonight? It wasn't as if there were any other weight-loss classes in the vicinity. So the pickings should be rich. Or not, looking at the class. A total of five, so far. This franchise was going to go bust before it had even got going.

Trudie glanced at her watch. Almost half past. So, that was it. A total of five for the first class. Oh well. Time to get this show on the road.

'OK,' said Trudie, clapping her hands together and

moving to the centre of the class. 'Let's settle down so we can get started.'

Settle down? No one was even talking.

'Well, good evening, ladies and our token gentleman.' Trudie pasted on a large smile. 'You have made an important decision to come here tonight. Possibly the most important you'll ever make. For tonight you will be starting your epic voyage on the sea to a new beginning. As with all journeys, there will be hard parts. There may be some turbulence or perhaps even some seasickness but ultimately your arrival is what's important. Your destination? Planet New You!'

She'd been working all afternoon on that speech and the reaction. Not a thing. Not even a smirk. This class had all the excitement of a graveyard.

'Now, I know it's a shock when you first get weighed,' said Trudie, attempting to drag some life into the proceedings. 'But this is a brand-new class so everyone's at exactly the same stage. In fact, at New You! we encourage you to cheer each other on. Celebrate your triumphs and share your disappointments.'

Fatties of the world unite. God help me, how much longer before I can go home?

'You've all got your welcome packs, in which you should find your diet booklet, a tape measure and a motivational DVD from Dr Ramsbottom, the founder of New You! Inside your diet booklet you'll find a chart where you can discover your personal daily calorie allowance. This calorie allowance will help you achieve a healthy weight loss without going hungry. And I know what a struggle that can be!'

Trudie gave them her false, tinkly laugh, but everyone was still dumbstruck. Perhaps they knew that she'd never been overweight in her life. The thought of being the same size as some of these people made her feel ill.

'And then, at your weekly class, you'll get weighed and we'll check on your progress. Best of all, you'll get a half-hour aerobics class with me each week to kick-start your weight loss!'

Trudie, still wearing her wide grin, stared at everyone and they stared right back.

'Normally I would now give you a small talk about tips for the week and how to keep on track but we seem to be running a bit behind, unfortunately. Not to worry, that just leaves more for next week!'

She felt her shoulders sag and briefly dropped her grin.

'Let's just get on with the workout, shall we?'

Just think of the money, Trudie told herself. No job satisfaction to be had here.

These people weren't going to achieve anything.

Chapter Five

Oh My God, thought Kathy. I'm going to die.

Her pulse couldn't possibly maintain this high rate. Her lungs were going to explode. And she must have strained every muscle in her body. This was it. Kathy Baker RIP.

She was attempting to jog on the spot but the hall was going blotchy in front of her eyes. Just work to your own pace, that Trudie woman had said. What pace? Kathy's body hadn't seen this kind of movement since PE at school.

She wasn't normal, that Trudie. That manic smile of hers. And as for that body? No one was that trim and perfect in real life. Perhaps she'd been nipped and tucked. Anyway, she was the devil. And nobody over the age of twelve should wear a pink tracksuit.

Not that Kathy was particularly proud of her own workout outfit. It was a man's T-shirt and baggy tracksuit bottoms She wasn't sure when she'd started preferring men's clothes to her own. But what did she expect at seventeen stone?

Seventeen stone! Hell's bleeding bells! She was enormous. No wonder she couldn't jump around. There were probably seismic shakes going off all over town as she attempted to leap up and down. She must have been fooling herself all this time. At 5 feet 7 inches, perhaps she had thought she could carry a bit of extra weight. But this wasn't just a bit extra. This was a whole six stone of flab.

What the hell was she doing here? Kathy tried to copy Trudie's complicated routine. She was on the stage at the front of the hall. They could all see her clearly enough but everyone kept crashing into each other. Perhaps it was all the sweat obscuring their view. Kathy felt she was dripping buckets. It didn't help that she had no coordination either.

Finally the agony stopped and Trudie told everyone to lie on the ground to do some stretches. Kathy wasn't sure if she was going to be able to get up again. Maybe they would bring in one of the cranes that littered the town centre to hoist her up and out of the roof before gently depositing her back home. Or into the nearby cemetery.

As instructed, Kathy took a deep breath in and out and attempted to stretch her leg out at a 90-degree angle. Her heart was still pounding. Her head was thumping. And she wasn't sure if she had just dislocated her hip joint.

They all struggled to stand up before Trudie finally released them from the jaws of hell.

'Well, that was great! Really well done, everyone. Give yourselves a round of applause!'

A few looks were exchanged amongst the victims before a few half-hearted claps could be heard.

'That's the spirit!' continued Trudie.

You had to admire her, thought Kathy. Perhaps the world was a happier place when you could slip into Lycra leggings and not look like a large sack of potatoes.

On the way out, everyone was given three carrier bags full to capacity with cereal bars and milkshakes.

'Have a good week, everyone!' said Trudie. 'You've taken your first step to a New You!'

Kathy left as quickly as her aching body would allow. She savoured the sweet, fresh night air for a moment before realising someone was standing next to her.

'God, that was grim,' said Kathy, giving the other woman a grin. They were both around the same age. 'Hi, I'm Kathy.'

'I'm Violet,' muttered the dark-haired woman, going bright pink. She was very pretty, thought Kathy.

'I thought we were gonna have to call for an ambulance when she started doing that jogging on the spot,' Kathy went on. 'I swear my heart stopped beating at one stage.'

Violet gave her a small smile but didn't say anything.

'You going towards town?' asked Kathy.

Violet shook her head. 'Sorry.'

'No worries. I'll see you back here next week, then. If we can put up with the torture again! Good night.'

Kathy gave a hearty laugh but it wasn't returned. The girl had scurried away.

Probably couldn't wait to get away. Sometimes Kathy really hated herself. Why couldn't she just be natural instead of Peter Kay on speed?

Kathy turned and slowly walked home, dreading the lonesome flat that was waiting for her.

*

Violet headed in the opposite direction to her car, wishing she was naturally chatty like Kathy. Why was everyone else able to be so natural and engage in conversation, when she couldn't string two words together?

She got inside and dumped the bags on the passenger seat before trying to calm her racing pulse. Fifteen stone! She blew out a long sigh. She was probably the fattest one there, apart from that one man in the class.

She placed her hands on the steering wheel, noticing how her engagement ring glinted in the light from the streetlamp. It was a nice ring. Not quite the diamond solitaire that she had always dreamed of but an emerald was still a good sign that Sebastian loved her. Even if he didn't realise that she had never really liked emeralds.

Fifteen stone! She was going to be the fattest bride the world had ever seen. Deep in misery, Violet drove home, desperate for something to eat to take away the pain and humiliation of the evening.

Home always made her feel better. It was an end-of-terrace Victorian cottage. There were only two bedrooms and the kitchen was tiny but the lounge had been knocked through into the dining room and it was a lovely, sunny space with patio doors leading on to a small garden.

She had managed to get the deposit with an inheritance from her uncle who had passed away four years previously. It had been her sanctuary from the outside world ever since. There were some lovely authentic features, like the real fireplaces. They were tiny but then it only needed a few logs to keep the room warm.

She wished Sebastian was waiting for her with a hug but he was working late that evening and would head back to his own flat to sleep. So she trudged up the small path to the front door before letting herself in.

'Hello!' she called, ever hopeful that Sebastian had changed his mind.

But only darkness and silence greeted her.

Violet dumped the carrier bags full of shakes and cereal bars on the kitchen counter and felt her stomach rumble loudly. She had gone to the club without having dinner first. And she still weighed fifteen stone.

The first two weeks of the diet sounded horrendous. Two shakes or cereal bars and then a healthy, nutritious dinner. But a quick flick through the diet booklet confirmed her suspicions that the dinner should be made up of lots of vegetables, fish and brown rice. No cheese, chocolate or anything else that tasted nice.

In despair, Violet threw open the fridge door, grabbed the unhealthiest things she could find and ate them all. Cheese, butter, cream, chocolate and even a frozen cheesecake that hadn't quite defrosted by the time she got round to devouring it. She ate until she felt sick.

And she cried the whole time she was eating. She was never going to lose weight, she told herself. She just wasn't strong enough.

Edward nodded goodbye to the ghastly Trudie before leaving. He had made it. He had got through the aerobic session alive.

The weigh-in didn't hold any humiliation for him, after being weighed by the doctor a few days previously. He had taken her advice and looked up the class. OK, so it was all a bit girly but he was prepared to give it a month. He tried not to think about the

40

doctor's words to him the other evening. He was fine. He wasn't ill, after all. He tried not to remind himself how massive he felt in his tracksuit bottoms and how far his stomach was hanging over the waistband.

Edward was impressed that the class included a workout. He just hadn't realised quite how unfit he really was. OK, so fielding the boundary at cricket wasn't exactly aerobic but he considered himself in a reasonable physical state even if he couldn't run between the wickets.

But he couldn't fool himself any longer. Not having seen that psychotic bimbo Trudie bouncing around. She had barely broken out into a sweat while Edward felt as if he was having a mild coronary. He must have lost about half a stone already in sweat. At least, it felt like it. His T-shirt was clinging to him, dripping wet. He felt revolting.

He strode to his car, his head held high. He was fine. Nothing at all the matter with him. He could cope with this every week. It was only a workout for women, after all.

He only briefly clutched his pounding chest before he let his hand drop. He glanced up and down the road to check nobody was nearby. And then he threw up.

As Maggie drove home, she tried to lift Lucy's low spirits.

'It wasn't that bad,' said Maggie, trying to put some life into her voice.

'It was crap,' muttered Lucy.

Maggie steered the car around the roundabout. She was nearly seventeen stone. She was enormous. No wonder she felt so unwell most of the time.

'I thought Trudie was nice,' she added.

41

'I thought she was a right bitch,' replied Lucy.

So did I, agreed Maggie. But she didn't say so.

She was still in shock that Lucy had wanted to go with her. She had tried sneaking out of the house whilst Gordon was in the garden, saying something about a quick trip to an evening sale at Debenhams.

But Lucy had picked up that she was lying and had begun to raise her voice while asking endless questions about where her mother was going.

'Keep your voice down,' Maggie had said, in a low tone. 'I don't want your father knowing.'

'What?'

'There's a new diet club,' said Maggie, trying to ignore Lucy's groan. 'I know, I know. Been there, done that. But I need to lose weight. So for God's sake, don't tell your dad where I've gone.'

'Why?'

'Because he'll say it's a waste of time and money.'

'Is it?'

Maggie looked at her daughter. 'Possibly, but I'm desperate, love.'

Lucy looked at her for a while before saying, 'OK. I won't tell Dad – if you let me come with you.'

Maggie's eyebrows shot up. 'Really? Why?'

'Look at me, Mum. I don't think Cheryl Cole's quaking in her shoes, is she?'

'Cheryl Cole needs a bloody good meal inside her.'

'Please, Mum. I want to lose weight too.'

Maggie knew her daughter needed to lose a few pounds. Nothing like her own massive excess, but perhaps it would help. So they went together.

'You never know,' said Maggie, turning the car into their road. 'This might be a whole new beginning for us both.'

Maggie hoped her words were true. But she knew deep down that this new diet club probably wouldn't make any difference.

When they got home, Gordon looked up from the sofa with a smile. 'How was the shopping?' he asked, keeping one eye on the football match on the television.

As Lucy stomped upstairs, Maggie smiled back at her husband. 'It wasn't great,' she said as she sat down next to him.

'Have one of these to cheer yourself up,' said Gordon, handing her the biscuit barrel.

Maggie sighed and helped herself to a chocolate digestive.

Lucy shut her bedroom door and threw herself on the bed.

She had spotted Nicola Bowles and her gang on the drive home and had slumped down in her seat to avoid being seen, though she didn't know how they could miss her at over twelve stone. No wonder they took the mickey out of her. She was the size of an elephant.

How the hell was she going to lose three stone? She glanced down at her stomach, straining against the T-shirt and leggings. It would take years to get rid of all the fat she was suffocating under.

Her mum had been surprised that she had wanted to go to the stupid weight-loss class. But Lucy was getting increasingly desperate. She wanted so much to be the lively teenager that she knew was buried deep inside somewhere. She didn't tell her mum how unhappy she really was. How one day last summer she had sat down in the bathroom with a packet of

Nurofen and had stared at the pills, wondering what would happen if she swallowed them all. In the end, she put the packet back in the bathroom cabinet and felt even more miserable. If she didn't have the strength to attempt suicide, what hope was there for her to lose three stone?

She grabbed her sketchpad and skipped through all the fashion designs until she found the page she had scribbled on a few days ago.

Lucy had drawn a silhouette of herself as she was at present. And then had drawn her dream silhouette inside it. That was her goal. The dream body shape. The kind of person who could wear skinny jeans and cropped tops. Who could wear any fashion they liked.

But Lucy knew it was just a dream and would never come true. It was too hard to achieve on her own and there was nobody else to help her.

Chapter Six

The morning after the weigh-in, Violet had a job interview. She had six pieces of toast with butter and marmalade in deference to the horror ahead. The diet would start later. Now she had to worry about what to wear.

Glancing at the kitchen clock, she realised it was nearly half past nine. Only an hour until the interview. She hurtled upstairs in a panic about her outfit and then had to spend ten minutes sitting on the bed, trying to get her breath back before opening the wardrobe door.

First things first. She needed to put on the control pants. She had bought a pair for the Christmas party at work but had bottled out of going, saying that she had the flu. Violet had never been a party kind of person, especially since she had put on so much weight in the past couple of years.

She got the knickers out of the packet. Great big ugly beige things that looked like bicycle shorts. She heaved and toiled and eventually got them over her fat knees, but there was no way they were going to make it past her thighs. She lay on the bed, yanking at the knickers but only succeeded in breaking a couple of nails.

It was no use. She was too fat. She gave up and spent the next five minutes trying to get the damn things off.

Still huffing and puffing from the exertion with the underwear, she squeezed into her black trousers. The waist button was straining but if she didn't breathe too deeply it should stay put. She regretted not getting a bigger size of the magic knickers but even they were a size twenty. Her stomach bulged through the trouser material. She would have covered up the rolls of fat by doing up the matching jacket but the buttons wouldn't meet in the middle so she gave up.

Heading downstairs, she glanced in the hall mirror and sighed with self-pity. (It was only a small one. She had no need for full-length mirrors.) Her long, black hair had gone impossibly fluffy from a quick wash and blast with the hairdryer. As normal, she'd only bothered with a sweep of mascara. Her cheeks were rosy from the heat and Violet could feel the beginning of sweat patches appearing under the jacket.

So she had the window down in the car on the way into town to cool down, even though it was only the beginning of May and the temperature wasn't that high yet.

She hovered outside the office, trying to pluck up the courage to go in. In the end, apathy won over her desire to run away. What was the point in fretting? She wasn't going to get the job. So she went inside, not caring either way.

Mason & Mason was a large company, which

appeared to be doing rather well, if the office decor was anything to go by. It was all glass and mirrors. Violet had to keep averting her eyes to avoid seeing her own reflection.

She was given a visitor's pass by the receptionist and told to wait. The interview was with Mark Harris and someone would come down to collect her.

A fierce-looking blond woman appeared. 'You here for the interview?' she barked.

Violet nodded, a bit scared.

'You'd better come with me.'

They both stepped into the lift.

'You're the fifth one he's seen today,' the woman snapped.

'Sorry,' muttered Violet.

'Not your fault,' she said. 'But I've got better things to do than show people in and out of the building all morning.'

On the third floor, the doors opened and they went through the office. It was bright and modern, full of smoked-glass panels, streamlined beech desks and brightly coloured chairs, all fighting for space amongst the exotic plants. The walls were adorned by fake Monet prints and motivational photographs of a man running up a steep mountain towards his goal and a possible heart attack.

They entered a messy department, which seemed at total odds with the rest of the building. The desks were strewn with paper; computer magazines were piled high on top of filing cabinets; and boxes filled with the insides of various computers were littered all over the floor.

Amongst the debris were the staff, all with their heads down and looking very busy. The woman showed Violet into an office.

'He'll be here in a minute,' she informed her and then left.

Violet stood inside Mark Harris's office, trying to compose some witty answers to the normal interview questions. Where did she herself in five years' time? What assets could she bring to this secretarial role? But her mind drew a blank.

'Right,' came a male voice from the doorway. 'Let's get this over with.'

Violet spun round and stared. It took her a moment before she realised where she had seen him before. She couldn't believe it. It was the handsome man from Marks & Spencer. The man whose cake she had snatched.

Mark Harris's eyes had widened as well. 'It's you!' he said, pointing. 'The phantom cake thief!'

Violet gulped, the tears filling her eyes. She was so embarrassed. Of all the dumb luck, this was the worst. She waited for him to start shouting at her to get out. But he didn't. He stared at her for a beat and then handed over a plastic cup.

'I took a guess at white coffee. Hope that's OK.'

She watched him walk around to the other side of the desk and sit down. Normally good-looking people flustered her. And Mark Harris was definitely a man to fluster women.

She wasn't sure what made him so attractive. His black hair was too wavy, and slightly too long as it curled around his neck. His face was creased with too many lines for his relatively young thirty-odd years. But beneath that olive skin he had a kind of sensual magnetism.

Violet, however, was beyond being flustered. She was humiliated. She didn't know what to do. Or how to get out of there quickly. This was terrible. Awful. Her cheeks burned with mortification.

'Look, sit down,' he said, gesturing at the chair on the opposite side of the desk from him. 'Please.'

She sank into a chair and stared down into the coffee. Beam me up, Scotty. If the ground could swallow her whole right now, that would be the answer to her prayers.

'So, it says here you're Violet Saunders,' he said, looking at the paperwork in front of him. 'Is that right?'

She nodded, still staring down at the coffee.

'I just need to get it right for the police when they come.'

Violet whipped her head up and found his green eyes twinkling at her.

'Well, at least I can see your face now,' he told her. 'I was only joking about the police, by the way. Shall we get on with the interview?'

She stared at him, trying to figure out what he had just said. He was joking about the police. He really did want to interview her. The agony would have to last a little longer. She simply needed to fluff the meeting, fail to get the job and get the hell out of there.

'I'm sorry about the cake,' said Violet, finally finding her voice.

'PMT, was it? Least of my worries, to be honest.' He shrugged his shoulders. 'Anyway, you did me a favour. It was a leaving present. But I'm not sure Felicity ever ate anything anyway so you saved me wasting a tenner.'

Violet didn't reply. The humiliation was still rushing through her body.

'So you're out of work at the moment?'

She nodded.

'It says here you got made redundant before Easter.'

She nodded again.

'I don't suppose you've got any IT experience, have you?'

This time she shook her head.

Mark Harris stared at her for a beat. 'Are you always this quiet?'

She thought about it and nodded once more.

His rumpled face split into a warm smile. 'Are you sure you're going to be able to answer the hotline if you're always this quiet?'

Violet blinked at him. 'The what?'

'You know, the job you applied for. The Hotline Assistant job.'

She had no idea what he was talking about but he didn't seem to notice.

He leant back in his chair, putting his hands behind his head. 'Basically, you'd be answering the phone to our sales force when they are having trouble with their computers,' he told her. 'You log the call on the computer and then field the calls on to the rest of the department. Not exactly a laugh a minute but that's probably why the pay is so low.'

Violet finally plucked up the nerve to string a sentence together. 'I was sent here for a secretarial position.'

'You were?' He frowned and picked up the phone. 'Cecilia? Mark Harris here. I've got a Violet Saunders in front of me. Says she's a secretary, nothing to do with IT. Right. God, they are useless. I see.'

He hung up and muttered a few words in a language Violet didn't recognise.

Then he blew out a sigh. 'Your agency is bloody hopeless. Turns out there's a secretarial post in the marketing department that you should have been sent for. I should warn you, though. They're not as much fun as us nerds. A right bunch of smarmy slimeballs.'

So the humiliation could have been avoided if her useless agency hadn't messed up. Violet sighed and shook her head.

Mark Harris was watching her. 'You should think about swapping agencies. They're rubbish. You should have seen the bunch of weirdos they've already sent me today. All thought they were the next Bill Gates. Far too over-qualified for this role.'

So it had all been a complete waste of time. Like everything in her life. Except Sebastian.

Suddenly aware of a long silence, Violet looked up to find Mark Harris studying her. He stared at her for a long time until she was so uncomfortable that she shuffled in her seat.

He broke out of his reverie and smiled. 'So? What about it?' he said. 'Think you can handle it?'

She was shocked. 'You're offering me the job?'

Despite the cake thing. And the complete lack of experience.

'If only to keep you out of prison,' he said, still smiling.

'But I can't do it,' stammered Violet.

'You can answer the phone, can't you?' He leaned forward on the desk, staring at her with his green eyes. 'Look, I'm desperate. Felicity left yesterday. Gone to be a footballer's wife or something. Vacant position for a vacant girl. She didn't even pick up the phone when it rang. Too busy painting her nails. Surely you can improve on that?'

Violet didn't know what to say. But she was

desperate. She needed a job to pay the mortgage. And the food bill. And the giant credit-card bill for the stupid New You! diet club as well. Surely just sitting there answering the phone wouldn't be too bad?

'You want to start tomorrow?'

She looked up at him and, after a brief internal struggle, finally nodded.

'Great. See you in the morning at nine o'clock sharp.'

And that was it. Interview over. Violet had a new job.

She just needed the new body to go with it.

Chapter Seven

Kathy was fed up. She'd had one shake for breakfast. Make that one disgusting, undrinkable diet shake for breakfast. Now it was mid-morning and she was desperate for something to eat with her coffee. Like a danish pastry. Followed by an iced bun. And a doughnut.

'Was it one sugar?' called Mavis from the kitchen.

Kathy rolled her eyes. 'Two, please.'

She had worked in the shop for over a month and they had had coffee every morning. But then, Mavis was about one hundred years old, so perhaps she was entitled to be a little vague.

'There you are,' said Mavis, making her slow way back across the small shop.

Kathy took the mug from her. 'Thanks.'

She took a sip and winced. There was no sugar in the drink. And it didn't taste like coffee either. The fact that the charity shop raised funds for the Alzheimer's Society was, perhaps, rather apt.

Luckily, it was a subject close to Kathy's heart. Her

mother had suffered from dementia for many years. Sadly the strain had got too much for her dad, who had passed away a few years previously from a heart attack.

In the end, Kathy had to move in with her mother and take charge. As the years passed, whole weeks went by when she didn't recognise Kathy. Her mother lived in her own world, quite content.

But Kathy wasn't. She was an only child and the strain of losing her dad and the slow decline of her mum was overwhelming. So she began to comfort eat – and had never stopped.

Not even when her mum had looked at her one day and said, 'You're a bit fat, aren't you?'

Kathy had sobbed herself to sleep that night. And most nights since.

She had expected to feel a little relieved when her mum passed away from kidney complications at the end of the previous year. But the only relief was that her mother was no longer in pain. Now, the pain was all Kathy's. There was no focus in her life. And no family either. In the end, she couldn't bear the solitude and moved away. A new start and hopefully a new life.

She sold the family home and rented a cheap flat on the edge of town while she decided what to do with her life.

But she'd been in the area for a month and was desperately lonely. She thought the job would help her socially but Mavis wasn't exactly party central. And the weight-loss club was terribly quiet too.

Now that she no longer had her mother to take care of, Kathy's life was empty. As empty as the shop she found herself working in. No company at home; no customers to chat to during the day. Some evenings, Kathy felt like screaming at the unfairness of it all. But instead she bottled up her desperation and found comfort in food. Glorious food, which was always available, always there to soothe her pain.

Kathy sighed and took another sip of her drink. The shop was too quiet to make any money. It needed a complete overhaul to drag it into the new century, let alone the new decade, but Mavis was apt to be offended by any suggestion of change. So Kathy turned up each day, smiled at the infrequent customers and then went home.

'Would you like a chocolate digestive?' asked Mavis, fishing a packet out of her handbag.

It was the first sensible thing she'd said all morning.

Maggie was bored as well. She'd opted for a cereal bar for breakfast. It had needed two cups of tea to wash away the taste and to get some moisture back into her mouth. And there was no way she could have a cup of tea without a little something on the side.

So it was only ten o'clock in the morning and she had already eaten her way through the packet of cake bars that she had bought earlier in the week.

The television blared out from the corner of the lounge. There was nothing else for her to do. The house was immaculate and it was too early to attack the garden. Not that there was much weeding to be done there either. She had hoovered every room the previous day. There wasn't an inch of dust anywhere in the house. Except in her brain.

Maggie felt like a prisoner in her own home. Gordon had never wanted her to go back to work when Lucy was growing up and Maggie had enjoyed spending the time with her daughter. But long gone were the days of gossiping with other mums outside the school gates. Lucy was all grown up and had left school two years ago. Whilst she was moving on with her life, Maggie's had ground to a halt. She didn't know what she wanted to do and so did nothing, day after day.

Not that Gordon had complained at all. As long as his dinner was on the table every night, he didn't care. It wasn't as if Maggie could even talk to him about it. They barely spoke at all about themselves these days. The topics of conversation rarely ventured beyond Gordon's business and Lucy. Then, as soon as dinner was over, the television was switched back on and they settled down in front of the soaps with the biscuit tin.

Maggie crumpled up the cake packet and flicked channels. At least the *Jeremy Kyle Show* made her feel better. The day's topic was, 'He slept with my mother and now she's pregnant!'

Those people had real problems, Maggie told herself as she reached for another packet of biscuits.

The classroom was quiet. Everyone was concentrating on their fashion designs.

The lecturer bent down to talk to Lucy. 'Hi,' she said in a low voice. 'How's it going?'

Lucy crumpled up her piece of paper. 'Crap. I can't get the sleeves right.'

She had been starving hungry after that ridiculous shake for breakfast and consequently pigged out on burger and chips at lunchtime in the college canteen. Now riddled with guilt, she couldn't concentrate at all.

The lecturer smoothed out the paper. 'Let's have a look.'

Lucy shrugged her shoulders. The military jacket she had drawn was different but wearable. The design could grace any number of Top Shop stores.

'It's great,' the lecturer told Lucy.

'It's not good enough,' snapped Lucy, angry with herself.

'For who?'

'For me.'

The lecturer smiled. 'You're a perfectionist, Lucy. And that's good. But you've also got to start believing in your work.'

Lucy shrugged her shoulders. What was the point?

'Why else would I suggest you apply for Central Saint Martins?'

Lucy stared up at her, her blue eyes wide with shock. 'You're kidding, right?'

The lecturer shook her head. 'You're gonna walk your A levels in a month's time. You'll get top grades. Listen to me, you've got real potential. And I'm telling you to go for it.'

Lucy sat back in her chair. She couldn't imagine it. Her at Central Saint Martins College of Art and Design? The same London design college where Stella McCartney went. And Matthew Williamson.

But she'd be like a baby elephant crashing around in such a trendy college where everyone was going to be thin and gorgeous.

'It's time to start believing in yourself,' the lecturer told her.

Lucy sighed. If only it were that easy.

Wednesday night was practice night in the cricket nets. A two-hour session to get ready for the season ahead. Truth be told, practice night consisted of half an hour of bowling practice and two hours getting drunk in the clubhouse afterwards.

Edward was trying to nurse his pint through the evening to stop himself having more than one but the lads kept buying him one round after another.

There hadn't been time to cook dinner between leaving work and heading out, so he had grabbed a cheeseburger, fries and onion rings on the way. But now that the baskets of chicken and chips had arrived at the table, he still couldn't stop himself tucking into the food.

The practice session hadn't been great. His energy levels had slumped and he had been barely able to make the run-up when bowling. Which was hardly surprising when he was so tired these days he drove everywhere, unable to walk any distance at all.

'Come on, big guy,' said Mike. 'What's wrong with you?'

'Yeah, you big miserable bastard,' said Pete, replacing the empty glass with a full one. 'You been given six months to live?'

Edward rubbed his chest but smiled back at his friends. If only they knew.

Chapter Eight

Violet was quaking as she got dressed into the same black trouser suit as the previous day. She hadn't worn a skirt since school. And there were no high heels in her closet. No skinny stiletto was going to support her tree-trunk legs. Just sensible black shoes.

She paired her suit with yet another black top. All her tops were black. Apparently, black was slimming. But nothing hid her double chin. Or her nerves.

She'd scoffed half a loaf of bread that morning, just to steady herself. The diet would have to wait for another day. Friday would be diet day. Thursday was going to be stressful enough without having to worry about food.

Sebastian had stayed over the previous night but had left before seven o'clock. He liked to hit the gym before starting work at some investment bank in the town. She'd never quite understood what his job entailed. His work parties were a complete nightmare, full of braying men and skinny women all talking about their iPads and flash cars.

Violet lived only a couple of miles from the office but hadn't contemplated walking. She never walked anywhere. It was far too exhausting. So she inched her way into town in the rush-hour traffic. Car-parking spaces were a duel to the death at ten to nine in the morning but she finally found one and headed towards Mason & Mason.

She was quaking at the thought of the new job. New people to talk to. New people to stare at her and think she was some kind of fat freak. And as for Mark Harris . . . her stomach churned just thinking about seeing him every day.

She took a deep breath and went in. She was just about to step up to the receptionist when a familiar voice spoke behind her.

'So you decided to come back, I see.'

She turned round to face her new manager. He was grinning at her. Violet felt her cheeks grow warm as she flushed pink.

'Come on then,' he said.

She followed him as he walked towards the lift with a swagger in his step. She stayed silent in the lift, not wanting to say anything wrong.

Once on the third floor, she followed Mark to the department. This was her new workplace. There was a group of four desks, one of which was empty. The desks were divided with a low partition.

Mark gestured at the only empty desk. 'This is you. Feel welcome to get rid of anything personal that Felicity left behind. Rest assured, she took all her Peter Andre photos with her.'

Violet looked down at the desk. There was a huge sheaf of papers pinned to the two walls of the parti- tion. Most of them seemed to be photos of cute cats wearing bows. And naked firemen with strategically placed helmets.

'Right,' hollered Mark above the hubbub of conversation. 'This is Violet. She's taking over from Felicity. All right?'

A few nods in reply but everyone stayed silent.

Violet was embarrassed at the attention. She glanced at the three people who were seated around her. One of them was the grumpy woman whom she had met the previous day.

'This is Julie,' said Mark. 'She's our database manager. Don't ask her about her kids 'cos she'll tell you. And don't try to take any of her Maltesers if she's having a bad morning. You two should get on famously.'

His eyes twinkled at her and Violet found herself blushing even more at his hint of chocolate theft. She looked at Julie and tried to smile, but Julie didn't smile back.

'This is Wendy,' Mark carried on, indicating the dark-haired girl sitting next to her. 'She's good at emails and all things to do with the internet. Just back after giving birth to her very own Messiah six months ago.'

Wendy gave them a weary smile. 'I've also got a toddler. I haven't had a full night's sleep for two years.'

'And this is Anthony,' Mark said, pointing at the young guy who had been playing on his BlackBerry until that point. 'Fresh out of university, thought he'd gain valuable experience in IT before hitting the big time in the City of London. Poor sod is only now finding out what he's let himself in for. He covers all the hardware stuff.'

Anthony nodded in greeting before hiding back behind his screen.

'So?' carried on Mark. 'Everything OK this morning?'

'Corum is up and running again,' said Julie.

'Corum is the sales reps' database,' Mark told Violet. 'So no more problems?'

Julie shrugged her shoulders. 'Probably but that's what you get for buying a piece of shit software.'

Mark seemed to shrug off her rudeness. Perhaps she was always bolshy.

'Much as I'd love to take full credit for Corum, it wasn't my decision to buy it. Because I'm not that stupid, contrary to what you're all thinking. Wendy?'

'Email crashed again overnight but it seems to be OK. The server went down but hopefully we're all OK now.'

Mark nodded and looked at Anthony. 'What about you?'

Anthony gave a dramatic sigh. 'Six laptops to fix. Two have broken screens, one had Cherry Coke poured on to the keyboard, two have broken power sockets and one was dropped down the stairs.'

'Accidentally, we presume?' said Mark, turning to look at Violet. 'So, that's it. Any questions?'

She tried to figure it all out. 'How many sales reps are there?'

His eyebrows shot up. 'Good question. About five hundred in total. They're all field-based around the country so you never get to meet them. Some will ring twenty times a day. Some you'll never hear from. Most of the younger reps seem pretty clued up about computers but the older reps resent having to use anything modern.'

'So everyone's got a laptop?'

'And a printer.'

Violet thought hard once more. 'And we answer questions on everything?'

Mark nodded. 'Absolutely. They'll call if something's not working or they don't know how to use or find a certain function on the laptop. But don't worry. Just pick up the phone and then pass it on to one of the other guys. If they're busy, take a message and tell them we'll get back to them. OK?'

She nodded.

He pointed at the black telephone on her desk. 'That's the hotline. It'll always ring at your desk first, although anyone can pick it up.'

Violet jumped as the phone suddenly rang and looked up at Mark. 'What do I say?' she asked, feeling panic stricken.

'"Good morning, Hotline" is normally a good start,' he said, grinning at her. 'Go on. Off you go.'

Oh God. She wasn't ready for this. But he was watching so she picked up the ringing telephone and spoke into the handset.

'Good morning, Hotline,' stuttered Violet.

'Thank God! You've got to help me!' screamed a woman down the line. 'I can't believe what's happening! My screen has gone mad! It's swirling around and around. I think it's going to explode! There's something wrong with it. It's a brand-new laptop – it shouldn't be doing this. You've got to sort it out!'

How was she supposed to handle this? Thankfully, the woman took a breath in which Violet managed to interrupt with, 'Could you hold for one moment, please?'

She covered the mouthpiece with her hand and looked up at Mark. 'She says her screen has gone mad. It's swirling around and it's brand new.'

He took the phone from her and spoke.

'Hello? Who's this? Hi, Mary. OK, what happened?' Mark suddenly broke into a smile. 'That's your screensaver. If you nudge the mouse slightly it will disappear. You see? Well, it's for security so nobody can see what's on your screen. It'll appear when you leave the computer for a long time. That's OK. You're welcome.'

He put the phone down and shook his head. 'Welcome to the department. You've just had your first hopeless case. If you need confirmation, look at Anthony's mouse mat.'

He gave her a quick smile that lit up his face before going into his office and closing the door.

This left Violet alone with the other three members of the department. Her desk was opposite Anthony's. She could just see his eyes above the low partition between them.

'You wanna see?' he said, holding up his mouse mat high above the partition.

It read, 'BANG HEAD HERE'.

She smiled at the joke.

'You wait,' said Wendy, from the desk next to Anthony's. 'I had someone ask me how to play the other side of a CD yesterday.'

'Do you know anything about computers?' barked Julie.

'I've used Windows and Microsoft Office,' Violet told her.

She sniffed. 'That won't get us far.'

'That's a wealth of knowledge compared to Felicity,' said Wendy. 'She couldn't even switch her own computer on, let alone help anyone else with theirs.'

'We'll see,' sniffed Julie.

Violet shrank back in her chair and stared at the

phone as it rang out once more. With a deep breath, she picked it up and said, 'Good morning, Hotline.'

'Hi,' said the male voice at the other end of the line. 'I'm trying to print but the computer says it can't find the printer. I need someone to fix it now!'

'Could you please hold,' said Violet and covered the mouthpiece once more.

She thought back to Mark's descriptions and guessed that Anthony was probably the most likely recipient for the phone call.

Wendy leant across her desk. 'Do you want me to show you how to transfer a call?'

Violet sighed with relief. 'Yes, please.'

Wendy showed her how and Violet transferred the call to Anthony's desk.

'What?' he said, looking at Violet as he picked up the phone.

'This customer has a problem with his printer,' she told him.

He sighed and pressed a button on his handset.

'Can I help you?' he said, his tone no different to the snappy one he had used on Violet.

Anthony listened for a minute before speaking. 'Is the printer switched on?' Another pause. 'Well, you have to let it warm up first.' Finally, 'You're welcome.'

Anthony slammed down the headset, muttering, 'They really are useless. I'm too busy for these idiots.'

It seemed to be a general theme within the department as the morning went on. Everyone appeared to be overworked, each of them sighing whenever a call was passed on to them. Especially Julie.

After yet another growl and scowl in her direction, Violet fled in the direction of the coffee machines. She had just got a Mars bar out of the vending machine when Wendy came into the kitchen.

'Sorry if we're all a bit tetchy,' she said, smiling. 'There's always so much work to do. It's crazy. They keep taking on more and more sales reps but don't add any more staff to the department. I think Mark's pulling his hair out.'

Violet took a sip of coffee.

'And don't worry about Julie,' she carried on. 'Felicity used to drive her mad. She'll tar you with the same brush but Ant and I think you're a big step in the right direction. At least you can answer the phone!'

'Thanks,' muttered Violet.

But the compliment didn't sit well. Did she mean a big step or just big?

Violet took a big bite of Mars bar and pushed the thought away. Hopefully she would be able to prove to Julie that she could do this job. And maybe she could prove it to herself at the same time.

Chapter Nine

This was it. D-Day. It was Friday and the first day of Violet's diet.

Write down everything you eat, said the New You! leaflet. Her list for today was going to read cereal bar, milkshake and some kind of healthy dinner that she hadn't quite got round to thinking about yet.

As soon as the hotline phone was silent, she got the cereal bar out of her handbag and stared down at it. Apparently it had zero fat. She took a bite. Zero taste too. The cereal bar fell apart as soon as she touched it and scattered crumbs all over the desk.

Violet sighed and crunched on the bar without enjoyment.

Mark had been talking to Anthony about some new laptops and glanced across at her over the partition.

'Looks like that stuff you insulate your loft with,' he told her with a frown on his face.

Violet swallowed hard. Tasted like it too.

Her boss shook his head and went away again.

Wendy peered around the corner. 'Is that Dr Shaker's Dream Bar?'

Violet shook her head. But Wendy was waiting expectantly so she had to carry on. 'I've joined a New You! Club,' she said, very quietly.

'Ooh! You'll have to tell me how you get on,' said Wendy. 'I'm desperate to lose my baby weight.'

Wendy was tiny and didn't really need to diet.

'What's for lunch?' asked Wendy.

'Some kind of shake.'

'The strawberry ones normally taste better than the chocolate ones.'

Two hours later, Violet decided that Wendy was wrong. The lunchtime strawberry shake tasted bad. It looked bad. And the smell was pretty grim too.

The diet booklet had suggested making every meal an event so Violet had poured it into a plastic cup. Poured might have been an exaggeration. It had sort of plopped out of the carton in one gooey mass. She contemplated slicing one bit off at a time but in the end decided to gulp it down. The goo lodged in her throat and Violet was close to gagging by the time she got to the end.

Feeling sick, she glanced up as Mark headed past the desks.

'What is this? Weird things you can eat at work day?'

Violet shook her head. 'Lunch.'

'Want me to garnish it with a Crunchie bar?'

She scowled at him. 'No, thank you.'

Yes! screamed her body, as he carried on walking away. For the love of God, yes!

Time passed quickly on the hotline. Suddenly it was Friday afternoon and everyone was talking about their plans for the weekend. Violet kept quiet and listened in, as normal. She wasn't sure what Sebastian had planned for their weekend.

The phone rang but she had managed to quell her fear of the hotline. Each time, she picked up the phone, listened to the problem and passed on the call. It wasn't exactly taxing on the brain. Plus the customers had no idea what Violet looked like so that was another big worry off her hands.

Violet picked up the receiver. 'Good afternoon, Hotline.'

'For God's sake!' shouted the male voice down the phone. 'This laptop you've given me is bloody useless! What kind of crap is this? It fails all the time. I want a brand-new one sent to me this afternoon.'

Violet looked up but Anthony was away from his desk.

She took a deep breath. 'I'm sorry but the person you need to speak to isn't here at the moment. Can I take your name and ask him to call you back?'

'For God's sake!' shouted the man. 'What's the point in ringing if there's no one there to help. Christ! A five-year-old has got more brains than you . . .'

On and on he raged and Violet shrank lower and lower in her seat. The customer was very aggressive and getting nastier by the minute. She bit her lip, trying not to cry.

'And another thing—' shouted the man.

But he never got to finish. The receiver was suddenly snatched out of her hand by Mark, whom she hadn't realised had been standing nearby. He listened for a minute before putting the phone down, cutting the line.

Violet was shocked. The man would ring back even

madder, surely? She stared up at Mark, who shook his head at her.

The hotline rang but Mark held up his hand and picked up the phone himself.

'Yes?' he snapped. He listened for a short while before speaking. 'If you ever talk to my staff like that again, I'll have you sacked and then I'll hunt you down and cut your balls off with a rather blunt knife. Understand?'

Then he slammed the phone down and muttered what sounded like swear words in a foreign language.

Violet was still upset but had managed not to cry by biting down on her lip.

Mark perched on the edge of her desk and looked down at her.

'Look, you're going to get idiots like that from time to time,' he said gently. 'But you don't have to listen to them. You don't take that kind of crap from anyone, OK?'

He sat close to her until Violet had no choice but to raise her eyes to meet his. He looked at her for a moment, his sea-green eyes holding hers. Then he walked away, leaving her to stew over his words.

On Saturday morning, Violet lay in bed and waved the third finger on her left hand. It was a week since she had become engaged to Sebastian and she was still getting used to wearing the ring.

'You like it?' said Sebastian, lying on his side and watching her. 'Do you know what we should do to celebrate?'

Violet's mind flitted briefly towards the chocolate gateau in Marks & Spencer.

'We should go and tell my parents.'

The chocolate cake exploded.

'Really?' Violet stammered.

'Absolutely. After all, they're going to be your family too, aren't they?'

Violet hadn't quite realised that was part of getting engaged. It wasn't that Sebastian's family were unpleasant. At least, not in an obvious way. They just made her feel uncomfortable. But perhaps marrying their son would change all that.

So Violet gave Sebastian a fake smile and nodded enthusiastically.

They arrived at his parents' house just before noon.

As Sebastian rang the doorbell, Violet wiped her sweaty hands on her trousers and fixed a smile on her face.

The door was thrown open with a cry of 'Darling!' Sebastian was then swept into a smothering hug by his mother. Miriam Parkes was very slim and perfectly coiffed. She finally released her son and glanced over to give Violet a large smile. But it didn't reach her eyes.

'Hello, Violet,' she said in her posh voice. 'How are you? Do come in, both of you.'

Sebastian's mother Miriam always sounded as if she had been born with a plum in her mouth but she and her husband only lived in a suburban semi. It was all cream carpets, gold accessories and china tea cups.

Donald, Sebastian's father, put down his Saturday *Telegraph* and glanced up.

'Hello,' he said, standing to greet them.

He shook his son's hand awkwardly before doing his normal dither of whether to hug or kiss Violet. In the end, they did neither and just smiled at each other in embarrassment.

'Do sit down, everyone,' said Miriam. 'Coffee?'

Sebastian and his father tiptoed the conversation around the previous weekend's football results whilst Miriam fussed around in the kitchen.

She eventually returned with a tray laden with cups and plates full of Victoria sponge.

Sebastian grabbed his drink and took a large glug of coffee. 'Needed that,' he said, leaning back against the sofa.

Miriam tutted and shook her head. 'They work you too hard at that office. You must rest properly, darling.'

Sebastian smiled. 'I'm fine, Mum.'

Sebastian was always fussed over by his mother. He was the crown prince, the only child of a couple who had started their family late in life. Therefore, he was adored and smothered in equal measure.

'You had that flu in December and the body needs time to recover. Especially a gentle constitution like yours. Did you get that echinacea I sent you? Your immune system will still be fragile and you mustn't catch another cold otherwise you'll be suffering for months to come.'

Sebastian put down his cup and took Violet's hand in his. She hoped he didn't notice how sweaty it was from nerves.

'Enough of the doom-and-gloom talk. I have some good news for you.' He smiled at his parents.

Miriam's face clicked up in expectation.

'Violet and I are engaged!' said Sebastian with a flourish.

'Darling!' cried his mother, leaping up from his chair to hug her son. 'How wonderful!'

'Yes,' barked Donald, staying put in his seat. 'Congratulations, son.'

Miriam then gave Violet a very awkward hug before moving quickly back to her armchair.

'When's the big day?' asked Miriam.

Sebastian and Violet looked at each other. They hadn't got round to planning the wedding day yet.

'Not sure,' said Sebastian. 'We only got engaged a week ago.'

'And you didn't call before now?' said Miriam with a pout.

'We wanted to come and tell you face to face,' said Sebastian, knowing how to placate his mother.

Miriam nodded. 'Of course,' she said, smiling once more.

'Where were you thinking of having the reception?' asked Donald.

Violet had thought of a few ideas regarding the big day and turned to say as much to Miriam but Sebastian placed a hand on her knee. 'I'll answer that, darling.'

Violet nodded. Of course. This was his family. It was right that he should be the one discussing the details with them.

'Actually we were wondering if you had any ideas,' Sebastian said.

Violet was stunned. Why did they need to ask Sebastian's parents for ideas?

Miriam smiled at her son. 'Well, you'll get married at St Winifred's, naturally.'

Sebastian nodded.

'So the reception can be at the Hyde Country Club.'

'Good choice,' said Donald, nodding.

In fact, everyone was nodding with approval. Apart from Violet, who had never even heard of these places.

She looked up and found Miriam watching her.

'Obviously, I know the unfortunate story of your parents,' said Miriam. 'Have you any other family to help with the arrangements?'

Violet took a deep intake of breath. But Miriam was right. There was no one. She shook her head.

'Oh dear,' cooed Miriam. 'Well, we'll cope. And I suppose we could fill your half of the church with some of the more distant members of our family. Great-uncle Geoffrey, for example.'

'Absolutely,' said Sebastian.

Miriam turned to face Donald. 'A lot of the aunts and uncles are getting on a bit so the heat of summer is really out of the question. Autumn is a busy time for me, what with the bazaar and flower festival.'

'Indeed,' murmured Donald.

Violet glanced across at Sebastian but he was staying silent. She couldn't believe he was going to let his parents choose the venue and now the date for their wedding.

'I know!' said Miriam. 'New Year's Eve. The Christmas rush at church will be over. It'll be lovely with the tree and we won't have to buy flowers for the church. Plus we won't have to attend John's dreadful New Year's Eve party for the tenth year running.'

'Hear hear!' barked Donald.

'Perfect,' said Sebastian, turning to Violet with a beaming smile.

Violet was so stunned she could do nothing but fix on a fake smile and stay silent.

Grateful of the excuse to escape, Violet got up to return her empty tea cup to the kitchen.

Unfortunately, Sebastian's mother had followed her into the room and was standing guard at doorway.

'A wedding,' said Miriam. 'How exciting. I can't wait to tell everyone.'

Violet nodded her agreement.

'Can I see the ring?'

Violet held out her left hand and watched Miriam peer forward for a closer look.

'Lovely,' declared Sebastian's mother. 'Emeralds are so classy, aren't they? But then Sebastian did always have good taste.'

Violet carried on nodding and smiling in reply.

'I suppose you'll want to lose a bit of weight for the wedding,' said Miriam, giving Violet a quick once-over.

Violet stopped nodding and blushed bright red, mortified.

'You could always try those slimming pills,' Miriam carried on, not noticing or caring about Violet's embarrassment. 'One of the ladies at my lunch club has lost a couple of stone in a month. Your mother was a large woman, was she?

The mention of her mother brought tears to Violet's eyes. She had been slim, a dark-haired beauty. Nothing like her fat daughter.

'It's a shame because you've got ever such a pretty face.'

Thankfully Sebastian chose that moment to appear. 'Any more of that cake?' he asked.

Miriam's smile snapped back on. 'Of course, darling.' Then she turned to look at Violet. 'You must both have a second piece.'

She went back into the lounge with Sebastian to sort out the plates, leaving Violet to calm down both her red cheeks and her racing pulse.

But somewhere amid the embarrassment was a flash

of anger. How dare Miriam dismiss the death of her parents as 'unfortunate'?

Violet was the only child of parents who had adored her. Then, when she was twelve, they had both been killed in a car accident. It hadn't been unfortunate. It had been catastrophic.

Not only did Violet suffer the deep grief of losing her parents, but her life suddenly changed dramatically. She was torn out of school and away from her friends to live with her mother's sister Mary and her husband Joel. They were the only family willing to put up with an orphaned twelve-year-old. Violet had no choice but to go.

Her parents' death had been a cataclysm and Violet hadn't been truly happy since.

Apart from now, she reminded herself. She was engaged. She was getting married to the love of her life. But her heart sank once more as she thought of Sebastian's parents' country club and all their cronies.

She would have preferred a small wedding. Intimate and stylish. But Miriam had already mentioned a guest list of at least a hundred. And that was just off the top of her head. It was made up of a lot of people who didn't know or care about Violet.

She tried hard to think about who she would want at her wedding. The only person who popped into her mind was Uncle Joel. But he had died four years ago, just before Aunty Mary.

And now there was nobody who cared. Nobody except Sebastian in her life.

Sebastian was smiling as they drove home later that afternoon.

'Well, that's all sorted,' he said. 'Mother says she'll

book the church and reception so at least we don't have that stress on our hands.'

But Violet was beginning to panic. A fat bride. A porky, obese bride waddling down the aisle in front of one hundred guests who didn't know her. They would all be whispering, giggling, laughing at her. She could feel her pulse racing at the thought of it. She couldn't do it. Oh God. All those people.

She took a deep breath and looked at her fiancé. 'We could always elope,' she found herself saying.

'Elope?' He sounded quite shocked. 'Don't be ridiculous. My family has been getting married in St Winifred's for generations. And you know what Mother's like with foreign food.'

Sebastian was right. It was ridiculous. As usual, Violet was being an idiot.

But what about us? a little voice inside her asked. What about what we want? What I want?

But Violet stayed quiet.

Chapter Ten

Trudie stared at the fat freaks before forcing a smile onto her face.

Right!' she said. 'Who wants to be weighed first?'

Nothing. Not a smile, not a whisper. That was a bit bizarre. The first weigh-in after her victims began their diets normally bought a brief joy at the very least.

She pursed her lips and then pointed. 'You! Edward! You can be first.'

Start with the fat boy. He'll have lost quite a bit already. That might spread a bit of excitement.

She strode over to the scales and waited as he lumbered his way over to her. Trudie tried not to shudder. Thank God, her husband Trevor was nice and slim. Not like this elephant. Imagine sleeping with that? Trudie gulped down her nausea.

'So? How was your first week? It's always exciting when you get your first results, isn't it?'

Edward nodded. Whatever, mate. Save your breath. You're going to need it to blow up your next date.

'Step up on the scales for me.'

Edward took a deep breath and stepped up.

There was a moment whilst the machine registered the weight and then beeped its final results.

Trudie frowned at the screen and then up at Edward.

'You've only lost two pounds,' she told him.

She waited for him to tell her that the computer must be wrong but his face was filled with guilt. He obviously hadn't bothered at all.

'I would have expected you to lose far more than that in your first week,' she told him. 'Especially at your significant weight.'

Edward coloured a deep shade of pink. 'It was a friend's stag weekend,' he said, sounding a little hoarse. 'Maybe I had a few too many beers.'

'Followed by twenty kebabs?' Trudie pursed her lips together. 'I expect better from you next week. Unless you have another social gathering you want to tell us about?'

Edward shook his head and lumbered away.

What a loser. Thank God for the Trevors of the world. Men like Edward should never make it past the sperm count.

Lord, here was the menopausal mother. Hopefully she'd had a better week.

'Hello, Maggie. How was your week?'

'A bit difficult, if I'm honest.'

Couldn't prise your hands off the sherry bottle, could you?

The woman looked even more wretched than usual in tracksuit bottoms and an aerobics T-shirt that was far too tight on her.

'Dieting is meant to be difficult,' Trudie replied. 'Otherwise everyone would be thin, wouldn't they? Hop on the scales for me.'

Maggie stepped up and they waited for the beep.

Trudie looked at the screen and then back up at Maggie.

'Not another one,' she snapped. 'You've only lost a pound. What happened?'

'It was Lucy's birthday,' said Maggie quickly.

When in doubt, blame the fat daughter.

'Did you eat the whole cake yourself?' said Trudie, not waiting for a reply. 'Try harder next week.'

I see that you were so impressed with your first couple of chins that you've added another one in the past week. What was wrong with these people? Couldn't they see how disgusting they looked?

Maggie stepped aside to make way for her daughter. Oh good, it's the birthday girl.

'I hope you didn't have too good a birthday,' said Trudie.

The teenager scowled back in reply. Stroppy mare. At least when I do a handstand, my stomach doesn't hit me in the face.

'Step up on the scales for me, please.'

Just as expected. Another loser but not in the most important way.

'You haven't lost anything,' Trudie said to Lucy. 'Not a single pound.'

Lucy shrugged and then walked away.

Not my fault you can't handle life without McDonald's, is it? Honestly, thought Trudie. They've spent all this money and not bothered. Makes me wonder why I should.

The next fatty wandered up. At least Violet was a bride-to-be and had a real goal to aim for.

Or not, Trudie realised, as the scales beeped their results.

'You've lost one pound,' Trudie finally said into the silence that stretched out between them.

Violet scuttled away before Trudie could say anything else.

She'll be lucky if the groom doesn't dump her before the wedding day.

Last up was the jolly fat lady. The joker of the pack.

'Hello!' boomed Kathy, as she arrived in front of Trudie. 'Don't bother to ask about my week. I was so hungry that I ended up in the bakery most days. Their sausage rolls are to die for.'

Trudie glanced down at the scales.

'Not a single pound off,' she snapped, with increasing frustration. 'Nothing to show at all. Have you anything to say for yourself?'

Kathy fixed on a smile. 'I know. It's disgraceful. I even bumped into a homeless guy yesterday. He said to me he hadn't eaten in a week. I told him, "I wish I had your willpower." Boom! Boom!'

Trudie sighed. Yes, keep talking. I always yawn when I'm interested.

It was unbelievable. She had never had such a total class failure. Head office was not going to be impressed. These bunch of fatties were going to make her look bad. She ground her teeth in irritation.

'Right!' she barked as Kathy sat back down. 'We need a team talk.'

She strode to the middle of the group and stared down at them all.

'I would have expected far bigger losses this week from every one of you,' she said in her sternest voice. 'Especially as you're in full detox fortnight.'

Everyone shuffled in their seats.

'Don't you want to lose weight and be nice and slim

like me? Don't you want to stop feeling fat and unwell all the time? Don't you care that my commission is based on how much weight you lose?'

Maggie and Kathy glanced at each other before looking back at her, eyebrows raised.

But Trudie didn't care. 'Right! I'm going to have to work you really hard this week to make up for it. Now stand up straight and put your hands on your waists.'

If you can find them, that is.

Chapter Eleven

Violet woke up on Wednesday with good intentions to stick to the diet. Especially after the humiliation at Trudie's class the previous evening. And it worked for a whole hour.

Because she never normally had breakfast, the hunger didn't kick in until 10 a.m. At which time, she was up to her eyes in hotline calls. Not that they were very exciting, unfortunately.

The job was very monotonous. Pick up the phone, say hello, find out their name and a rough idea of the problem. Then pass it on to the relevant team member. Job done. It made her job at the accountants' firm seem like nuclear physics.

Once in a while, the call became interesting. Like when someone screamed that their world was falling apart because they couldn't get into their emails. Or when she overheard her colleagues negotiate the fine line between advice and sarcasm.

She had just passed a phone call across to Anthony

after a man had rung saying he had lost the letter H key from his keyboard.

Violet tuned into what Anthony was saying.

'I can send you a replacement H key. It just clicks into place. I suggest you don't let your cat sleep on the laptop in future.' There was a small pause. 'Well, I think the vet's going to have to deal with that.'

Anthony put down the phone and let out a sigh. Their gazes locked briefly and Violet gave him a sympathetic smile. Anthony rolled his eyes and turned back to his computer screen.

'God, I'd kill for some chocolate,' Wendy said suddenly. 'But I mustn't. I'm trying to be good. I put on a stone with Calum and I just can't shift it.'

'You don't need to lose weight,' snapped Julie from across the desk. 'I keep telling you, you look fine.'

'I never had this trouble when I had Jack,' said Wendy. 'My stomach snapped back straight away. Perhaps it was the breast feeding. But Calum wouldn't even try to get on to my tit.'

Violet noticed Anthony get up rather swiftly and head into the store cupboard where he kept all the computer parts. That was his sanctuary away from the girly talk, which was usually initiated by Wendy.

'Chocolate's my downfall,' said Wendy.

Violet thought that all food was her downfall.

'You'll never lose any weight eating between meals,' said Julie. 'Do you know how many calories there are in a Mars bar?'

Violet didn't even know the meaning of between meals.

But, as usual, she kept quiet. It was interesting to hear slim people talk about their struggle with weight.

'I'm gonna go low-carb,' said Wendy. 'You know, like the Atkins diet.'

'You'll die of clogged arteries,' snapped Julie. 'All that butter and red meat. Your heart will go into cardiac arrest.'

'No, there's a new diet out,' said Wendy, grabbing a magazine from her handbag and flicking through the pages. 'It's like the Atkins diet but without all the fat.'

'But what does that leave?' said Julie, rolling her eyes. 'Are you just gonna eat meat all day?'

'I think they let you have a lettuce now.'

'Very nutritious,' said Julie. 'Gimme that magazine.'

Wendy reluctantly handed it over.

Julie was silent for a minute before tutting. 'Look at that,' she said, holding the magazine aloft so she could point at the opposite page. 'Samantha from that new pop group says she eats normally. But do you know what she does? Sprinkles charcoal over every meal.'

'Charcoal?' Violet couldn't stop herself from stammering out loud.

Julie nodded. 'The same stuff that we put in our fireplaces, this girl is adding to her food. It absorbs all the bad fats in the body, apparently.' She threw the magazine back across to Wendy. 'These girls are bonkers.'

Wendy stared at the photo of the charcoal-eating singer. 'But doesn't she look great?'

'Who looks great?' said Mark, coming to stand between Violet and Wendy.

'Samantha from Popstars,' said Wendy, holding up the photo for him.

'Bit skinny,' he said, making a face. 'I prefer women

to have a few curves rather than look like they can't even cast a shadow.'

'She eats charcoal,' said Julie to Mark. 'To make herself thin.'

'Thought she looked like a bunny boiler.' He peered closer at the photo. 'Plus she's the colour of a lobster. I rest my case.'

And off he strode.

'Did you see that girl he met in reception last week?' hissed Wendy to the girls. 'Think he took her to lunch. Really tall.'

'So? He's got to be over six feet,' replied Julie.

'Yeah but she was gorgeous. Tall but curvy. I reckon she was a model.'

'Humph,' said Julie, rolling her eyes. 'I bet she didn't eat anything at lunch though.'

'What happened to the last girlfriend?'

Julie gave a snort of laughter. 'Tossed out like the rest of them. He doesn't keep them hanging around for long.'

'They're always beautiful though,' said Wendy with a sigh.

Violet picked up the hotline as it began to ring once more, grateful not to hear any more about Mark's love life. Or about Mark in general. Something about him made the hairs on the back of her neck rise. Whenever he looked at her, she could swear he knew what she was thinking. The fact was that he had seen her at her absolute worst and it still mortified her.

Later on, she mulled over Wendy's thoughts about dieting. Perhaps she should go low-carb too. People on the internet were reporting huge weight losses really quickly. And that's what she needed. A quick fix to get rid of all the flab.

The thought of a life without potatoes, bread, rice

and cereal was a bit daunting, but the promise of losing a stone in two weeks was just too much to resist. She needed a big start to her weight-loss campaign. And this was going to work, wasn't it?

She printed out a menu for the week. All you could eat was meat, fish, eggs and non-fat dairy stuff, which sounded great. Plain bacon in the morning would be weird without buttered bread, but she normally skipped breakfast anyway.

By lunchtime Violet was ravenous. She'd already had her New You! cereal bar but that barely touched the hunger inside. What was she supposed to eat? So she went into McDonald's and had a double burger but discarded everything apart from the meat. The bun and salad went in the bin. Yet she was starving that afternoon so she had her shake as well.

Dinner that evening was a bit more of a problem.

'What are you doing?' asked Sebastian, leaning against the kitchen door and watching her.

'I'm looking for something to eat,' she told him, closing the fridge door. She took a deep breath. 'I'm sort of trying a carb-free diet for a week.'

His eyebrows shot up. 'Why?'

'I told you. I want to lose weight for the wedding.'

He gently shoved her to one side and opened up the fridge door. 'Great,' he said, before straightening up. 'Let's have a fry-up.'

So they had fried eggs, bacon and sausages. She wasn't sure if that was strictly within the diet but it sounded close enough. Sebastian wolfed down two slices of bread and butter but Violet just about managed to resist the temptation.

Think of being skinny, she told herself. Think of the

wedding dress. Think how wonderful you and Sebastian will look together once you're no longer fat.

The following day, she followed the same diet of no breakfast, burger but no bun and a fry-up of steak and eggs. That night Sebastian added chips to his plate. Violet's mouth was salivating but still she held firm.

Violet had begun to suffer with headaches. And she wasn't the only one. Wendy was moaning as Julie handed her some paracetamol.

'It's no wonder you feel crap,' she barked at Wendy. 'You're not eating properly.'

'I am.'

'Of course you're not. You had a single chicken breast for lunch.'

Wendy gulped down some pills and water. 'I'll be fine. As soon as the protein hits the fat in my body then I'll start losing weight. It's all very scientific.'

Julie gave a snort and went back behind her computer monitor.

Wendy leant across to whisper at Violet, 'James told me I have the breath to kill six rhinos this morning.'

Violet gave her a small smile and wondered whether Sebastian would feel her breath was smelly too.

She was starving by the time she reached home. Sebastian suggested another fry-up. Violet nearly wept. She was overdosing on protein. She needed carbohydrates, had to have them. Plus she hadn't been to the loo properly for days. She felt weird, weak and a bit sick. Her body felt alien. Something had to give.

So she waited patiently until Sebastian went for a shower later on. She stayed still until she heard him step into the bath and switch the water on. Then she ran into the kitchen and wolfed down a huge bowl of cornflakes. It was glorious, even better once she'd added the sugar on top. As she heard him come out of the bathroom, she quickly washed the bowl up and put it back in the cupboard. He was none the wiser.

But the guilt was huge when she saw Wendy the next day. What was wrong with her? Why couldn't she stick to any diet?

'Hi,' said Wendy in a small voice. 'I failed my diet.'

'Oh dear,' said Violet, relief flooding through her. 'What happened?'

'We had a curry.'

'I think it's only the sauce that's fattening.'

'What about the large rice and two peshwari naan breads? All to myself.' She gave a loud sigh. 'I just couldn't do it any more. And nor could James. He said he didn't know what was worse, my breath or my wind. It had to be the constipation that made it so bad.'

Violet noticed Anthony quickly left his desk again.

Later that evening, alone in the house, Violet ate a massive bowl of pasta. She ate and ate until her stomach screamed at her to stop. It was wonderful. Her body was craving carbohydrates like a starved maniac. As she waited for the water to boil, she wolfed down a couple of pieces of bread and butter.

Another diet, another failure. Perhaps it was time to go back to the shakes and cereal bars. And this time they would work. Hopefully.

Chapter Twelve

Kathy stared at the tiny figurines.

She had been scrabbling around in the back of one of the kitchen cupboards, trying to find her sieve. Her intention had been to make a healthy banana loaf but all ideas of baking were forgotten once her fingers touched the small tin. She drew it down from the shelf and took it into the lounge.

Kathy sank on to the sofa with a sigh. She knew what was inside. She knew it would upset her to look at them. But she couldn't stop herself.

She lifted the tin lid and stared down. There was a clay Father Christmas and Snowman both looking a little grubby and well used. The Happy Christmas plastic sign was very worn too.

The decorations had been used on top of her family's Christmas cake for as long as Kathy could remember. As a child, she remembered being allowed to stir the cake mixture in the big bowl before her mother poured it into the baking tin. She could still imagine that gorgeous smell wafting through the house as the cake firmed up in the oven.

As an adult, Kathy had taken over the mantle of making the Christmas cake after her father had died. Under her mother's guidance, Kathy would bake and decorate the cake. Some years her mother would remember it was Christmas. Some years she would look at Kathy vaguely for clarification. But Kathy continued baking the cake, year after year, determined that the family tradition wouldn't die out.

Even the last Christmas, when her mother was in hospital, Kathy had still made the cake and taken it in with her to show her mother. That was the day she found her mother had lost consciousness. The day the doctor had told her that she would probably never get up again. Two days after Boxing Day, she died.

Kathy stared down at the figurines. Who was there for her to bake for now? Who would know about the silly tradition apart from her? Maybe she wouldn't bother next time. After all, it was only she that would know.

Each special day was hard to get through. The first Mother's Day. The first Easter. And now it was her mother's birthday. Kathy had felt so low that she couldn't even face Mavis and the shop so she phoned in sick. Mavis was so kind and concerned that it made Kathy feel even worse.

Kathy had planned to stay in all day but the figurines had changed all that. Now she knew what she had to do.

She made the long drive in her car back to her old home town. Along the way, she picked up a small posy of flowers. She parked the car and took the short walk to her mother's grave in the cemetery. She placed the flowers next to the headstone and stared down at the ground for a while before straightening up.

She walked to a nearby bench and sat down, trying not to cry. She was so low, so grief-stricken. And the only person who would have been any help right now was her lovely mum. It felt a very long time since her mother had held her, had hugged her. Since anyone had held her, she realised.

There had been a few low-life boyfriends but nobody special. Initially they were all attracted by the jolly fat woman with the cheeky smile and bright brown hair. But it was exhausting being amusing all the time. Sometimes Kathy just wanted to sit quietly and not have to be on show.

She stayed on the bench in the graveyard for a long time. So long that the time ran away with her and she realised that she probably wouldn't be home in time to go to the diet club that evening. Not that Kathy cared. Missing one week wouldn't make any difference.

The way she felt, nothing was going to make any difference to her life. She sat on the bench until darkness fell and then made the long drive home.

Maggie had been trying really hard to stay on the shakes and bars. Honest, she had. The trouble was, by the time she got to the afternoon she felt ill and exhausted, with a hideous headache.

According to the New You! booklet, the first fortnight was supposed to be tough. It was meant to be an extreme detox to cleanse the body of its evils and get it ready for all the healthy stuff ahead. The cereal bars and shakes were full of nutritious goodness to help the body.

'Rubbish,' muttered Maggie, clutching her head.

She even lay down on the bed, holding her stomach and willing it to stay calm. This was good. Hunger was good. She had all these extra fat reserves waiting to be used up. Her body could cope with a little starvation. Her stomach howled in fury.

But it was no use. Maggie couldn't settle. So at four o'clock, she headed back downstairs and wolfed down half a loaf of bread. Then she went into the lounge and sank on to the sofa in carbohydrate-induced delirium.

It had been the same routine nearly every day. Starve then binge. Repeat daily until the next weigh-in.

Trouble was, the next weigh-in was that evening. Maggie couldn't care less. Not only did she have the headache from hell, she was also bent double with hideous period pains. The last couple of months, her period had been really heavy.

Then, as she was staggering around the supermarket the previous day, Maggie had had her first hot flush. Standing in the bread aisle, she was suddenly aware of a deep heat glowing from her face, neck and chest. She had to fan herself with a magazine to stop herself from passing out. In the end, she went to the freezer section and stood by the open freezer chests to cool herself down.

So that was it. The menopause was on its way. Just the night sweats, mood changes and lack of sex to look forward to. Maggie sighed. Not that she and Gordon had any kind of sex life these days. A quick cuddle at the weekend, if she was lucky. But more often than not they couldn't be bothered.

At least she had already achieved the maximum weight gain. She hoped.

*

93

Lucy had had a terrible day at college. Nothing went right. The lack of calories during the day was making her brain fuzzy. She'd screwed up design after design, nothing being good enough. It was rubbish.

She hadn't heard from St Martins so the lecturer had obviously been lying to her, trying to make her believe that she was good enough when she really wasn't.

To top it all, she had run into Nicola Bowles and the gang on the way home. If only she had enough money to buy a car, then she could drive past them and never have to meet them in the street. But no, she had to travel on the bus and the gang were always hanging around the bus stop near the local shops.

They were laughing hysterically at something as Lucy got off the bus. She was certain it was her.

'Hey, Fatso!' yelled Nicola. 'Saw your mum today. Runs in the family, does it? Being fat bitches?'

Lucy felt a sting of hatred shoot through her and tried to carry on walking. But the gang of girls blocked her path.

'That's right,' sneered one of the girls. 'I heard your momma's so fat they had to grease a doorframe and hold a Mars bar on the other side to get her through.'

The gang fell about laughing, screaming their glee in Lucy's face.

'Yeah,' said another girl. 'Your momma's so fat that when she walked by my TV, I missed the *EastEnders* omnibus.'

More hysterical laughter followed. Lucy tried to change direction but they blocked her path once more.

'Your momma's so fat, even Dora can't bloody explore her,' said another girl who was pushing a pram.

The young mum was still thinner than her, Lucy thought.

Then Nicola Bowles stepped right up so her face was close to Lucy's.

'Your momma's so fat, she died. Or she will do if she don't get her stomach stapled. Or is that you? Are you the one who needs one of them gastric bands, you fat bitch?'

Lucy's anger boiled over and she gave Nicola a large shove to move her out of the way.

'Ooooh!' the gang cooed as she strode away from them.

Lucy half ran up the road, praying that they wouldn't follow her. That they wouldn't see the tears streaming down her face.

She slammed the front door shut behind her and stalked into the lounge, where she found her mum sprawled on the sofa. For a second, she thought Nicola's prediction had come true and her mother had passed away. Then she saw Maggie move and realised she just been asleep.

'What's with you?' Lucy snarled, hating both herself and her mother for being so weak.

'Don't feel very well, love.' Maggie was struggling to sit up.

'Aren't you going to that diet club tonight?'

Maggie cleared her throat. 'Not sure I'll be up to it. What about you?'

'Don't bloody care,' said Lucy. 'Stupid bloody diet doesn't work anyway.'

She stomped upstairs and threw her college bag down on the bedroom floor. Once the door was firmly closed, she drew out a box of doughnuts and bit into one. She had to have calories. She was starving.

Besides, it didn't sound as if her mum was going tonight and there was no way she was going to see that Trudie on her own.

She switched on her TV and pushed in a DVD to watch. She watched Jennifer Aniston bounce around the screen for a while before throwing the remote across the room in despair. Stupid bloody actresses. Why couldn't she look like them? Eat like them? What was wrong with her?

Lucy hid the empty doughnut box underneath her bed. Later on, she would creep downstairs to hide the evidence in the bottom of the wheelie bin.

Edward's department had just signed a big deal for a new computer system. The IT sales guys wanted to take them out for a couple of drinks to celebrate. He didn't mind. His social life started and ended with the cricket club. Apart from that, Edward spent his time on the sofa with his beloved Sky+ box.

He grabbed his briefcase before stopping to rub his chest. It was probably only indigestion from the Cornish pasties at lunchtime. At least, that's what he told himself.

His mother had fussed over him at the weekend, telling him he looked terrible.

'You need to start looking after yourself,' she had told him. 'You've not got any colour.'

'It's only May,' Edward told her. 'Why would I have a suntan?'

His mother had shook her head. 'You don't look well. You're carrying too much weight.'

'I'm fine, Mum.'

She had fussed over him ever since his father had passed away four years previously. His dad had suffered numerous minor strokes over the years but the last stroke had been a major event and he had not survived. Now Edward's mum was convinced he would go the same way as his dad. It was the same every time he popped home to see her, which was why the visits were becoming less frequent.

The celebration with the IT Department was certain to turn into a meal at the local Indian with a lot of booze attached. His mind briefly flickered on to the diet club. But business was business. Besides, he could be humiliated at the diet club by that stick insect Trudie or he could have a laugh with his workmates. No contest.

He didn't feel too guilty about not attending the diet club. Everyone else would be there, wouldn't they?

Chapter Thirteen

Violet hadn't gone to the weigh-in class either. After her disastrous low-carb diet failure, she had been too embarrassed. It would never have worked. Besides, she hated getting weighed in public. It was too stressful.

Anyway, she had enough on her plate that week as they were going to a wedding at the weekend. One of Sebastian's colleagues was getting married. Violet was hoping to pick up some tips for their own wedding day. But it wasn't feeling like their wedding any more. Sebastian's parents had completely taken over.

'I'm just saying,' Violet told Sebastian as they drove to the church. 'It would be nice to have had some consultation before your mother increased the guest list to a hundred and ninety.'

'Who cares?' said Sebastian, fiddling with the air-conditioning temperature. 'The more the merrier.'

'But I don't know most of them.' Violet was trying not to let her voice whine.

'Nor do I,' he replied. 'Look, just let Mum sort everything out. It takes the stress off you, doesn't it?'

'But perhaps I want the stress,' said Violet. 'Perhaps I'd like some involvement in my own wedding day.'

Sebastian swung around to glare at her for a moment. 'She's doing all this for us,' he snapped. 'You could be a little more grateful. After all, Mum has a busy life too.'

'I know,' said Violet. 'But how much is this all going to cost?'

'Your inheritance kicks in next year so we can pay it all back then.'

Sebastian bringing up the subject of money startled her somewhat. It seemed that her inheritance was being spent before Violet had even received it.

Having spent many miserable teenage years with her aunt and uncle, she certainly never expected to receive any inheritance from them. Her uncle had left a small legacy, enough to put a deposit down on her lovely house. But a year afterwards, her aunt had also passed away. With Violet being the only remaining family member, the whole estate passed to her.

It was only when she was summoned to the solicitors that Violet was told she stood to inherit an astounding £120,000. It seemed an extraordinary amount, especially when her aunt had been so cruel in the years following her parents' accident.

But her aunt had still had the last laugh. The final kick in the teeth was her will. Yes, she'd left Violet her money. But Violet wasn't able to access it until she was thirty, by which time she would be deemed trustworthy.

Did she want this reminder of her cruel aunt? Of all those awful years? Not really.

Of course, she had daydreamed about what to do with the money. A long trip somewhere, perhaps around the world. She could pay off a large chunk from the mortgage, leaving her with a bit more money each month. She had even considered going to university so she could get more meaningful work. But nothing concrete, no definite plans.

'Maybe we should just give it all to a cats' home,' she said, only half joking.

Sebastian looked horrified. 'You can't waste it! That's for our future.'

Violet shrugged her shoulders. 'We both work. We don't need it.'

'If we invest it carefully, we could be millionaires in ten years. Then retire early.'

I don't care about being a millionaire, thought Violet. Not unless it makes me thin. But then she had an idea.

'Maybe we could travel round Europe,' she said, voicing an idea she had long thought buried. 'We could go to Italy. I saw a programme years ago. It looks wonderful.'

'Don't be silly, pumpkin.'

'But why not?' she pressed. 'With that money, we could take a gap year from work and travel around, immerse ourselves in different cultures.'

'Are you mad?' he snorted. 'Why would I want to see how other people live? That doesn't interest me. Unless they're pouring my cocktail in a fancy restaurant or hotel.'

Perhaps it was best that the money was going towards their wedding, thought Violet. After all, it was supposed to be the most important day of their lives. They could work out what to spend the rest on at a later date.

'About the wedding,' she began. 'I am grateful for

your mother's help but we didn't even have the chance to choose the food for the evening buffet.'

Sebastian suddenly became angry and gripped the steering wheel. 'If Elizabeth had survived, she would have been able to plan her wedding,' he said in a steely tone. 'But, as you know, she didn't and so my mother only has my wedding to look forward to.'

The subject of Elizabeth was brought up whenever Sebastian needed to defend his mother's actions. His baby sister had died soon after birth and was the reason that Sebastian was so smothered by his mother.

'But it's my wedding day too,' Violet said in small voice.

'You're being totally unreasonable,' he snapped. 'I don't know what's up with you today. After all, it's not like there's anyone on your side to help, is there?'

Violet clenched her fists on her lap but didn't reply. She was probably wrong about her desires for the wedding. She was usually wrong about everything else.

But he had brought her parents into the argument so she sulked as well. The remainder of the journey was spent in sullen silence, with Sebastian continuing to ignore her once they were outside the church.

It was quite a smart occasion, despite being held in a tiny church. Violet felt dowdy in her normal black batwing top and trousers. Even her sparkly jewellery did little to liven up the outfit. Everyone else was in lovely, bright dresses and fascinators.

The bride and groom had also been blessed by glorious end of May sunshine. It was like a mini heat-wave and Violet could feel the sweat beginning to form under her arms and around her waist. She prayed it didn't show through the top.

Sebastian's colleagues stood around, braying at each other. The men were all going on about their jobs. She had no idea what they were talking about. But worse were the looks from the women: a mixture of envy and pity. She shuffled from foot to foot and wished she had called off sick so she could hide at home.

Thankfully, it was soon time to sit down and concentrate on the service.

Sebastian was still making a point of ignoring her so Violet stared down at the Order of Service. It was a thick, cream card with gold embossed swirls for the edging. It looked and felt expensive. But Violet preferred the home-made ones she had seen in a bridal magazine. She wasn't certain how Sebastian or his parents would cope with home-made.

Everyone stood up for the bride as she appeared. As well as the posh stationery, it appeared she hadn't skimped on her dress either. It was a beautiful but elaborate gown, embroidered with sparkling beads. The strapless bodice clinched in her tiny waist before cascading into a massive, full skirt with an extra-long train. It swamped her tiny frame but she looked beautiful.

Violet felt a stab of panic as everyone murmured their approval. They were all saying how wonderful the bride looked. What on earth would they say about her in seven months' time?

She took a deep breath. It was OK. It would be fine.

Sebastian kept his eyes on the altar and didn't turn to look at her, even though she knew he could feel her watching him.

The service was lovely, everyone remembered their lines and the only slight hitch came as the vicar declared them husband and wife. The handsome groom stepped forward to kiss his beautiful bride. But he never got the chance.

She hissed at him, 'You're standing on my bloody dress!'

Hardly a serene bride but Violet put it down to nerves.

Afterwards, everyone stopped for photographs outside the church. Again, as she hid at the back of the group, she was filled with panic at the idea of being the focus of everyone's attention.

They made their way back to the hotel and everyone got stuck into the booze. Violet sipped nervously at her non-alcoholic drink whilst everyone else downed their alcohol at an alarming rate. Especially the father of the bride, who told everyone in his speech exactly how much the wedding had cost him, including having to pay for his daughter's new silicon breasts.

Violet thought that she would have wanted the ground to swallow her up if that had been her. But the bride, also a little drunk by now, didn't seem to mind. In fact, she roared with laughter and jiggled her new chest up and down to show everyone that it was money well spent.

By the time the disco started, the bride was so drunk that she screamed across to her husband, 'Maaarrttttiiiinnn! It's our first dance! Come on!' Then they proceeded almost to consummate their marriage on the dance floor while Westlife crooned over the speakers.

It was hideous and Violet was desperate to get out of there. But Sebastian was in his element, knocking back the wine and laughing uproariously with his posse, most of whom were from his office. She knew he was still making a point of ignoring her and she kept being elbowed out of the way until she was moved to the outside of the group.

She tried to nod and smile along but found herself unable to fake laughter at their inane jokes. Perhaps it would have helped if she were drunk too but she was driving so she was sober. And miserable.

A couple of the girls started asking about her wedding dress. Violet shook her head, saying she hadn't decided yet. But she knew what they were thinking. Where is she going to get a dress that fits?

A secretary who worked with Sebastian said there was an outsize bridal dress shop near her. Great. Violet's cheeks burned as she smiled politely. The woman was trying to be helpful but Violet was beginning to feel ill.

In the end, she couldn't bear the scrutiny so she went to the ladies' toilets and locked herself away in a cubicle. There, she tried to take deep breaths to compose herself.

It must be wonderful to have self-assurance, thought Violet. To be confident amongst people. She had never had that luxury. Violet had spent her whole adult life trying to hide in a corner, trying to be invisible.

She heard the door sweep open and the clink-clink of high heels on tiles.

'This is so bloody dull,' crowed one of the girls.

Violet recognised her voice as one of Sebastian's work colleagues. She couldn't remember her name.

'Why don't we just leave?' whined her friend. 'That bitch Samantha won't notice. She's out of her head on Bacardi Breezers.'

'Very classy for a bride. Look, just give me another half-hour.'

'Is that how long it will take you to get a snog off Sebastian?'

They both giggled.

Violet gaped at them from behind the door.

'He's all right, I suppose,' said one of the women.

'All right? He hit the ugly tree on every branch, I reckon.'

They both giggled.

'But his body's quite fit.'

'Yeah and you owe me five pounds if you don't get to kiss him.'

'You're mean. Fancy making me a bet when I was drunk.'

There was a short silence whilst they fiddled around in their handbags, presumably to find and renew their make-up.

Violet stared at the closed door in front of her. Her Sebastian? Her saviour? Ugly? No, he wasn't. Was he? No, she was sure of it. Why else would she be with him?

She shocked herself with a sudden thought. Perhaps she could do better? OK, so maybe her fiancé wasn't a handsome man like, say, Mark from work. He was drop dead gorgeous. All the girls said so.

But Sebastian wasn't a hobbit, even if he was a bit shorter than she was. Yes, he could be childish on occasion but that was only because his mum had smothered him when he was growing up. And yes, he did cheat on her. But that was because he and Violet had had a row and he had gone off and got drunk. Besides, he always hated it when she disagreed with him about something.

Sebastian was lovely, she told herself. He was everything. And he was the only man who had ever wanted her.

'What about his fiancée?' came a voice from outside of the cubicle.

The other girl gave a snort of derision. 'Did you see the state of her? What does she look like?'

'Why is he marrying her?' asked the friend.

'Out of pity, I expect. Or maybe she's loaded with money. It certainly isn't for her looks.'

They giggled once more.

'What will she look like as a bride?'

'She'll probably need to hire a marquee. To wear, I mean!'

They both hooted with laughter and were still giggling when they left.

Violet stood up, trying to take it all in. She held on to the wall for support, her head reeling. Then she turned around and retched into the toilet.

Thankfully there wasn't much to come up as she had picked at her dinner. But she retched over and over again. Finally, she flushed the toilet, put down the lid and sank down.

Violet felt the tears roll down her cheeks. Those two bitchy girls had been right. What had she been thinking of, going around looking like she did and not doing anything about it?

And what was Sebastian doing with her? Violet found herself getting angry. How had she let herself get so gross? Her weight was overshadowing any happiness she might feel. Getting married was supposed to be the happiest time of her life. She could spend a fortune on a beautiful dress and make-up but she still wouldn't look her best. Or anywhere near it. She'd look a right royal mess.

Everyone was thinner than she was. Except for the others at the diet club, Violet reminded herself. But even there she had failed. She hadn't attended the class that week. They would all get thin and Violet would stay the same. Forever fat. Forever miserable.

She didn't know how long she sat in that toilet. Presumably someone would notice that she was missing eventually. But no one came looking for her.

As she sat in that cubicle, many girls came and went. Some were drunk. Others just wanted to reapply their lipstick. But all seemed happy and confident.

Violet stood up, smoothed down her clothes and stepped out of the cubicle. Alone in the ladies', she stared at her reflection. She had two choices. She could be a fat bride whom everyone laughed at. Or she could be slim and happy on her wedding day.

Violet knew at that moment there was no choice. She didn't want to feel this way any more. She had had enough.

She gave herself a deadline. She vowed to change her body by Christmas. Before Sebastian gave up on her and before her body gave up under the strain and stress of living like this.

It was time.

Chapter Fourteen

Kathy worked the Saturday shift in the shop to make up for being absent on Tuesday. It was a little busier at the weekend but the time still dragged.

Thankfully, Mavis didn't work on Saturdays. Unfortunately, she was replaced by a different pensioner called Cheryl, whose conversation skills were the complete opposite of Mavis's restraint.

'I said to the ladies,' she was saying as another exciting story from the WI emerged, 'if you want to have buns as light as mine, you've got to sift. There's no other way.'

Kathy smiled and nodded but said nothing.

She was still feeling very low after the anniversary of her mother's birthday and nothing seemed to budge her out of her fog of grief. The shakes and cereal bars didn't help. In fact, she was ignoring them altogether and overcompensating in the evenings.

Today she had woken up with the intention to be positive. To try to eat healthily. And her resolve lasted until Cheryl unearthed the box she had carried into the shop that morning.

'Ta-dah!' she said, whipping off the lid with a flourish.

Kathy's mouth dropped open. There they were, about a dozen of them. A sort of doughnut-looking cake, with some kind of cream in the middle, glistening with shiny icing.

'They're whoopie pies,' Cheryl told her. 'I've been practising all week for the bazaar and I need to try them out on someone.'

Kathy wanted to say no. But that would have caused offence and she didn't want to upset Cheryl. Plus she could smell the sugar.

'Cupcakes are so over,' said Cheryl, shoving the box under Kathy's nose.

Kathy selected her choice and took a bite. It was extremely sweet. Extremely fattening too, no doubt. But what the hell.

She nodded at Cheryl who, she noticed, wasn't eating. Cheryl was the shape of a lamppost but seemed happy to let Kathy pig out in front of her.

'It's wonderful,' mumbled Kathy in between bites. 'Aren't you having one?'

'Oh no,' said Cheryl. 'I only do gluten-free.'

Unfortunately, the whoopie pies seemed to trigger a sugar craving of extreme ferocity. For the rest of the weekend, Kathy scoffed cakes, biscuits and chocolate in vast amounts. Living alone, she could binge in glorious solitude. She had totally fallen off the slimming wagon. Not that she had ever really got started.

It all came to a head on Monday night. Kathy was trying to finish up the last of the bad stuff in her fridge. She had already decided to head back to the slimming class the following evening but the fridge needed to be clear of anything fattening if she were to start afresh. So she used extreme amounts of cheese and cream in her pasta supper and then finished off the three tubs of ice-cream she had bought the previous week.

Clutching her distended stomach, she went into the bathroom with the intention of running a nice bubble bath to relax in. But then she remembered the weigh-in which was only twenty-four hours away. What was the point of spending all this money just to be told that she was still huge?

Then Kathy had a thought. What if the food could disappear? What if she could eat without putting any weight on?

So Kathy made herself sick for the first time. And swore it would be the last time as well.

Afterwards, she sat in the bath and sobbed. What was wrong with her? Was she now making herself ill just so she could carry on eating fattening foods? Was she mentally ill as well? She knew Alzheimer's could be hereditary. Perhaps she was beginning to show the early signs?

But she knew that dementia wasn't the reason. She was just being a total pig. What would her mother have said if she were alive? Probably that she was developing an eating disorder and needed to sort herself out.

Kathy kept crying until there were no tears left to come. But from the misery came determination.

It was time for her to take action.

Edward had been in the queue at the fish and chip shop on Friday night when he had begun to feel strange and unwell. His skin suddenly felt clammy and his pulse was racing. Perhaps it was food poisoning from the burger at lunchtime. He changed his mind about the fish and began to walk out of the shop.

Then the chest pain began. It started in the middle of his rib cage but quickly began to spread out around his body. He could feel his heart thumping, hard and loud.

Oh God. He was having a heart attack. And then everything went black.

He woke up in the ambulance with an oxygen mask on. He tried to take it off but the paramedic shook her head.

'Leave it on,' she told him. 'You need the air.'

He closed his eyes and tried not to panic.

Many hours later, the doctor stood by his bed in the A and E cubicle and told him what was wrong. 'It was an angina attack.'

Edward breathed a sigh of relief. It hadn't been a heart attack. He was fine.

But the doctor's face told him otherwise. 'Your blood pressure is sky high. We're going to give you some beta-blockers to slow down your heart.'

Edward nodded.

'You were lucky,' the doctor told him. 'It was angina and not that big an attack. If you don't change your lifestyle, next time you might not be so lucky.'

Edward stared at him.

'If you don't change your way of life, there might not even be a next time.'

Left alone in the cubicle, Edward mulled over the shocking words. It was just an angina attack. Well, not just. He had thought he was going to die. And he hadn't yet lived.

But if he didn't start taking his health seriously,

he was going to end up back in hospital. And he didn't want it to be in the mortuary. He'd been given a warning. A flashing-bells, screaming-siren warning.

It was time to be a man and face up to his future. Otherwise he might not have one.

Lucy was feeling uncomfortable. She had squeezed herself into a black denim skirt that was a size fourteen but it was far too tight. She couldn't be bothered to change it once she'd left the house so she carried on to the bus stop.

God, but she was hot. It was almost June and she was in black tights so that her legs wouldn't look too fat in the skirt. Plus the waistband was digging in so hard that it was making her stomach hurt. She had hidden her lack of waist with a large black top with long sleeves.

She waited in the morning sun, willing the bus to arrive soon. Especially once Nicola Bowles' gang appeared around the corner. Thankfully the bus was trundling down the road and Lucy stuck her hand out, desperate to get the hell out of there.

But there was a little old lady taking her time to get down the steps and once it was Lucy's turn to get on board, the other girls were nearly there.

Lucy quickly stuck her leg up to climb the steps and heard a loud rip. Her skirt suddenly felt much looser. She glanced down and saw that the side seam had split all the way up to her thigh. Mortified, she had no choice but to swiftly cover her exposed leg with her big college bag. She showed the bus driver her student pass and went to the back of the bus. Getting off would have meant facing the other girls and they would have seen her burst skirt.

So Lucy sat on the bus, tears trickling down her face, her skirt open all the way up to her knickers. She had no choice but to wait on the bus when it reached the town centre and return back home. The journey took over an hour, during which Lucy finally admitted to herself that something had to change. That she couldn't and wouldn't carry on like this. She would rather die than be this miserable. And she really did want to live.

Maggie sank on to the sofa, still wearing her raincoat. For once, she didn't feel like reaching for the biscuit tin for comfort. She was in too much shock for that.

She had booked an appointment with her doctor, figuring that the tiredness and increased need to go to the loo in the middle of the night were all symptoms of the menopause.

But when Maggie had asked for a prescription for HRT, the doctor had shaken her head.

'It's not the menopause I'm worried about,' she had told Maggie. 'It's your diabetes.'

'My what?'

'You've got type two diabetes,' the doctor said.

Maggie was aghast. 'Are you sure?'

The doctor gave her a small smile. 'I ran a few extra tests with your blood sample.'

Maggie tried to rally. 'But that's the mild form of diabetes, isn't it?'

The doctor's smile dropped. 'There is no such thing as mild diabetes. All diabetes is serious and, if not properly controlled, can lead to serious complications.'

Maggie bit her lip. 'What do I do about it?'

'You should lose weight and exercise more. But in

the meantime, I'm going to start you off on some medication.'

Maggie had driven to the chemist in shock and was still clutching her paper bag full of pills.

It was the worst possible scenario. She had turned into her mother. Not the pettiness or guilt-inducing, woe-is-me act. No, Maggie had taken on the physical attributes of her mother, who had lost sight in her right eye in her early sixties due to her diabetes. Maggie's mother was also on a daily injection of insulin.

Maggie shuddered. She hated needles and injections. Luckily she was on the pill form of medication.

She rang Gordon while she waited for her prescription. But he was busy with a client. She assured his secretary that she was only calling about that night's dinner. It sounded stupid but she so rarely rang her husband during the day that she didn't want Gordon to panic.

In fact, she'd decided not to tell him at all. He didn't need to know. She didn't want him to think any less of her. To think that she was menopausal and now so dangerously overweight that she had to be medicated.

Tears rolled down Maggie's cheeks. She felt as if her life was over when it was only halfway through. The front door burst open and Maggie quickly stuffed the pill packet into her handbag. Brushing away the tears, she tried to fix on a smile.

'You all right, love?' she asked as Lucy came into the lounge.

Then she realised Lucy also had tears rolling down her cheeks.

'What's the matter?' she said, taking her daughter in her arms.

'I tore my skirt,' sobbed Lucy.

Maggie looked down and saw the skirt was split nearly up to Lucy's waist.

'It's only a skirt,' she said to her daughter.

'It's not the skirt, it's me!' cried Lucy. 'I'm too fat. Nothing fits. I'm disgusting. I hate myself. I don't want to be this fat any more.'

Maggie held her daughter for a long time until she finally began to calm down.

'You're not disgusting,' Maggie said. 'And nor am I. We just let things get out of hand, didn't we?'

Lucy nodded as Maggie held her close.

'How about we go back to that diet club tomorrow night?' said Maggie.

'Yes,' said Lucy, the tears still rolling down her cheeks. 'I can't go on like this.'

'Me neither,' said Maggie, letting herself join in the tears. 'So let's start afresh, eh?'

Lucy nodded.

And the mother and daughter pact was made.

Chapter Fifteen

On the Sunday morning, Violet had woken up with piggy eyes and a stomach ache from all the stress of the previous evening at the wedding.

Sebastian was struggling with a horrendous hangover and was still snoring in bed. Violet wanted some fresh air so left him to it. For once, she had no appetite. After the previous night, she wasn't sure it was ever coming back. The women's bitchy comments still lay heavily on her.

She even walked rather than get in the car. It was only a short walk to a nearby Sunday market in the town car park. The warm morning air felt quite refreshing. Once arrived, she headed to the fresh fruit and vegetable stalls. She hardly ever touched fruit, always going instead for the quick and more tasty option of chocolate. Violet counted the pineapple on her Hawaiian pizza as one of her five a day. But that morning, she treated herself to a banana and began to munch on it while she wandered around in the early summer sunshine.

Violet found herself reluctant, for once, to scurry back to Sebastian. He hadn't said anything about her disappearing for hours on end to the ladies' toilet. And when she had finally joined him back at the party, he was too busy with his friends to notice how upset she was.

Sebastian was so drunk that she practically had to carry him up the stairs to bed. He then made half-hearted attempts to make love but thankfully passed out before things got too far.

He'd been too out of it to recognise her misery. So Violet lay awake for most of the night, fighting the demons inside. She was determined to take control of her eating for ever. She just didn't know how.

She passed a secondhand book stall, casually picking up a horror novel before putting it back down again. That wouldn't help her think more positively.

Then a pink book caught her eye: *Isabella's Guide For the Elegant Bride*. She picked it up and stared at the cover. It wasn't particularly well thumbed, almost new in fact.

'I bought that by mistake,' someone suddenly said.

Violet looked up to see the stallholder, nodding at the book in her hand.

'I wanted to know about table pieces for my wedding but it wasn't much help.'

But Violet couldn't stop thinking about being an elegant bride. How wonderful it would be if she were suddenly stylish. And thin, obviously.

At least it would pass the time whilst Sebastian recovered from his hangover. So she handed over a two-pound coin and slowly made her way home. Sebastian was still groaning from the bed upstairs so she left him to it and curled up on the sofa with a cup of tea and the book.

The author was Isabella Marigiano. In her photo, she was blond and beautiful, like a young Grace Kelly. The book turned out to be over twenty years old but Violet was still intrigued. She knew nothing about being elegant.

'There is nothing more elegant than a simple Italian wedding,' read the first line.

Oh God. Violet checked the front cover. She'd picked up a book for Italian brides.

'There are six rules to achieve eternal elegance,' she read on. 'Both at your wedding and throughout your life. Learn them, live them and you will have style forever at your hands.'

Violet glanced at the first rule. It was about food. She was just about to read on but Sebastian staggered downstairs demanding attention and carbohydrates so Isabella would have to wait. But Violet was intrigued. Perhaps she would get time to read a little more during the week.

She looked at Sebastian, slumped on the sofa, clutching his forehead.

'I feel awful,' he whined, running a hand through his blond hair.

'Poor you,' said Violet but not really meaning it.

'Get me a bacon buttie, would you?'

Violet waited a minute for an apology, before realising he wasn't going to say sorry for completely ignoring her the previous evening. He had never apologised for his moods or anything he had done throughout their time together. Apart from sleeping with another woman, she remembered. Then he had said sorry. In Sebastian's eyes, he was always in the right. Or so he thought. Violet went along with it because it was easier than having another row. Anything for a quiet life.

She stared at him. Was he ugly, as those girls had said? She couldn't see it. Of course, he wasn't looking his best that morning. But he was her man. He was everything.

She sighed and went into the kitchen. Violet piled a plate high with bacon butties but only helped herself to one round. Something had clicked inside her. She didn't know what and didn't know how. But this time, she was determined that the diet would work.

This time she was actually looking forward to Tuesday. Despite minimal weight loss so far, she was willing to learn. Finally, she wanted to learn the secret of being thin.

And Violet knew just the woman to help her.

But Trudie was very out of sorts that Tuesday evening. She had barely said two words to anybody. Before the weigh-in began, she spoke to them all.

'I'm so glad you could all be bothered to turn up this week.' Her voice was heavy with sarcasm. 'I don't know why you made the effort.'

She paused for effect.

'Especially as not a single one of you turned up last time.'

Violet blushed, even though she realised that no one else had gone to the weigh-in last week either. But she wasn't to be deterred. Feeling brave for the first time in her life, Violet slowly walked up to be first for the weigh-in.

'Blimey,' Kathy called out after her. 'You're a bit keen, aren't you?'

Violet attempted a smile at Trudie but she scowled

back. Perhaps it was her time of the month. They both looked down at the weight the scales were showing.

Trudie gave a massive sigh.

'I know,' Violet told her, holding up her hand. 'But I really want to do this now.'

She even sounded as if she meant it this time.

'Really?' Trudie replied, her voice laced with scorn. 'You really, really want to lose weight now, do you? Even when you haven't bothered to do anything about it during the last month?'

Violet felt embarrassed but knew she deserved the ticking off.

'Well, no,' she mumbled. 'But I'm getting married and I want to look good on my wedding day.'

'Not much chance of that,' Trudie muttered. 'Unless you're going for the World's Fattest Bride record.'

Tears of shock stung Violet's eyes. She couldn't believe Trudie was being so cruel.

'Now wait a minute,' said Edward, coming to stand next to them. 'I don't think there's any call for you to be mean like that.'

'Shut up, lard arse,' snapped Trudie. 'What are you going to do? Smother me with your moobs?'

Violet glanced at Edward who was looking equally stunned.

'Some girl in the office caught your eye, has she?' carried on Trudie, still scowling at Edward. 'Still, if she gives you the cold shoulder, you can always go drown yourself in more beer.'

Edward paled as her words struck a nerve. Eventually, he managed to bluster, 'I really think you ought to apologise to Violet and myself.'

Everyone was glancing at each other, wondering where all this was coming from.

Trudie held up her hand. 'Listen up, fatties. I've had enough. I have up to thirty people sometimes at my other classes. It's not worth my time or the petrol to come here and see you lot. You'll never achieve any kind of weight loss and that'll make me look bad.'

'Well, that would be a real shame, wouldn't it?' said Maggie, who had noticed Violet's eyes filling with tears and had come over to give the girl a bit of support.

'Wake up and smell your menopause,' Trudie snarled at her. 'You're overweight. Deal with it.'

'Don't you speak to my mum like that,' said Lucy, standing next to her mother.

Trudie gave a mirthless laugh. 'Don't suppose you're getting any boy action with an arse that large. The boys would rather use their hormones on some size-eight slag from the council estate.'

Lucy took a deep breath in horror before bursting into tears.

'Now listen,' barked Kathy, coming to stand in front of them. 'You can't talk to us like that.'

'Nobody's listening to you,' snapped Trudie. 'Nobody laughs at your jokes, thinks you're funny or gives a damn about you. You'll probably die alone, surrounded by empty cake boxes.'

Kathy gasped and bit her lip.

'You're horrible,' sobbed Lucy.

'Newsflash! I don't care,' shouted Trudie. 'None of you is worth my time and effort. I've got other classes where people are serious about losing weight.'

'And where you can earn a lot of money off them,' said Edward, scowling at her.

'Of course!' cried Trudie. 'What do I care about your obesity levels? You lot will never achieve anything.'

With that, Trudie swanned out.

'Ding dong, the witch is dead,' said Kathy, putting an arm around Violet, who was still upset.

'What a bitch!' said Maggie, trying to mop up Lucy's tears.

The reign of terror was over. But it also meant they were now on their own. Not knowing what else to do, Kathy suggested they went to the pub on the corner. Nobody was really in the mood to socialise but they all went with her anyway.

Once the drinks were ordered, they found a table and sat down.

Violet was still feeling incredibly wounded by Trudie's words. All her new-found optimism had disappeared. She glanced up briefly to find Maggie smiling at her.

'Congratulations on getting engaged,' she said.

'Thanks,' Violet replied, feeling perfectly miserable.

Everyone else looked up from their drinks.

'When's the big day?' asked Kathy.

'New Year's Eve.' Violet allowed herself a pity sigh, remembering what Trudie had said about her being the world's fattest bride.

'That Trudie was a bunny boiler,' snapped Edward, who had been quiet until then. 'Forget about her.'

But even Violet could see Trudie's words had wounded him.

'Exactly,' said Kathy, putting her glass down with a clatter. 'All in all, it was a perfect class tonight.'

'But we'll never see Trudie again,' stammered Lucy.

Kathy nodded. 'Like I said, a perfect class! She was a complete witch and not the least bit helpful. Christ, I could write her sum knowledge of diets on a Galaxy bar wrapper.'

'Have you seen they're doing Galaxy counters now?'

said Maggie, her eyes lighting up. 'Little circles of chocolate. Yum!'

'The day they brought back Wispa bars was the happiest day of my life,' said Kathy. She took a sigh. 'That's sad, isn't it? My happiest days shouldn't revolve around food.'

They all nodded in agreement.

'Bloody sod's law that I had finally decided to do something about my weight, to be serious about it, I mean,' said Kathy. 'And what happens? The witch leaves us in the lurch! Now what am I supposed to do?'

'Exactly,' said Maggie.

'Maybe we don't need her,' said Edward.

'I tell you something,' said Kathy. 'I'm not wasting any more money on tasteless crap like those bars and shakes.'

Everyone was nodding in agreement.

'I need normal food,' said Maggie.

'Couldn't we help each other?' said Lucy, looking a little shy at her suggestion. 'Seeing as we're all in the same boat.'

'The same overloaded fat boat that's sinking, you mean,' said Kathy, grinning.

Lucy gave her a small smile in return. She found Kathy really funny.

'It can't do any harm,' said Maggie.

'Why don't we meet up Thursday night?' said Edward. 'Strike whilst the iron's hot and all that.'

'And maybe get some ideas in the meantime?' said Kathy.

Edward nodded. 'Something like that.'

Kathy nodded. 'OK with me. But not here. I can't talk about weight loss in a pub that's going to tempt me with Baileys and a large packet of pork scratchings.'

'I'm afraid I only live in a tiny flat,' said Edward. 'No room to get everybody inside.'

'Me too,' said Kathy.

They both looked at Maggie but she was shaking her head.

'My husband's not very supportive about diets,' she told them. 'I don't think it will be possible.'

'So where shall we meet?' asked Lucy.

Everyone slowly turned to face Violet, who hadn't spoken for a while.

'I've only got a small house,' she said.

'A house? That will do fine,' said Maggie.

'Great,' said Kathy. 'What's the address?'

Violet felt she had no choice. Everyone agreed to meet at her home in forty-eight hours' time. Violet knew that Sebastian was out at some work do on Thursday evening so the place would be free. But she felt uncomfortable about everyone being inside her house.

'So we'll all have a think about the best way to get this weight off, shall we?' said Maggie.

Everyone nodded, each promising to do some research on healthy-eating plans.

Violet sighed. This obviously wasn't going to work. What could five fatties achieve on their own?

Chapter Sixteen

After what appeared to be the end of the weight-loss club, Violet spent the next morning googling every kind of diet known to man. Work was pretty slow that day so she had loads of time in between calls to waste.

She had typed the word diet into Google and got a massive 129,000,000 results. Her jaw dropped at the mind-boggling range of eating plans in front of her.

There were women advocating eating only baby food. Or juices. Or soups. Or a combination of eggs and grapefruit. Or just breakfast cereals. Or drinking maple syrup and peppered water all day, every day and nothing else.

Some recommended low GI. But what was the difference between GI and GL? Instead of dieting, why not detox? Or body cleanse, whatever that meant? There were metabolic diets, Nordic diets and Frenchwomen diets.

Violet could discover her blood type and eat according to that. She could eat only protein or become a vegan. She could drink special tea to cleanse her colon. Or green tea. Or no tea and coffee at all because they were bad.

Vegetables and fruit were best. Then there was a different website saying that vegetables and fruit were terrible for the diet. Brown rice was great. Or brown rice was the devil. It was all so confusing.

But as Violet delved deeper, she found that perhaps she didn't have to diet at all. There were pills to pop to make you thinner. She could get hypnotised into getting thin. Or have acupuncture. Or have major surgery or gastric bands inserted into her stomach.

She took a long, deep breath. Definitely no surgery. She hated her body but there was no way she was going under the knife.

She sighed and wondered whether it was worth all the effort to look up any kind of healthy-eating plan. Nobody would turn up tomorrow night and that would be the end of it.

Except the doorbell rang at 8 p.m. on Thursday night and there was Kathy, clutching what appeared to be an envelope.

'Did you get one?'

Violet nodded. The letter had arrived in the post that morning.

'"New You! would like to apologise for the conduct of their personal consultant, Ms T. Recks,"' mimicked Kathy with a hoot of laughter. 'Who do you think blabbed?'

Violet shook her head. 'I don't know.'

'Oooh, this is nice,' said Kathy, going into the living room.

Violet had flicked a duster around and hoovered when she had got home from work. She supposed that counted as a workout. Anyway, she was exhausted afterwards so it must have done some good.

To Violet's surprise, everyone else turned up soon after. It was a different kind of diet club. This time they were in charge. It felt a little naughty.

'So, the bitch is back,' said Kathy, waving the letter at them.

'I rang them up yesterday morning,' said Maggie.

'Mum!' whined Lucy, rolling her eyes.

'She can't get away with talking to us like that.'

'Shame they tell us we've got to go back otherwise we've wasted our year's worth of subscriptions,' said Kathy.

'Do we have to?' said Lucy, looking worried.

'I guess we've got to get weighed,' said Edward. 'And the aerobics might be good for us.'

'Yes, but what about bloody Trudie?' said Kathy.

'Sod her,' muttered Lucy. 'I'm more worried about me than her.'

'I think that's right,' said Edward. 'And hopefully she'll behave herself from now onwards.'

There was a short silence whilst everyone remembered what Trudie had said to them about their weight. Her cruel jibes still hurt.

'I've brought a bottle with me,' said Maggie, brandishing the wine. 'Thought it might help. Drown our sorrows and all that.'

Violet grabbed some wine glasses and the drinks were poured. The girls took a gulp of wine and tried to relax. Edward shuffled in his seat awkwardly. He wasn't allowed to drink because of his medication.

Somebody cleared their throat but no one spoke, until Kathy could bear it no longer.

'Anyone for a top-up?' She refilled her glass, having

drained it with nerves. 'You're not drinking?' she said to Edward.

He shook his head.

'I hope you don't mind me saying,' said Maggie to Edward, 'but you don't look very well.'

'I was ill at the weekend,' said Edward, after an awkward silence.

'Oh dear,' they all murmured.

'Nothing serious, I hope,' said Maggie, out of politeness.

Edward opened his mouth and then closed it again. He seemed reluctant to talk but the women waited patiently. After all, misery loves company.

'I had an angina attack on Friday,' he finally told them.

'That can be very painful,' said Maggie, thinking about when her mother had had an attack the previous year.

'I ended up in A and E,' said Edward with a sigh. 'It's because of my weight.'

Everyone nodded in sympathy whilst he turned a light shade of pink.

'That's nothing,' said Maggie, feeling sorry for him. 'The doctor says I've got diabetes.'

'Mum!' said Lucy. 'You never said!'

'Nothing to be proud of, love,' replied her mother. 'I'm on medication but I've got to get my act together. I'm fat, fifty and flabby.'

'You're not that bad,' Kathy told her.

'I'm pretty sure I am, but thanks.' Maggie shrugged her shoulders. 'It's embarrassing, isn't it? To have to admit that you've eaten your way into a serious health condition.'

Edward nodded in agreement. 'They say I could be

heading for a heart attack. How did I end up at twenty-one stone?'

Everyone else knew. Because they were the same.

Lucy sank back into her chair. 'I feel really bad now,' she said. 'My reason for losing weight is all about vanity.'

'So?' said Kathy. 'What's wrong with that?'

'But I do get a lot of headaches and I'm always so tired,' said Lucy.

'Me too,' said Kathy. 'But then, look at the size of me!'

But nobody laughed at her forced jolliness because they were all overweight.

'I get bullied too,' Lucy told them.

Maggie was shocked. 'Why didn't you tell me?'

Lucy shrugged her shoulders. 'There's a group of girls that go on and on at me. You can imagine what they say.'

Maggie put her arm around her daughter's shoulders, which were shaking with suppressed sobs.

'That's why I don't go out much,' Lucy said, looking directly at her mum. 'I'm too self-conscious about how I look. I stay in because I'm so miserable. And I'm miserable because I don't go out. I should have got my act together but I'm still fat.'

'Sweetheart,' said Kathy. 'I'm fat, thirty and single. It doesn't get any more desperate than that.'

'Thirty's not old,' said Maggie.

'It is on the singles scene,' said Kathy.

'But you're lovely-looking,' said Maggie, in full mum mode.

Kathy gave her a grin. 'I'm not just a sex goddess, you know. I do have eyes in my head.' But her smile faded. 'I've had so many blind dates off the internet where the bloke has done a runner. One look at me and they're off.' Kathy bit her lip and Maggie realised the jolly act belied a soft centre.

'They were obviously idiots,' said Edward, and then blushed.

'Exactly,' said Maggie.

'I've always been big,' Kathy told them. 'But when I was taking care of my mum, I didn't look after myself properly. Fry-ups and big tubs of ice-cream seemed the easiest thing when I finally got round to eating.' She snorted a sad laugh. 'Trouble is, Mum passed away in December and I'm still eating rubbish.'

They stared into their wine glasses for a while before Lucy spoke.

'What about you?'

Violet looked up and found everyone looking at her. She blushed but realised she had to speak. After all, everyone else had revealed their innermost desolation.

'I've always been big,' she told them in a quiet voice. 'Well, since I lost my parents when I was twelve. I was sent to live with my aunt and uncle. My aunt Mary was horrible but also huge. A fat, smelly weirdo obsessed with the Bible. Every plate had to be finished otherwise it was a sin, because of the starving children in the world. And it was always stodgy stuff like dumplings or pies.'

She bit her lip, wondering if she had talked for too long.

'Go on,' said Maggie gently.

'I remember we had to do some kind of project at school on our bodies and everyone had to be weighed. I'd been living with my aunt and uncle for two years and I was already three stone heavier than anyone else in the class. All the other kids laughed at me and I started getting picked on. That's what turned me into a comfort eater and my weight problems got even worse.'

'Do you still see them? Your aunt and uncle?' asked Edward.

Violet shook her head. 'They died a few years ago.' She looked around at everyone. 'And now I'm engaged.'

The women smiled at her.

Violet found tears suddenly filled her eyes. 'And I'm miserable,' she told them, trying not to sob. 'I can't go down the aisle looking like this.'

'Come here,' said Maggie, putting her arm around Violet. She was now holding both Lucy and Violet in a maternal hug.

'Well, those bloody shakes and cereal bars won't do us any good,' snapped Kathy. 'There's nothing but E-additives in them.'

Maggie nodded. 'I was thinking about going on that juice diet. That's all healthy fruit and veg so it must be good for you. Plus you get really good results in the first week and I need to get these pounds off fast.'

'I'll join you, Mum,' said Lucy, wiping her eyes.

'There's a whole double page spread in my magazine about it. We'll have a look when we get home.'

'I'm going to cut out the beer,' said Edward.

'I was thinking of going carb-free,' said Kathy. 'Everyone's doing it.'

Violet didn't tell them about her failure to go carb-free. Perhaps Kathy would do better than she had.

Instead, she got up and dug out the pile of slimming magazines she had bought at lunchtime.

'I've been through them all,' Violet told them.

And it was true. Such was the boredom of work

131

that she had read every page. The other staff hadn't been impressed, but what else was there for Violet to do?

'Oooh!' said Lucy, snatching a celebrity diet magazine. 'Look how much weight she's lost!'

It was yet another soap actress who had lost weight by way of a personal trainer and dietician, and was now plugging her brand-new fitness DVD.

'She looks like the living dead,' said Maggie with a sigh.

'So what do we do now?' said Lucy. 'Shouldn't we just join another club?'

'After all the money I've just forked out for bloody New You!' spluttered Kathy. 'You must be joking.'

'But I give up so quickly,' said Lucy. 'I can't do it on my own.'

'And that Trudie's no help.'

'Look, why don't we still go next Tuesday,' said Edward. 'But maybe come back here afterwards and have a chat.'

'You mean, end the evening on a positive note after Trudie's inevitable sarcasm?' said Kathy with a grin.

Edward smiled back at her. 'Absolutely.'

'But we won't be having those horrible shakes and bars, will we?' said Lucy.

Kathy shook her head. 'We'll have to work out something else.'

'Let's all keep in touch by phone or text,' said Maggie.

So they took each other's mobile numbers for emergency texts and then agreed to meet up the following week back at Violet's house.

Their secret diet club was formed.

Chapter Seventeen

Violet sat alone after everyone had left. She stared at the magazines scattered across the coffee table.

Amongst the weird and, quite frankly, dangerous diets that had been listed, she had noticed a familiar pattern begin to emerge. For women, 1,500 calories was regularly quoted as being the optimum amount for steady weight loss. For men, the calories allowed increased to 2,000.

On top of that, anything with a fat content of over 5 g per 100 g was to be avoided on a daily basis. Less than 5 g of fat was acceptable as the body, it seemed, needed a little fat.

So the scientific part seemed fairly easy to understand.

The problem was that the weight loss would only be about one to two pounds per week. It sounded slow but Violet thought that perhaps she would be less hungry on this regime.

There were other tips in the magazines too, like writing down everything you ate each day. Not for

133

ever, just whilst losing weight. And a lot of experts recommended planning what to eat at the beginning of each week.

Violet sank back into the sofa. Fifteen hundred calories per day. It didn't seem much when split down into separate meals. But what to eat? It was all such a minefield. And there was so much choice. Too much.

She picked up Isabella's book on bridal elegance and read her thoughts on food.

'You must eat three meals a day,' she read. 'Breakfast is important so do not miss it, even if you only have time for some fruit. Stuffing yourself with latte and cannoli later in the morning is not elegant and is terrible for the figure.'

Violet never ate breakfast. She was always too lazy or in too much of rush in the morning. But perhaps it was time to start afresh.

Write everything down, she remembered. So the following day she did.

For breakfast, Violet had an over-ripened, medium-sized banana. It was brown and a bit yucky but it did keep the hunger pangs at bay. And it was only 140 calories.

Later at her desk, she bit down on a Twix bar, scowling; 245 wasted calories and it was only half past ten in the morning.

It was the boredom that had tempted her, made her think constantly of food and nothing else. No wonder everyone else in the department was so slim. They were all burning off calories, scurrying around, being busy.

She took another bite. She was more bored than the most bored person in the most boring job. She picked up the phone, forwarded the call, put down the phone. Ad infinitum.

She thought back to Isabella's words she had read the previous evening. 'If you get hungry between meals, eat fruit. No biscuits, crisps or such rubbish. They are common. Fruit and vegetables are marvellous for the skin. Who wants to be a bride with bad skin?'

Violet took the last bite of the Twix before throwing away the wrapper. She had made her decision. No more chocolate. She had to do this.

'Right,' said Mark, coming to stand at the end of Violet's desk. 'I'm bored. What gossip have you got for me?'

Violet stared up at him. 'Not much, I'm afraid.'

'It's early yet,' he said, smiling at her before looking across at Anthony. 'What are you up to?'

'Nothing,' said Anthony, a little too quickly.

Mark rolled his eyes. 'Please tell me that you haven't hacked into the payroll database again.'

Anthony became a little rattled. 'I'm only trying to prove how easy it is.'

Mark muttered something his breath which Violet couldn't quite catch.

Wendy and Julie returned to their desks, clutching their hot cups of coffee.

'Where's mine?' asked Mark.

'In the machine,' replied Julie, sitting down.

'Sometimes I have trouble remembering why I employ you,' said Mark. But he was smiling as he walked away.

'I have trouble remembering why I work here,' Julie told the team. 'But I'm pretty certain it isn't because of the large salary.'

Violet couldn't help smiling. She found she enjoyed the easy banter between her work colleagues.

At lunchtime, she visited a bookshop and bought a book that listed the calories of every single food imaginable.

The information in the book was terrifying. A Starbuck's blueberry muffin was a whopping 460 calories. With her usual grande latte at 262 calories, that was almost half her daily allowance of calories in what she had previously classed as a snack!

A typical Friday night takeaway of fish and chips was 900 calories. Her Saturday night sweet and sour Chinese was 700 calories. Her weekend breakfast of croissants and jam didn't bear thinking about when a standard size croissant was 215 calories. And it didn't even fill her up, Violet realised. She wondered about her average weekend calorie total. It made her feel ill.

Everything she had thought about food was rubbish. It needed a radical rethink. She needed to be much more careful with her calories otherwise there would be none left for dinner at the end of each day.

After the bookshop, she went into Marks & Spencer. She didn't dare visit the cake aisle to see how many calories her favourite chocolate gateau was. Plus it would be just her luck to run into Mark. Instead she grabbed a healthy 259-calorie sandwich. It usually required crisps and a Coke to go with it but she managed to hold herself together and picked up a piece of fruit instead.

On the way home after work, Violet went to the supermarket to stock up. It was a bit of a scrum at that time of the evening but she needed healthy meals and the corner shop wasn't much good for that.

Normally she grabbed the food in a frenzy and then headed straight to the tills. This time she read all the ingredients, checking the calories and fat content. It took her nearly an hour to find everything she needed.

In the queue for the checkouts, Violet noticed how full her shopping trolley was. Yes, it was all ready meals, diet soft drinks, yoghurts and fruit but it still seemed a lot, considering she was on a diet. How was she going to lose weight eating all of this?

She was still aiming to stick to 1,500 calories a day. She had worked out on the computer during the long stretches of boredom at work that she had actually been consuming 3,500 calories on a typical day. Gulp. If Violet had been a marathon runner that would have been OK. But she barely moved so it was just massing around her stomach and hips.

Now she was getting organised and was aiming for 250 calories for breakfast, 350 for lunch and 450 for dinner. With a couple of pieces of fruit, some milk and a low-calorie dessert each day, that was it. Violet prayed it would be enough.

That evening, she waited for the microwave to ping that her low-calorie meal was ready. With three minutes left to go, she idly opened the fridge door and stared in.

One idea that was commonly repeated in the magazines and on the internet was to clear the fridge and kitchen cupboards of anything that wasn't healthy. Violet looked in the fridge. It looked like food heaven but she knew it was dragging her downwards towards her current hell.

She grabbed a dustbin liner. She had to take control. She had to start to lose weight properly. And sensibly.

She began to shove all the food into the bag. In went a glorious cheesecake. Some blocks of heavenly cheese. It was heartbreaking but it had to be done.

She wanted a life with Sebastian. And if that meant doing without, then she would just have to cope. Violet tried not to cry.

She would have kept any healthy food back, of course. But it turned out there wasn't any apart from the fruit and ready meals she had just bought.

She stared at the half-empty fridge and closed the door. Then she opened a cupboard and began to add all the crisps, cakes and biscuits to the bin. She kept going until the shelves were empty and only a large packet of peanuts remained. They were protein so that should be OK.

Violet closed the door, opened it once more and added the peanuts to the overflowing bin bag. Who was she kidding?

Her microwave pinged ready. It wasn't the worst thing she had eaten but it was pretty miserable. Stodgy enough to keep the hunger at bay but not very satisfying. Healthy, but she didn't feel any nutrients rushing around her body.

After dinner, Violet continued to vet the whole kitchen. From cooking ingredients – all that cooking chocolate had to go – to the biscuit barrel, which held on tight to its buttery shortbread before finally releasing its hold. Nothing was sacred. Every food with any fat went in the bin. Violet was in a food frenzy.

She tied up the two large bags of food waste and put them in the front garden, ready for the refuse collection the following Monday. Then she quickly closed the front door and went back into the lounge.

Well, that was that. Out with the old and in with the new. A new beginning. A new you! Violet gave a snort of derision at herself and the sorry mess she had got herself into.

She tried to distract herself with the television but by this time, her favourite soap had been and gone and she was left channel-hopping to find something else to watch. She quickly skipped past the cooking channels and landed on some lifestyle programme. A woman, skinny and botoxed, was talking about the merits of a decent manicure.

Violet glanced at her fingernails. They weren't in bad condition but in the frenzy of food clearing she had torn one of them. She opened up the sideboard where she knew there was an emery board lurking and stared.

It was one of Sebastian's Easter presents that she had forgotten about. A big, beautiful box of luxury chocolates. She picked up the box. This wasn't mass-produced rubbish. This was expensive chocolate. This was . . . oh, what the hell!

She ripped off the cellophane and tore the box open, inhaling the heady scent of cocoa. But then she stopped. And slowly stood up, still clutching the box. She took it into the kitchen and placed it in the sink. She drew out a bottle of bleach and squeezed it all over the chocolates. Every last, glorious one.

She stuffed the gooey mess into a carrier bag and placed it outside with the rest of the rubbish. Violet felt a little shaky as she sat back down but quickly recovered. She was OK. She would survive.

Violet's week crept by. The hunger pangs weren't too bad, she realised. Certainly not as bad as when she tried to survive on just cereal bars and shakes. Her stomach was beginning to realise that it could survive on 1,500 calories a day and so, in turn, was the rest of Violet.

She could do this, she told herself. She would do this. She had to do this.

On Sunday, Violet found Sebastian staring in the open fridge.

'We're getting a bit low for food, aren't we?'

Violet wanted to tell him about her food clearout but he had been quite scathing about the New You! class.

'Well, the aerobics sounds quite good,' he had conceded, as he thumbed through Dr Ramsbottom's leaflet. 'But the rest of it sounds like a load of twaddle.'

Not feeling brave enough to let on, Violet had let the subject slide. He hadn't asked her how much she weighed and there was no way she was going to tell him. As far as Sebastian was concerned, she was still out on a Tuesday night at the New You! class. He didn't know that everyone would be coming back to the house afterwards for a post-Trudie discussion.

'Well, seeing as there's nothing to eat, I'm going to order an Indian.'

Violet opened her mouth but in the end said nothing. It was her fault that there was nothing for Sebastian to eat in the fridge.

She ordered tikka masala for herself but managed to avoid eating too much of the gloriously creamy and fantastic sauce.

'Have an onion bhaji,' said Sebastian, wafting the packet in front of her nose.

She took a deep breath. 'I'm full, thanks.'

He frowned. 'You can't be.'

'But I am.'

'Go on. Have a bhaji.'

Violet shook her head.

'You know you want to.'

Finally she took the damn thing just to get it out of her face. But when Sebastian left the room to go to the bathroom, she crept into the kitchen and put the bhaji in the bin. She didn't know what his problem was but she wasn't going to ruin her diet.

She was in control, she realised. And she liked it.

Chapter Eighteen

Trudie was late. The god of traffic lights had not smiled down on her that evening. She hated being late almost as much as she hated ugly people, cellulite and women who wore pink slogan T-shirts calling themselves angels when they were three stone overweight.

She shoved the door open and strode into the hall but there was no one there. Idiots, she thought. Why would I expect this class to be keen and get here on time?

She opened up her large bag to bring out her folder of notes. On the top was the letter. The severe reprimand from head office. What a joke. As soon as Trudie made enough money she was going to dump New You! down the toilet where it belonged. She'd had enough of chubby tubbies and their problems. They made her feel ill with their wobbling chins and pitiful excuses.

It was all so unnecessary. Didn't they have any restraint? Any resolve? Her mind briefly flitted towards Trevor, her husband. What had he been thinking? It was only a cricket match, for God's sake. He didn't need to drink beer whilst watching it.

'But it's a one day international,' he had whined.

'So?' Trudie had replied, pouring the beer down the sink. 'It's Monday. You know we don't drink alcohol during the week.'

How else did he expect to maintain his trim figure? Lord knows, she had already had to ban butter, cheese, chocolate, crisps and cooking oil from the house.

Even more worrying was the fact that Trevor had tried to initiate sex later on in bed.

'It's still only Monday,' Trudie had told him, before turning her back on him. Had he completely forgotten the rule about no sex during the working week? She couldn't have less than eight hours' sleep a night.

She put the scales down on the floor and stood, waiting. Wondering if any of them would bother to turn up.

The door opened and in came the bride-to-be.

'Good evening,' called Trudie.

She hated having to make the effort to be nice but head office had threatened her with the sack if she couldn't keep her mouth shut. She was only being honest with them the previous week. Didn't they deserve that?

'Hello,' murmured Violet, heading towards the safety of the chairs.

'It's lovely to see you again,' Trudie carried on.

Violet sat down, waiting for the others to join her.

'How are the wedding plans going?' called Trudie across the empty space.

Violet shuffled in her seat. 'Fine, thank you.'

'Good, good. Weddings are lovely, aren't they? So romantic.'

143

Violet looked down at her feet.

You should be embarrassed, thought Trudie. How romantic is yours going to be if you can't even squeeze through the church door?

The main door was pushed open once more to reveal the mother-and-daughter act.

'Good evening,' Trudie said to them, the grin still in place.

Maggie tried to return her smile and failed. 'Good evening.'

Lucy glared at Trudie and followed her mother to the chairs.

Was it they who had stitched her up and whined to head office? They would pay. They would all pay once they started the aerobics session. She had planned a particularly brutal one. Hopefully she might kill a few of them off and then she could close the class altogether.

The main door opened again.

'Good evening,' said Trudie, smiling at the mouthy one.

Kathy gave a snort of laughter. 'Whatever, love.'

Trudie tried not to scowl at her back.

Then the fat boy Edward appeared, grunted his greeting at her and that was it. They were all there.

Trudie took a deep breath and went to stand in front of them. They were all muttering under their breath, probably about how much they had eaten in the past week. She cleared her throat to get their attention.

'Well, good evening once more,' she said with a fixed grin.

When no one answered, she felt her smile faltering.

'I would like to take this opportunity to apologise for my outburst last week. I've been on antibiotics for

144

a chest infection and I'm afraid I reacted quite badly to them. Side effects, the doctor told me. As you know I'm normally one hundred per cent professional so I promise you it won't happen again.'

Only because jobs were scarce on the ground right now. It was a pain that Trevor didn't get the pay rise she had been banking on. He would have to try harder as well. Now she was stuck with these losers for the rest of the year.

But in the meantime, she had to keep them sweet.

'So, now that we're all friends again, who would like to be first to be weighed this week?'

Dead silence until Kathy said, 'What the hell,' and followed Trudie over to the scales.

She kicked off her shoes and stepped up. 'Better find out how much weight I've put on.'

There was a short silence as everyone watched her face drop.

'I'm afraid you've put two pounds on,' said Trudie in a pitying tone of voice.

'No worries,' said Kathy before scuttling away.

Didn't she care? And didn't she need a licence to be that fat in public?

Next up was the menopausal mother.

At least she hadn't put any weight on. But she hadn't lost any either.

Maggie gave her a smile that was full of fear.

But Trudie fixed on a rictus grin. 'Not to worry. Next week will be better, I'm sure.'

About as sure as I am that you're stuffing your face in front of *This Morning* each and every day.

The daughter had also put on two pounds.

Lucy scowled at her but Trudie let it wash over her. Teenagers were always a pain. In fact, all children were. There was no way Trudie was ever having children. Think of the damage it would do to her body.

The fat man strode up, looking a little smug. Perhaps it was he who shopped her to head office.

'I take it you won't be talking to us in a rude way ever again,' said Edward before he stepped up on the scales. 'Otherwise you'll see a side of me that you won't like.'

What was he going to do? Drop his trousers for her?

But Trudie was the one looking smug when Edward's weight registered that he had put on another pound.

Only the bride to be left. Violet came over, not making any eye contact.

Trudie wasn't bothered. She would be past caring, if she had ever cared in the first place.

The great heifer stepped up on the scales. Then she took a deep breath and looked up.

Trudie gave her a pitying smile and glanced at the scales.

That can't be right, she thought.

She sighed. 'I'm sorry, but could you step off the scales and then back on? They seem to be malfunctioning.'

Violet did as she was told and then waited once more.

But the scales registered the same weight.

Trudie looked up at her in genuine amazement. 'You've lost five pounds!' she said, aware that her tone was high and screechy.

Violet gave a start and took a quick look at the screen. It was true. She was now 14 stone 9 lbs.

'I don't believe it,' she said.

Nor do I, thought Trudie.

Violet went back to the chairs in a daze whilst everyone congratulated her.

Well, don't let it go to your head, thought Trudie. Your body's still such a disaster that the UN have set up a helpline.

Besides, the wretched woman would probably put it all back on within a week.

Chapter Nineteen

The whole group was nearly at bursting point as they staggered through Violet's front door after the class had finished.

Violet closed the front door behind her, trying to make sense of it all. She had lost five pounds. How? Well, she knew how. But that much? So soon? She couldn't believe it.

'Well done!' said Maggie, sinking on to the sofa and still trying to catch her breath from the ruthless aerobics session.

Trudie had been severe in her punishment and they were all trying to calm their hammering pulses.

'How did you do it?' asked Kathy, her face bright red.

Violet was still in a daze and stared around at everyone as she sank on to the sofa.

'But I had an Indian takeaway,' she stammered.

'Every night?' asked Lucy.

'That's the diet for me,' said Edward with a grin.

Violet shook her head. 'It was only on Sunday.'

'So what did you eat the rest of the week?'

'Yeah, spill the beans,' said Kathy. 'Five pounds off! That's bloody amazing!'

They were all looking at Violet with eager anticipation.

She shrugged her shoulders. 'I just counted calories. It wasn't very exciting but at least I wasn't starving hungry.'

'Did you have carbs?' asked Kathy.

Violet nodded. 'I had pasta one night. Oh and a shepherd's pie on another night.'

'That's what I should have done,' said Kathy, rolling her eyes. 'Instead of trying to cope with yet another faddy bloody diet.'

'Just think what we could have lost if we'd done the same thing,' said Maggie, looking at Lucy.

'Except we did that stupid juice diet,' said Lucy with a grunt.

'It was a complete nightmare,' said Maggie.

'In what way?' asked Kathy.

'We worked out that the reason everyone loses weight so quickly is because the juices are so disgusting that you don't want to drink them. So we went back to eating all the bad stuff again.'

'And I had a McDonald's yesterday,' said Lucy, also looking glum.

Kathy sighed. 'I failed too. Carb-free, my arse. I can't do without bread or potatoes. It's just not physically possible.'

She looked at Edward who gave a large sigh.

'I had eight pints on Saturday night,' he told them. 'And then a chip kebab. Maybe two.' He then looked at Violet. 'You did really well.'

Violet was a little uncomfortable at all the praise

149

being heaped upon her. It wasn't as if she had found the secret to the universe.

'I'm going to be so good this week,' said Kathy. 'No cheating.'

'Me too,' said Lucy. 'But there's always something naughty to eat at home. I've got no willpower.'

'What do you suggest?' asked Maggie.

Violet realised that Maggie was talking to her, asking her for advice.

'Well, I cleared out my cupboards,' she told them, somewhat embarrassed. 'I thought it would be easier if there wasn't any rubbish in the house for me to eat.'

'Right!' said Kathy. 'That's what I'm doing too.'

'What else did you do?' said Maggie, leaning forward and eager to learn.

'Well,' said Violet, clearing her voice and growing pink. 'I tried to stick to fifteen hundred calories each day.'

'What did you eat?' asked Kathy.

'Fruit or cereal for breakfast and a readymade sandwich under three hundred calories for lunch.'

'What about for dinner?' asked Maggie.

'Only ready meals. You know, the low-fat ones.'

'Which ones?'

So they wrote down the meals she had eaten.

'They're not very exciting,' Violet told them.

'Who cares?' said Kathy. 'I'm desperate.'

'So just fifteen hundred calories,' said Lucy.

Violet nodded. 'It is actually quite a lot of food if you're not eating rubbish.' She glanced at Edward. 'I read that men are allowed two thousand calories, especially if they're active.'

He nodded thoughtfully. 'That's what I'll aim for then.'

'How much do you think we'll lose?' said Maggie, who now had a gleam in her eye.

Violet bit her lip. This wasn't really her area of expertise. But she managed to recall a few things from her search through the internet and magazines.

'There's no quick fix,' she told them. 'I think we'll all have an initial big loss if we stick to fifteen hundred calories but then it goes down to a loss of one or two pounds a week. We've got to be patient.'

'But I want to be thin!' whined Lucy. 'Now!'

'If you lose two pounds a week, it will only take two months to lose a stone,' Violet found herself saying, before wondering where all this was coming from.

'That's all right,' said Maggie, nodding her head.

'I've been this fat for so long,' said Kathy. 'I can wait a bit longer to be thin.'

'Those crash diets are rubbish,' said Maggie. 'I always put on far more weight than I started with.'

As everyone nodded in agreement, Violet realised that perhaps she hadn't been alone in her healthy-eating troubles.

'Anything else?' said Kathy.

Violet hesitated before speaking. 'I also read that we should take our measurements. Now, at the beginning. Chest, hips and waist. Not here!' she said quickly, as the women in particular looked horrified. 'But it should give you a boost to see the tape measure go down as well as the scales.'

Everyone nodded. And Violet felt a little proud of herself that she had managed to give them some advice.

'What about alcohol?' asked Edward, but inside he knew what the advice would be.

Violet shrugged her shoulders. 'I guess it still counts as calories. Everything does. All food and drink has some kind of calorie.'

And so they went away, planning to copy her meals for the following week to see how they all got on.

She still couldn't quite believe it. She, Violet Saunders, giving advice on healthy eating and living. She nearly snorted at the irony.

Chapter Twenty

Kathy had been really determined that this would be the start of a healthy regime. Violet had lost five pounds. She must be able to do the same thing, surely? Wednesday was a blank canvas just waiting to lead her into a new and exciting life.

Unfortunately, fate threw a spanner in the works. Kathy had been left alone in the shop for the past week while Mavis was off with a flu bug. She was now better but Kathy woke up on Wednesday morning feeling rough. She was running a temperature and coughing like a smoker on eighty a day.

Kathy felt dreadful, with barely any energy to drag herself into the kitchen. What if she really deteriorated and nobody knew that she was lying on the floor with a high fever, unable to move?

She called in sick as she could barely stand up, let alone be on her feet all day in the shop. Then she fell back on to the sofa and growled at daytime TV.

There was nothing worse than being ill when you lived on your own. No one to put a cool flannel on your forehead and make you a cup of tea. Nobody to get you a boiled egg and soldiers or a nice soothing cold drink for your sore throat.

Kathy felt even more lonely than usual. What would she give to have a lovely boyfriend fussing over right now? Kissing her fevered brow? The only man she spoke to on a frequent basis was Mr Perkins, who came into the shop on a Thursday morning and flirted with her. Unfortunately Mr Perkins was in his late eighties and had so many bristles coming out of both ears and nostrils that he could fill a duvet with them.

The only other man that Kathy came into regular contact was Edward from the class. He was kind and funny, not too shy to talk in front of a bunch of women. He had nice eyes too. Plus he also had those wide shoulders that could protect you from anything. But he was out of her league. Once he got slim, he would never look at a woman like her. Especially as she would probably fail the diet and stay fat.

She rubbed her forehead. She didn't know why she was thinking about Edward in a romantic capacity. It must be the fever.

If Kathy had had any energy, she would have been really cross. Why did she never get any of those horrific stomach bugs which sounded awful but where most people seemed to lose half a stone in a day? No, she had to catch proper flu which entailed lying prostrate on the sofa and eating ice-cream to soothe her throat whilst watching old films on the TV.

Feed a cold or starve a fever. She had both so she had better keep eating. Maybe she would sweat a few pounds off with the high temperature but she didn't think so. Not when she discovered how comforting cheese scones and butter could be.

Afterwards, she felt even more depressed. It was ridiculous. She ate too much because she was depressed about her weight. And she was depressed because she ate too much.

It was a cycle that had taken years to perfect. And Kathy wasn't sure it could ever be broken.

Edward was also feeling awful but not because of summer flu. He was sitting in a traffic jam but could feel his heart racing again. He knew it wasn't because of any exertion because he'd been in the car for half an hour.

He glanced at the clock on the dashboard. Quarter of an hour had gone by and his heart was just starting to calm down. He had tried not to panic, determined to ignore it. This time he wasn't giving in. He was on medication for the angina and that would just have to do.

Talking to his mother at the weekend hadn't helped.

Yet again she had gone on and on about how grey he looked until finally he had confessed to his angina attack. Prepared for a hysterical outburst, he was surprised that none came. Instead, she snatched the packet of biscuits from the table in front of him and dumped them in the bin.

She held up her hand to his protests.

'No!' she told him. 'I've lost your father. I'm not going to lose you too. And I certainly won't be encouraging you to eat any more. No more cakes, biscuits or rubbish when you come here. If you can't take care of yourself, then I'm going to.'

He placed his hands on her shoulders. 'It's all right, Mum. I get it.'

Her lips begin to tremble and her eyes filled with tears.

'It's OK,' he told her as he pulled her into a hug. 'I'm going to lose weight. I promise.'

At the time it had been a small white lie but he knew it was time to get serious about his health. After the weight-club meeting the previous evening, he had gone straight to the twenty-four-hour supermarket and picked up a whole load of fruit and low-fat ready meals. He then went home and threw out everything fat-laden in the house.

He was now on two thousand calories a day and he would just have to learn to exist on it. In actual fact, it was quite a large amount of food. More than enough to feed him each day. So it was in with the healthy cereals for breakfast and out with the fry-ups.

He had already decided not to hang about at the cricket club that week. He wasn't going to drink any alcohol for a fortnight to see if that made a difference. Edward knew he'd get some stick from his mates but he had to do this.

But he also knew that just eating healthily wouldn't be enough. On the way home from work, he was making a detour. His stomach was rumbling, desperate for its dinner, but he knew it had to be done. If he was going to get healthy, he'd do it the right way.

His pulse was beginning to calm down as he drew into the car park. He got out and lumbered his way towards the front door. He knew what to expect. And he was right.

The skinny receptionist fixed on a Hollywood smile. 'Hi. Welcome to Grove Gym. Can I help you?'

He knew what she was thinking but he had to start somewhere.

So he smiled back and said, 'I'd like to join the gym, please.'

Lucy grabbed a piece of toast before going to college. But unlike every other morning, she didn't smother it in butter and chocolate spread. A quick slick of marmite was enough. It was a little dry to eat but Lucy didn't care.

She grabbed a banana and an apple from the fruit bowl and stuffed them in her bag. No more chocolate. No more crisps. Her moment of shame on the bus had been a turning point and the split denim skirt was hanging up outside her wardrobe to remind her.

'Are you going to the supermarket later?' she asked her mum.

Maggie nodded. 'Healthy ready meals all round.'

'What about Dad?'

'I'll buy him the full-fat versions. He won't twig.'

Lucy swung her bag on to her shoulder. 'I'm grabbing a salad from the canteen for lunch.'

'Watch those calories!' shouted her mother as she swung the front door closed.

Lucy smiled as she walked down the front path. This was a new beginning, of that she was sure. She just had to be strong and not succumb to temptation.

Unfortunately, the guy in front of her on the bus had bought his breakfast from McDonald's and the smell drove her so crazy with lust that she had to move seats. As she left the bus, she also tried not to inhale the delicious aroma wafting out of the bakery near the bus stop.

On automatic pilot, she found herself in the newsagent's and reaching out for a chocolate bar to keep her going until lunchtime. Just in time, Lucy remembered her fruit. So she picked up some sugar-free gum instead. If she needed something to chomp on, that would have to be it.

She was queuing up to pay when she glanced at the young guy who had just bought a can of Red Bull and was leaving the shop. They locked eyes briefly before he looked away and hurried out of the shop. It was Robert, the guy whom she had slept with the previous summer.

Lucy recognised the look on his face. It was mortification mixed with embarrassment. She hoped it was because he had never called her. But she knew deep down that he was probably embarrassed at having slept with her in the first place.

She paid for her gum and left the shop, trying to hold herself straight. Well, stuff Robert. So what if he was embarrassed? So was she, come to think of it. He was no looker and hadn't exactly been fantastic in bed. She would find herself a decent boyfriend, a gorgeous guy who was funny and intelligent. A guy who would think himself so lucky to have her that he would never stop telling her so.

Lucy nodded to herself. That was it. That was her goal. Stuff Nicola Bowles and her cronies too. Stuff the world. Lucy was on a mission.

This was it. No turning back.

Maggie hated the house once everyone had left. It always felt so empty without them there. After years of hectic family life, it had all suddenly calmed down. Lucy was grown up and at college. Gordon's garage was an established business and didn't need her input now. Which left Maggie at a loose end.

She ate her toast whilst listening to the radio. She always had either the radio or television switched on. It filled the silence in the house.

After breakfast, she headed for the supermarket. The food shopping was fairly easy. Lots of healthy ready meals for her and Lucy. More calorific meals for Gordon. Of course, he could do with losing a few pounds as well, but he hated dieting so there was no chance of his eating the same as her and Lucy. He wouldn't realise that their meals were different. He was normally too busy chatting about his hectic day at the garage.

It was OK for Gordon, thought Maggie. Her days were never hectic.

Next to the checkouts was a large display of exercise DVDs.

Maggie thought back to what Trudie had said during Tuesday night's class.

'Exercise is the key,' Trudie had told them, hardly out of breath while everyone else was looking for an oxygen tank. 'It shifts the fat faster than anything.'

Maggie threw the DVD into her shopping trolley. It had to be better than daytime TV.

She headed home, her heart sinking. An hour had passed. What to do for the rest of the day?

She unpacked the shopping, trying not to glance in the cupboards which were still filled to capacity with biscuits, cakes and treats. Gordon had a sweet tooth so she wasn't able to clear them out like the others had. Maybe she wouldn't buy any more in the future. Let him run down the pile she had stashed inside the cupboard. If she and Lucy weren't going to eat any of it, it would take Gordon a good few months to get through all their supplies.

She glanced at the last bag of shopping to be

unpacked. It was more biscuits and cakes. All for Gordon, of course. More sweet, lovely, comforting things to be eaten. Including a box of fresh doughnuts. Gordon loved his doughnuts. She always brought him one to go with his cup of tea when he got home from work.

But this was a box of eight. Special offer, the label said. Buy four, get four free! Eight delicious doughnuts. Maggie licked her lips. No, she was fine. She could do this.

She headed into the lounge and switched on the television. Slotting in the DVD, Maggie wondered if she worked out all the time whether she could eat whatever she wanted. Like a marathon runner or an Olympic athlete. The only gold Maggie knew she could win at the moment was an overeater's competition.

Maggie closed the curtains and stood in front of the television. She was still wearing her jeans and jumper but she couldn't be bothered to change.

It was lucky she hadn't made the effort, Maggie told herself five minutes later. She could barely finish the warm-up. The instructor was telling her to copy everything, but the stretches were impossible. The side lunges hurt her knees. A quick march on the spot jiggled the fat around her middle.

In the end, Maggie watched the rest of the DVD from the sofa. The beautifully toned instructor bounced around her fitness studio in her teeny tiny shorts and top. It must be wonderful to be that thin and not have to worry, thought Maggie.

She went into the kitchen and made herself a cup of tea. But as she picked up the mug, she sighed. Then she picked up the box of doughnuts as well and took them both into the lounge with her.

Chapter Twenty-one

The morning after the weigh-in, Violet still couldn't believe that she had lost five pounds. How? Why? It was all a mystery.

She supposed she must have somehow eaten less than normal. It didn't feel like it. Different, yes. But she hadn't been starving hungry. She thought she had eaten loads, too much even. It was all very odd.

She found a tape measure after the others had left and had taken her measurements. Big fat rolling skin measuring oh so many inches. There was still such a long way to go. But this second week would be better. She would eat healthily once more. She just had to be strong. And patient.

Talking of patience, when was the new shopping precinct in the centre of town ever going to be finished? Violet's car was inching forward in the queue at snail's pace. The traffic was getting worse and worse.

Violet arrived at work still feeling quite bouncy. Five pounds off! Did it show? Was her waistband any looser? No. But it must have gone from somewhere.

She arrived at her desk and put down her handbag.

'Good morning,' said Mark, coming out of his office. But his usual smile was missing.

'Morning,' muttered Violet, sitting down.

'Wendy's off sick,' Mark told her, with a grimace. 'Some hideous stomach bug she caught from one of her kids. She went into too much detail and put me right off my breakfast.'

Violet nodded, not knowing what to say.

'And the email system is off line.'

Violet realised the stress levels in the office were humming on full blast.

'How long will the system be off?'

'God knows,' he said, running his hand through his dark hair so it stuck up a little. 'Couple of hours, we think.'

The hotline phone inevitably rang.

'You're going to be inundated,' he told her, with a shake of his head.

He continued to hover whilst Violet picked up the phone.

'Hello, Hotline. Can I help you?'

'I can't get into the email system,' said the female voice down the phone.

Normally Violet would have passed the call on to Wendy and just let her tell them that the email wasn't working. But Wendy wasn't there. Julie and Anthony were already on the phone. It seemed a bit ridiculous that she couldn't just simply advise the customer what the problem was.

So she took a deep breath and said, 'I'm afraid the email is likely to be down until midday. But if you have any problems this afternoon, please phone back.'

162

She finished the call and looked up to find Mark still standing over her, with his eyebrows raised.

Violet waited for the inevitable bawling out but it never happened. Instead he nodded at her, allowing himself a small smile, before walking away.

The morning continued with barely a moment to pause for breath. The hotline was red hot with people panicking about their emails. But Violet continued to field most of the calls.

Then she received a call from one of the managers, who had put on his most pompous voice and asked what the exact problem was. At that point she had to pass on the call to Anthony.

Afterwards, Anthony peered over the divide between our desks. 'That guy is such a tosser,' he said, referring to the last phone call.

Violet nodded. 'I'm sorry. I didn't know what to say to him.'

He passed over a piece of paper. 'If they're really pushing for the technical answer just use any of these words at random. That soon shuts them up.'

She peered at the piece of paper. 'Right. Thanks.'

'Go on then. Let's see if you can sound convincing.'

'Oh! Well,' she said, looking at the paper. 'You seem to have an encrypted gateway. The stack has failed, I'm afraid.'

Anthony grinned. 'Excellent!'

'Are you teaching Violet to lie to the customers?' said Mark, suddenly appearing out of thin air.

Anthony nodded.

Violet cringed, fearing his wrath. But Mark broke into a smile. 'Excellent. Keep up the good work!'

She didn't even have time for a lunch break, so busy was the hotline with calls. So Violet ate her lunch at the desk. Not wanting to buy ready-made sandwiches every day, she had bought some low-fat crackers and very-low-fat cheese. It was pretty taste-less but at least it kept within her calorie count for lunch.

'What's that?' said Mark as he passed by. 'Part of a dry wall cavity?'

She ignored him. Hadn't he seen anyone eating healthily before?

Violet was just finishing her last cracker when she became aware of Julie glancing over.

Finally, Julie spoke. 'You did OK this morning. With the email stuff, I mean.'

Violet was shocked. Julie didn't even speak to her normally, let alone give out praise.

'Thanks,' she managed to stammer. 'It seems silly me being bored when I could take the heat off you guys. You all seem so overworked.'

It was sheer, unadulterated flattery. But Julie seemed to preen a bit at the words.

'We seem to have more and more customers but the same amount of staff to support them all. It's crazy.'

Violet nodded in agreement and then decided to be a little bit brave once more.

'If you ever wanted to show me some basic proce-dures on your database, I'd be happy to field some of your phone calls as well.'

There. She'd said it. She waited for Julie to throw her computer in disgust. But she didn't. She narrowed her eyes briefly, at which point Violet mentally ducked. But then she gave a nod.

'Will do.'

She said it so quietly that Violet almost missed it.

'Thanks.'

Later on, she was regaling Sebastian with the news from her exciting day.

'It was so funny,' she told him. 'Anthony's given me all these words like transmission and migrated and you just say a few in order. It totally fazes the customers!'

But Sebastian wasn't laughing. 'All sounds a bit unprofessional to me,' he snapped. 'I'm starving. That ready meal was crap. What's for pudding?'

'Erm, I'm not sure.'

She hadn't dared to tell Sebastian about her cupboard overhaul.

She took the plates into the kitchen feeling a bit deflated. Why couldn't Sebastian support her in the new job?

But he was probably just tired. After all, his job was a lot more important than hers.

Chapter Twenty-two

Violet had had a reasonable week but still didn't feel confident at the second weigh-in. She still wasn't sure if the previous week's weight loss had been some kind of fluke.

Trudie looked as if she believed the same thing, especially when Violet bravely stepped up on the scales first.

There was a short silence before Trudie looked up at her with her lip curled. 'Another five pounds off,' she snapped.

Violet reeled from the wonder of losing ten pounds in two weeks.

'Are you sure you haven't had one of those gastric bands fitted?' asked Trudie with a frown.

Violet looked at her, horrified, and scuttled away.

With nothing to lose but his dignity, Edward quickly got up to get weighed next.

'Right,' he said. 'Let's get this over with.'

He had stuck to the two thousand calories but who knew if it had worked? He had no idea what he was going to do if it hadn't.

He took a deep breath and stepped up on the scales. There was a short silence and then Trudie looked up at him.

'You've lost half a stone,' she said, staring at him as if he were from an alien planet.

'Excellent!' he said, beaming at her.

'Me next,' said Lucy, standing up. 'I've been really good too.'

She stepped up on to the scales briefly and then stepped off before giving a scream of joy.

'I've lost four pounds! And I had a piece of cake yesterday! Think how much I would have lost if I hadn't had that!'

'Well,' said Trudie, trying to gather her thoughts together. 'Let's try and not have any cake next week.'

'I won't if you won't,' said Lucy, grinning at her.

Maggie smiled at her daughter as she returned to the chairs and gave her a quick hug. Then she looked at Kathy.

'You had a bad week too, did you?' said Kathy.

Maggie nodded. 'Terrible.'

'No, you didn't,' said Lucy. 'We were really good. We only had those healthy meals in the evening, followed by a yoghurt.'

Maggie hung her head in shame. 'Yes, but I had already eaten for Britain the rest of the day when everyone else was out.'

Lucy shook her head. 'I don't believe it.'

The others persuaded both Kathy and Maggie to get weighed anyway. Thankfully both their weights had stayed the same.

'I'm very disappointed in both of you,' Trudie told them, finally able to criticise someone and get it out of her system. 'You've really let yourself and the whole class down. You must do better next week. For me, if not for you.'

'Wicked old witch,' muttered Kathy as Violet handed them a mug of tea when they were back home.

'At least you didn't put on any weight,' Edward told them.

'Yeah but you've all done so well,' said Kathy.

'I ended up in hospital,' Edward reminded her. 'I have to lose weight otherwise I'll be straight back there.'

When he gave Kathy a small smile, she found herself blushing and had to look away. She had had all sort of feverish dreams about Edward whilst she was ill. Now she was trying to forget about them.

'And I'm getting married,' Violet told her. 'I've got a goal.'

'Me too,' said Lucy. 'I've had a miserable time in college being fat. I'm not going to be fat at university as well.'

'I've been lying on the sofa with flu feeling sorry for myself but that's no excuse,' said Kathy.

'Yes it is, you were ill,' said Maggie. 'Every time I'm with the family, I eat really well.'

'That's good,' said Violet.

Maggie shook her head. 'But it's a lie. Every time Lucy or Gordon go out, I end up shovelling as much food as I can down my throat. When they get back home, I go into serene goddess mode again.'

Lucy looked shocked but didn't saying anything.

'I made myself throw up after eating once,' Kathy found herself saying. 'That was when I decided I'd had enough.' And then she burst into tears. 'Everyone's doing so well,' she sobbed.

'I'm not, am I?' said Maggie, giving her a hug.

'Why am I so rubbish at everything?' Kathy hiccuped, trying to calm down.

'You're not,' said Violet.

'It's all right for you to talk,' snapped Kathy. 'You're losing weight.'

Violet blushed red, but found herself being a little bit defensive. 'Look, I stuck to my calorie count,' she said, trying not to snap back. 'Didn't you?'

To her horror, Kathy ducked her head in shame. 'I'm sorry. I didn't mean to bark at you. It's not your fault.'

'That's OK,' Violet said quickly. 'I know how difficult it is.'

'Do you?' said Kathy, with a throaty cough that she had yet to get rid of. 'You've lost ten pounds.'

'Yes, and I've got another sixty to go,' Violet told her. 'This isn't easy.'

Kathy began to say something but it was lost in a cacophony of coughing. Violet went and got her a glass of water.

'Thanks,' Kathy was finally able to croak. 'Sorry, folks. Hopefully germ-free now.'

'Poor you,' said Maggie. 'Are you OK now?'

'I don't think I'm quite up to running a marathon,' said Kathy with a smile. 'But then again, when was I ever?'

'So?' said Maggie, looking at Violet. 'What's happened to make you into a diet goddess? I mean, I understand the calorie counting. But how come you've just gone straight into it without any difficulties? What happened to you?'

Violet sighed. 'The most awful night of my life.'

They all stared at her. But it was time to be honest. Really honest. So she told them about hiding in the toilets at the wedding and what she overheard the women saying about her.

'Those bitches!' said Lucy.

Violet sighed. 'I'd like to say it was the most embarrassing moment of my life but even that wasn't it.'

Everyone was waiting and watching her. Oh well. She had nothing to lose but her dignity and that had gone a long time ago.

'I was feeling really low one day and I went to get my favourite chocolate cake from M and S. To eat it all myself, obviously. But there was only one left and some guy was holding it. So I snatched it out of his hands and ran away with it.'

Lucy and Kathy giggled.

Violet shook her head. 'That's not the really bad bit. The guy is now my boss.'

Even Edward was shocked at this. 'You have to see him every day?' he spluttered.

Violet nodded.

'What's he like? Did he say anything?'

'He's OK. He made a little joke and that was it.'

'And?' asked Maggie.

'I've told you everything,' said Violet, sighing.

'No. Was it the milk chocolate cake with the sprinkles or the white chocolate gateau?'

It raised a smile from Violet. It was funny how she felt she could speak freely in front of these relative strangers. Perhaps it was the fact that they were all in the same boat, all fighting the weight issue. But Violet could really could speak her mind with them. It was quite liberating.

'How did we get here?' said Kathy, shaking her head.

'Long journey,' said Edward, blowing out a sigh.

'Via every drive-thru McDonald's,' said Kathy.

And they all laughed again.

'Look,' said Violet. 'I've done nothing special. It's not rocket science. I'm just keeping a close eye on my calories. And I write down everything so I know I'm not going over my limit.'

'It was easier than I thought,' Lucy told them. 'The food's not very exciting but it works. Honest.'

'Yeah, but you've got a young metabolism,' said Maggie. 'You're not old like me. The weight's going to fall off you really quickly.'

'I'm no spring chicken though, am I?' said Edward. 'But I lost half a stone and I wasn't even hungry.'

'Pig,' muttered Kathy, before giving him a shy smile.

'I joined a gym and I didn't touch any alcohol either,' said Edward, still grinning. 'And I'm not going to this week either.'

He was really pleased with himself. The effort had been worth it.

'Why don't you both start afresh tomorrow?' said Violet. 'But you've got to be honest with what you're eating. Just between us. Everyone's in the same boat so if one of us messes up then we'll rally round, OK?'

Violet didn't know where all these words of wisdom were coming from but everyone was nodding eagerly with her.

'You're going to email me what you eat every day, OK?'

Everyone was still nodding.

'And if you cheat, you're only cheating yourself. Get over this week and move on. And keep busy. Try not to obsess about food.'

So the pact was made and email addresses were exchanged.

After they left, Violet sat down on the sofa and glanced across to Isabella's book of elegance. There was nothing much on the TV so she flicked through the pages instead.

Rule Number One, she read. Food should be healthy and delicious.

Hmmm. So far, so bad. Her ready meals were OK but nothing to get her tastebuds zinging.

'Food should be fresh and easily cooked,' it continued.

Lord knows what Isabella would think about the microwaved, low-fat lasagne she had just eaten.

'A bride who eats healthily is a bride full of life. But not to an extreme. Look at Sophia Loren. The ageless Italian beauty is quoted as saying, "Everything you see I owe to spaghetti." Her advice, like her beautiful figure, still holds good today. A simple Mediterranean diet is healthy and will help you lose weight.'

Violet googled Sophia Loren and stared at her photos. There were a lot of black and white photos of her in the 1960s where she had a fabulously curvy body. Slim but with va-va-voom curves.

Her search led on to other gorgeous Italian women. Monica Bellucci again had curves which could stop traffic. Elisabetta Canalis had even ensnared George Clooney with her Italian sex appeal. They all had figures. Trim but curvy with defined waists as well as a decent size chest and hips. Healthy but not Hollywood stick insects. Imagine looking like that on a daily basis?

But hey, hadn't she just lost ten pounds? Where did it go? Did it just ooze out of the skin? Violet stopped that train of thought before she felt ill.

But now it was possible the loss would slow down to two pounds a week. But that would make her nine stone by the time of the wedding. She snorted. As if she would ever weigh that!

But something had clicked since the humiliation of that wedding. Her healthy-eating plan was working. She was losing weight. She felt a little tingle of happiness deep inside. And hoped it would last.

Chapter Twenty-three

Violet was still feeling smug as she went into work the following day. Ten pounds' worth of smug, self-satisfied weight loss. But alas, the good feeling didn't last long.

She was so bored at work that she found her thoughts heading back to food. The hotline stayed quiet and there was nothing to distract her. Nothing to lead her thoughts from the sugar craving. She had to have sugar.

Violet sat up straight in her chair. No, she didn't. Think fat bride. Think enormous bride. Did she want to feel like that? No! A thousand times no! She had to be strong.

Her phone beeped with a text from Kathy.

'How many calories in a massive bowl of Coco Pops?'

Violet googled the calorie count before replying, 'Standard bowl is about three hundred and eighty.'

'Bloody hell!' came the reply. 'And it was full fat milk.'

'Try changing to semi-skimmed,' she replied.

Violet's phone beeped once more but this time the text was from Maggie.

'Emergency!!! Help!!!' read the message.

Violet quickly rang the number. 'What is it?'

'I'm in the kitchen,' panted Maggie. 'Help me. I've got a cream eclair in my hand and I'm not afraid to eat it.'

'Right,' Violet told her, putting on a stern voice. 'Keep hold of the eclair and walk towards the kitchen bin. Open it and then drop the eclair in there. Now close the lid.'

'OK,' said Maggie. 'I've done that.'

'Good. Better now?'

'Yes. Thanks. It's silly, I know. I can do this.'

'Yes, you can,' Violet told her.

Maggie rung off. Violet stared at the phone for a while before calling Maggie again. This time she took a while longer to answer.

'Hello?' came the muffled voice.

'You got the eclair out of the bin, didn't you?'

Maggie choked on her eclair in shock. 'How did you know?'

'Because we've all done it. Have you eaten it all?'

'I swear to God, I was only on the first bite when you rang.'

'OK. Drop it in the bin again. Now go to the sink and get the washing up liquid. Take it over to the bin and cover the eclair in the liquid. All over. No spot untouched.'

'Done it,' said Maggie. 'God, I'm useless. I only lasted through breakfast.'

'It doesn't matter,' Violet told her. 'Why don't you keep yourself busy? Is there anything you can do to take your mind off food?'

'I was going to clean the kitchen.'

'I think you should stay away from the kitchen.'

Violet put down the phone and looked up to find Mark standing over her.

'That sounded very perverse,' he said, breaking into a smile. Instantly his face lit up and she remembered how attractive he could be when he wasn't frowning.

She blushed. 'It was one of my diet group.'

'Washing-up liquid? What a waste of a good eclair.'

And off he went. He was right, too. But then Mark had probably never been big in his life. Violet had overheard him mention going to the gym on a couple of occasions so perhaps that was why his body was strong but slim. He was also six feet tall so could probably carry a few extra pounds without worrying about it.

Violet looked at the time. Three more minutes had dragged by.

She glanced around at everyone else. Everyone was busy and concentrating. They weren't eating rubbish because they were occupied. They didn't have time to eat. She had all the time in the world. Violet began to get twitchy.

The hotline stayed silent. She glanced at Mark's office door. It was open and she could hear him shouting down the phone at someone. She heard the slam of the phone. And then all was quiet apart from the tapping of keyboards.

Violet looked around her desk. There wasn't even anything to read. There were no distractions.

Come and buy me, beckoned the Mars bar in the vending machine.

She made up her mind. She stood up. Then she sat back down again. She could do this. She could be strong.

Then she stood up once more and headed towards the corridor and chocolate. But her feet swerved suddenly and Violet found herself at Mark's office door.

She was just about to back away quietly when he appeared in the doorway and made her jump.

So did Mark. He barked out some incomprehensible word in shock.

'You nearly gave me heart failure, lurking like that,' he told her.

Violet cleared her throat. 'Erm, it's just I was thinking . . .'

Her voice trailed off, along with her courage.

'Well, that's very interesting,' Mark replied with a smirk. 'Now if only we could get our customers on to advanced thinking then one day they might even achieve common sense.'

His glib tone and lack of chocolate made her snap.

'Look, you've got to give me something to do! I'm dying out here!' she told him. 'No wonder everyone leaves the job. It's so bloody boring. And if I stay bored, I'm going to eat and I am not going to end up a fat, lardy bride. No bloody way! You pay me to work here, so give me something to do! I'm not a thick person. I have a brain. Let me use it! I can't be a fat bride! I won't! I just won't!'

Violet finally shut up, the embarrassment coursing through her cheeks. Dear Lord, what was the matter with her? Mark was staring at her as if she were some kind of psychopath.

Perhaps it was the lack of sugar in her bloodstream. Maybe she'd gone into withdrawal mode. Her eyes certainly felt a bit bulgy. Perhaps that's why Mark stared at her for a while longer before brushing past.

He was probably going to get security to have her thrown out of the building. Violet hung her head in shame.

But instead Mark walked up to Anthony. 'Have you got a spare laptop you can give to Violet to use? Set up just like our customers have it?'

Anthony nodded and went into his stock room. He came out and handed a laptop to Mark.

'Here,' said Mark, placing the computer in her hands. 'Use this. Learn about the systems. Get yourself taught. Knock yourself out.'

He walked back to his office door but stopped and turned around. 'And eat a cake or something. Steal one if you have to.'

His eyes twinkled as he gave Violet a knowing grin before disappearing out of sight.

Her cheeks still throbbing, Violet scuttled back to her desk and switched on the laptop. Anthony gave her a list of passwords and she spent the rest of the afternoon nosing around the software.

It wasn't until she was driving home that Violet realised she hadn't eaten a thing all afternoon.

She was feeling smug until she played the answerphone message on the home number.

'Violet? It's Miriam.' As always, the sound of Sebastian's mother's voice made her shudder involuntarily. 'How are you getting along with your search for a wedding dress? I only ask because my sister has kindly given me her daughter's dress. Never been used. And I think she's the same size as you. No point wasting money, is there? I'll pass it to Sebastian and see what you think.'

Violet let her stomach rumble. She might never eat anything again. She had put off the whole dress thing for so long. But with six months to go, it was time to get organised.

She spent the evening looking through bridal magazines. But the models were all so thin, so elegant. So not how Violet felt. Everything was strapless, with a lot of skin on show. She felt terrified about having to expose that much of her body. Where were the dresses that went from the neck all the way down to the ground? With added boning and built-in magic pants?

Violet had seen a large and swanky-looking bridal shop in the centre of town. So the following lunchtime, she went along and stared in at the window. The mannequins were dressed in swathes of ivory taffeta and big flounces. It wasn't the style of wedding dress she had considered for herself but she had to start somewhere.

Violet took a deep breath and went in.

The sales assistant sitting behind a desk looked up from her notepad. 'Yes? Can I help you?'

Violet could feel the beads of nervous perspiration forming on her forehead and under her arms.

'I'm getting married,' she stammered. 'And I was wondering if I could try on some dresses? To get an idea of what suits me.'

The assistant was about to reply when someone else came through a curtain nearby. It was another bride-to-be coming out of the changing room. She was a Gwyneth Paltrow lookalike dressed in a slinky nightgown style. A posse of sales assistants cooed and fussed over her. She really did look sensational.

The woman behind the desk turned back to Violet.

'You'll need an appointment,' she told her. Then she

looked Violet up and down and lowered her voice. 'But I'm not sure we have anything here that would suit you. Might I suggest Madame Pomfrey's Bridal-wear across town? She caters for brides of larger sizes.'

Violet recoiled in horror, tears filling her eyes. She quickly fled the shop, renewed in her resolve to lose weight.

Chapter Twenty-four

Edward was striding out on the running machine at a fast walking pace. There was no way he was up to running. He didn't think his heart could take it. But he was power walking and although his pulse was racing, this time it was in a good way. At least he hoped it was.

He'd lost half a stone in a week. He couldn't quite believe it. It had been easy. And cheaper now he wasn't buying takeaways every night. OK, so the meals weren't exactly as tasty as a Chicken Dhansak with Bombay Potatoes and a couple of naan breads. But he could cope. For him it was a no-brainer.

He knew he had made a promise to his mum to get better but he actually needed to do it for himself. He didn't want to feel ill any longer. He wanted to have energy, a bit of get-up-and-go inside. If he was ever lucky enough to find himself a girlfriend, it would be nice to think that they could do things together, other than sitting on the sofa eating themselves into oblivion.

Edward found he hadn't really missed alcohol for

the past two weeks. He knew he would have to be careful when he began to drink again but for now he was coping. It hadn't been as hard as he had imagined.

Routine helped, he found. He would have cereal for breakfast, then go to work and have a ready-made sandwich for lunch. Some fruit in between meals if he was feeling hungry. Then home via the gym.

A gym bunny was running on the machine next to him. She was in tight Lycra shorts and a teeny top. He glanced over as her ponytail swung back and forth. Her make-up was still immaculate even though she had been running for ten minutes. Edward considered her to be too high-maintenance. He liked normal women. He wanted somebody with whom he could laugh and whose company he could enjoy without worrying that he wasn't wearing the latest shirt. Someone he could go for long walks with without having them moan that their high heels were stuck in a muddy field.

He knew he had a way to go before he was up to any kind of long walk. But since joining, he had been to the gym every night after work. It wasn't about getting his money's worth. It was what Violet had said earlier in the week. Something had clicked inside his head.

Determination had set in. He had had enough of feeling ill. He wanted more from life.

And this time he had decided he was going to get everything he had dreamed of.

Lucy was on top of the world. Not only had she lost four pounds in a week but she had also received a letter the previous day telling her that she had been accepted at CSM in the autumn. It was a provisional place but if her A-level results were OK she was on her way. She was thrilled.

She had looked up the college a thousand times on the internet. Central Saint Martins College of Art and Design had a reputation for being one of the leading design colleges in the world. And it was in London. How cool was that? She would be studying fashion in the fashion capital of the world.

Unlike this dump, thought Lucy as she stared around the shoe shop where she worked every Thursday evening and all day on Saturday. She didn't think Manolo Blahnik was quaking at the competition. It was a small shop which sold really cheap shoes. But at least it gave her a bit of extra money each week.

She spotted Nicola Bowles and her gang hanging about outside and quickly scuttled into the back room. You're not hiding, Lucy told herself while she tried to control her breathing. You're just avoiding a confrontation, that's all.

She peeked out through the doorway but the gang had moved on. Lucy sighed with relief before telling herself to get a grip. She only had three months left of torture and then she would be free of the shop, of the town but, most of all, free from the bullying.

She would swagger up and down Bond Street and Oxford Street, in her element because London would become her city.

And she would be thin. In her mind's eye, as she imagined herself wandering the corridors of the fashion college and bumping into Stella McCartney, she was thin. Thin and happy.

Lucy bit down on her apple. No more chocolate bars

or crisps to snack on. She had her goal. And she was going to achieve it.

Maggie was delighted for her daughter.

'I'm so proud of you, love,' she said after Lucy had bounced into the kitchen with the offer letter from CSM.

But now it was Friday morning and Maggie was alone once more. On Violet's advice she had cleaned the house from top to bottom. Once she had done that, Maggie had turned out every drawer and cupboard in her kitchen and organised those too. Anything to stick to her calorie ration and not to binge.

Lucy had made both of them lunch. Since her mother's confession at the diet club, Lucy had tried to make some of her determination rub off on Maggie. So, in the fridge for lunch was a ham and salad sandwich. Lucy had placed a banana and an apple next to it and told her mother, 'That's all you're eating until I get back from college.'

Maggie was determined not to let her daughter down.

In the end, to fill the next hour, she watched the exercise DVD once more. This time, she joined in. She put on the normal tracksuit bottoms and T-shirt she wore to Trudie's class and drew the curtains. This was a sight that the neighbours shouldn't be privy to.

It was dreadful. Worse than dreadful. Maggie ended up marching on the spot whilst the beautiful people in the DVD bounced around without a drop of sweat on their perfect bodies.

Maggie tried to keep to the beat of the thumping music but she felt hopelessly uncoordinated and old. Really old. Nevertheless, she stayed with the programme to the very end, if only to use up some of her endless spare time.

It took another hour for Maggie to recover, lying down on the sofa. Eventually she dragged herself upstairs and changed into her normal clothes.

As she came back downstairs, Maggie eyed the bags in the hallway. Some were destined for the charity shop. Perhaps she could take them to Kathy's shop. Others were for the dump.

She looked at them and sighed. At least it would give her something else to do.

Kathy was still waiting for her moment of diet revelation. She was wondering whether it would ever come. Everyone else was doing so well, she thought. Well, perhaps not Maggie, but Lucy, Edward and Violet were all losing weight.

But Lucy had her mother, Edward had a wide social circle and Violet had her fiancé. Kathy was alone. And lonely.

Even the shop didn't help. Mavis was beginning to slow down as she approached retirement and now only worked two days a week. Kathy found she even missed Mavis's chatter during the day. There seemed to be no difference between her lonely flat and the empty shop.

The bell rang as the door swung open. Kathy looked up and saw Maggie staggering through with a couple of dustbin liners.

'Hi,' said Maggie. 'Do you need some more stuff to sell?'

'Always,' said Kathy, fixing on a grin and heading across the shop to help with the bags.

Maggie handed over the bulging bin liners.

'It's all good stuff,' she told Kathy. 'Mainly kitchen bits that I've never used. You know, those gadgets that are supposed to make your life easier but end up cluttering up the drawers and cupboards.'

'I know,' said Kathy. 'That's great, thanks.'

Maggie looked around the shop. 'Pretty quiet today,' she said.

Kathy nodded. 'Afraid so,' she said. 'Business isn't very brisk.'

'Shame really,' said Maggie. 'There aren't any other decent charity shops nearby so you think people would come in.'

'I know,' replied Kathy.

'It needs a better sign outside,' said Maggie. 'And brighter windows too. I thought the place was closed down when I first saw it.'

Kathy nodded. The whole place needed overhauling.

'Must be difficult when it's so quiet,' said Maggie. 'I find if I'm not busy, I end up eating everything in sight.'

'Me too,' agreed Kathy.

'Hence the clearout,' Maggie told her. 'Once I've finished in the lounge this afternoon, I'm moving on to the airing cupboard, our bedroom and then the loft.'

'I find myself dusting shelves just to relieve the boredom,' said Kathy.

'It's such a shame you don't get much business. It's a good-sized shop,' said Maggie. 'Mind you, I didn't know it was here until you told me.'

'I know,' said Kathy. 'We're stuck down a side street which nobody seems to use. It's not a great position.'

'Will it have to close if business carries on being so quiet?'

Kathy nodded. 'We only just cover the rent at the

moment.' She put on another bright smile. 'But I'm sure your kitchen gadgets will draw in the crowds.'

Maggie smiled back but left soon after.

Kathy didn't want to think about the future if she didn't even have the shop to go to. She had enough trouble with the hours in the day as it was. She found herself emailing or texting Violet quite a bit. Misery loves company or safety in numbers, she wasn't sure which. She knew she was probably being a pain but the contact helped.

Kathy didn't want to let the group down but she wasn't really eating that well and knew the next weigh-in would show it.

Chapter Twenty-five

Violet was actually beginning to find work a little more enjoyable.

With her new laptop on the desk, it meant that, between calls, she was able to learn about the different software packages. It was great to be able to use her brain.

Unfortunately though, the lunches were becoming monotonous. She stared at her crackers and sighed. She didn't know what else to do, but something had to give. Otherwise she would go crackers herself.

'I'm just popping out for some lunch,' she told Anthony.

There had to be something more appetising to eat than those bloody dry biscuits. She wandered the streets for a short while but didn't fancy mass-produced sandwiches. The greasy smell of a burger joint hung in the air but she quickly walked in the opposite direction.

Finding herself in a part of town that she normally didn't visit, she suddenly breathed in the heady smell of garlic and spices. Something smelt wonderful. She took a left up a small alleyway, following her nose.

The wonderful aromas were coming from a tiny Italian delicatessen called Gino's. It must have expanded its trade at some point because it also seemed to serve coffee and food. Gino's was packed with lunchtime diners. Suited businessmen and -women filled the small number of tables and chairs. Others had spilled on to the tables in the street to bask in the June sunshine.

Violet felt warm in her black suit and top but her stomach was rumbling too much for her to care. Everything looked so delicious. She stared at the food on display, wondering what was healthy and how everything would taste. She must have stood there for some time until a familiar voice spoke.

'Now this is real food.'

She turned to find herself face to face Mark Harris, her boss.

'Much tastier than that rubbish you've been eating,' he told her, smiling.

Violet's mouth had gone dry. What was he doing here?

Then came a shriek of 'Marco!' from the other side of the counter.

A wizened, older woman of about eighty years old was carving her way through the crowds towards them.

'Ciao!' she said, coming to stand next to Mark.

Violet stared in amazement as he bent double to get his cheek close enough for her to kiss.

Then Mark began to speak. In Italian. And Violet's stomach did a backflip. It was as if he were another man. And she realised 'Marco' was stressed-out, scary

Mark Harris. And that muttering he had been doing under his breath in the unintelligible language was Italian.

She looked at him properly for the first time and realised that, with his dark hair and green eyes, he could be Italian. And that the summer sunshine was beginning to turn his skin darker.

He caught her staring and smiled. 'Come with me,' he said.

Feeling she hadn't much choice if she wanted to keep her job, Violet followed him through the crowd and into the back kitchen. But he carried on walking until they found themselves in a small courtyard.

It was hemmed in by four walls, covered with plants scrambling up to the sky. Few windows overlooked the garden. The walls were trapping the heat of the midday sun.

Terracotta pots, in all shapes and sizes, filled every wall, spreading into the middle until they reached a round iron table and chairs. In the middle of the table were a bunch of sweet peas in a jam jar being used as a vase.

'It's beautiful,' stammered Violet, hardly believing that five minutes previously she had been in an air-conditioned office. Now she had been transported into a beautiful courtyard.

'Nonna likes to have as many pots as she can.'

'Nonna?'

'She's the lady who greeted me.' He pursed his lips. 'Let me get this right. She's my mother's cousin's mother. Is that right? Yes. I think so. Everyone in the family just calls her Nonna.'

Mark sat down at the iron table and gestured for Violet to do the same.

'Who was Gino?' she asked.

'Nonna's husband. Their son, Gino Junior, runs the café. Nonna's come over from Italy to help out for a while.'

'So you're Italian?'

'Half. My mother was Italian. My father is English. Hence the Marco. And the Mark, I suppose.'

'And your parents live here in England?'

His handsome face dropped. 'My mother passed away a couple of years ago.'

'I'm sorry,' said Violet.

'Thank you. My father is still alive but he spends most of his time in Italy. As did I when I was growing up.'

He was so relaxed, so completely different to the man in the office. Violet wanted to ask him more but didn't want to be too intrusive.

Nonna came into the courtyard with a tray of drinks. Mark quickly stood up and took them from her. She gave Violet a nod and a smile as she sat down next to Mark.

'*Bella signorina*,' she said, before giving Mark a wink.

She then rattled off a couple of sentences in Italian. She was obviously talking about Violet, who looked at Mark for clarification.

'She thinks you have a beautiful face but very sad eyes.'

Violet blushed pink and hoped they wouldn't see in the sunlight.

Nonna suddenly pointed at Violet's engagement ring and shook her head.

Mark raised his eyebrows at her and Nonna explained herself to him in Italian, gesticulating at the ring and shaking her head again.

They both turned to look at Violet.

'What is it?' asked Violet.

'It's nothing,' he told her with a small shrug. 'She just doesn't think emeralds are a good idea for engagement rings. Says they're bad luck.'

Violet gulped. Was it true?

Mark shook his head at her. 'Don't worry. It's just superstitious rubbish, I'm sure.'

Then he rattled off a few sentences of his own in Italian and Violet found herself trying not to melt in lust. She had always found Italian to be the sexiest language to listen to. Her whole life she had wanted to go to Italy but had never yet had the opportunity. Or the courage.

Once he had finished talking, Nonna turned to Violet and smiled. She patted her hand and then slowly stood up and went back into the kitchen.

Violet looked at Mark. 'What did you tell her?'

He stretched out in the warm sun like a cat and she found she couldn't stop herself staring at his lithe body.

'I told her you were trying to lose weight but that you've been eating rubbish and I want her to show you how to eat properly.'

Violet found herself snapping, 'Do you think I got to this size by not knowing about food?'

'Not real food, from what I've seen. Food should be enjoyable. Rich in colour. Full of flavour. Are you telling me those horrible crackers, milkshakes and all those other things I've watched you eat are any of those things?'

Violet didn't reply.

'I thought not. Sit. Enjoy. Learn.'

And then he was silent. And so was Violet. It was mortifying to have been dragged out there like a child, no matter what his intention was. How dare he teach her about food?

Violet sat and tried to sulk for a few minutes but it was impossible. She could smell the flowers and herbs from the nearby pots. Bumble bees were buzzing about from flower to flower. The sun was beating down and it was just far too glorious a day to be sulking.

In the end she turned her face to the sun and closed her eyes, enjoying the warmth on her skin.

Eventually Nonna returned and placed a plate in front of her. It had two pieces of bread in the middle, surrounded by some salad leaves.

'Bruschetta,' said Nonna and pointed at the bread topped with tomatoes. 'Classica.' Then she pointed at the one topped with black goo. 'Con crema di olive.'

Violet glanced at Mark's plate which appeared to be a massive helping of meats and salad.

'Antipasto,' Mark told her.

'Buon appetito,' said Nonna and patted Violet on the hand once more before disappearing.

Violet looked at Mark, not sure what to do.

'You heard the woman,' he said. 'Eat.'

So Violet took a small bite out of the classic bruschetta. And her taste buds exploded. There were basil and tomatoes and perhaps a touch of garlic. It was like an release of summer into her mouth. It was spectacular.

She glanced up at Mark.

'Good, eh?' he said, tucking into his lunch.

Violet nodded and tried the olive bruschetta. It was just as good but completely different. Less grassy, more salty. But she couldn't work out what the taste was.

'It's the capers,' Mark told her.

Violet didn't care what it was. It was fantastic. She

found herself trying to slow down but she couldn't help but wolf down the food until the plate was empty. Even the lettuce leaves tasted different – peppery. It was all wonderful.

Then she sat back and stared at the empty plate. The guilt had begun. Nothing that tasty could be healthy. No way. She'd just wrecked her diet.

'What's the matter?' asked Mark. 'Didn't you like it?'

'It was fantastic,' she told him.

'So why do you look like you're going to cry?'

She hesitated and then remembered he'd seen her crying and snatching chocolate cake out of his hands. What the hell, she thought.

'Because I've just ruined my diet,' she told him.

'Haven't you been listening?' he said. 'This is good stuff. Fresh and full of vitamins and nutritional stuff. It's healthy. Trust me. How do you think I stay so trim when I eat here all the time?'

She stole a glance at his flat stomach before looking away.

'Look, I didn't bring you back here to wreck your diet,' he told her. 'Just to show you that food can be delicious. And enjoyable. Italian food isn't all heavy cheese and pizza, you know.'

Violet didn't reply. Her mind was racing with thoughts of the new Mark. And with the concept of the healthy but tasty food.

'What area do your family come from?' Violet asked, desperate to change the subject.

'A small village in the hills near Sorrento.'

She couldn't stop a sigh from escaping her lips. 'I was hoping to go to Sorrento for my honeymoon. But it's the wrong time of year.'

'When do you get married?'

'New Year's Eve.'

'You're right. You want to go now or in early autumn.' He smiled. 'I'm going there in August to stay with the family. There's always a big crowd during the summer holidays.'

Italy had always been a dream. But they couldn't go in January. And Sebastian had already decided on the Caribbean. He had booked for them to stay in a bland, massive complex which had everything from watersports to ten restaurants. Sebastian assured her that they didn't need to leave the resort and see any more of the island, even though Violet would have quite liked to visit the local villages.

'Couldn't you change the wedding date to keep your honeymoon?'

Violet shook her head.

'Shame.' Mark looked at her. 'Nonna was right. You do have the saddest eyes I've ever seen.'

She shrugged her shoulders. 'Maybe I'm just not happy with myself.'

'You're in love. You're getting married. Doesn't that make you happy?'

Violet nodded, trying to convince herself. 'I will be once I've lost weight.'

He frowned. 'So you think that once you're thin, your life will be perfect?'

'Of course.'

'I see.' His eyes devoured her face once more. 'But remember, your eyes will be just as blue whether you're big or small. I just hope they're not as sad.'

Violet didn't know what to reply to that so she stayed silent.

They left to go back to the office soon after. Mark

wouldn't accept any money for the food. Nonna chatted away in Italian as they left. Violet smiled and nodded but didn't understand a word. Except *'bella'*. But she thought that meant beautiful so that couldn't be right.

Back at the office, Violet sat down at her desk, watching Marco head back into his office. Mark, not Marco, she quickly reminded herself. It must have been the hot sun muddling her.

Once she was home that evening, she went straight for Isabella's book. Her unexpected lunch with Mark had got her mind churning with all things Italian.

Violet had never finished the first chapter which was all about food. So she let Isabella enlighten her.

'Food should be healthy and delicious,' Isabella said. 'Food should fit into your life. Not be a chore. But it should also give you pizzazz. Energy. Italians love their food and they look marvellous because of it.'

Talk about bigging yourself up. Her mind briefly flitted to Mark's smooth skin before tearing itself away again.

'If you get hungry between meals, eat fruit. If you eat fatty rubbish, you will look terrible.'

Violet didn't need to look at her skin to know how bad she looked.

'Start with simple fresh foods and you cannot go wrong. Stock your pantry with good quality pasta, olive oil, tomatoes, onions, garlic, lean meat, fish and seafood, and herbs like oregano, basil and parsley. Allow yourself a little parmesan but avoid the mozzarella.'

It all sounded a bit of a hassle. But it might be worth a try. After all, Italian food was fantastic. That smell in the delicatessen at lunchtime had been wondrous.

She got on the internet and downloaded a couple of pasta recipes for future dinners before stumbling across pasta salads as well as rice salads. That would liven up her lunchtime menus.

But Violet realised she had to be careful with portion sizes. She measured out the specified amount of pasta for a typical dinner of 450 calories. And it wasn't much. The portion sizes she had been giving herself before she had started losing weight would have fed a whole family.

The following day, Violet stocked up at the supermarket once more. But this time, her trolley was stuffed with fruit and vegetables and not so much ready-made stuff. Plus lots of different ingredients for a bit of home cooking.

Once home, she started on a pasta recipe for dinner. It was quite simple, with just a tomato-based sauce but lots of garlic and basil to bring out the flavours. She had forgotten the parmesan cheese for a quick covering but it was still tasty. Violet even felt quite impressed with herself.

The next evening, she cooked Sebastian a recipe for stuffed chicken breast.

'What's this?' he said, swallowing hard.

It was a little dry, admittedly. But Violet didn't think it was that bad.

'Chicken stuffed with porcini mushrooms,' she told him.

'Where's the sauce?'

'The recipe didn't come with it.'

He made a face and pushed the food around on his plate.

'Do you want some gravy?' asked Violet.

'Only to drown myself in.'

'I'm trying to be healthy,' she told him.

'We've got to eat,' he snapped back. 'What's the harm in a chicken kiev? Or a pizza?'

'They're both high in calories,' she said. And fat. And everything else.'

'I keep telling you to stay the way you are. Just stop all this healthy-eating crap. It's driving me mad.'

Sebastian loved her as she was. But Violet didn't. It was a shock to realise that and even admit it to herself but it was true. She wanted to be thin. For herself.

For me, she told herself. Me. It wasn't a word Violet used very often. But perhaps she should try to get used to it.

Chapter Twenty-six

'Wow,' said Violet to Edward as he sat down. 'You've lost a stone in two weeks.'

They had just experienced another positive Tuesday night weigh-in. Trudie's lip had curled into a self-satisfied smile, thinking it was all down to her dreadful bars and shakes. Nobody was willing to put her right.

Edward went a bit pink as he reached forward for his cup of tea but he was smiling. 'Only seven more stone to go,' he said.

'Tell us your magic secret for losing seven pounds a week,' said Maggie. 'I only lost three.'

'What do you mean you *only* lost three pounds?' said Lucy, smiling at her mum. 'I'm really proud of you. You've turned it round.'

'Thanks, love.'

Maggie was secretly overjoyed. The food hadn't tasted great but it had kept her going longer than the other faddy foods she had tried.

But her biggest challenge wasn't food. It was the fitness DVD she had bought. It ignited something deep in her. A passion to move her body. It was so hard that Maggie could still barely move to the music but she found she loved it. The music, the energy. She got a little further through the DVD each day. Next week, she was determined to get all the way through it without needing a sit down.

Maggie thought that perhaps she wasn't getting quite so out of breath when she walked up the stairs. It was a start.

'Plus I've tidied the whole house,' said Maggie, smiling.

'It shut that witch Trudie up, didn't it?' said Lucy with an evil grin.

'Yes,' said Maggie. 'But I need Edward to tell me his secret so I can figure out what to do next.'

'First of all, I have the most to lose out of all of us,' said Edward. 'So it's going to come off the quickest. Second, I've joined the gym. I've been cycling and power walking every day for an hour and a half. I'm knackered but I tell you, I've never slept so well as this past week.'

'Right,' said Maggie. 'I need to up my exercise once I've finished the spring cleaning.'

She glanced at Kathy but she had been ever so quiet that evening. Even more so than Violet. Unfortunately she was the only one not to lose any weight and had endured another humiliating ticking off from Trudie.

Edward carried on. 'So I'm just going to keep eating the same stuff and exercising and hopefully it will keep working.'

'You can tell you've already lost weight,' said Lucy, who was feeling very generous as she had lost another three pounds. That was half a stone already. She was thrilled. Already her skirts and jeans were a little looser around the waist.

'Thanks,' said Edward, but he knew it was true. One of the jowls under his chin had begun to recede. But it wasn't the real difference. That was inside. He could sense his body begin to feel better now that the strain was easing from his vital organs. His pulse wasn't racing so much.

He also knew that he had a long way to go. But he would get there. He had to.

Kathy noticed how much more Edward was smiling. Plus he'd lost the grey colour he had had a few weeks previously. He was a nice guy and would look really good once he'd lost a few more stones.

Kathy wished she could borrow some of Edward's drive and determination. She was drawing blanks with her motivation, despite Violet's positive texts and emails. It was no good. She'd eaten like a pig and the scales had shown it.

'Are you all right, love?' asked Maggie. 'You seem a bit blue.'

'I'm fine,' said Kathy, putting on a bright smile.

But her face couldn't maintain it. Everyone watched in dismay as her smile faded.

'What is it?' said Maggie, putting her arm around Kathy.

It was the touch that did it. Kathy was so desperate for any kind of human contact that she burst into tears.

Everyone else exchanged worried glances. Kathy was always so jolly and funny; something dreadful must have happened. Violet went and made a strong cup of tea. Lucy knelt down in front of Kathy and put her hand on her knee. Edward leant forward in his chair but said nothing.

Violet returned with the tea and sat down. Then they waited and listened until Kathy's sobs gradually subsided.

'I'm sorry,' she said, eventually.

'Don't be stupid,' said Lucy.

'It doesn't matter,' said Violet.

'Tell us, pet,' said Maggie.

'You can trust us,' said Edward.

Kathy took a deep breath to try and steady herself. 'It's so hard to admit,' she started, wringing her hands together. 'But I'm lonely. My life is so empty.' And then she had to suppress sobs that threatened to rise up once more.

'You've just moved to the area, is that right?' asked Maggie.

Kathy nodded.

'It's hard when you don't know many people,' said Lucy. 'I'm scared stiff about going to university and trying to make friends all over again.'

'Trouble was,' said Kathy. 'I was lonely before I moved here. My mum was diagnosed with Alzheimer's about ten years ago. Dad tried to cope but it was all too much and his heart couldn't take it. I had to move in with Mum because her mind had deteriorated so much she wouldn't have been safe by herself.'

'Better that she didn't hurt herself,' said Maggie.

Kathy nodded. 'But it was so hard, just watching her deteriorate day by day, year on year. She didn't know who I was by the end. I celebrated Christmas with her but she didn't have a clue, bless her.'

Kathy wiped away another couple of tears.

'In the meantime, my social life went down to nothing. I only saw Mum and the doctor. Nobody else. I was so lost when she died that I felt I had to get away. Start afresh. But you're the only people I've met, apart from Mavis in the shop. And she's old and batty.'

'Well, you've got us now,' said Maggie, with a firm note in her voice.

'Yeah,' said Lucy. 'Just when you thought your life couldn't get any more shit!'

Everyone giggled and the tense atmosphere eased.

'Lucy's right,' said Violet. 'It is hard to make new friends. Look at me, I've lived in this town for years and I still hardly know anyone. My size didn't help. I wasn't exactly wanting a hectic social life looking like this.'

'But you've already lost a stone,' Kathy told her.

And it was true. Violet had lost a further four pounds.

'I know,' Violet told Kathy. 'But it doesn't help all those years I wasted before.'

'I agree,' said Edward. 'I play cricket every weekend during the summer but it's not as if I can hoof it round a football pitch in the winter. So I used to stay in with a lot of takeaways.'

'I'm sorry about your mum,' said Maggie to Kathy.

'It must have been like being orphaned,' said Violet, knowing how Kathy would be feeling.

Kathy nodded. 'It would have been Mum's birthday a month ago and I just hit a bad patch that I can't seem to climb out of.'

'Of course you did,' said Maggie. 'You can't think about dieting and all that when you're feeling so low. You're still grieving for your mum. Give yourself a chance, love.'

'But I do want to lose weight,' said Kathy.

'And you will,' said Violet. 'After all, if we can do it, so can you. We're no different. Just try not to worry about it at the minute.'

'Keeping busy is good,' said Edward. 'After my mum lost my father, she never stopped. Joined that many classes, just so she didn't have time to be lonely. She's always off to play bridge or learn how to embroider or whatever.'

Kathy nodded. 'That's why I joined New You!' she said. 'To try and meet people.'

'And you have,' said Maggie.

'If you don't include Trudie,' said Lucy with a small giggle. 'Because she's not people, she's an alien from the planet bitch.'

'Tell you what,' said Edward. 'Why don't you come and watch us play cricket when we're next at home? We're rubbish but at least it'll get you out of the flat.'

'And I was thinking about doing that ridiculous army fitness thing at the park later this week,' said Maggie. 'There was an advert in the local paper. I've got to do something to keep busy once I've finished tidying the house. Why don't you join me and stop me looking a total wally all by myself?'

Kathy smiled at them. 'Thanks, everyone.' Her mouth trembled as she fought back the tears. 'You've all been so kind.'

'I think it must be because we're friends now,' said Maggie, giving Kathy a quick hug.

And everyone realised it was true.

Chapter Twenty-seven

Work had become manic and Violet had no time to spare. Not that she missed the endless boredom. But now she was almost constantly on the phone.

Deciding she needed a mid-morning coffee to keep her going, Violet offered to get everyone a drink from the machine. It also meant that she could nip to the ladies briefly. She had now decided that the fat wasn't melting off her. It was pure water. She was needing a toilet break every hour.

While she was standing in front of the vending machine, Violet's phone rang. She saw who it was and rolled her eyes.

'Violet? It's Miriam,' said Sebastian's mother.

'Hello,' said Violet, her heart thumping. She hoped it wasn't bad news about Sebastian.

'Hope you don't mind me calling you at work but I've had the most marvellous idea. Wendy from church had doves when her daughter got married. What do you think?'

'Doves?' stammered Violet.

'When you exit the church, you can have ten doves released into the air. Someone at my Pilates club had the same thing for her daughter and said it was wonderful.'

'Ten doves,' repeated Violet in a stunned tone. Good grief.

'Well, they actually release double that amount but apparently you lose quite a few in the trees and power lines. But it will look super. Everyone will be very impressed.'

Violet was speechless which Miriam unfortunately took as positive.

'Wonderful! I'll get it organised. Toodle-oo!'

Violet stared at the phone for a beat before ringing Sebastian. She explained the dove idea to him, whereupon he snorted a laugh.

'It's not funny,' Violet told him. 'I thought we wanted a nice, simple day. Can't you have a word with her?'

'It's not worth the hassle,' he said. 'It doesn't matter, does it?'

No. It was only their wedding. But who would end up paying for all this rubbish? Violet knew the answer to that question as well.

But Violet also knew she wouldn't bring up the subject of money. She had always sought to please everyone and hated confrontations. So it was best to let it slide. Doves and all.

She sighed as he rang off and stared once more at the vending machine.

'That wasn't a customer phone call, was it?'

Violet spun round and came face to face with Mark.

'No.'

But Mark was waiting for her to speak, she realised.

'It was just my fiancé.'

'Ah,' he nodded. 'How are the wedding plans?'

Violet blew out a sigh. 'Complicated.'

'As long as the food is excellent, that's all that matters.' He gave her a warm smile. 'Italian weddings are all about the food. It's the best way of celebrating with family and friends. And everybody normally eats outside. Weather permitting, of course.'

Violet bit her lip. 'What do the guests eat?'

He shrugged. 'We start with antipasto. You know, olives, salami, prosciutto, stuffed mushrooms and so on. Then on to the pasta, salads, soups, meats, fruits and the dessert, of course.'

Violet's mouth gaped open.

'Sometimes there are as many as twelve different courses.' He grinned at her. 'Nobody goes home hungry from an Italian wedding.'

'Wow,' sighed Violet.

It sounded fantastic. She could just imagine having a relaxed day full of food, friends and sunshine. Not that she had too many friends, apart from her weight-loss club. But it certainly sounded better than a dreary country club with Sebastian's parents' snooty friends.

'Is that for me?' asked Mark, pointing at the vending machine.

'Er, no,' she said, picking up the plastic cup. 'Sorry.'

'Thank God,' he said, peering into the synthetic froth. 'No Italian has a cappuccino after ten o'clock in the morning.'

'Why not?'

He thought for a minute. 'It's a breakfast drink. It would be like having cereal for lunch.'

Violet had briefly considered the cereal diet a while back but said nothing.

'Next time we're in Nonna's deli, remind me to get you a ristretto. Now that's proper caffeine.'

And he wandered out again.

Next time? She shook her head and pressed the button for the next coffee.

But Violet was still thinking about Mark's words as she headed out for a breath of fresh air at lunchtime. Not that she wanted to go back to the delicatessen and bump into him again. Hell, no. But she needed some olive oil for a recipe and that was probably the best place to get it.

Olive oil was hideously high in fat and calories but the salad recipe required just a tiny drizzle. Violet figured that if she was only allowed a small amount, she had better make it count.

So she found herself back at Gino's, inhaling the intoxicating scent of Italian food. The queue was huge again. But as she waited patiently in line, Violet felt a touch on her arm. She looked round to find Nonna standing next to her.

'Ciao,' said Nonna, her smile revealing a few missing teeth.

'Hi,' said Violet.

To her embarrassment, she was dragged out of the queue by the little old lady and was taken to the end of the food counter.

Nonna rattled off a question in Italian which Violet translated, or hoped, to be a query of her order.

'Olive oil,' said Violet, very slowly.

Nonna led her by the hand to a large shelf unit nearby which had hundreds of bottles fighting for space on the wood. She brought down a bottle and handed it over. Violet stared at the label. 'Olio di oliva', it read.

Nonna made a hissing noise and then mimed a frying action with her hand before giving her the thumbs up.

'Cooking?' guessed Violet.

A nod was given in reply.

Nonna then brought down a different bottle from the shelf. The label read 'Olio extra vergine di oliva'. Ah, the extra virgin olive oil. This was the stuff Violet had read about in Isabella's book.

Nonna took Violet over to the counter and pointed at the salads. Another thumbs up. Then she took her into the kitchen and pointed at the stove before shaking her head. OK. Violet understood. The extra virgin olive oil was no good for cooking. Just for salads.

Violet nodded her understanding and said thank you.

Nonna patted her hand and smiled. She was really very sweet. Violet wondered if Mark knew how lucky he was to have a family as warm and friendly as this.

Having paid for her goods, and received an unexpected kiss on both cheeks from Nonna, Violet headed back to the office with her goodies. With her mind on all things Italian, she made a brief detour into a bookshop and bought some more cookbooks to flick through.

At home, Violet studied one of the low-fat cookbooks she had bought. Quite a few of the recipes were Italian, such as spaghetti bolognese. Probably not quite as authentic as Nonna would have liked but it had to be better than a ready meal.

So the following evening, Violet cooked her fiancé the spaghetti bolognese.

'This is all right,' he told her, between mouthfuls.

She smiled and thought how wonderful that

Sebastian couldn't tell that it was made with extra lean mince and that both the beef and the onions had been dry fried. The sauce was also low in fat. OK so she'd added a splash of red wine, but the herbs and stock cubes had also enriched the sauce.

'I don't know why you've been bothering with all that healthy stuff you've been trying to force feed me,' said Sebastian after finishing his plate. 'This is much more like it.'

Violet should have been pleased that he couldn't tell the difference but his words still bothered her.

'Don't you want me to lose weight?' she asked.

'What's the point?' he said. 'It doesn't matter to me. And if you're going to put it all back on again then we might as well save ourselves the bother.'

Violet took a deep intake of breath. Did he really think she was going to fail? But then, did she really believe she would succeed in losing all her extra weight?

Sebastian was so different to the friends she had made from the weight-loss club. She had never thought about them as friends until Kathy's disintegration at the last meeting but it was true. Staying positive for each other was what kept her going. Hopefully all the way to her target of ten stone.

Violet took the plates into the kitchen, thinking how much easier it would be if Sebastian was also positive about her weight loss. Positive like Mark, for instance. He never seemed to question her capability, either at work or regarding her diet. Why couldn't her own fiancé feel the same way?

They were quite different, Mark and Sebastian. Certainly in looks. Mark was dark where Sebastian was blond. Mark was tall, Sebastian short. Mark was good-looking whereas Sebastian was perhaps not quite so handsome.

Violet frowned. What did it matter if Mark was better looking? Sebastian had always been her dream man, the one she wanted to share the rest of her life with.

Besides, it was personality that counted. Mark oozed charm but he was Italian! Weren't all Italian men professional charmers? Yes, he was also kind and funny. Sometimes a little too frank in conversations but at least it encouraged her to be honest with him in return.

Sebastian had other gifts, that was all. It wasn't his fault he had been smothered by his mum when he had been growing up. It wasn't his fault that his sister had died so young and left his parents devastated. All that was bound to have an effect and make him perhaps a little immature at times.

She shook her head as she tidied up the kitchen. She didn't know why she was trying to justify her love for Sebastian. After all, he had asked her to marry him! She glanced at her emerald engagement ring and tried to forget about Nonna's warning. It was just an old wives' tale.

Sebastian came into the kitchen. 'What's for pudding? The football's on in a minute.'

'I'll just get it,' said Violet, reaching into the freezer for the lemon sorbet she had made the previous evening. Sebastian could always cover his with chocolate sauce if he wanted.

She glanced at a nearby stack of papers on the counter. Hopefully Sebastian wouldn't find *Italian for Beginners* hidden underneath.

Chapter Twenty-eight

Maggie had badgered Kathy about the fitness class until she finally conceded defeat. So now she sat in the car, waiting for Maggie to arrive.

Apparently it was a fitness class run by some army commandos or something. Maggie had told her that Lucy had said a blunt no way but that she would feel better with company. Out of the goodness of her heart, Kathy felt unable to say no.

Kathy felt better in herself but was still embarrassed about her collapse in front of the others earlier that week. Revealing her inner misery had been the worst moment. But then, she realised, everyone else had revealed their lowest points too. Perhaps she needed to get everything off her chest to feel better and move on.

It was eight o'clock in the evening on a Thursday night in high summer. The weather should have been glorious but the heatwave had broken and it had been raining nonstop for twenty-four hours.

It was getting later and later and Kathy was

beginning to hope that Maggie had forgotten all about their meeting. But no such luck. At that moment, Maggie arrived on the other side of the car park.

Her heart sinking, Kathy switched the engine off and got out.

'Nice weather for it!' said Kathy brightly.

Maggie tried to smile. 'I'm a bit nervous.'

Kathy let her face drop. 'Thank God! So am I. But think of all those calories we're going to burn off.'

They walked across the car park together.

'How are you?' asked Maggie.

Kathy nodded. 'A little better, thanks.'

She just wasn't sure how long that good feeling was going to last.

They joined a large group of people who had gathered on the edge of the park. Kathy could see them all bouncing around, like a litter of overexcited puppies.

'Welcome!' boomed a very muscular man in army combats. 'I'm Sergeant Steve Coldfield but you can call me Sarge.'

Maggie and Kathy gave a nervous giggle.

'That's Sergeant Roger Cartwright.' Another Action Man nodded his greeting. 'Right. Help yourself to a bib. Blue if you're a beginner. Red if you're fit. And green if you're super-fit.'

There was a huge pile of blue bibs, left untouched by the rest of the class. The majority were wearing green bibs, with some red bibs dotted about. Maggie and Kathy grabbed a blue bib each. Kathy found it barely fitted across her chest and noticed Maggie hadn't been able to use the velcro at the sides either.

It reminded Kathy of all those hideous games lessons

at school where she was the last one to be chosen by the team captains.

'So?' said Sarge, coming to stand next to them. 'You want to get fit? Become more active?'

'Absolutely,' said Maggie, lying through her teeth.

Kathy stayed quiet. The only active thing about her was her imagination.

'Come on, Blue Fourteen. Let's see some enthusiasm!' he barked.

Kathy looked around and then realised he was talking to her. Her bib had a large fourteen painted on it. She was no longer a name. Just a number.

'How about it, Blue Fourteen?'

Kathy gave him a small thumbs up, unable to speak for terror.

'Right!' he boomed, now addressing the rest of the class. 'We'll start with a gentle jog over to the other side of the park as a warm-up. Let's go!'

The rest of the class began to trot across the grass. Maggie and Kathy exchanged a look of sheer fright. Jogging? Oh no.

As soon as she began to move, Kathy remembered that she should have invested in a sports bra. Her boobs were nearly hitting her in the face. But at least that took her mind off the pain in her legs, which had never run anywhere since she was a child. She found herself slipping and sliding on the mud.

And this was a warm-up? Her cheeks were already bright pink, her pulse thumping hard and loud. Next to her, Maggie was also panting but didn't look too miserable about it. The class had disappeared over the horizon, leaving just them and Sergeant Roger.

'Come on!' he shouted at them. 'Pick your feet up.'

Kathy was wheezing and gasping for air.

'Make the effort! Get moving!' he screamed.

Kathy found she was so anxious to get away from him that they made it over the hill to where the main group had gathered. As they got nearer, Kathy realised that the rest of the group were springing up and down in star jumps.

'Glad you could finally make it,' boomed Sarge. 'Give me twenty press-ups.'

Maggie and Kathy glanced at each other before gingerly getting down. Kathy's hands squelched in the mud as she laid them flat on the grass. She copied Maggie, who was on all fours and bending her face towards the ground.

'All the way down, Blue Fourteen,' said Sarge, pushing on the back of Kathy's head until her nose went into the mud.

'That's one! Nineteen to go!'

Kathy inhaled some mud up her nostril and gagged. But Sarge wouldn't let her get up or even pause for a second. She had to carry on until she had completed all twenty push-ups.

By now, everyone else had swapped to sit-ups. And that was the next instruction to Kathy and Maggie. Lying down, her back freezing on the cold ground, Kathy wondered if she would have to throw away her clothes once she got home.

Each time, she struggled to sit up, her stomach twinged in agony. As did her back. And her neck.

By the time Kathy had finished and had stood up, the sergeant was shouting once more.

'Right! Go and touch five trees and then return here. Now!'

Everyone sprinted off at high speed except Maggie and Kathy.

'You didn't start quick enough for my liking,' roared Sarge at them. 'Give me ten squats.'

Maggie and Kathy looked at each other not knowing what he meant. So Sarge showed them and made it look so easy. He was bouncing around like Tigger on speed. Kathy knew it wouldn't be painless and was proved right. Her whole body was jiggling and her thighs were burning in agony.

Kathy just wanted to die. Please don't let me live through another forty-five minutes of this, she prayed.

But the horror carried on. Once the rest of the class had rejoined them and completed a couple of dozen star jumps, he shouted at them to get going.

'Sprint!' he roared at everyone, causing a dogwalker nearby to jump out of her skin. And the dog to start barking at the group.

Kathy tried to sprint. Honestly she did. But she was beginning to feel nauseous from the exercise.

'It's too much,' she croaked, staggering to a halt. She clutched her pounding heart, fearful it would explode.

'Too much?' Sarge bellowed at her. 'I did fourteen weeks in Afghanistan. Get moving!'

Kathy lurched off once more, in pursuit of the class. Even Maggie seemed to be faster than she was. As usual, Kathy was the last. She was the most unfit, she told herself. The slowest. The most useless.

The sergeant was cruel, taking full advantage of the ghastly weather. He got the group to crawl around on their stomachs like snakes. The mud was seeping into every pore, into every nook and cranny. There was a game of tag where Kathy couldn't even catch anyone. There were more press-ups, more jumping, more squats.

By the end of it, the tears were streaming down Kathy's cheeks. But nobody noticed them with the rain pouring down. She didn't even have the energy to wipe them away.

'Give me ten more press-ups,' shouted the sergeant.

Everyone squatted down once more. Kathy dropped to her knees, her legs unable to hold her any longer. She put her hands on the ground and then sort of stayed there. She felt so ill, so nauseous.

And then the sergeant pushed her face into the mud once more. Except it wasn't just mud. There was a different smell. The dogs had been there too.

Kathy got up, clutching her hand to her mouth. She staggered over behind a tree and retched and retched. At least it replaced some of the mud on her trainers.

'You all right?' puffed Maggie, coming to join her.

Kathy shook her head, still recovering.

'That's it,' screamed the sergeant. 'Session over. Get out of here.'

The fit, skinny people were looking muddy as well, but they were all on their exercise high, bouncing along with glossy skin and skinny bones.

Maggie and Kathy looked at each other, at the mud plastered into their hair. At the bright red cheeks, the sopping-wet clothes. The sheer mess of each other.

And then they laughed and laughed until they slid down into the mud, their legs unable to hold them up any longer.

Eventually, they staggered over to Kathy's car. Kathy opened up the door and looked down.

'Bloody hell,' she said. 'My seats are going to be ruined.'

And they began to laugh once more.

Chapter Twenty-nine

Violet had decided not to share her good news with Sebastian about losing a stone in weight. He was still a bit funny about the whole weight-loss thing and it was easier to keep quiet rather than rock the boat.

Besides, it probably wasn't noticeable. She was wearing the same clothes, though they were a little baggier, especially her trousers. The tops had always been baggy so they still hid the rolls of fat underneath.

But she caught Wendy looking at her later that week.

'You OK?' she asked.

Violet nodded. 'Fine, thanks. Why?'

'You haven't caught that bug I had, have you? You look tired.'

Julie peered from around her computer screen. 'She doesn't look tired.'

Wendy put her head to one side. 'Well, something's different.'

'Cheekbones,' said Julie suddenly. 'You've lost weight.'

They both looked at Violet, waiting for an answer. So she gave them a little nod to let them know they were right.

'How much?'

'A stone,' said Violet, somewhat embarrassed at the attention.

'Good for you,' said Wendy.

Violet was secretly thrilled that someone had noticed. She made a mental note to have a good look in the mirror. So in the ladies' loos, later that morning, she did. And yes. She had cheekbones. The fat hamster cheeks had receded somewhat. Shame about the rest of the body. What was that thing everyone said about losing weight from the top downwards? Why on earth couldn't it be the other way around? Especially as most women wanted to lose the inches from their tums and bums. Oh well. At least it was something.

At lunchtime, Violet headed for the small supermarket in the centre of town. The recipe she wanted to cook that evening was salmon with zucchini. She had got the recipe from the low-fat cookbook she had been using. The salmon steak was already at home but she had no idea what zucchini was and had forgotten to google it. The teenagers in the supermarket were also clueless.

She glanced at her watch but still had half an hour left of the lunch break. So Violet headed for Gino's cafe to see if Nonna could enlighten her. She took a quick look around, to make sure that Mark wasn't already there. Sighing with relief, she joined the back of the queue, which, as usual, was winding its way out of the door.

However, as soon as she moved inside the

delicatessen, she spotted Nonna ploughing through the lunchtime crowds towards her.

'Ciao!' beamed Nonna, giving Violet a kiss on each cheek. Then she rattled off some Italian words and waited patiently.

Violet smiled, nodded as if she understood every word she was saying and finally spoke. 'Zucchini?'

'Sì,' replied Nonna and led Violet away from the queue towards the back of the counter. Violet was somewhat embarrassed at having to stand with all the other staff, most of whom appeared to be Italian and possibly related to Mark. But they nodded and smiled at her as they went past.

Nonna gestured towards the brightly coloured vegetables in front of them. She reached down and brought out a courgette. Ah, thought Violet. Zucchini was Italian for courgette. No wonder she hadn't been able to find it in the supermarket.

She watched Nonna feel the courgette before shaking her head. Then she squeezed another and nodded.

'Bene,' she muttered, giving Violet a large smile as she handed over the vegetable.

Violet felt now was the time to attempt a little Italian, if only to be polite and say thank you. 'Grazie,' she said, rhyming it with 'patsy'.

'Ah!' cried Nonna, clapping her hands together with joy. 'Parla italiano, eh?'

Nonna appeared overjoyed that Violet was now attempting to speak her language. Violet made a face and shrugged her shoulders as if to say, not really.

But Nonna had taken her hand and squeezed it, as if to reassure Violet. 'Grazie,' said Nonna, over-pronouncing the word as she rolled the 'r' and spread out the middle part of the word.

Then she smiled and Violet realised she was waiting for Violet to repeat the word. She cleared her throat. '*Grazie*,' said Violet, this time copying the Italian pronunciation.

Nonna beamed as she nodded her head. '*Bene*,' she said.

Violet had no choice but to smile back at the old lady. She was grateful her efforts had pleased Nonna.

Violet handed over the money for the courgette and left, waving at Nonna as she went. At least she hadn't completely embarrassed herself.

Her mobile rang as she headed back to the office. It was Kathy.

'So what should I have for dinner tonight?' she asked. 'I've got a pie in the freezer but I don't think you'll let me have that.'

'I'm having fish,' Violet told her. 'Salmon with steamed vegetables. Try slicing some fresh garlic and ginger over the salmon before you wrap it in foil to bake in the oven. It's really nice.'

'Can I have a baked potato with it?'

'Only if it's no bigger than your fist and you don't smother it in butter.'

'You're mean and nobody likes you,' replied Kathy, before chatting away about the salad she'd had for lunch.

The phone calls continued for the rest of the week. Violet even received one from Edward about the pros and cons of breakfast cereals.

But nobody seemed to be going hungry, least of all her, Violet realised. The fish and vegetables were tasty and full of flavour. And if her stomach did rumble, she had stocked up on plenty of fruit.

The strawberries were so sweet at that time of year

that they really didn't need sugar. Maybe they warranted a big dollop of double cream but she managed to cope with a blob of 0 per cent Greek yoghurt and a drizzle of honey. In fact, Violet's stomach was pretty much fooled most of the time. It seemed the damage was mostly in her head.

Boredom was certainly the biggest problem. Finding her mind wandering longingly to the corner shop for a huge bar of chocolate one evening, Violet picked up Isabella's book to distract herself.

The first chapter had been all about food. She reread Isabella's instructions about buying fresh food and concentrating on lots of lean meats and fish with plenty of fruit and vegetables.

Then she read the second chapter.

'Rule Number Two,' said Isabella. 'Drink water all day. Most Italians drink at least one litre of water per day, sometimes two. It is marvellous for the skin. And brides should be glowing as they walk down the aisle.'

Violet considered what she drank at the office each day and realised that it all came out of the vending machine. If it was hot, it was coffee. If it was cold, it was Diet Coke. At home it was cups of tea and more Diet Coke. Perhaps it was time to rethink.

'Wine is served at dinner but there will always be a pitcher of water on the table as well. Do not drink alcohol to excess. This is not becoming in any woman, especially brides.'

Violet thought briefly about the wedding she had attended with Sebastian and how drunk the bride had been. It had not been elegant.

Isabella carried on: 'If you must, a little champagne is acceptable.'

How wonderful to be so refined that the only alcohol

you allowed yourself would be champagne. What a great life Isabella must have led. A champagne-swilling style guru.

So Violet bought a two-litre bottle of water at the garage on the way to work the following morning and began to drink. And drink. And drink until she thought her insides were going to explode.

She also pored over recipes with an Italian twist. Most of them required fresh herbs which were a little pricey, especially if they were used sparingly. She knew she could freeze the leftovers but Violet had always wanted terracotta tubs of herbs in her garden. Her mind went back to Nonna's pots in the courtyard. How wonderful to be able to go outside each evening and pick some fresh herbs.

The English summer was actually behaving itself and becoming hot and humid. Perhaps she could buy a few pots at the weekend and start her little Italian kitchen garden.

Violet asked Sebastian about it the following evening.

'What do you want to go to a garden centre for?' he said, frowning.

'No reason,' said Violet. 'I just thought I could get a few herbs and things. Now that the weather is so warm.'

'Why bother? I suppose this is to do with that fat club, is it?'

Violet frowned. 'No. It's to do with me wanting to do a bit more cooking.'

He raised his eyebrows at her snappy tone of voice but didn't reply.

Violet stalked into the kitchen and stared out of the window. The garden was completely overgrown. A few roses had pushed through from somewhere but the rest was a total tangle of weeds. There was probably no space for her pots anyway.

But she was upset. Why couldn't Sebastian be supportive instead of rude? And if his opinion of the other members of the diet club was that low, what did he really think about Violet?

Chapter Thirty

Trudie waited for the compliments as the fatties arrived. But nobody mentioned her tan. Not even an admiring glance. What was the point of spending time in the sun if nobody told her how good she looked?

They were just jealous, that was all. Besides, it wasn't as if any of this lot would be lying on a sun-lounger on a mini-break to Spain any time soon. The news would declare an unexpected solar eclipse if that happened.

'Who's first?' she called out.

Trudie picked at a rough bit of skin on her hand. She wasn't going to peel, was she? That would be a disaster. She must put on some more moisturiser when she got home.

The fat man came up first with a superior look on his face. Don't know what you've got to be smug about, thought Trudie as Edward stepped up on to the scales. You'd still take up two seats on an airplane.

'Seven pounds off,' she told him.

'Excellent,' replied Edward with a smile. 'That's another half a stone.'

Trudie tried to return his grin but couldn't be bothered. He genuinely seemed pleased to still be that fat. She supposed that if ignorance was bliss than Edward must be the happiest person alive.

Her back cried out to be scratched. She was certain it was beginning to peel. It was all Trevor's fault. She had told him to rub the moisturiser in thoroughly each night but he was always too drunk to do it properly.

She focused on the teenager Lucy as she stood up on the scales.

'Another three pounds,' she snapped.

'Ha!' yelled out Lucy in triumph before walking away.

You don't have to shout in my face, thought Trudie. Just wave your Asbo about.

She knew all about that generation. Getting pissed on their brightly coloured kiddie drinks. Just like Trevor, she realised. Her face screwed up into a scowl as she remembered how drunk he had become each day on their holiday.

The bride-to-be Violet had also lost three pounds. Trudie had watched a couple getting married on the beach. A very different affair to her own wedding. That had been a quick march down to the register office by her parents. Of course, it turned out she hadn't been pregnant after all. But she had known she was going to marry Trevor at some point so it was a good idea to get the papers signed. He had been the best prospect at school, both good-looking and intelligent. He was the one who was going places, who would take Trudie out of boring suburbia.

To her eternal disappointment, it turned out he

actually wanted to stay in the same town and do a boring job in a boring office. Something to do with insurance; Trudie had never been interested enough to ask.

Menopausal Maggie came up for her weigh-in.

'Five pounds off,' muttered Trudie.

This was so annoying. Of course, she wanted them all to do well. She received her commission when they dropped the pounds. But where was the fun in that? She enjoyed their misery.

Trudie began to feel a little brighter as Kathy came to stand in front of her. This was better. This was the one who hadn't lost any pounds during her time at New You! Kathy shouldn't feel too bad, thought Trudie as she stood up on the scales. A lot of people had no talent in life.

She took a double take at the scales. No, it couldn't be. She looked up at Kathy.

'You've lost four pounds,' Trudie told her, trying to smile but failing.

Kathy bit her lip and looked like she was going to cry. Trudie would cry too if she had lost four pounds but still had five stone to lose.

Five stone overweight. Trudie shuddered as Kathy walked back to join the rest of the group. There was no way she would ever let herself gain any weight. Unlike her mother who had spent most of her life plump and seemingly happy with it. It was disgusting.

Trudie had deliberately chosen the resort in Spain for its gym and sports facilities. Each morning she had pounded away any fatty residue from the all-you-can-eat buffet on the running machine, followed by two aerobic sessions.

Trevor had only seemed interested in the all-inclusive

drinks. He even tried to tempt her towards the pool bar that first afternoon. Was he mad? There was no way she was going to lower herself into a public pool where children had been playing and splashing about. The pool was probably diluted with all their wee.

So she just watched in disgust as Trevor drank himself into oblivion from dawn to dusk each day. It was almost as if he couldn't bear to be with her when he was sober.

Chapter Thirty-one

'It was hilarious,' Maggie was telling the group.

Kathy was also giggling. 'Honestly, you should have seen the state of us by the end of it.'

'You threw up!' cried Maggie, wiping away a tear from laughing so hard.

'That's cheating!' said Lucy, giggling. 'That's not the way to lose weight properly, is it?'

She turned to Violet, who smiled back at her, and thinking how nice it was to see Kathy appearing a lot happier.

'I've lost four pounds!' said Kathy, still amazed. 'I never thought it would happen. I mean, I've stuck to the breakfast and lunches. And the fruit instead of biscuits with my cuppa. But the dinners have been a bit borderline, calorie wise. I can't believe it!'

'We knew you could do it,' said Edward.

Kathy blushed a little and couldn't stop herself from beaming.

'It must have been that army fitness camp, as well,' said Maggie.

'Did you see Trudie's face!' said Lucy with glee. 'For once she couldn't have a go at any of us!'

'She looked as if she'd swallowed a lump of lard,' said Maggie with an evil grin.

'Well done,' said Violet. 'Anyone for a cup of tea?'

'I'll help,' said Maggie, following her into the kitchen and opening up the fridge. 'Where's the milk? Oooh! Look at all your healthy food. No wonder you're doing so well.'

Violet blushed and put the teabags in the mugs.

'What's that garlic bread and pizza doing in there?' said Maggie, frowning.

'To keep my fiancé happy,' Violet told her.

She sighed, wondering if she should confess. Surely it wouldn't do any harm?

'Sebastian doesn't want me dieting,' said Violet, pouring out the hot water into the mugs.

'But he knows how unhappy you are?'

'I think so.' Did he? Violet wasn't certain. 'But it makes it a bit difficult.'

Maggie took a deep breath. 'Snap,' she said.

Violet looked at her.

'Gordon hates me dieting as well.'

Violet shook her head. 'It's mad, isn't it? Surely they should be supportive?'

'I don't know what my husband's problem is,' said Maggie. 'Or how to get round eating the same food as he does.'

'That's the easy bit,' said Violet, bringing out the milk.

Maggie glanced at the plastic bottle and raised her eyebrows. 'I thought whole milk was banned. Semi-skimmed or skimmed only.'

Violet gave her a small smile. 'I decant my

semi-skimmed milk into the whole milk container. Then he doesn't realise what he's putting on his cereal and into our tea and coffee.'

'My God! That's brilliant!' said Maggie. 'What else?'

'I've been starting to cook healthier versions of our favourite dinners, like spaghetti bolognese. But I've been draining the fat off the mince and using low-fat sauces. He hasn't a clue!'

'All very cloak and dagger,' said Maggie. 'We'll have to compare notes later.'

They headed back into the lounge and Violet put down the tray of mugs on to the coffee tables.

'I'm sorry but I'm going to have to use your bathroom,' Maggie told Violet. 'I've never weed so much in my life. It must be all water that's dropping off me. Five pounds this week!'

She did a little jig and then stopped before breaking into a giggle. 'I don't want to scare the neighbours into thinking there's an earthquake.'

Maggie knew it was the combination of exercise and healthy food that was working for her. She was using the exercise DVD every day but was beginning to find it a little monotonous. So she was also heading out every afternoon for a walk. She had even bought new trainers, in case she ever felt like jogging. Not that it was very likely, of course.

Maggie gave them all a grin before disappearing.

Edward had lost another half-stone.

'I had to buy a belt for my suit trousers,' he told them. 'They're huge.'

'My God, you're doing so well,' said Lucy.

He shrugged his shoulders. 'I've picked up the speed on the running machine, though I'm still walking. I really want to get fit. Even if it's only for the cricket.'

He turned to Kathy. 'You should come along and watch us. We're at home this weekend. It's the club at the end of Grove Street.'

Kathy nodded, grateful for the invitation. The weekends were still a struggle for her. But she wasn't sure about being with Edward on her own, away from all the others. Wouldn't it be a bit awkward? Maybe he would be embarrassed at being seen with her? After all, he'd lost loads of weight. She was still a lard arse. With four pounds off, admittedly.

There was a sudden hoot of laughter from upstairs.

Violet got up to see what was going on when Maggie burst through the door.

'What the hell is that hanging on your bedroom door?'

Violet remembered that she had received the second-hand wedding dress from Sebastian's mother and had forgotten to hide it away. She wasn't bothered about Sebastian seeing it because there was no way she was ever going to wear something as monstrous as that.

Violet sighed. 'It's a wedding dress that Sebastian's mother gave to me.'

'Show us!' cried Lucy and Kathy at the same time.

Violet shook her head. 'It's awful.'

'She's right,' said Maggie, still grinning. 'It's big flouncy layers of silk, satin and lace. It's truly hideous.'

'Go on!' said Kathy. 'Put it on for us!'

Violet shook her head.

'It's only us,' said Lucy. 'We won't laugh.'

Feeling somewhat bullied into it, Violet went upstairs and changed into the dress. It was a bit loose now that she had lost weight but she didn't need a mirror to know that it was awful. Did Sebastian's mother really want her looking like this?

She tripped her way down the stairs and into the

lounge. Everyone burst out laughing, except Edward who shot tea out of his nose instead.

'Bloody hell!' snorted Kathy. 'It's dreadful!'

'I know,' said Violet. 'Plus I think it's jinxed. Apparently the wedding was called off which is why it's brand new.'

'Someone paid money for that?' said Lucy, shaking her head.

'You're not going to wear that, are you?' asked Maggie. 'I mean, you can't. It's hideous.'

'I might not have a choice,' Violet told them.

And then she found herself telling them about the snooty woman in the bridal shop. Suddenly everyone had stopped laughing.

'That bitch!' said Lucy.

'Some of those bridal shops are really snobby,' said Kathy. 'Just ignore them. If they don't want your business then sod them.'

'Exactly,' said Maggie.

Lucy was fingering the material. 'The silk is a nice quality, though. You could probably use that.'

'And do what with it?' asked Kathy.

Lucy looked up at Violet. 'If you like, I can make a few sketches for you. Give you a few ideas for a homemade wedding dress.'

'Really?' said Violet. 'That would be great.'

Lucy blushed but in her heart she knew she could do something better than the monstrosity that was in front of her. This was a side effect of weight loss that nobody spoke about. Lucy now felt she had something to offer the world.

'I've finished college now so I've got some spare time before I start in September. If you don't like any of my designs, just tell me. I won't be offended.'

'I'm sure they'll be great,' said Violet, before heading back upstairs to change back into her normal baggy clothes.

Maggie nudged her daughter with her elbow. 'My daughter. The great designer!'

'Shurrup!' said Lucy, nudging her back.

But they were both smiling.

Everyone was really happy that evening.

'I'm staying on fifteen hundred calories forever!' said Kathy.

'I've bought a calorie-counting app for my iPhone,' Lucy told them. 'It's brilliant and tells me exactly how many calories everything has and lists the fat content too.'

'I can't wait to be a size twelve!' said Maggie. 'Actually, I can't wait to be a nice size fourteen. I'd be thrilled to get to that.'

'Just remember that the quick fixes don't work,' said Violet as she came back into the room. 'We can do this but it must be slow and steady. The crash diets work briefly but then it all goes on again.'

'With some more added to it,' muttered Kathy.

'We can't go through life only drinking juices or not eating a potato or piece of bread ever again. That's just not realistic,' Violet told them. 'Now we've got to carry on but only aiming for a loss of one or two pounds a week.'

'But that'll take me for ever,' said Edward.

'We might all lose a few more pounds than that,' Violet told them. 'Because of our weight, it's going to fall off a bit quicker.'

'Excellent,' muttered Lucy.

'The thing is,' said Maggie. 'I'm not sure those

ready meals are any good. I know I have healthier lunches and all that but I need a decent meal in the evening.'

Violet nodded. 'I know. I found that too.'

'So what now, boss?' asked Kathy.

Violet realised they were all waiting for more words of dieting wisdom.

She cleared her throat. 'I was looking up some healthy dinner recipes on line. Breakfast and lunch are fairly easy. I tend to stick to fruit or cereal in the morning and then a sandwich or cracker biscuits for lunch. But we need variation. Actually, it's me that needs variation, otherwise I'll get bored and then I'll pig out, if I'm not careful.'

'Exactly.'

'I've bought a couple of low-fat recipe books,' she told them. 'The food is mainly Italian but I can share the recipes with you, if you want? They need fresh herbs and the odd splash of wine to liven them up but they taste much better. But you must measure out all of your food. I don't know about you but I was eating gigantic portions. Way too much.'

They all pored over the recipes.

'Ooh!' said Maggie, salivating at the photo of linguine with garlic, prawns and spinach. 'How can that be only four hundred calories?'

'You gotta make that for us, Mum,' said Lucy. 'And the spicy meatballs.'

'I can't believe you're allowed those parmesan shavings on top,' said Kathy. 'I thought cheese was full of fat.'

Violet flicked through to the notes at the back of the book. 'It says if you get a really nice bit of parmesan, you don't need to use so much. It's quality, not quantity that makes the difference taste-wise.'

And she knew just the right delicatessen to buy it from.

Chapter Thirty-two

Kathy parked her car and walked slowly towards the cricket pitch. She wasn't sure that she really wanted to be there but what else was there to do on a sunny Saturday afternoon in July? Especially when she was renting a poky, first-floor flat without a garden. Besides, she had promised Edward and didn't want him to worry if she didn't turn up.

She had fretted over what to wear. Summer clothes were the worst fashion for the single overweight lady as the thin material showed off any sweat or rolls of fat and a big, baggy cardigan to hide everything wasn't an option. So Kathy settled on a bright pink T-shirt which didn't cling quite as much as it used to and a pair of black linen trousers so wide legged that if the wind got up, she would take off. With a pair of sparkly black flipflops on her feet, she basted up with suntan lotion and felt almost brave enough to watch Edward's team in action. Or at least hide and watch the action from the sidelines.

She slowly walked around the edge of the field

towards the pavilion which seemed crowded and noisy. Everyone seemed to know everyone else and they were all laughing and gossiping.

Not knowing anyone and feeling shy, she settled herself on the scorched grass a little way from the pavilion and took the opportunity to hunt Edward down with her eyes. She found him just beyond the wicket on the other side of the field.

From far away, Kathy could see Edward's full silhouette and realised how much he had trimmed down. The weight had gone from everywhere, especially around his waist. He appeared more defined, slimmer. He was beginning to get a good shape on his body now that he had lost almost two stone.

The ball flew out in Edward's direction and he caught it easily, causing celebrations as the wicket fell. His strong forearms were tanned from the time spent out in the summer sun.

As the next batsman headed out on to the field, Edward and his team were huddled together discussing tactics. They were all laughing and Kathy suddenly felt jealous that he had such a wide circle of friends.

Then the players split up, with Edward tossing and catching the ball before turning around to bowl. She watched him run up to the wicket. For all his extra weight, he could move quite well and the batsmen were having problems staying in.

Men are so lucky, thought Kathy. OK, so Edward was over six feet tall, but why could men get away with extra weight and women not? Still, a sneaky glance at the scales this morning had confirmed her suspicions that she was still losing weight and she certainly felt better about herself than she had for a long while.

She found her mind casting back to her younger days when her dad used to play cricket whilst she and her mum helped sort out the cricket teas in the clubhouse. Happy days, thought Kathy. But they seemed a long time ago.

A huge roar from the pavilion indicated that Edward had bowled out the last member of the other team and that it was his side's turn to bat.

Kathy watched Edward behind the safety of her sunglasses as he made his way over to the clubhouse to wait for his turn. He was certainly a popular member of the team, with everyone slapping him on the back and cracking jokes.

He suddenly caught sight of Kathy and waved before beginning to walk over.

'Hi!' he said, throwing himself on to the ground next to her. 'Glad you came.'

Up close, she could see how much weight he had lost from his face as well, making him look younger than he had done when they had first met. He appeared to have had a haircut too. His blond hair was neater than she remembered.

'Hello,' she replied. 'You did well out there.'

'Thanks, but you haven't seen my lack of batting skills yet.'

'Is it that bad?' she asked.

'Unspeakable,' he told her, before glugging down some of the can of Diet Coke he was holding. 'God, but it's hot. I thought I was going to melt when I cycled over here today.'

Kathy raised her eyebrows. 'You're cycling now?'

He grinned at her. 'Bought a bike off eBay and I go everywhere on it, even to work. It's true what they say. It does get easier.'

He had lost another five pounds that week.

Kathy nodded. 'Nice to be out in the sun as well.'

Edward picked up the wistful tone in her voice and looked at her.

'I'm always either stuck in the shop or in the flat,' she explained. 'I get so little daylight that I'm in danger of getting scurvy.'

He broke into a grin and Kathy was glad the sunglasses hid her cheeks which were growing pink. His round face was becoming a handsome one.

'What happened to your arm?' he asked, looking down at a vivid bruise near her wrist.

Kathy rolled her eyes. 'The kitchen cupboard doors fall off if I forget to treat them gently. And I'm not very gentle when I'm hungry. I obviously don't know my own strength.'

'Is it your own flat?'

Kathy shook her head. 'Rented. I'm still working out what and where to buy my own place.'

Edward frowned. 'Can't you complain to your landlord?'

She shrugged her shoulders. 'The rent's pretty low and I don't want to do anything to rock the boat.'

'Look, I'm at the gym in the morning but how about I come over tomorrow afternoon and fix the doors?'

Kathy began to shake her head. 'I don't want you to go to any trouble. It's not worth it, honestly.'

'You can't keep hurting yourself. It's not right,' said Edward, as a roar came up from the cricket square indicating that another wicket had just fallen. 'Anyway, I'm up next so you've no time to argue. Text me your address and I'll see you around four-ish. OK?'

Kathy didn't have time to reply as Edward had

already got up and was heading towards the pavilion for his pads and bat.

At least it meant she wasn't at a loose end on Sunday morning, she realised the following day with a duster and bin liner in her hand. Thank God, Edward wasn't turning up unexpectedly and had pre-warned her. OK, so the flat wasn't that bad but it wasn't exactly immaculate either.

By mid-afternoon, she had just sunk on to the sofa, having finished her blitz, when there was a knock on the front door.

'Hi,' said Edward, smiling and waving his toolbox at her. 'Bob the Builder here.'

'Come in,' said Kathy.

'Hey, this isn't bad,' Edward said, taking a look around. 'It's bigger than my place.'

'The size comes at a cost,' she told him. 'It overlooks an industrial estate at the back so I get woken up most mornings by the lorries thundering in.'

'Mine isn't exactly a room with a view either. Now what about these dodgy doors?'

'It's not that bad,' said Kathy but Edward was already marching into the kitchen to have a look.

Edward went to open one of the higher cupboard doors and found it came clean off in his hand. He raised an eyebrow at Kathy.

'OK, so it's really bad,' she told him with a rueful smile. 'I just didn't want you to go to any trouble. Let's have a cuppa first, though.'

They made small talk about the previous day's match whilst they sipped their tea. But Edward was soon up and working on the doors, ignoring her protestations. She watched him as he tightened up the hinges of every cupboard in the kitchen. Some of the doors were in such a mess that he had to either replace the screws or sort out the hinge.

An hour later, he had finished.

'All safe now,' he told Kathy.

'Thank you,' she replied. 'I won't have to worry every time I come in the kitchen. Or get hungry.'

'Something smells lovely in here,' he said. 'I've been trying to work out what it is for the past hour.'

'You must mean the basil on the windowsill,' Kathy told him. 'I bought a pot to liven up my spaghetti bolognese.'

'You make it yourself?'

Kathy nodded. 'I got the recipe from Violet. It's really good.'

'I miss home cooking,' he replied with a sigh. 'I only moved out of home a couple of years ago but Mum's cooking is great.'

So was mine when I had someone to cook for, thought Kathy, trying not to get emotional in front of him.

Edward rolled his eyes. 'I'm such a typical bloke. By the time I get in from work and the gym, I can't be bothered to cook so I've still been surviving on those low-fat ready meals.'

'Well, you're looking good on them.' Kathy blushed as soon as the words were out of her mouth. 'I mean, you've done well with the weight loss so far.'

'Thanks,' he said. 'To be honest, I've just transferred my evening meals from takeaways to microwave food.'

She made a face. 'Doesn't sound very appetising.'

Edward leant back against the kitchen counter. 'Not really. Especially as Mum still does a mean roast for us all.'

'How big is your family?'

'I've got two sisters and two brothers.'

'Wow,' said Kathy.

'They're all married and I've got a handful of nieces and nephews too. When we get together, there's barely any room in my mum's house to sit down.'

Kathy suddenly had a wistful longing to be in a family house full of life and laughter. How lovely that would be.

'Anyway, it's been a while since I got some home cooking inside me,' said Edward.

Kathy glanced at the clock. 'Look, I know it's not quite six o'clock yet but I was going to make myself some dinner. How about I treat you to my low-fat spaghetti bolognese as a thank you for sorting out the kitchen for me?'

'Are you sure?' asked Edward, breaking into a smile. 'I wasn't dropping any hints, if that's what you were thinking.'

'I know,' Kathy told him.

'I don't want to put you to any trouble.'

Kathy shrugged her shoulders. 'The mince comes in a big packet so I was going to have to freeze the rest anyway.'

Whilst Edward went to the bathroom and washed his hands, Kathy put on some music and began to fry the mince.

'What happened to the shower head?' said Edward, coming back to lean against the door of the kitchen.

He was so tall and broad-shouldered that he seemed to fill the kitchen and Kathy found herself having to concentrate on the food so she didn't keep looking at him.

'The shower?' she replied. 'I think it's so clogged full of limescale that it couldn't cope with the weight and fell off this week. Luckily it missed my head whilst I was in the bath.'

Edward pursed his lips. 'Look, I haven't got anything with me to fix it at the minute. But I can come back another time, if that's OK with you?'

Kathy looked at him. 'Is this a ploy to get some more home cooking?'

His face split into a grin. 'You saw through my master plan.'

'So I get my flat fixed and you get some decent food?'

He nodded. 'Exactly.'

'I see.'

Kathy found herself smiling too as she turned back to her recipe.

Chapter Thirty-three

Once August had arrived, everyone had been going on holiday. Violet had always hated the summertime, the heat being absolutely no good for someone in her shape. Even with approaching a two stone weight loss, it was still a bit of a struggle. But not as much as it used to be, she reminded herself.

Especially as the sun was continuing to shine. Her garden lawn was as parched and brown as everyone else's. And the nights were still warm enough for Violet to need only a sheet over her.

The hotline began to quieten down as everyone headed off on their holidays. So the department began to take some time off as well. Wendy had gone camping in Cornwall. Julie went to Greece. Even Anthony had found a fellow nerd to visit California with.

Violet didn't have as much holiday entitlement as everyone else as she hadn't started with the company until May and was saving up the rest of her holiday for the honeymoon at the end of the year. But she didn't mind. The air conditioning was a welcome relief from the heat.

Mark left in the second week of August to visit his family in Italy. Violet found herself quite wistful at the thought of those narrow Sorrento streets and warm Mediterranean sea, and she found it was strange not having him suddenly appear at her desk all the time.

But Violet took the opportunity to visit Gino's delicatessen more frequently whilst he wasn't around. As soon as she stepped inside the café, Nonna's face lit up and she came over to kiss Violet's cheeks. This was their accepted way of greeting now.

'*Ciao, bella,*' said Nonna, beaming up at her.

'*Ciao,*' replied Violet. 'Er, parmesan?' she asked, before remembering what she had learnt online the previous evening. '*Per favore.*'

Violet knew her accent wasn't very good but Nonna's eyes lit up at her wretched attempt to say please.

'*Sì,*' she replied, taking Violet by the hand.

Violet thought she was being led behind the counter as normal, but instead she was taken through the kitchen and back outside into the courtyard.

Nonna gestured for her to sit and went back inside.

Violet sat at the small table and gazed around as the heat from the sun warmed her back and shoulders. There was a small breeze which made the strands of an ornamental grass flutter in a nearby pot. Bumble bees hovered in the air before gliding from flower to flower in their search for nectar.

Violet raised her face to the sun and watched an aircraft slice through the cobalt-blue sky, leaving a fluffy white vapour trail in its wake.

She sighed. It felt like a holiday just being in this

courtyard. She really had to do something with her garden, if only to try to make it as relaxing as this.

And it was nice to just sit there without the hotline ringing or having the burden of the 'big day' bear down on her. The wedding was creeping ever closer and the budget was increasing daily. She didn't believe that expensive cars were required to ferry them about everywhere. And did she really need the most expensive and extravagant flowers in her bouquet and at the reception?

Violet inhaled the scent from a pot of freesias nearby. They were one of her favourite flowers. Why couldn't she be brave and tell Sebastian that she would rather have freesias instead? After all, she would be carrying the bouquet.

She realised she was going to have to tackle the issue of the wedding at some point. Things couldn't continue to spiral out of control. She was dreading the conversation with Sebastian but feeling a little stronger too, these days. Perhaps it was time to speak up.

Nonna returned, bearing a tray with two glasses of cold water and a plate with various wedges of cheese placed on it.

Violet took the drink from Nonna and thanked her, once more in Italian. Then she waited patiently whilst Nonna sliced off various bits of cheese. A piece was held out for Violet to try.

'Parmigiano,' she was told.

Violet smiled and took the small wafer-thin slice of cheese. It tasted lovely and strong. She looked at Nonna and smiled, wondering whether to give her a thumbs up or not. But Nonna was shrugging her shoulders, as if to say it was nothing special. Then she handed over another piece of cheese.

'Pecorino,' she said and gave a noise like a sheep's bleat. Violet was a bit stunned until she understood what Nonna was getting at. It was cheese made from sheep's milk, she guessed.

This cheese also melted in her mouth. Why were the Italians so good at this kind of thing? And why was cheese such a sin for dieters? It just wasn't fair.

Finally, the last piece. Nonna didn't say anything this time, so Violet took the slice with a nod of thanks. The taste exploded in her mouth. The other cheeses had been great but this was mecca. This was fantastic.

She nodded frantically at Nonna, who was looking smug.

'Parmigiano Reggiano. Reggiano,' she repeated with emphasis.

Violet understood. It had to be reggiano, whatever that meant. Without that, it was nothing.

Violet mimed the shape of a wedge with her hands.

'Sì,' said Nonna.

But they took their time over their cool drinks, enjoying the companionable silence. Until Violet glanced over to see Nonna nodding and smiling at her.

Nonna began to speak in Italian and Violet quickly picked up on the name Marco. She tried not to gape as she recognised the Italian word for woman amongst the quick sentences. Nonna seemed to be talking about Mark and his girlfriends. From the tone of Nonna's voice, she obviously hadn't approved of many of them.

Nonna glanced once more at Violet's engagement ring. Violet braced herself for the bad-luck talk but Nonna was rummaging around in her apron pocket. To Violet's surprise, she drew out a black and white photograph and passed it across the table.

Violet studied the photograph. It was of a bride and groom, many decades ago.

'Gino,' said Nonna, pointing to the handsome groom, who was smiling at the person taking the photograph. Then she pointed at the bride and then to herself. It was Nonna's wedding day.

'Bella,' said Violet, describing Nonna the bride.

Violet peered closer. Nonna was staring up at her groom with such a look of love in her eyes that Violet found her own eyes pricked with tears.

As she went to return the photograph, Nonna grabbed Violet's hand and started gabbling away in Italian again. Violet didn't understand every word but gathered that Nonna loved Gino very much. That they had had a very happy marriage. That the love was everything.

They sat in silence for a little while longer before Violet exaggerated looking at her watch, indicating she had to head back to the office. Back in the shop, Nonna sliced off a lovely big chunk of Parmigiano Reggiano. Violet couldn't wait to shave a few pieces off to try out with the summer spaghetti she had seen in a recipe book.

There was a brief tussle about the money, which Violet won by holding out the change until Nonna had to accept it. She not only received the usual kisses from the old lady as she left but also a warm hug.

It wasn't until Violet arrived back at the office that she discovered that Nonna had actually got the last word. There were a few extra packets in her shopping bag apart from the parmesan. Nonna had popped in some olives, tomatoes and a pepper which, when added to pasta, tasted wonderful.

That evening, Violet sat on her sunny patio and ate

her delicious pasta with a small glass of wine. Somebody somewhere was having a barbeque and the sound of laughter drifted into her garden. Birds were singing in the late sunshine and the sun was still warm on her face.

She finished her pasta and thought briefly about Mark, wondering if this was the kind of thing he was eating in Italy and whether he would be eating alone like her or whether he would have company. Female company.

She actually blushed, even though she was sitting alone and he was hundreds of miles away. What on earth was she doing thinking about Mark of all people? It must have been all that food. That was all.

Chapter Thirty-four

'I think this will do,' said Maggie, throwing the travel rug and her beach towel down on to the sand.

At the last meeting, the girls had decided to head out to the seaside on the Bank Holiday Monday. Unfortunately Edward had a charity cricket match on that day but at least it meant that they could have a good gossip and slip the straps down on their tops without embarrassing him.

The weather had still not broken and the sun was blazing down as they spread out on the beach. The beach was busy but not so crowded that they were hemmed in on all sides. Children laughed as they ran in and out of the waves lapping at the shore. It was a perfect summer's day.

Violet stared in wonder at the others' summer clothes. They were all so confident in their shorts and little tops, even though they were big like she was. Well, she corrected herself, none of them were as big as they were. Violet had lost two stone, as had Lucy. Edward was nearly up to a four-stone loss. Kathy and

Maggie had each lost two and a half stone as well. The pounds were coming off now that everyone seemed to have found their healthy-eating groove. They had worked out that they had lost a whole person's weight between them.

'These shorts are getting big,' said Lucy with a grin. She held out the waistband to see how much gap there was between her skin and the material. 'And I only bought them at the beginning of the month.'

'Back to Primark this week then,' said Maggie, smiling back at her daughter.

The sun was blazing hot and everyone began to strip down to their swimwear. Everyone except Violet.

'Aren't you hot?' asked Kathy, as she lay back on her beach towel in her black swimsuit.

'I'm OK,' said Violet quickly.

'I love my new swimming cossie,' said Lucy, stripping off her T-shirt to reveal a bright blue tankini and matching bottoms.

'Is that because it's a smaller size?' asked Kathy.

'Size twelve and baggy,' said Lucy, grinning, before she lay back on her towel. 'Soon to be a size ten bikini.'

Lucy was thrilled with her quick progress. In the old days she had associated food with happiness but now there were extra delights which didn't involve sugar, such as all the fashion opportunities opening up in front of her. She was even beginning to break free of black and colours were making an appearance in her wardrobe.

Maggie looked across to Violet. 'Haven't you got a costume with you, love?'

Violet shook her head. She was too ashamed to admit she didn't even own a swimsuit.

'I used to hate undressing on the beach too,' said

Maggie, guessing why Violet was uncomfortable. 'But a few years ago I couldn't stand it any longer and had to begin peeling off some clothes. Mind you, over two stones off and I feel better about my body than I did.'

Despite her own two-stone loss, Violet didn't feel any different about her body.

'The sun's lovely,' said Lucy, putting on her sunglasses.

'I bet it's hot at Edward's cricket tournament,' said Kathy, stretching out on her towel.

'Was it an all-day thing?' asked Maggie.

'Till at least six o'clock,' said Kathy. 'Poor Edward will have fried by then in this heat. Did I tell you what a great job he did with my kitchen cupboards?'

'You did. And did he fix that shower for you as well?'

'Yes, it was so kind of him.'

It had been the second Sunday that Edward went to Kathy's flat. She had tried to talk him out of it, telling him that he wouldn't have enough time and that she could live with the few tatty areas in her flat.

'Actually, I have a sneaky reason for coming to see you,' Edward had told her.

Kathy's heart had begun to thump a little harder.

'Did you know you burn calories even whilst doing DIY?' he said, breaking into a grin.

Kathy switched on an automatic smile and tried to ignore her confused feelings.

She had cooked him another meal; this time it had been griddled steak, salad and healthy chips. She found she was beginning to look forward to his company on Sundays and dreaded the day he decided he was bored of her.

'He's a good man,' said Maggie.

'Yeah,' said Lucy. 'He'd make someone a wonderful boyfriend.'

Kathy rose up on to her elbows and found the three other women looking at her with grins on their faces.

'Shut up,' she said, and lay back on the towel. 'Anyway, I've told you. I'm soooo over men.'

'So what are you telling us? You're a lesbian?' said Lucy.

'No. I just seem to attract only the idiot members of the species. I know it's my fault.' She looked over to Violet. 'You're lucky. You're one of those nice quiet women that men fall for. I've got a gob bigger than the Thames on me. I'm not one of those dainty types.'

'I wasn't always quiet—' Violet stopped suddenly as she realised her statement was true.

'What happened?' asked Maggie.

Violet gave her a small smile. 'It's too nice a day to talk about depressing stuff.'

'Rubbish,' said Kathy, sitting up. 'It's only us. Get talking.'

And then it will stop me talking about Edward, Kathy told herself.

Violet sighed but they waited patiently until she was able to speak.

'I had a lovely childhood. Normal stuff with parents, lots of friends and parties. It was great.'

'But then you lost your mum and dad,' said Maggie.

Violet nodded. 'My aunt was so weird. I put on so much weight eating her stodgy food and getting ever more miserable. I was in my teens, I needed a bra and all that kind of girly stuff explaining, but she didn't really talk to me. So I had to wear a vest until I stole some money out of her purse to buy myself a bra. I used to wash it in the bath and dry it in my room so she wouldn't know.'

'OK, so she didn't know about bringing up a girl,' said Kathy. 'But was she never kind? Did she ever talk to you?'

'Only about religion. It was all thee and thou and grace before meals.'

'I bet the other girls were right bitches to you,' said Lucy, speaking from experience.

Violet nodded. 'They were awful. I was fat and wore old-fashioned hand-me-downs. Great big ghastly kaftan things.'

'So in the end, you just withdrew into yourself,' said Kathy.

Violet nodded again.

'Couldn't you have escaped to university?' asked Maggie.

'No money,' said Violet. 'I was good at languages and was desperate to study and then travel. But it was no use. My aunt said it was an extravagance and they'd already spent so much money feeding and clothing me, it was time for me to get a job and get out. Basically she'd had enough of me by then.'

Maggie shook her head in dismay.

'So I went to work and, as soon as I could, I moved out into a tiny flat.' Violet found that now she was talking she could barely stop. 'My uncle unexpectedly died of a heart attack a few years ago and left me a small amount as an inheritance. Enough to put a deposit down on my lovely little house. My aunt never came to visit. But within a year she was dead from cancer. I didn't grieve. She had never shown me any love. Had never hugged me. She was a horrid woman.'

There was a short silence whilst they digested everything she had said.

Suddenly Violet smiled. 'But something weird happened, after she died. It turns out that the house was worth a bit of money and all the money comes to me next year when I'm thirty.'

'Cool!' said Lucy. 'You could do all that travelling now.'

'Or go back to university and do your studies,' said Kathy.

'What do you want to do with the money?' asked Maggie.

Violet realised that she wanted to do all those things and more. But instead of telling them, she shrugged her shoulders. 'Sebastian says it's sensible to put the money down on a house.'

Lucy frowned. 'But you've already got a nice house.'

Violet didn't know what to say so she buried her face in the coolbag she had brought with her and began to unpack the healthy lunch she had insisted on preparing for them.

The others oohed and aahed at the aromas and colours of the food. Violet had brought individual bowls of salads for each of them. Crisp lettuce had been mixed with slices of plump tomatoes, red onion, black olives and crumbled feta cheese. A small drizzle of extra virgin olive oil made the leaves glisten.

'What's the black stuff?' asked Lucy, pointing at a piece of discoloured feta.

'Balsamic vinegar,' Violet replied. 'You'll like it. It adds a nice flavour. There's also breadsticks to munch on and some fresh melon and strawberries to finish with.'

'Fantastic,' sighed Kathy, picking up a fork.

'This is lovely,' Maggie said, in between mouthfuls.

Violet had to agree that her cooking skills were improving. The quality of ingredients helped. She had picked up balsamic vinegar that weekend from the delicatessen, making sure that the label specified 'aceto balsamico tradizionale di Modena', which meant that it had been made to the traditional methods and was the real thing.

Of course, all this Mediterranean food tasted better in hot sunshine. But her senses, especially taste, were being roused from their slumber by all the new flavours she was now treating her body to.

They were all sucking on the juicy strawberries when Maggie sighed. 'Maybe I should go to university,' she said with a wistful tone in her voice.

'What would you study, Mum?' asked Lucy.

'I don't know,' Maggie said. 'But I've got to do something. You're all grown up and off to London. I'm going stir crazy at home by myself.'

She was keeping occupied with her exercise but knew it wasn't enough to satisfy her.

'Can't you go back to work?' asked Violet.

Maggie shook her head. 'Gordon's very proud that his business does well enough that I don't need to work. So he feels better but that leaves me with nothing to do.'

'I know!' said Kathy, sitting up with a start. 'I'm going to be on my own in the shop when Mavis retires at the end of the week. But the Alzheimer's Society says I can go on taking care of the shop if I can bring in some more business. Why don't you come and help? I can't work in the shop on my own. Not that there's any customers most of the time. But think what a laugh we'll have!' Her face fell.

'But there's no money in it, I'm afraid. It's all volunteer work.'

'Are you sure?' asked Maggie.

'God, yes! I've got so many plans to get the shop making more money but it's impossible with Mavis there. She didn't even want us to have an electronic till installed.'

'OK,' said Maggie, with a nod. 'You're on.'

'Mum! You've got a job!' said Lucy, grinning.

'Great!' said Kathy. 'Let's celebrate with an ice-cream!'

'No!' cried everyone else.

'I meant a healthy, low-calorie ice-lolly, of course!' Kathy leapt up. 'Who's helping?'

'Me,' said Lucy.

Violet and Maggie stayed behind and looked out to the waves.

'I love the sound of the sea,' said Maggie.

Violet nodded. 'My boss is Italian and has been telling me about the sea near the village where he comes from.'

'Oh, the Med is lovely. As warm as a bath and that clear you can see the fish swimming in it. You've never seen it?'

'Not yet.'

And Violet realised how much it pained her not to have travelled by the age of twenty-nine.

'How's the sneaky diet working?' she asked Maggie.

'Brilliant! Thirty-four pounds off and counting! But I've been thinking that I really need to talk to Gordon. He's got to understand about me getting fitter. If he doesn't like me losing weight, then it's tough. It's my body.'

Violet nodded in agreement, realising that she ought to be thinking the same way.

They sat in comfortable silence, watching families dash in and out of the sea. People were playing football on the sand. The beach was getting busy as people realised that it was perfect summer weather.

'Here you go,' said Lucy, coming back with Kathy and the ice-lollies.

'I even asked the bloke the calorie count of each one,' said Kathy. 'The ice-cream man wasn't impressed but we've got fruit lollies to cool us down.'

'Only sixty calories each!' said Lucy.

There was a short silence whilst they enjoyed the fruity lollies in the sunshine.

'What's in the bag?' asked Maggie, once they'd all finished.

'Something for Violet,' said Lucy with a grin. 'From the beach shop.'

They threw the bag into Violet's lap. She looked down at it and then back up.

'For me?' she asked, growing red.

'Go on!' urged Lucy. 'Have a look.'

Violet reached into the plastic bag and drew out a flowery swimsuit.

'It's a bit old-fashioned,' Lucy told her with a grimace.

'But we figured it would do for today,' said Kathy. 'We guessed your size.'

Violet glanced at the label. It was a size eighteen. She didn't know what to do or think. 'Thank you,' she stammered.

'You'll have to try it on,' said Kathy.

'The ladies' loo is just there,' said Lucy, pointing up the beach.

259

Violet slowly stood up and headed off, holding the carrier bag in her hand.

'You bullied her into it,' Maggie hissed at them.

'It's for her own good,' said Kathy.

'I don't think she's even got a costume,' said Lucy. 'She's wearing a thick T-shirt and black trousers in eighty degrees. She must be roasting.'

'She's lost two stone,' said Kathy. 'Maybe we should take her out shopping at some point.'

Lucy nodded. 'Definitely.'

'One step at a time,' said Maggie. 'Let's start off slowly with her. Poor girl's had a rough life so far. She's only just starting to open up to us.'

'Gently does it,' said Kathy, nodding in agreement.

'It's nice to see her starting to come out of her shell though.'

'Here she is!' cried Lucy after five minutes.

Violet came to stand next to them, still wearing her T-shirt and trousers.

'Didn't it fit?' asked Kathy, her face dropping.

Violet nodded.

'Have you got it on?' asked Lucy.

Violet nodded once more.

Lucy opened her mouth to say something but Maggie shook her head at her daughter. So they all sat quietly whilst Violet began to slowly pull down her trousers. There was a pause and then she peeled off her T-shirt.

Violet stood on the sand, waiting for the roars of laughter. But none came. She glanced at the other people on the beach but nobody was even looking at her. It was OK. She would be OK. One small step on the sand meant one giant leap forward for Violet.

'Right!' said Lucy, leaping up. 'Last one in buys the next round of ice-lollies!'

And off she ran towards the sea.

Kathy also stood up. 'Come on, girls. Can't let the youngster have all the fun.'

Maggie and Kathy began to walk towards the sea before pausing and turning back.

'Come on, Violet,' called Maggie.

Violet slowly began to walk up to where they were standing. Kathy linked one arm with Violet's and Maggie linked the other. Gradually they broke into a jog, taking Violet with them. By the time they got to the sea edge, they were all giggling.

In the sea they began to splash each other with the cold water. Violet found herself laughing and joining in. She was in a swimsuit in the sea having fun. And somewhere deep inside, she felt a little spark of something. Of life.

Something had happened when she began to lose weight. She was starting to find her voice. And her life.

Violet wasn't sure she could stop it now. Or that she even wanted to.

Chapter Thirty-five

Lucy sat on the train and watched the miles thunder past. It was Induction Day at the college and she was so excited she could barely sit still on the hour-long train journey.

She fiddled with her scarf, whipping it off and then putting it back on again. The mornings and evenings were getting a little cooler as August had finished. But she was happy with the rest of her outfit. She was now in size twelve skinny jeans, a white long-sleeved T-shirt and a battered leather biker jacket which she had found in a vintage shop.

Her mother had told her that the quick two-stone weight loss in two months was down to her youthful metabolism. But Lucy also knew that it was because she had stuck rigidly to the diet. With only one stone to go, the weight loss had slowed to only two pounds a week. So Lucy knew she had to up her game. For the past week, she had dug out some old exercise DVDs and begun to use them each morning. Her dad was starting to go nuts about the noise coming through the ceiling but she didn't care. She knew she would need exercise to shift the last stone and, anyway, she wanted to tone up.

She was going to be in London, to live in London – the coolest city in the world! She would tone up by walking everywhere. There was so much to see. She wanted to look at the vintage fashion galleries in the Victoria and Albert Museum. She wanted to window shop down Bond Street and mooch through the thousands of departments in Selfridges. She wanted to walk across Abbey Road where the Beatles had stepped out before her. Lucy wanted to see it all.

As she bounded off the train at Paddington, she glanced at her reflection in the window and was happy with herself. It was a nice feeling – a new feeling for her.

Her skin was so much clearer now that she was no longer eating all that junk food. And her hair had been given a new lease of life with two inches off the bottom. She no longer straightened it every day; the new cut had given her hair life and movement. But Lucy still hadn't been satisfied until she had dyed her dull brown hair. Now her burgundy red waves shone in the morning light.

She got on the tube to Charing Cross and managed to find a seat. She was staring around the carriage, trying to take it all in, when she locked eyes with a guy opposite her. He gave her a flirty smile as he got off at the next station. Lucy's stomach gave a little flutter. He had been eyeing her up, she was sure of it.

It made her a little sad to realise that he probably wouldn't have been quite so flirty when she was larger. So many people noticed only the fat and not the person inside. These days she was no longer invisible.

Lucy had narrowly avoided Nicola Bowles and her gang as she walked to the station that morning. From the other side of the street, they had done a double take at her new clothes and burgundy hair, even shouting out something about 'tomato head'. But if that was the best they could come up with these days, Lucy found she didn't care so much. She was travelling up to London to begin her studies at a fashion college. What were they going to do today that would even come close to that?

At Charing Cross, she walked the short distance to the college. The reception hall was packed with newbies, all looking young and lost. Lucy joined the back of the queue to register herself. College was starting in a few weeks' time but she was glad to get a good look around the place first.

The queue took an age to shuffle forward and it had been a long time since her early breakfast so Lucy grabbed an apple out of her bag and took a bite. The loud crunch caused the tall guy in front to turn around.

'Smart move,' he said, his voice revealing a soft American accent. 'I forgot to bring anything with me.'

Lucy looked at him for a beat. Floppy dark hair almost covering grey-green eyes. A tall, strong body. A nice smile that crinkled the corners of his eyes. A distressed denim jacket covered his T-shirt, which was matched with beige cargo pants and trainers.

She rummaged about in her college bag and drew out a second apple. His eyebrows shot up as she handed it to him.

'Thanks,' he said, before taking a bite. 'You starting a fruit stall in that bag of yours?'

She shook her head. 'You're American?'

'Canadian. But I'll let you off this time.' He held out his hand. 'Todd Carter.'

'Lucy Walsh.'

'What are you studying, Lucy Walsh?'

She liked the way he said her name. 'Fashion design. You?'

'Industrial design.'

'Sounds good.'

The queue kept shuffling forward as they learnt a bit more about each other. Yes, they were both staying in the halls of residence. No, neither of them knew London that well. Yes, they were both eighteen.

Lucy found herself relaxing in his company and on the hallowed turf of her design college. She fitted in. She was OK. She was going to be just fine.

Maggie knew Lucy was getting home late from her induction day but she still felt nervous for her daughter. It was like the first day of school all over again.

She had managed to keep busy during the day. Maggie was particularly enjoying her afternoons now that she had started to jog during her walks. She had built up to two minutes of walking to one minute of jogging. Maggie loved the feeling of getting fitter.

The door opened but it was only Gordon, filling the house with a certain, mouth-watering aroma.

'I got a curry, love,' he told her with a big smile. 'For a treat.'

'But we had a curry on Saturday night,' she told him. 'I was thinking of doing fish for dinner.'

'We're celebrating,' he said.

'Celebrating what?' Maggie snapped. 'Our obesity levels?'

Gordon frowned. 'I don't know what's the matter with you these days. You've always got the right hump.'

Maggie sighed. 'Sit down, love. We need to talk.'

'What about my balti?'

'Stuff the bloody balti!' shouted Maggie.

Gordon sank on to one of the dining-room chairs, his eyes wide. They weren't one of those couples that shouted. Or really talked, Maggie realised.

Maggie took a deep breath. 'I didn't mean to shout,' she told him. 'But . . .'

Maggie's voice trailed away as she realised Gordon's lip was trembling and his eyes had filled with tears.

'What is it?' she said, kneeling in front of him.

'You're leaving me, aren't you?'

Maggie was flabbergasted. 'What? No! Of course I'm not.'

He shrugged his shoulders. 'I know the signs. You're bored and you're losing weight. You've got another fella.'

'Of course I haven't,' she told him.

'But you've got your eye on someone.'

Maggie took a deep breath. 'The only thing I've got my eye on right now are those poppadoms. But I need to lose weight.'

'Then you'll get thin and get a new man. It happened to a bloke in the pub.'

She took his hands in hers. 'I don't need a new man. I'm happy with the one I've got.'

Gordon tried to smile but it was forced. He didn't yet believe her, she realised.

'I'm happy with you. I love you,' she told him.

'But you'll get thin, attract all the men and then bugger off and leave me.'

'Don't be daft,' said Maggie, realising for the first time that her husband could be as insecure as she was. 'I'm just not happy within myself.'

'Why not?' asked her husband. 'You've got a lovely house, our daughter's got a bright future in front of her. You've got everything you wanted. You're not going to stop eating altogether, are you? Some women get a bit obsessed that way.'

'I am not an anorexic,' cried Maggie. 'I don't have an eating disorder. I have diabetes!'

She took a deep breath in the silence that followed. Gordon was staring at her in amazement.

'The doctor says I'm morbidly obese. I've got diabetes and I have to sort myself out. Do you want me to end up like my mum? Always in and out of hospital?'

Gordon sank back in his chair in shock. 'You never said.'

Maggie shrugged her shoulders. 'Didn't want to admit it, even to myself.'

'So that's why you're off the takeaways?'

She nodded. 'I've lost two and a half stone with the help of my club. But that's not enough. I need your support, love. I can't do this on my own. I need to lose at least three more stone. I have to. I don't want to be ill.'

Gordon studied his wife, taking in her beautiful blue eyes and stroking her soft cheek. 'I don't know what I'd do if I lost you.'

Maggie's eyes filled with tears. 'I'm not going anywhere, you big numpty.'

'Can I tell you something too?' said Gordon,

suddenly shuffling in his seat. 'When I went to the doctors in the winter when I couldn't shift that bad cough, he told me I had to lose weight as well.'

Maggie shook her head. 'We just got lazy and didn't take care of ourselves.'

'Too busy bringing up kids and getting a business up and running.' Gordon suddenly sat up straight in his chair. 'Right. Well, that's changing from now on. No more takeaways. No more cakes and rubbish after tea in the evenings.'

'It's OK,' Maggie told him. 'I've got lots of recipes for some lovely meals. We won't even realise that we're eating healthy stuff, I promise. It doesn't matter how long it takes for us to get these pounds off. Lucy's already lost two stone. We can do this. We have to. But everything has to change.'

'It will,' he said, standing up and taking her with him.

They hugged for a long while, holding each other.

'One more thing,' said Maggie, looking up at him. 'And don't shout. I'm not doing it for the money but to help out a friend from my slimming club. I'm going to work in the Alzheimer's charity shop during the week. I've got all that marketing experience from when we started the garage and I thought it would help get some more money coming in for them.'

She waited for Gordon to blow his top but he didn't. He eventually nodded and said, 'OK then.'

'And I want to go ballroom dancing again.'

Gordon's eyebrows shot up.

'I want to do something with you,' Maggie told him. 'I miss dancing with my husband.'

'Me too,' he told her, giving her a quick kiss.

They sat down at the table, the takeaway laid out between them.

'We'll eat this but then that's it,' Maggie told him.

'Last meal for the condemned man?' said Gordon, before quickly adding, 'Only joking, love.'

'And I want to start going for a walk after dinner,' Maggie said. 'Just you and me. Not with the television on so we can't talk. I want us talking. And some time alone with you.'

He reached over and took her hand. 'I like the idea of alone time,' said Gordon, waggling his eyebrows suggestively at her.

'Stop it, you fool,' said Maggie, blushing.

But they were both smiling.

Edward was also enjoying himself. He was glad he had invited Kathy to the club after the cricket match on Sunday. They were sitting at the bar, both enjoying a gin and slimline tonic.

'The lads took the mickey a bit about my new drink regime,' he was telling her. 'But in the end they just got bored and started on someone else.'

'You don't care? About their mickey taking?'

Edward shook his head. 'I'm not going to be bullied into doing something I don't want to. If I want to be healthy, then I will be. Once I've set my mind on something, that's it. I rarely waver.'

He had found that as he lost weight, his confidence had begun to soar. Edward was actually beginning to like himself.

'You don't want to sell me some of that self-confidence, do you?'

Edward smiled at her. It was nice that she had finally dropped that forced jollity and was beginning to open up to him.

'You're doing just fine. Another three pounds off this week.'

Kathy nodded. 'I'm too impatient, that's my problem.'

'It'll be worth the wait,' he told her. 'For both of us.'

He thought briefly about his family. His mum was thrilled at the change in him, going on about her 'handsome boy' and wanting to know all the details. His sisters were more interested in the girls in the weight-loss club and how often the name Kathy cropped up in his conversation. They were on full radar and it had got him thinking.

As the barmaid came to clear their glasses away, he gave her a smile. 'How are you, Meghan?'

'I'm as fabulous as always,' she told him, with a wink. 'Though I've got to say, you're starting to become a little more fabulous yourself.'

She ran a hand up his arm and he flexed the bicep that had begun to appear after his daily visits to the gym.

'Hubba, hubba,' she cooed. 'You're turning into quite a hunk, Edward.'

He smiled at the joke and then across at Kathy but found she wasn't smiling back at him.

All right, Kathy told Edward silently. You can stop dribbling into your drink now.

Men. They were all the same.

Why did she care anyway? It was only Edward. Edward whom she found herself thinking of most days – most hours, if truth be told.

She watched the barmaid sashay away from them, having neatly destroyed the cosy ambience that had appeared during the past hour.

Kathy fixed on a smile and regaled Edward with the hilarious stories of Mavis's last week at work. He laughed along with her, basking in her faked jolliness.

Kathy's smile didn't drop until she was home, alone once more.

Chapter Thirty-six

By early September, Violet was feeling excited about how loose her trousers had become. She had now lost nearly two and a half stone.

She had mentioned to Sebastian about having to go down a dress size but he seemed reluctant for her to go out and spend lots of money on new clothes.

'We're spending enough on the wedding,' he told her.

And who's fault is that, Violet wanted to reply.

'But look at me!' Violet said, holding out a vast expanse of waistband. 'They barely stay up.'

'You'll probably put the weight back on,' he snapped back.

Violet took in a sharp intake of breath and tried to hold back the tears. He was being so cruel. Did he not know how much this meant to her?

But suddenly Sebastian was holding her and saying sorry over and over.

'I'm just so stressed at the minute. Money's really tight.'

Violet was still struggling not to cry. 'But I thought you were going to make loads of money with that share-investment thing?'

He had mentioned a get-rich-quick scheme over the summer which Violet had thought sounded very dodgy. But, as usual, she had kept quiet.

'It turns out it wasn't quite such a sure thing as that,' said Sebastian, looking sheepish.

'Are you out of pocket?'

'Only by twenty grand,' he said.

Violet was horrified. It was so much money to waste. How could he have been so gullible?

'Thank goodness our windfall comes in next year,' he told her, suddenly breaking into a brilliant smile.

Violet smiled back but her heart wasn't in it.

'But that takes it down to a hundred thousand pounds,' she said aloud. And that was without the grand extravaganza of the wedding. What would be left to spend?

She hadn't planned what she was going to do with her inheritance. Since when had it become *their* inheritance? Not that it really mattered, she supposed. Of course it would be theirs. They were going to be husband and wife. He was probably right about not wasting money on clothes.

So the following morning, she fastened the waistband of her trousers with a safety pin and tried to flatten the folds of material that bunched around her stomach.

Anyway, she didn't have time to think about money. The hotline calls were now coming thick and fast and Violet was dealing with about a third of them, without having to pass them on to other members of the department. She was learning to recognise people's voices and what kind of problems they were most likely to be getting. She loved dealing with people after years spent pushing paper at the accountants.

Mark called her into his office later that week. He had only come back from his holiday the previous weekend and his skin was still golden. It made his eyes look even greener than usual.

'Sit down,' he told her. 'You're handling more of the calls, I notice.'

'Not too many,' Violet said quickly.

He smiled. 'You're not in trouble, if that's what you're thinking. The others have all been praising you.'

Violet raised her eyebrows in surprise.

'Yes,' he nodded. 'Even Julie.'

She was thrilled.

He sat back in his chair, enjoying her pleased reaction. 'Nonna tells me you were in the deli quite a bit whilst I was away.'

'Only a couple of times,' said Violet, hoping he didn't think she was stalking him. 'I needed some cheese and figured they would have the tastiest.'

'How did you two get on?'

'A lot of hand gestures and miming,' she replied.

He smiled. 'Well, you must be doing something right. My customers keep telling me how helpful you are. My staff do likewise. Even Nonna's on your side. She says your accent is excellent.'

'How was Italy?' she asked, desperate to change the subject.

'Lovely,' he told her. 'You should go, especially right now. The sky is so blue.' He looked at her for a beat. 'Same colour as your eyes, I realised when I was out there,' he added.

Violet blushed. Embarrassed at the unexpected

compliment, she quickly stood up to make a speedy exit. Alas, it wasn't quick enough. Under the swift movement, the safety pin gave way and sent her trousers down around her ankles.

Mortified, Violet snatched the material to make herself decent once more.

'So you do striptease as well?' said Mark, now grinning. 'Now I can see why you're so popular.'

Violet fled out of the office, clutching at her trousers. But not quick enough to avoid the sound of Mark chuckling. She was so embarrassed. And angry. He must have thought she was an idiot.

That night at home, Violet took the hall mirror down from the wall and brought it upstairs to her bedroom where, with the curtains shut, she let the trousers fall to her ankles.

She thanked God for the small mercy that her long black top hid most of her torso and thighs. But what if it had ridden up slightly? Would Mark Harris have had a glimpse of her big, baggy, black knickers? Oh Lord.

She was cross that she had embarrassed herself. And angry at Sebastian for not letting her buy any new clothes. But Sebastian was away that weekend playing golf, and she couldn't keep letting her clothes fall down in public. She needed to buy some new trousers, if only for decency's sake.

But shopping for clothes had always been a nerve-racking experience. Violet had always picked up clothes and paid for them without trying them on first. There was no way she was brave enough to face any changing-room trauma.

She needed help. So she took a deep breath and

texted the girls. 'Does anybody want to go clothes shopping with me tomorrow?'

Maggie, Lucy and Kathy all replied in the affirmative and they met up in the morning for a pre-shop skinny latte.

Violet told them about her trouser-dropping experience and they all squealed with laughter. In the end, she had to join in. Perhaps it was a little bit funny.

'Where do you want to go for a new pair?' asked Kathy.

'I normally go to Preston's,' Violet told them in a small voice.

The others exchanged a look.

'Their clothes are, like, soooo old,' Lucy told her.

'Even I wouldn't shop in there,' said Maggie. 'And I've got twenty years on you.'

Preston's was the shop where Violet normally got her clothes. It was a place for ladies who were advanced in age as well as measurements. The clothes were dull and plain. And suited her just fine, or so she had thought.

'Haven't you ever been to Evans?' asked Kathy.

Violet shook her head.

'At least their stuff is up to the minute,' said Lucy. 'Even if it is for us porkers.'

'Hey!' said Maggie. 'Not quite so porky these days, if you don't mind.'

With nearly three stone gone from her body, Maggie was finding bones and muscles she had forgotten existed.

'You're right,' Lucy told her. 'I'm almost a size ten these days. Top Shop all the way for me.'

Violet let them lead the way into Evans. She realised that, despite their similar weight issues, the other women were always dressed more fashionably than she was. But she was still riddled with nerves.

They headed into the shop and immediately everyone was cooing over various garments. Violet spotted a smart black trouser suit which was very reasonable in price.

'Would you like to try that on?' asked one of the shop assistants.

Violet nodded. The others were still ploughing through the clothes rails so she followed the lady into the changing room which was thankfully separated into single cubicles.

She changed out of her elasticated, baggy tracksuit bottoms and tried on the trousers. But something was wrong. Violet finally glanced at myself in the mirror and realised the trousers were far too big.

'How are you getting on in there?'

It was Kathy who had suddenly appeared outside the cubicle.

'I think they're the wrong size,' Violet told her.

'Can I come in?'

So Kathy came in and looked at the enormous trousers.

'I'm normally a size twenty,' Violet told her. 'I must have picked up the wrong size.'

'But that swimsuit we got you at the beach was a size eighteen. You've got to remember you're losing weight now!' chuckled Kathy. 'I'll get you the right size.'

And she disappeared again.

Violet found herself frowning at her reflection. A size eighteen? Was it so hard to believe?

The size-eighteen trousers not only fitted but were a bit loose. But she wasn't mentally ready for a size sixteen yet. Violet also had to try on a smaller jacket as the original one swamped her.

She was still admiring her new form in the mirror when Lucy asked to come in.

'Look,' she said. 'Tell me to bog off if you think I'm being bossy but these tops would go great with your skin. Do me a favour and try them on. Please?'

Lucy held out a couple of bright garments. Violet felt she had no choice but to take them. Then the curtain swished closed once more.

Violet stared at the tops. One in particular caught her eye more than the others. It was a plain turquoise top with a small ruffle down the front. It was the colour that stole her heart. Surely it was too bright for her to get away with?

But she couldn't stop her hand from reaching out towards the top. She slid off the jacket and her baggy T-shirt and pulled the turquoise top over her head. She had just put the jacket back on when Lucy begged to come in.

'Oh my God!' she squealed. 'I knew it! I knew that was the colour for you.'

Violet slowly turned round to face the mirror, expecting to experience the normal sinking feeling. But it didn't come. Lucy was right. The turquoise suited her. It was such a change from her normal black that she couldn't believe it was her.

Now Kathy had joined them. 'Wow! You look great! You've got to get that!' she said.

And Violet found herself nodding along in agreement.

Maggie appeared holding another couple of tops, one pink and the other navy striped. So Violet tried those on as well. In the end, she bought all three tops plus the trouser suit.

The tops were half price in the summer sale so she didn't feel quite so guilty over the money. Why should she feel guilty anyway? Sebastian would never see her work clothes so he wouldn't have to know.

'We've bought loads of new stuff from Primark,' said Lucy. 'You should go in there.'

'We didn't want to spend too much money. Especially if we're going to drop another dress size,' said Maggie.

'Which we are,' said Lucy.

'Definitely,' said Kathy.

Everyone was pleased with themselves that Saturday.

Back home, Violet checked Isabella's thoughts on style, which was Rule Number Three in the book.

'Only ever wear clothes that you love. Take pride in your appearance. Coco Chanel said that a woman should be two things: classy and fabulous. Your clothes should make you feel the same.'

Violet went through her wardrobe and drawers, picking out the clothes that didn't make her feel fabulous. In the end, there was only her new trouser suit and tops hanging up in the wardrobe, with everything else piled high on the bed, ready to be thrown out.

She had found herself throwing out most of the baggy clothes that had always made her feel huge and shapeless. They were all too large for her now, anyway.

It was time to start looking fabulous. And it was tough if Sebastian didn't like it.

Chapter Thirty-seven

With some trepidation, Violet went into work on Monday morning. She was a little nervous about her new, bright top and sitting in traffic for half an hour didn't help.

'That traffic's getting worse,' she said, just making it to her desk for nine o'clock.

'Wow!' said Wendy. 'Look at you!'

Even Julie peered round the side of her computer screen. 'Nice top,' she said.

'You've lost loads of weight,' said Wendy.

'Thanks.' Violet was blushing bright pink but felt grateful for the compliments.

Wendy was squealing so much at her appearance that, in the end, Mark came out of his office to see what the commotion was. His eyebrows went up on seeing the new Violet.

'Very nice,' he said, looking her up and down. 'It's good to see you out of your funeral colours for once.'

Violet felt embarrassed at the attention and was pleased when the hotline began to ring.

Later that night in the bath, Violet read a magazine article that Kathy had given her.

'You've got to read this,' Kathy had said. 'Apparently your shoes reflect your innermost self. It's all very *Sex and the City* but it does make sense.'

The article was fascinating. Apparently the type of shoes you wore reflected your personality. So someone with a very extroverted personality would wear very bright shoes.

Violet dripped her way from the bath to the bedroom, wearing only her towel, and opened the wardrobe doors. What did her three pairs of shoes say about personality? Well, they were all dull, black and flat. Was that how Violet saw herself? Dull and flat? She didn't have a single pair of feminine, sexy shoes.

Violet sank on to the bed as a dreadful thought hit her. Was that because she had never seen herself as either sexy or feminine?

She didn't sleep very well that night. She couldn't get the stupid article out of her head. Consequently, she was late heading to work and got caught up in yet more traffic.

'This is getting silly,' said Violet, finally arriving more than ten minutes late for work.

'It's the new one-way system,' said Anthony.

'I heard it won't be finished for another year,' said Wendy.

'It's taken me nearly an hour to get into work,' Violet told them. 'And I live about two miles away.'

'You're lucky,' said Anthony. 'You can walk if it gets too bad.'

'Walk?' squeaked Violet. 'Are you mad?'

And she laughed.

But later on that morning, she wasn't laughing.

There was an article in the paper about applications for the London Marathon needing to be submitted for the following April. There followed tales of heroism so colossal that Violet felt guilty for her laziness. People with no eyes, only one leg and even some over the age of ninety were able to run twenty-six miles. And Violet? She had no excuses. She was healthy and young. She should be in her prime, not suffocated by fat.

So Violet came to a decision. She would take the bus to work. Because the bus station was quite a way from the office, that would mean a small walk at either end of the journey, but she had made her mind up. The exercise would do her good. After all, look how well Edward had been doing by going to the gym.

Unfortunately, her shoes weren't really up for walking, no matter how dull and flat. So at lunchtime, Violet wolfed down her home-made salad and headed to a nearby department store. In the sports department, she purchased a pair of trainers. OK, they were black, but they did have a tiny Nike swoosh in glittery pink as well. It was a start.

With ten minutes left of her lunch hour, she hurried back through the store with her purchase. Taking a shortcut through the shoe department, Violet suddenly stopped dead in her tracks. The summer sales were still on and there, amongst the flipflops and sandals, were the most beautiful pair of shoes she had ever seen. They were a thinner, more elegant type of gladiator sandal. They were turquoise and shiny. They gleamed as if they had been polished. They were magnificent. And Violet had never worn anything like them in her entire life.

Despite the time, she couldn't stop herself. She was

drawn to them. She had to touch them, to feel them, to try them on. To her surprise, Violet had gone down a shoe size. Did feet retain fat as well? It was all very bizarre.

But the size fives were wonderful. She didn't walk about in them, just stared down at her feet in wonder. The shoes were so lovely that she could put them in a display cabinet and just look at them.

Violet frowned. The beautiful sandals also highlighted her toenails, which she never painted. That would have to change. Perhaps she could get some nail varnish from the chemist? But a quick glance at the time confirmed she was cutting it close so she paid for the shoes and went back to the office clutching her precious purchase.

'What have you bought?' asked Wendy, nodding at the bags.

'Trainers,' Violet told her. She paused. Then found she couldn't stop herself. 'And the most beautiful pair of shoes I've ever seen.'

Wendy's eyebrows went up at her excited tone. 'Let's see them.'

Violet drew out the shoebox and took off the lid. There they were, nestled amongst the tissue paper. Her fabulous shoes.

'Oh my God!' screeched Wendy. 'They're gorgeous!'

'Lemme see!' said Julie, suddenly appearing around the side of the desk.

She picked one of the shoes out of its box and stared. Then she looked at Violet and gave her what must have been the first smile that year.

'Bloody hell!' she said. 'You start off all quiet and wouldn't say boo to a goose. Now you've gone all Carrie Bradshaw on us!'

Violet blushed.

'What next? Handbags?'

In unison, they all stared at Violet's black, dull, practical handbag. The girls looked back at her and Violet nodded at them, knowing that next on the list was a new handbag.

'Put the shoes on,' Wendy urged.

Violet muttered about her toenails not being painted but nobody appeared to be listening.

'I've soooo got to get a pair of those,' said Julie.

They were so busy staring at her feet that nobody noticed Mark joining the group.

'New shoes?' he said, muscling his way through to see what was going on.

'You wouldn't understand,' said Julie. 'It's a girly thing.'

Violet's eyebrows shot up. Her? Girly?

She locked eyes with Mark and gave him a tentative smile. He stared down at the shoes and whistled.

'Very sexy,' he said and smiled at Violet in such a way that she blushed bright red. She quickly took the shoes off again.

But back at home that evening, she teetered around the lounge in them. She even brought the mirror in from the hall and put it on the floor just so she could see her feet. The shoes were expensive and impractical. She couldn't even walk properly in them yet. But Violet was beaming. They were gorgeous.

But something still wasn't quite right. The following lunchtime, Violet purchased foot cream, emery boards and various shades of nail varnish. In fact, every lunchtime that week saw Violet return from lunch with yet more purchases. A new pair of shoes for work which were still black but were Mary Jane types with a heel.

A new purple patent handbag which was shiny and fabulous. Navy trousers and a pink top for work.

Sebastian was away at a conference for the week so each night Violet held her own private fashion show. Just her and the mirror.

By the time she was cooking Sunday roast for Sebastian and his parents, Violet felt different somehow. A little younger. A little more modern.

'Are those jeans new?' said Sebastian, glaring at her legs as she placed the chicken on the table.

'Only Primark,' she lied, even though they were from Debenhams.

Miriam sniffed at the food in front of her. 'What have you done to the chicken?'

'Oh, I added a touch of garlic and rosemary,' said Violet. 'Just to make it a bit different.'

It had smelt divine whilst cooking. She had even roasted the vegetables in the same pan, using olive oil and fresh herbs to give them flavour.

'It's certainly unusual,' said Miriam, wrinkling her nose.

'It's low fat,' said Violet in a dull tone.

'Pass the gravy,' said Donald.

Violet watched as he drowned out the lovely flavours with the packet sauce that Sebastian had insisted she make.

'It would be nice to have some normal bloody food around here,' snapped Sebastian, scowling at the roasted vegetables.

'Poor darling. You mustn't go without all the time,' cooed Miriam, before glancing across at Violet. 'An eating disorder isn't attractive.'

'I don't have an eating disorder. I'm trying to eat more healthily,' said Violet, suddenly feeling a bit

285

brave. 'After all, I need to lose weight for the wedding, don't I?'

She met Miriam's eyes and felt a little thrill as Sebastian's mother was the first one to look away.

It was a small victory that she would pay for later as Sebastian was still going on about the new jeans that evening.

'I had to get something new,' Violet told him. 'Everything was so baggy. You don't want me greeting your parents in tracksuit bottoms, do you?'

'It wouldn't bother me, pumpkin,' he replied with a shrug of the shoulders.

But it was really starting to bother Violet. As was being called pumpkin.

Chapter Thirty-eight

Lucy was hunched over her drawing pad as she worked at the dining-room table. It was a little odd being at home on her own, as her mum was working in the shop. But she didn't mind.

It was quite a tough assignment that she had given herself. Violet's ghastly wedding dress was hanging up over the door and Lucy was desperate to tear it apart. But that was the problem. What to do with the pieces that remained? Violet was a hard one to figure out and certainly to design for.

Lucy had a feeling that Violet was secretly a classic dresser. She could just imagine her in crop trousers, ballet shoes and a plain top. Perhaps with a sleek, black bob. Not that Violet would ever get rid of that long curtain of hair that she hid behind.

Lucy wondered whether the bride could be persuaded to have her hair up in a classy chignon on her wedding day. And she was thinking that a simple but slightly sparkly sheath dress would be perfect. She was already over halfway to her weight-loss goal and Lucy had no doubts that she would reach her target.

So nothing fancy, nothing too frilly. But the lace on the great meringue of a dress hanging in front of her was quite pretty. Perhaps that could go over the top in a fine layer.

Lucy leant back in her chair. She considered adding a few beads to up the glamour factor. Her favourite shop in town was a small haberdashery that stocked hundreds of beads, buttons and trimmings.

She glanced out of the window. It was a nice autumn day and she really had nothing to do until university started in ten days so Lucy decided to head to one of the local bridal shops and have a nose around for inspiration. Then perhaps she could go to the haberdashery and buy a few bits and bobs.

She stepped out of the front door, putting the earpiece in as she went down the front path. Her parents had bought her an iPod to celebrate her good exam results and she had downloaded the Gym Bunny workout music from iTunes almost immediately. It was great to walk to, the beat causing her feet to pound the pavements at a fast pace.

She turned the corner at the end of the road and carried on striding out, her mind occupied with designs for Violet's wedding dress. With the music on and her head down, her feet led the way into town.

Before she reached the shops, Lucy's eyes suddenly caught sight of a pair of pink trainers on the pavement. She didn't need to look up to know whom they belonged to. She recognised the graffiti and grubbiness. It was Nicola Bowles.

But Lucy found the fear that had long haunted her

had evaporated. It must have disappeared along with all those pounds. She found she was a different person now, both inside and out. She had always been scared to go out, to socialise with other people. Now she couldn't wait to get to London and all it offered. She would talk to anybody and everybody if given the chance.

She was dressed in new skinny jeans and boots, only half a stone away from her target. She was on her way to a fantastically trendy university in London to study design. She was happy with herself and excited about the future. What did she care what Nicola Bowles thought of her? And did it really matter anyway?

She, Lucy Walsh, had nothing to worry about. She could hold her head high. She was OK. She was better than OK. She was loved by family and friends. She was talented. She was young. She was fine.

She stole a quick glance at Nicola. Why had she never noticed that muffin top over the waistband of her jeans before now? The hair with its split ends and bad roots? What was so special about her?

Out of curiosity, she glanced up into Nicola's face. Her face was screwed up in animosity and she was obviously saying something to her. But Lucy couldn't hear her above the iPod. And why should she listen? Nicola Bowles had nothing to say that could ever interest Lucy.

So she sidestepped Nicola and carried on walking into town, away from her past and into her future.

Maggie and Kathy were covered in paint.

'At least I'm not ruining any of my nice new clothes,' said Maggie, gazing down at the large T-shirt she was wearing. 'This was the only one of my large clothes that I kept. Time to start again, I reckon. Another dress size, another new wardrobe.'

They had decided to give the shop a complete overhaul. So they had put up signs saying it would be closed for a fortnight.

'Not that there are any customers anyway,' Kathy had said.

But Maggie was hopeful. A lick of paint, some modern lighting and a new layout in the window might do the trick.

'This pale yellow is absolutely right,' Maggie declared, stepping back to look at the wall she had just painted.

'Very cheerful,' said Kathy, who sounded anything but.

She had been in a funny mood all week, thought Maggie.

'How are you getting on with the bike?' she asked.

'Fine,' replied Kathy.

Maggie had found Lucy's bicycle in the garage and offered it to Kathy.

'My legs aren't long enough,' Maggie told her. 'You should take a ride down the river path. Gordon and I went for a walk along there last night. It was gorgeous.'

It really was, thought Maggie, allowing herself a smile. She and Gordon had walked along hand in hand until it was nearly dark. It was lovely to be able to talk about their work days as they strolled along. The weight loss had not only given her a boost, it had given their marriage one as well.

'Gordon's already lost half a stone and he's only been on the diet a week,' said Maggie.

Kathy didn't reply so Maggie continued chatting to fill the silence.

'As Gordon says, it's not really a diet. It's a long-term healthy-eating plan. Maybe that's why it's worked. I've already lost nearly four stone. OK, so I've got another three to go but I feel so much better.'

Maggie's palpitations were a thing of the past and she had increased her weight loss back up to five pounds that week by jogging each day. She was up to ten minutes' solid running at a time and the weight was dropping off her.

She and Gordon were joining a dance class and Maggie couldn't wait. Lucy was going to sew some sequins on her new skirt so that Maggie's sparkle count was high enough.

'Did I tell you I can see my feet again?' said Maggie with a chuckle. 'I've lost so much off my chest and stomach I can finally see the ground. Which also means I have to start painting my toenails again.'

When there was no reply from Kathy, Maggie bent down to pick up the paint tin and carried it over to where she was painting the opposite wall.

'Right,' said Maggie. 'You can either tell me what's going on or you get this lot down your bra. It's your choice.'

Kathy gave her a small smile. 'Why are you picking on me?'

'Because Lucy's not here.' Maggie put down the tin of paint. 'How about a nice cup of tea?'

She went and put the kettle on. She returned with two mugs of tea and a packet of pink wafers under her arm.

'Thanks,' said Maggie, as Kathy relieved her of the biscuits. 'They're a godsend these wafer things.

Especially when you want something sweet but don't want to ruin your diet.'

Kathy took a sip of her tea but remained quiet.

'Are you watching the cricket again this weekend?'

Kathy shook her head. 'Season's finished.'

'Right. Is Edward still coming over to fix your flat?'

Kathy shrugged her shoulders. 'Don't think there's anything left to fix.'

Maggie took a bite of the wafer biscuit, thinking that Miss Marple could rest easy. Her detective skills were in no danger from this line of questioning.

'I was thinking that we could go back to that army workout on the common,' she continued. 'Now that we're thinner and fitter. Maybe you could ensnare one of them with those lovely brown eyes and your new figure.'

Kathy shook her head. 'Not really interested in men at the minute,' she said, staring into the distance.

'Apart from our lovely Edward,' said Maggie, slyly.

'Apart from him,' said Kathy, before coming out of her trance. 'No, wait a minute! Don't keep saying he's lovely, it distracts me. Besides, we only see each other now on a Tuesday night at the weigh-in. Hardly the start of a romantic relationship, is it?'

'Aha!' said Maggie in a triumphant tone. 'So you do want a romantic relationship with him!'

'Tell anyone and I'll cut your heart out,' snarled Kathy, but then she sighed. 'It's no use. He's not interested in me. Not like that, I mean.'

'Then we'll have to find you someone that is,' said Maggie, giving her friend a quick hug.

A dark gloom had come over Kathy since the cricket season had finished. There was no excuse to see Edward outside of the weight-loss club now. No cosy chats over dinner on a Sunday night. It was all at an end.

The only time she would see Edward now was with the other girls. Kathy found it wasn't enough for her.

She mulled over Maggie's words as she headed home on the bike. She found she was really enjoying the cycle ride to work. It was lovely to have some fresh air and clear her head. She tried to avoid the busy main roads and stuck to the pretty side roads and avenues.

She glanced at the cricket ground as she cycled past. She had gone there on Thursday evening to watch the last match of the cricket season. She had got off the bike but left the helmet on, worried about helmet hair.

She watched the game for about five minutes. Until Edward strode out of the pavilion to bat, that was. Then she got back on the bike and cycled away before he saw her. He probably wanted her to stop bothering him. After all, that flirting with the barmaid had been very cosy. Perhaps he wanted to get rid of the fat friend and go with the busty barmaid.

Kathy cycled for a long time that evening and had actually gone along the river path that Maggie had suggested. She worked out on the map when she got home that she had cycled around six miles that afternoon. The raspberry sunset streaked the sky. It was very romantic. But she had no tall blond man with kind eyes to share it with.

Edward had spotted Kathy cycling away just as he reached the cricket stumps. He had gone to wave at her before realising she was leaving the cricket ground.

She was probably bored with him; he understood

that. He had been far too pushy, inviting himself over every Sunday and then having dinner with her. She might have thought he was just going over there for the food rather than to enjoy her company.

Maybe he should leave her alone, he told himself. But he knew he really didn't want to.

Chapter Thirty-nine

On Monday morning, Violet left her car outside the house and walked to the bus stop. She was a little breathless by the time she arrived but felt OK.

The bus turned up, she paid her fare and sat down. It was quite nice to let someone else do the driving. Plus she could people watch to her heart's content. Or rather fashion watch. A woman got on with such a fabulous handbag that Violet almost asked her where she had got it from. And those shoes were nice. What about those bangles? Earrings? Her lipstick?

Everyone else must have thought that Violet was one of those nutters you often got on the bus, staring wildly at everyone. But she was just clocking their fashion choices. And wondering if she should flash her credit cards again that lunchtime.

But the small amount of exercise was good for her. She had flicked through Isabella's book the previous evening and realised she was now on Rule Number Four. Exercise.

'For *una bella figura*' – a fine figure, Violet translated – 'you must do a little walking each day. We Italians take the evening *passeggiata*' – walk – 'before dinner. It is good for both the digestion and the soul.'

Violet wondered whether her bus journey and short walk would impress Isabella. Probably not.

'You must do a little activity each day that makes you breathless. You may include *l'amore*, if you wish.'

Breathless? Sex? What it made Violet, to be honest, was a bit stressed. All that revealing of naked flesh and for what? The only time recently that Sebastian had made her breathless was with anger.

It was time to send out the wedding invitations. She had the invites for her work colleagues in her handbag. But the invitations had brought up the subject of which wedding list to choose.

It turned out that Violet's dreams of a few choice presents of candlesticks and other keepsakes didn't correspond with Sebastian's ideas. He wanted to ask for money instead.

'We can't,' Violet told him, aghast.

'Why not?'

'It's not right,' she told him. 'We don't need it with the inheritance coming next year.' She had a sudden thought. 'We could always ask people to give to charity instead, on our behalf.'

'You must be bloody joking,' said Sebastian. 'Some goat given to some loser in Africa? What's the point? And since when did you start disagreeing with everything I say?'

'I don't.'

'Yes, you do. Since you've lost weight, you've changed.' He bit his lip. 'I suppose you don't even want to marry me any more.'

Violet flung herself at his knees and stared up at him. 'Of course I do,' she stammered. Her heart was thumping at the thought of not marrying Sebastian, of being alone.

'I just don't think it's polite,' she told him. 'Asking for money like that when we already have so much of our own.'

He rubbed her hair. 'Let me do the thinking, pumpkin. It'll be fine.'

In the end, they had compromised on registering for gifts at John Lewis. Violet had spent a wretched couple of hours wandering around the home section with Sebastian, trying to choose cutlery and crockery that they both liked. He appeared as uninterested in the choices as she was so they had ended up choosing a set that neither of them really liked. Sebastian quickly got bored and wandered off, zapping the barcodes of ridiculous items such as cocktail shakers, a wine thermometer and a cricket bat.

Violet had glanced longily at the garden section. There were some raised herb gardens in grey that she would have loved. But Sebastian had begun to yawn and get restless so she didn't bother.

Violet dragged her mind back to the present and found that the bus hadn't moved very far. It was barely quicker than the car journey that she had been struggling with every day. The bus lanes made a bit of a difference but the whole town came to standstill at quarter to nine.

She glanced at her watch. She daren't be late again. She might get the sack. She realised in that instant that she really enjoyed her job. She liked using her brain and the responsibility.

She made a decision and stood up. It was only a short distance to the office. So she got off the bus and began to walk. There was something about walking past everyone in their cars that made her feel quite smug. She wasn't sure if the fumes were doing her lungs any good but she could feel her face glowing by the time she got to work.

She had just pressed the button in the lift to go up to her floor when Mark slipped his way through the gap, a little breathless. 'Good morning,' he said, panting slightly. 'Traffic's a nightmare this morning.'

'Good morning,' replied Violet, also still out of breath from her walk.

Her mind suddenly flashed to Isabella's words on what could make you breathless. Thankfully her blushes were hidden as her cheeks were already red.

'What have you been up to?' asked Mark, studying her rosy face.

'I got off the bus early to walk,' Violet told him as the lift doors slid open.

They walked down the corridor together until they reached the department. It was only just after nine o'clock.

Violet glanced over to Anthony, who was just finishing a phone call and rolling his eyes as he put down the receiver.

'What?' she asked him.

'Pbkc,' he told her.

Violet's mind panicked. Was this some new kind of technology that she hadn't yet grasped? Or even thought of?

But Anthony's face split into a grin. 'Problem between keyboard and chair,' he told her.

Once she got the joke, Violet smiled back.

She caught the bus home again and realised she had achieved about thirty minutes of walking, including the short stroll from her front door to the bus stop. So the following morning, she got off at the nearer bus stop once more to walk a little further. And then walked to the bus stop instead of the bus station on the way home.

Violet continued the walking each day and lost four pounds that week just from the extra exercise.

All the fresh air and extra movement triggered a yearning for carbs so Violet made some salads to take into work for her lunch. The possibilities were endless. Cold pasta, mixed with a small amount of good quality pesto, cherry tomatoes, cubed cucumber and a couple of olives. Cold rice mixed with sun-dried tomatoes and parma ham with the fat removed. She even took in some leftover lemon risotto, made with courgettes and a splash of white wine.

Gradually Violet became braver and got off the bus earlier and earlier each morning. By the following week, she decided it was barely worth the hassle of getting on the bus. So she walked past the bus stop and kept walking all the way into town. Half an hour later, Violet was at work and feeling proud of herself. So she began to walk home too. Violet lost four pounds that week as well.

But at the weekends, she had nowhere to walk to. Sebastian often played golf or squash but that excluded her so she began to find other ways to keep active.

First of all, she decided to attack the garden as autumn had almost arrived. Twenty minutes of weeding burned one hundred calories, apparently. Violet didn't know how many calories she used up as she wrestled with a particularly large and pointy thistle that had grown up near the patio. There were huge gaping holes around the garden by the end of the weekend as she tore up massive weeds and thorns. Then she dug over the soil in the gaps to get the garden ready for some new plants. Her arms burned and her back ached from the exercise but it was a good feeling. And she was happier being out in the fresh air than embarrassing herself at a step aerobics class.

'Why are you bothering? asked Sebastian, later that weekend.

'Because it would be nice if the garden didn't look like a jungle.'

'Who cares? It'll be on the market soon anyway.'

Violet spun round. 'Why?'

He grinned at her. 'I was hoping my wife would be moving in with me at some point.'

Violet thought about his bachelor pad, which was all cold chrome and black leather.

'It makes sense,' said Sebastian. 'To move in with me first. Then we'll sell the flat and get one of those new townhouses on the edge of town.'

Violet knew which ones he meant. Very tall. Very expensive. Not much character.

'But we can't afford one, can we?'

Did he notice the hope in her voice? The hope that it was well out of reach.

'We'll use your inheritance, naturally.'

Not knowing what to say, she went back into the garden and attacked the soil with added ferocity.

'What happened to you?' asked Mark, staring at her arms the following day.

It was Violet's first time of wearing a short-sleeved top. She was gradually getting used to baring a bit more flesh.

She glanced down. It looked as if she'd been dragged through a barbed-wire fence.

300

'It's Sebastian,' she told him, putting a solemn note in her voice. 'He flays me.'

Mark looked incandescent, his face creasing up into outrage.

'I'm joking,' she told him quickly.

Mark walked away still frowning whilst muttering Italian gobbledygook under his breath.

Later that week, she replaced the empty patches around the garden with some new plants. Then Violet decided to turn her attentions to her house.

That weekend, she began a major spring clean, or rather an autumn clean, of the whole house. Hoovering apparently burned up 193 calories in an hour. Dusting came in at 173 calories. Mopping floors also at 173 calories burned. And her house needed hundreds of hours to get clean.

How had she lived like this for so long? She had just vegetated in front of the telly and eaten and eaten. No wonder she had stayed so fat for so long. Exercise was a big help. In fact, during the month of September, when Violet's weight loss should have been slowing, she lost another stone in weight. It was falling off her body in shock at all the movement. But she felt so much better for it.

Exercise made her hungry but Violet still stuck to her healthy food. In the early autumn sunshine, she reminded herself of summer with a pasta dish with rich tomatoes, a slug of red wine and fresh basil. She even used a few shavings of Nonna's marvellous Parmigiano Reggiano to add some flavour. Cheese might be the devil's food if you're dieting but Violet was beginning not to stress too much about the odd nibble.

In fact, Violet was stressing less about all the calories and focusing more on enjoying fresh flavours.

But she was so busy enjoying her dinner that she was almost late, she realised as she hurried up the stairs to the local library. Sebastian always played snooker on a Thursday evening which left her free. In fact, he didn't even have to know about the class she had signed up for. Which was good because Violet really didn't want to tell him about it. It would provoke too many questions and she didn't know yet what her answers would be.

She scurried into the classroom and took a seat. It was odd meeting people who didn't know how large she had been. She was down to twelve stone. It helped, she found. The fact that they thought she might only be curvy rather than morbidly obese empowered her and brought her out of her shell.

Nobody in the classroom knew about her weight in the past. And nobody needed to know. Violet was now all about the present and the future. The past should stay where it was.

'*Buona sera!*' said the teacher as he entered the classroom.

Violet glanced at the paperwork on the desk. *Italian for Beginners* said the textbook in front of her.

She got out her notepad and began to write.

Chapter Forty

Maggie tugged at the hem of her top, trying to pull it down even further.

'You look beautiful,' whispered Gordon in her ear. 'Stop fretting.'

She let go of the hem and turned to face her husband. He was also looking very smart in black trousers and an open-necked blue shirt.

'Good evening, folks,' said the man on the stage, talking into a microphone. 'It's Friday night so I hope you've got your dancing shoes on.'

Maggie glanced at her feet. She was wearing brand-new black shoes with a small heel. They were a little tight but that was the least of her problems at that minute. Her arms were bare in the new sparkly evening top she had bought. The full black skirt stopped at her knees and she was wondering if her ankles looked fat.

Worst of all were the unexpected nerves. What if she had forgotten how to dance? What if she tripped up on the dance floor, fell flat on her face and revealed to everyone that she was wearing Spanx bicycle shorts underneath her skirt?

'Shall we?' said Gordon, turning to her and holding out his hand.

Maggie nodded and clutched his hand as they made their way out to the dance floor. The place was packed with couples of varying ages, all fighting for space as the music began.

Gordon put one hand in the middle of her back and clasped her other hand at a right angle to their bodies.

They began to move to the music and all Maggie's cares were forgotten. They had stepped back in time twenty years and it was just Maggie and Gordon. The music sang in her ears as Gordon swept her around the floor. She felt light on her feet for the first time in years, able to match his step with hers.

Maggie was in Gordon's arms. He smiled down at her and she felt a frisson of something. Romance? Passion, even? Definitely love. Maggie smiled back at him, feeling like a newlywed all over again.

Maggie felt herself come alive.

Kathy looked around the shop in the morning light, checking that everything was in place. It was the day of the Grand Re-Opening of the shop. A lick of paint, some new lights and a complete overhaul of the layout and window had worked wonders. It actually looked like a place into which customers might want to venture.

'My feet are killing me,' said Maggie, who was sitting down on a chair behind the till, rubbing her feet.

'You should have got the next size up,' Kathy told her, handing over a mug of coffee.

'Thanks,' said Maggie. 'The size sixes were too big. It'll be OK once they're broken in.'

'So you're going back there next week?'

Maggie nodded. 'Definitely. I felt about ten years younger.' She gave Kathy a rueful smile. 'Until I tried to get out of bed this morning. I've pulled muscles I didn't even know existed.'

'I'd have thought all that running would have helped.'

'Different muscles, it seems.'

Kathy wished that she too had found some new muscles but the weight was coming off gradually. Feeling slightly better about her weight loss, she had treated herself to a new skirt and knee-length boots to wear for the special opening.

'Nice boots,' said Lucy, who had been fiddling with the mannequins in the window.

'Thought I'd better make an effort in case the news-paper people show up.'

Maggie had persuaded Kathy to ring up the local paper about the shop re-opening to try and generate some extra publicity.

As soon as it was nine o'clock, Kathy unlocked the front door and stepped back with a nervous grin.

'Here's hoping that somebody actually comes in today,' she told Maggie and Lucy.

Kathy was secretly hoping that, amongst the crowds of people that she had been praying for, Edward might find time to pop in as well.

Lucy went outside and stuck a smile on her face. The weather was a little crisper, a sign that autumn had truly arrived.

She stared up at the shop window, secretly pleased with her work. She had grabbed an old denim jacket and reworked it with some new buttons and collar. Teamed with a pair of black leather trousers that someone had donated that week and a white T-shirt, she had created a young look.

It had been Lucy's suggestion that they change the inside of a shop to reflect a fashion boutique, hoping to attract the younger and wealthier crowd who might look for a vintage bargain.

She had helped behind the scenes, steaming and ironing clothes, figuring it would be all in a day's work when she had her own shop. Lucy had even fixed up a few of the clothes with different belts and buttons to make up some different designs. She found if she kept her hands busy with sewing, then they were also away from picking at chocolate.

She had only two weeks until she left for college and only a couple of pounds left to reach her target. Everything seemed to be coming together at once. She thought back to how she had felt at the beginning of the year. How miserable, how worthless she had thought herself to be. Now she was designing shop windows and filled with so much energy she thought she might burst.

Life was meant to be exciting and she couldn't wait for the future.

Violet arrived shortly after opening time and found Lucy outside.

'I found a fantastic skirt for you,' said Lucy. 'It's a designer pencil skirt. It's so you!'

Violet grimaced. 'Me in a pencil skirt?'

'Of course,' said Lucy, as if it were the most obvious

thing for Violet to wear. 'You've got that classic hour-glass that it was made for. Dead sexy too.'

Violet glanced at her reflection. She was quite pleased with her new jeans but wasn't sure her legs were up to a skirt yet.

Aware of Lucy watching her, she indicated the plate of brownies that she had made for the occasion and went into the shop.

'Fantastic,' said Kathy, taking one of the bite-size pieces.

'Lovely,' said Maggie, between mouthfuls. 'But I can't believe you're encouraging us to be so sinful.'

'I'm not,' said Violet, breaking into a grin. 'I've replaced the chocolate with cocoa powder and the butter with very-low-fat mayonnaise.'

'Mayonnaise?' said Kathy, now grimacing as she swallowed.

'You wouldn't know the difference unless I'd pointed it out,' Violet told them.

'I don't believe it,' said Maggie, staring at the plate. 'They taste just the same.'

Violet winked at them and was heading back outside when she bumped into a woman in the doorway.

'Excuse me. I'm from the *Daily News*.'

Violet turned around. 'The newspaper's here.'

Kathy wiped the chocolate crumbs from her mouth and fixed a smile on her face as she headed outside.

'Hello,' she said to the journalist. 'I'm Kathy, the new manager.'

Violet watched as Kathy chatted away, wishing she had that kind of ease with people face to face. She was still thankful that the hotline wasn't yet conducted over a webcam.

People gradually began to hover outside the shop,

drawn to the grand re-opening by some balloons and big signs that Maggie had had printed.

Violet watched the photographer take a few shots. She wondered if he covered weddings as well. Then she remembered the fancy photographer that Miriam had chosen. She had taken a quick look at the website. From the gallery of shots, it all looked a bit arty. A photograph of a single shoe. A flower head. None of it seemed real, plus it all came at a hefty cost. Miriam was heading down the route that thought the more expensive the service, the better.

Violet shook her head and focused back on Kathy.

'Donate, don't waste. That's our message,' Kathy was saying to the journalist. 'After all, giving us five pounds for a skirt or jacket would pay for one person to attend a half-hour session at a monthly meeting, providing information and support for both the people with dementia and their carers. It's so important to have outside contact.'

Violet wondered if she should just hand over her whole inheritance to the Alzheimer's Society. Lord knew, they would probably do something more worthwhile with it than Sebastian would.

Amongst the crowd that was gradually beginning to build up, both inside and outside the shop, was Edward.

He said hi to Violet and Lucy, before standing and watching Kathy chat to the journalist.

He realised that her face had lost its roundness as the pounds had dropped and now she had cheekbones lit by a pink glow. Her brown eyes sparkled and she had cut her hair a little shorter. She was very pretty and he found he enjoyed looking at her.

A photographer from the newspaper had arrived to take a picture to go with the article. He was trying to gather everyone together for a group shot and was getting a bit hands on with Kathy, manoeuvring her to the middle by placing his hand on her lower back. An inch lower and Edward would floor him with a punch.

As well as the weight-loss girls, a few of the regular customers had also turned up, including some of the pensioners.

'Right,' said the photographer, before holding up his lens. 'Everybody smile. And remember, tits and teeth, ladies. Tits and teeth.'

There was a shocked silence and a few looks exchanged.

'What did he say?' asked Mavis, who thankfully was slightly deaf.

'He said his name was Keith,' said Kathy.

Edward's shoulders were shaking as he tried to suppress his laughter. He locked eyes with Kathy who was also trying not to giggle.

As she turned back to smile at the camera, Edward realised he had to keep trying with Kathy. He couldn't let her go without a fight. She meant too much to him.

Chapter Forty-one

It was a momentous week. Lucy had reached her target of nine stone.

'And just in time for my leaving do on Friday night,' said Lucy, grinning.

She was moving into her university digs at the weekend and wanted to go out for a few drinks with her friends from college, as well as the weight-loss group.

Violet felt her stomach plummet. Going out was for other people. Other more confident and happy people. She always dreaded going to nightclubs with all those slim women and Violet as the token fatty. But the girls had started to talk about the hen night in December and, with only three months until the wedding, perhaps she should get a bit of practice in.

That Friday night, Violet stared at her reflection in the full-length mirror which she had finally purchased. The image in the mirror surprised her. Nearly as much as the fact that she was now a size sixteen.

She was wearing her brand-new, pale silver

embroidered camisole with straps thick enough to hide a bra strap. It was too pretty to resist. None of Violet's bras warranted any kind of display so she had found some courage and headed into Marks & Spencer's lingerie department. She had never been measured for a bra and it came as a shock to discover that she was now only a 38C. Up till then, Violet had been wearing a 42E and even that left massive welts across her back and shoulders.

She had just got paid so she treated herself to half a dozen new bras, three in white, two black and one nude. The matching knickers were pretty so Violet bought those as well. She had decided to throw out all her horrible old knickers, whose baggy material was beginning to show through her trousers.

So with new underwear, top, trousers and her favourite turquoise high heels, Violet was ready. She looked at her reflection and gave herself a little nod. She was all right. She could now see the full length of her body and she looked OK. It was time to stop hiding.

The front doorbell rang and Violet made her careful way down the stairs in her heels. She opened up the front door and found Kathy and Maggie standing on her doorstep with big grins on their faces.

'You look great,' they told each other at the same time.

Kathy and Maggie were also wearing black trousers and heels with different tops. Perhaps it was the uniform for going out.

'Those shoes are fabulous!' cooed Kathy at the turquoise heels.

'I know,' said Violet. 'But I can't walk in them.'

'Hang on to us, love.' Maggie held out her arm. 'You'll be fine.'

Violet was smiling but felt nervous. Yet it was a fluttery kind of nervous. As if this were a good thing, an important step. After all, wasn't this what everyone else did in their twenties? Went out and had a good time? Violet had managed to get through almost a whole decade without having any kind of good time.

'Lucy and Edward are meeting us there,' said Maggie.

'Where are we going?' asked Violet.

'Zizzi's for pizza and on to that club at the top of town.'

'You mean The Zone?' said Kathy, her eyebrows shooting upwards. 'Aren't we a bit mutton?'

'Never!' said Maggie with a grin.

She was masking her slight disappointment at having to miss her Friday night's dancing with Gordon. But Lucy was leaving at the weekend and then they'd have all the time in the world.

They met Lucy and some of her college friends at the pizza place. Lucy gave them a hug, already a little merry after a cocktail or two. Maggie, Kathy and Violet sat at the other end of the table from the teenagers and ordered a bottle of wine.

'Edward texted me,' shouted Lucy from the other end of the table. 'He's stuck at work but he's hoping to come along later.'

Seeing Kathy's shoulders droop, Maggie immediately poured out a large glass of wine for each of them. The wine helped the conversation flow, closely followed by the laughter.

Violet ate the pizza and tried not to think about the calorie content.

Kathy was also looking concerned but Maggie

thought that this wasn't about the calories and decided to change the subject.

'So how're the wedding plans?' she said to Violet.

Violet swallowed a piece of gloriously cheesy pizza. 'Sebastian's mother's doing most of the organising so I haven't had much to do, to be honest.'

'Lucky you,' said Maggie. 'It can be quite stressful organising a wedding.'

Violet kept quiet.

Kathy said, 'But you'd probably quite like to have a hand in your own wedding, wouldn't you?'

After a beat, Violet nodded.

'Can't you have a word with your fiancé?' said Maggie.

'He's happy with his mother taking charge,' said Violet, putting down her knife and fork. 'I shouldn't have eaten that.'

Kathy frowned. 'Once in a while isn't bad,' she said.

But Violet was still looking upset. 'I've got to do this. I've got to get to my goal weight.'

Maggie and Kathy exchanged a look at Violet's stressed tone.

'You're doing really well,' Maggie told her.

'You don't understand . . .' said Violet, leaving her voice to trail off.

Maggie and Kathy kept quiet and sipped on their wine, waiting for Violet to speak. But in the end, Violet shrugged and gave them a small smile.

'It doesn't matter,' she said.

'Tell us,' said Kathy. 'You know you can trust us.'

'It's not that,' said Violet, before taking a deep breath. 'Sebastian cheated on me.'

There was a sharp intake of breath across the table.

'When?' they said, trying to keep their voices low.

'Easter. Look, it's OK. We're engaged now and he's committed to me.'

'Should be bloody committed to hard labour for cheating on you,' muttered Kathy.

'How did you find out?' asked Maggie.

Violet sighed. 'She rang me.'

'What a cow!' spat Kathy.

Violet shrugged her shoulders. 'She was drunk. Apparently she never meant to hurt me.'

'I still don't understand why eating that pizza would upset you,' said Maggie.

Violet shook her head. 'Don't you see? If I'm slim and good-looking then our marriage will work.'

Maggie frowned. 'Surely it's not all about looks?'

'No. Yes. I don't know,' said Violet. 'Anyway, he loves me and that's all that matters.'

'If you can trust him,' said Kathy.

'I shouldn't have said anything,' said Violet, looking close to tears.

'We won't talk about it again if you don't want to,' said Maggie.

Violet nodded, unable to speak for a minute. She should have kept quiet.. After all, it wouldn't make a difference. Besides, there were no other threats now. She and Sebastian were fine.

'Can't wait to have a bit of a boogie tonight,' said Kathy, trying to cheer up the conversation. 'Get my moves practised for your wedding.'

'What entertainment have you got for the evening?' asked Maggie.

Violet blew out a long sigh. 'Sebastian's cousin has been booked as a DJ.'

'Great,' said Maggie.

'Not unless you like doing the Macarena,' said Violet, before taking a gulp of wine.

Maggie and Kathy drew the conversation back to the shop, telling tales of retail hell. All the time they kept filling up Violet's wine glass until she began to smile again.

By the time they left the restaurant, Violet wasn't the only one feeling a little tipsy. Lucy was beyond merry and well on her way to drunk and disorderly but she wanted to go dancing so they followed her to the nightclub.

Violet hadn't been into a nightclub for a very long time. And then she had only lasted half an hour during a Christmas party many years previously. It had been a miserable time but at least it was dark in there.

To her surprise, she found she didn't want to leave. She wanted to stay and dance away her troubles. Maggie and Kathy's reaction to Sebastian's betrayal had, in a small way, confirmed her fears that it *had* been a big deal and she had been right to be cross with him at the time. But that was all in the past now.

She trusted them with her secret as well. After all, they had all shared shocking things along the way. Violet felt she was amongst friends and was safe.

She caught her reflection in the mirrored walls as she entered the nightclub. She felt happier every time she caught sight of herself, she realised. How things had changed. How much she had changed.

The music pumped out as they hit the large, dark room. They headed for the bar and Violet downed an overpriced Bacardi Breezer to steady her nerves. Lucy and her friends were already on the dance floor and were gesturing for Violet, Kathy and Maggie to join them.

Violet carefully negotiated the sticky black floor in her high heels but she found that if she kept her feet still and wiggled everything else, no one noticed. Not that there was too much room to dance properly. It was Friday night and the place was jumping.

They all sang along with Beyoncé about her Single Ladies. Beyoncé and her bootylicious body. That was Violet's aim. She didn't want to be stick thin like Victoria Beckham. And she wasn't sure that was even achievable. But Beyoncé's curves were.

Violet hadn't drunk that much, just enough to take the edge off her nerves and relax her. She was enjoying herself. She was dancing! In public! Bits of her were still wobbling, she could feel them. But she didn't care.

Violet had missed out on this and so much more. On life, in fact. And she felt alive now. Really alive.

The beat went on. As the hours passed by and more Bacardi was downed, Violet finally lost her inhibitions and danced as if she would never stop. She lost herself in the music, thinking that it was her kind of workout. She'd always enjoyed music but it was great to relax and just dance.

'Damn girl,' shouted Kathy in her ear. 'You've got some moves.'

Violet smiled and carried on dancing. She'd just sung along to Lady Gaga with the others. She was born this way, said the lyrics. Perhaps she was. Reborn to become whatever she wanted to be.

Sometime later, Violet left the girls to head to the ladies' but it was a real crush on the dance floor now. She had trouble squeezing through everyone.

A large man nearby made some extravagant dance move with his hands and knocked Violet into another man's chest. She slipped in her high heels and lost her balance. The man's arms came out to hold her as she stood chest to chest with him.

Violet looked up and found Mark staring down at her.

'Hello,' he shouted.

'Hi,' she replied, very aware of his close proximity and trying to draw back a little. But she couldn't back completely away due to the press of the crowd. She was so near to him she could smell his aftershave, a sensual fusion of spices and citrus.

'You OK?' he asked. 'Did that guy hurt you?'

She shook her head. 'What are you doing here?' she mouthed at him.

'Out with the football team,' he said, his eyes burning into hers. 'I was watching you on the dance floor.'

Violet felt her cheeks grow warm.

'You look great,' he shouted in her ear.

'So do you.'

The words were out of Violet's mouth before she could stop herself.

But it was true. He was wearing a short-sleeved navy shirt which showed off his muscly arms and a broad chest. Someone knocked into Violet from behind and she was once more crushed against Mark's chest.

She looked up into his eyes and was suddenly conscious of breathing heavily. He seemed to fill the room with his height and wide shoulders. Even with her high heels on, he was still taller than she was. With Sebastian she had to stoop a little, with Mark she had to stare up.

Someone bumped into them once again and Violet automatically put her hands out against his chest to steady herself. Under her fingers, his chest felt hard with muscle.

They stared at each other, no longer keeping up the pretence of small talk. Mark looked at Violet and she realised he was going to kiss her. And she was going to let him. Right here. Right now.

Their faces began to draw closer. Her pulse was thumping now. The beat and music faded away until it was only him. She could think of nothing else.

He was staring at her mouth and then back into her eyes. She could barely breathe for the anticipation of Mark kissing her.

'Hello!' boomed a male voice at them. 'I thought it was you!'

Violet turned her face to find Edward standing next to them and quickly drew away from Mark.

'Hi,' she stammered, her face still flushed.

'Hiya!' screamed Lucy, staggering over to join them. 'Mum and Kathy are over there!'

Edward headed over to the others.

Violet glanced back at Mark who was still gazing at her, his eyes burning into hers.

'You on your way to the ladies'?' slurred Lucy.

'Yes,' said Violet, finally tearing her eyes away from Mark's.

'Who are you?' said Lucy, squinting at him.

'Violet's boss,' he shouted, glancing at Violet. 'I was just doing a staff appraisal.'

'You what?' said Lucy. She was completely smashed by now.

Violet took her arm and dragged her in the direction of the toilets. And away from Mark.

It would be fine, she told herself. Mark must have had a few beers. She had also drunk quite a lot. Blame it on the alcohol. It would be fine, she repeated to herself.

Kathy was also telling her pulse to slow down. It shouldn't have raced so fast when she spotted Edward ploughing his way through the crowds. But it did. He only had two stone left to lose and thanks to his many hours at the gym, his body was becoming more striking by the day. Kathy spotted quite a few girls watching him with approval.

Unfortunately, her happiness was short lived because they had to leave soon afterwards. Lucy had been sick and that was their cue to go.

The taxi dropped off Kathy and Violet first before heading back towards Maggie's home.

'I feel great!' slurred Lucy, her head in her mother's lap.

'You won't tomorrow,' said Maggie, stroking her daughter's hair with a smile.

She was determined not to cry when Lucy finally left for London. But Maggie knew she was bound to.

'I'm never going back to being fat,' Lucy carried on. 'I feel too good.'

'You don't think it's all those Bacardi Breezers that made you feel like that?'

Lucy giggled. 'Those bitches that bullied me. They're nothing, are they?'

'No, love. They're not.'

'I'm nine stone!' said Lucy.

'And beautiful,' Maggie told her daughter with a smile.

'Shame Edward came so late.'

'Something to do with his work. But there'll be other times.'

'Kathy seemed fed up.'

'She'll be OK.'

'Who was that bloke with Violet? Was that her fiancé?'

'No. She said it was her boss from work.' Maggie thought back to the man she had seen briefly through the crowd. 'Must have been the Italian one. He was gorgeous.'

'Bit old for me, Mum,' said Lucy, with a yawn.

'I wasn't thinking of you,' said Maggie, remembering the look on Violet's face as she had stood so close to him.

Chapter Forty-two

'Going to the chapel and I'm gonna get married,' Violet hummed as she walked into work on Monday morning. Over and over again, she played the tune in her head. And tried to ignore her heart.

'I'm getting married,' she told herself. 'Me. Violet Saunders. Fat, worthless Violet becoming Mrs Fabulous Parkes.'

And then she gave herself a good ticking off. She was no longer fat and she certainly wasn't worthless.

Her mind flicked back to Mark on Friday night. Mark standing so close she could feel his breath on her cheek. Mark's lips getting closer. She shook her head and sped up her walk. If she pounded the pavement hard enough, she could crush these stupid thoughts that kept spilling into her mind.

She sat down at her desk and watched Mark stalk past without even a greeting. She stared at his bottom until he disappeared out of sight into his office.

'I'm getting married,' muttered Violet, finally

drawing her eyes away from Mark's office door. She was marrying Sebastian. She loved Sebastian. He was everything. She was nothing without him.

Except, Violet realised, she wasn't nothing. She wasn't a useless lump. She had a life that she was really enjoying these days.

'I need a decent coffee not from that vending machine,' shouted Mark from his office door. 'Anyone want one?'

'Are you paying?' asked Julie.

'Sounds like it,' he muttered, before taking their orders. 'Violet can help me carry them back.'

Violet gulped. She had really been hoping to avoid any one-to-one conversation with Mark that day. But, as usual, she couldn't say no, so she found herself meekly following him out of the building.

'Your friend was having a good time on Friday night,' he said, breaking the silence as they walked along the street.

'Lucy? She's off to university so we were giving her a proper send-off.'

This was OK. She had just bumped into him on Friday night in a crowded nightclub. That was all. They could converse like adults. There was nothing to be ashamed about.

'What's she studying?'

'Fashion design. She's making my wedding dress for me.'

He grunted but said nothing as they turned into the small alleyway leading up to Nonna's delicatessen.

'*Buongiorno*!' he said to everyone behind the counter as they went in. He turned to Violet. 'I'm half asleep this morning. Do you want to grab a quick ristretto before we head back with the rest of the coffees?'

Violet nodded. She hadn't slept very well either since Friday night.

Mark gave the man behind the counter his order and they waited in silence as he crashed about with the coffee machine. After a couple of minutes, he handed them each a tiny espresso cup full of dark liquid. It was the famous ristretto he had told her about. Like espresso, it was only a shot of coffee. But it had far more guts than espresso. Violet downed the coffee in one gulp and then shuddered as she felt the caffeine coursing through her veins.

'What do you think?' said Mark, who had been watching her and waiting for a reaction.

'I think I've just had an electric shock,' Violet replied, her eyes clicking wide open.

She was just putting her cup back on to the counter when Nonna came rushing up to them, greeting them with Italian words and kisses.

'*Buongiorno*,' she said to Violet, kissing her on both cheeks. '*Come sta*?'

Normally Violet would have just nodded but, thanks to her evening class, she now knew that she had been asked how she was and the also knew the reply she should give.

'*Bene, grazie.*'

'Ah!' yelled Nonna, before glancing across to Mark who was staring at Violet in amazement.

But before he could speak, Nonna was rattling off more questions to Violet and they were able to hold a tentative conversation in Italian. Violet asked about limoncello, the lemon liqueur she had seen listed in a recipe for a healthy cheesecake. Nonna went on for so long about recipes that could include limoncello that Mark went off to order and pay for the coffees whilst they carried on.

Once he had walked out of earshot, Nonna appeared to change tack. Violet managed to understand most of what she was saying, including Nonna's rant about how none of Mark's girlfriends so far had been good enough for him.

Violet had forgotten the existence of Mark's many ex-girlfriends until then. According to the office gossip, there was a new woman in his life every couple of months and they were always fabulous-looking. But then again, why would he be single?

Seeing Mark returning to them, Nonna changed subject swiftly and asked Violet about Sebastian and the wedding. Violet was just talking about her wedding dress when Mark came to stand next to her, holding a tray of coffee cups.

'We'd better head back,' he told her.

Violet said goodbye to Nonna who gave her a warm hug and told her to come back soon.

'That was surprising,' said Mark as they walked away.

Violet shrugged. 'She always tells me to come back soon,' she told him with a sly smile.

'You know exactly what I'm getting at,' he told her, narrowing his eyes. 'You've been learning Italian.'

'Evening class,' she told him. 'It helps me order the right things from Nonna. I now know my polenta from my passata.'

'Good accent,' he replied, nodding as if in deep in thought.

'Thanks. I didn't want to come across as rude to Nonna by not speaking any of her language.'

'She's a pretty good judge of character,' Mark told her. 'I heard you telling her about your fiancé. I have to say, it wasn't how I had imagined him at all. I thought he would be a lot shorter. But I suppose women go for that whole macho, muscly look.'

'When did you see Sebastian?'

He looked puzzled. 'At the nightclub on Friday night.'

'That wasn't Sebastian,' she told him. 'That was Edward from my weight-loss club.'

Mark suddenly broke into a grin. 'Right. I see.'

She had to remember to tell Edward that her boss thought he looked macho and muscly. And so he did with nearly six stones lost; he was in great shape.

'So how many people are at this weight-loss club of yours?'

Violet found herself telling Mark about the various members and how well they had all done until now. Mark walked slowly to allow Violet time to tell him about how they met in her home once a week.

'Sounds like you've done a great job with everyone,' he told her as they walked through the office reception.

'They've mainly done it themselves.'

'Don't sell yourself short,' he told her. 'Without having you as the nerve centre, I doubt they would have done so well.'

Violet stepped into the lift, thinking about his words. Perhaps it was true. Perhaps they had all done better being part of a group.

As they arrived back in the department, Julie looked up from her desk. 'Have you heard about our pay rises yet?'

Mark shook his head. 'But what I do have is a coffee

for each of you, totally free of charge. Plus the new holiday entitlement for next year is in. Apparently, you will all receive 104 personal days next year.'

Everyone looked at each other in amazement.

'Really?' stammered Anthony.

'Yup,' said Mark. 'They're called weekends.'

He broke into a smile as they all groaned.

Julie sighed. 'I knew it was too good to be true. Stupid company.'

'I agree, Julie,' said Mark. 'And we know you only come in each day to dazzle us with your sunny disposition.'

He went back into his office whistling a happy tune as he left.

Wendy was deep in conversation on the telephone. 'So you've found the letter "a" on your keyboard,' she was saying. 'But you don't know how to get the circle around it?'

She rolled her eyes at Violet as she handed over the coffee. Violet sat down at her desk as the hotline rang out once more and the day swung into action.

Later, she immersed herself in a relaxing bubble bath reading Isabella's book. Violet found she had sailed through rules one to four and was now on to Rule Number Five, which was all about beauty.

'Every woman needs a hand with her beauty. Look your best and make the most of your features. Grooming is essential. Get regular haircuts.'

Violet put the book down on the side of the bath. She hadn't had a professional haircut in years. She just snipped the split ends off with her kitchen scissors. Anyway, she had never really bothered about her hair. Perhaps she could be brave and get a decent haircut. Perhaps it was time to be a little more adventurous.

Perhaps it was time to stop hiding behind her long hair and start living, she told herself.

Chapter Forty-three

Trudie glanced across at the weight-loss-club clients as she sorted out her paperwork in readiness for the weigh-in. Not that she actually considered them as clients once they had handed over their money. This group were more like some kind of weird science project.

After a pathetic start to their diets, they seemed to have finally realised that their bodies were disgusting and begun to get their act together.

She picked up on their conversation.

'I had such a hangover,' the mother Maggie was saying. 'But Lucy was far worse. Poor kid could hardly get out of bed on Saturday.'

'It was good though, wasn't it?' said Kathy the jolly one.

'I wouldn't know,' said the male. 'Bloody meeting went on so long that I missed most of the evening.'

Trudie bristled. What was this? The fatties heading out together? Fat friends united and all that?

She walked over to stand in front of them. 'Sounds

like you all had a bit of a party,' she said with a wide smile.

Maggie shuffled in her seat. 'It was Lucy's leaving do.'

Ah yes. The moody teenager had left the group. Trudie had been amazed that Lucy had actually hit her target of nine stone the previous week. Nobody had ever reached their target before, in any of Trudie's classes.

'Where did you go?' asked Trudie.

'Zizzi's and then The Zone,' replied Kathy.

'What a shame,' cooed Trudie. 'I've got tickets to the VIP room there. If I'd have known you were going, I could have met you there.'

The silence rang out as they realised how rude they had been by not inviting her. She was their class leader, for God's sake. Not that she would have been seen dead near this lot in public. But it was the principle of not being invited.

'Well, we'd better see how much damage all that pizza has done to your diets, hadn't we?' she said before nodding at Violet. 'You first.'

The bride-to-be followed her over to the scales.

'Eleven stone and eight pounds,' Trudie told her. 'You only lost one pound this week.'

She knew they wouldn't be able to keep up their rate of loss for too long.

Trudie pasted on a pity smile. 'Anyway, it could be worse.'

Violet sighed. 'How worse?' she muttered.

Trudie frowned. 'I don't know. It's just an expression.'

She watched Violet shuffle back to the chairs. She had nothing for her. No words of encouragement for any of them. What was the point? They were the ones who had let themselves get in that state, weren't they?'

Edward came over next to be weighed.

'Fourteen stone and eleven pounds,' she told him.

He smiled at Trudie. She didn't like it when people smiled at her unexpectedly. It unnerved her.

'Upped the running at the gym,' he told her, still smiling as he walked away.

I hear what you're saying, she thought. But I really don't care.

What was it with men and gyms? Trevor was going through a health kick as well. He was there all the time. Every evening and every weekend too.

Not that Trudie minded. He was finally getting toned and had lost that bit of paunch that she had nagged him about. But she would like to see him at least one evening a week. But no, he didn't come home until eleven o'clock at night and then went straight to bed.

Then he had hurt his back and wasn't able to perform his sexual duties in the bedroom on the one night designated per month. Apparently he'd damaged his back lifting some weights. Men were so stupid sometimes.

Maggie came over next.

'Twelve stone and thirteen pounds,' said Trudie.

'I'm down into the twelve-stone area,' beamed Maggie.

She seemed to be pleased that she was still so gross.

Finally, the last weirdo came up to be weighed.

'Thirteen stone exactly,' she told Kathy. 'Perhaps you should try a bit more exercise to speed up your weight loss.'

Kathy shrugged her shoulders. 'If God had wanted

me to touch my toes,' she told Trudie, 'He would have put them higher up my body.'

Then she walked away.

Trudie rolled her eyes. She only had one nerve left and they were all getting on it.

Chapter Forty-four

Maggie sighed. 'I have an empty nest,' she told the group, once they were safely out of Trudie's clutches.

Violet, Kathy and Edward nodded with solemn faces.

But then Maggie's face lit up. 'It's fantastic!' she told them. 'No rows. No thump thump of music through the floorboards upstairs. I don't have to watch *Hollyoaks* any more and can have Radio Four on instead without my daughter declaring it soooo boring.'

There had been a few tears for both Maggie and Lucy but they had managed to pull themselves together.

The house had seemed strange at first but then Maggie discovered that empty nest gave her and Gordon all sort of opportunities. They could now have an uninterrupted candlelit dinner at home followed by an extremely early but very sexy night under the covers. Since losing weight they had both found their sex drives improved dramatically and some of their new moves were causing Maggie's face to blush just thinking about it.

Thankfully her mobile rang before her thoughts betrayed her.

'Hello, love,' she said into the phone. 'I was just telling everyone how much I was missing you.'

Maggie gave everyone a big grin and a wink.

Lucy was sitting in her room in the halls of residence.

'Put me on speakerphone,' she told her mum.

The phone crackled at the other end and suddenly she could hear everybody.

'Hi, everyone!' called Lucy. 'I'm back!'

'You've only been gone a couple of days,' came back Kathy's voice.

Lucy giggled. 'I know! But it's going so quick.'

She was loving college life. She was sure the classes were going to be brilliant, she had made loads of new friends and even the tiny little single room she was living in was just perfect for her.

'How are you finding London?' asked Edward.

'It's fab,' Lucy told him. 'It's also noisy, dirty and just a little bit scary. But mostly it's great. The uni is brilliant. Everyone's so cool.'

A lot of the other students in her class were also from outside of London so everybody was in the same excited frame of mind.

'Plus a lot of the galleries and museums are free. It's great.'

'You should go to the Victoria and Albert,' said Kathy. 'They've got a great fashion collection.'

'We're going on Saturday,' said Lucy.

'What about the weight?' asked Violet. 'Are you keeping healthy?'

'Yes, sir! Mum gave me a set of scales to take with me and I checked this morning. I'm still dead on nine stone.'

'Well done,' said Violet.

There was a communal kitchen down the hall where Lucy was going to rustle up healthy pasta dishes for herself and some of the other girls. They couldn't believe she had lost three stone and had ever been that big. She had even found herself advising them on what meals to cook for themselves.

'What about exercise?' asked Edward.

'I'm walking everywhere,' Lucy told him. 'It's free, isn't it? We even walked all the way round Regent's Park last night and that's, like, huge.'

'Who's we?' asked Maggie.

'Just me and Todd,' said Lucy, before clapping a hand over her mouth in horror.

'Todd, eh?' cooed Kathy over the airwaves.

'Good to speak to you all,' said Lucy, suddenly in a big hurry. 'But there's somebody at the door. Gotta go!'

'Bye!' they all called out, except her mum who called out, 'I love you.'

'Love you too, Mum.'

And then she hung up.

Lucy flopped back against her pillows, sighing at herself. She knew they were gossiping about her and Todd back at Violet's house.

But what was there to gossip about? She had bumped into him almost as soon as she had arrived in London: it turned out that he was living just down the corridor from her. So naturally they were going to see each other most days. That was cool. It wasn't like he was anything other than a friend, was he?

Lucy chewed on her lip, wondering whether he would be at the student bar later that evening. Just for a friendly chat, of course.

Kathy turned to Maggie with raised eyebrows. 'Todd?'

'Canadian artist,' said Maggie. 'Very cool, apparently. But very nice.'

'Aw!' said Kathy. 'Ain't young love grand?'

'She wants you to keep texting her your measurements,' Maggie told Violet, thinking about her wedding dress.

Violet nodded.

'They must be changing on a weekly basis,' said Kathy.

'Are you sure you don't want to meet up with Lucy before the Christmas holidays?' asked Maggie. 'She's a bit nervous that you won't like the dress.'

Violet shrugged her shoulders. 'I'm sure the dress will be lovely,' she said. 'I trust Lucy's taste.'

'And she wanted to know what you're doing with your hair on the day?' said Maggie. She was still worried about Violet's complete lack of interest in her wedding dress.

'Actually, I was going to ask if anyone can recommend a decent hairdressers?' said Violet.

'Toni and Guy at the top of the high street,' said Kathy.

Violet bit her lip. 'Isn't it really trendy in there?'

'Why?' asked Kathy. 'What were you hoping for? A shampoo and set?'

Violet managed a small giggle.

'Have you asked Edward about the DIY?' Maggie asked Kathy.

Kathy shook her head.

'DIY?' said Edward, looking at them both.

Kathy was suddenly on mute so Maggie spoke for both of them.

'We need some shelves putting up in the shop. And my husband is useless with that kind of thing so we were wondering if you could give us a hand?'

Gordon wasn't at all useless at DIY but a little white lie wouldn't do any harm. Maggie had realised that Edward and Kathy needed a good shove in each other's direction.

'Of course,' said Edward. 'Just let me know what it is that you want.'

'Kathy can do that,' said Maggie, trying not to smile.

Edward nodded whilst Maggie kept her eyes on her mug of tea, determined not to lock eyes with Kathy whom she knew would be scowling at her.

Kathy was indeed scowling at Maggie. But only inwardly. On the outside she was all smiles and jolliness. Until Maggie came up with an excuse to stay behind to talk to Violet, leaving Kathy walking down the street alone with Edward.

'So, about these shelves . . .' said Edward, eventually breaking the silence.

'It's not important,' said Kathy.

'How about Sunday? The shop's closed then, isn't it?'

'It really doesn't matter.'

Edward stopped walking and grabbed Kathy by the arm. 'OK,' he told her. 'What's going on?'

'I don't know what you mean,' stammered Kathy.

He had such kind eyes. And that breadth of shoulder and rib cage made her heart sing. This was bad. She had enough on her plate without having a crush on Edward as well.

Edward released her and dragged a hand through his hair. 'Have I done something to offend you in any way? Because I've been racking my brains and I just don't know what's changed between us. But something has.'

Kathy's insides clenched. She was an idiot. And, apparently, not quite the fine actress she had considered herself to be.

'It's fine,' she told him. 'It's not you, it's me.'

Edward stared at her. 'Isn't that what people say when they're breaking up with someone?'

Kathy bit her lip and couldn't think of anything to say.

'I thought we were friends,' Edward told her. 'I was enjoying your company.'

'Me too,' said Kathy. 'Look, forget about it. I'm an idiot. An emotional wreck. Who wants company with that?'

'I do,' said Edward.

God, this was terrible. He must think her a total headcase.

'I'm sorry,' said Kathy, dropping her head. 'I never meant to upset you.'

'How sorry?'

Kathy lifted her head up to look at Edward.

'Are you so sorry that you'll be my date for the end of cricket season do? It's in two weeks' time.'

His date? Kathy gulped.

'Otherwise I'll have to take one of my sisters and that would be really embarrassing.'

Edward was smiling at her but Kathy's brief smile had dropped. So the only reason he wanted her to go with him was to stop him looking like some saddo? He was desperate so he thought of Kathy? Charming.

'It's a fancy-dress party,' carried on Edward, seemingly unaware of the pain his words were causing. 'So you don't have to wear a posh frock or anything.'

And now he was saying that she didn't own any nice clothes? Was that because she was still fat?

'You could just go as a witch,' said Edward, whose smile was beginning to falter. 'Or something like that.'

'I'll think about it,' snarled Kathy.

She walked away, hoping he wouldn't see the tears streaming down her cheeks.

Edward sighed as he watched Kathy hurry away.

His confidence was soaring as the stones dropped off him and he toned up. He knew he was looking good and was even aware of a couple of girls in the office starting to flirt with him.

Trouble was, Kathy had slunk into his heart when he wasn't watching and now he realised he didn't want to lose her.

But he seemed to have got it all wrong again.

There was every possibility that the party would turn into a horror show.

Chapter Forty-five

Violet was trying to feel confident as she swung the salon door open.

'Hi!' said the skinny teenager behind the reception desk with a wide smile. 'Can I help you?'

'I've got an appointment booked in the name of Saunders.'

The girl tapped her computer screen a couple of times. 'Violet? OK. Take a seat. Sarah will be along soon.'

Violet glanced at the other customers as she sank on to the long leather sofas in the waiting area. To her surprise, there was a broad range of ages and types, from yummy mummies and their perfect children to white-haired pensioners. The catwalk models she had assumed would be there were nowhere to be seen.

The combined heat of the hairdryers, sinks and people were making Violet's cheeks flush so she took off her scarf and coat, placing them next to her on the sofa.

She was wearing a pair of new jeans which were a size fourteen. No sooner did she buy a new pair of trousers than she was buying a smaller size. Over the new jeans she had on her latest, favourite purchase, knee-length biker boots. She had lost so much weight that she could finally get boots over her calves. It was bizarre which areas the body lost inches from. Her shoes had gone down another half a size as well.

A young salon assistant came to stand in front of Violet.

'Do you want to follow me?'

Violet duly trotted behind her to a large wardrobe, where her coat and scarf were hung up. In their place, a black cape was draped over her. Then she was led to sit in front of one of the thirty or so mirrors to wait for the stylist.

Violet glanced from side to side but every customer looked the same in their black capes. Only their faces differed. People looked relaxed, as if this wasn't at all anything special.

'Hi. I'm Sarah,' said a pretty blond woman coming to stand next to Violet. She talked to Violet through their reflections in the mirror. 'What can I do for you today?'

'I don't really know,' stammered Violet.

And she didn't, she realised. The idea had been a quick trim but now, sitting here amongst all these people, she wasn't so sure.

Sarah picked up a long strand of Violet's black hair. 'It's not in bad condition,' she said. 'How long have you worn it like this?'

'For ever,' said Violet, before giving Sarah a rueful smile. 'Sorry to be so vague. I've lost some weight and now it's as if my hair doesn't fit my new body.'

Her shoulders sagged. She must sound stupid.

But Sarah replied, 'I know what you mean. Look, you've got fantastic hair. It's thick with a slight wave so it would hold a really blunt cut. How brave are you feeling?'

Violet gulped.

'How about I trim it to here?'

She held her hand just above Violet's shoulder, holding out the six inches of hair that would be lost. Violet took a deep intake of breath but then found she didn't really mind. She'd shed the inches around her body, why not her hair too?

'Trust me,' said Sarah. 'It'll look brilliant.'

Violet was led over to a row of sinks where a different salon assistant washed and conditioned her hair. It was a total pampering experience, because not only was her back massaged by the long leather chair underneath her, the assistant also massaged her scalp whilst the conditioner worked its magic. It was wonderful.

Violet realised it was time to start spoiling herself with little experiences like this. Not extravagant days at the spa but small things like making sure her toenails were always polished and that she was wearing make-up. Things to make her feel more feminine.

Back at the mirror, Sarah chatted to her as her scissors scythed their way through Violet's hair. She asked Violet about her weight loss and Violet was able to tell her that she was three and a half stone down with only one and a half to go.

'That's amazing,' said Sarah.

And it was, Violet told herself.

But not nearly as amazing as her reflection once

Sarah had wielded her magic scissors and hairdryer. Violet couldn't quite believe it was her.

She was no longer hidden behind a black curtain which made her cheeks seem huge. Her hair was now shoulder length, a simple but classic cut, which gave her hair more bounce than it had ever had. No longer dead straight, it fell softly with the odd small wave. The parting was just off centre with some strands falling over her forehead and down the side of her face.

She bought the smoothing cream that Sarah had used before blow drying her hair but Sarah had also assured her that the hair would look good even when it dried naturally.

Violet thanked her over and over again, still not quite believing the transformation. She paid at reception and then wandered out of the salon in a daze.

She walked down the high street, unable to prevent herself from staring at her reflection in every shop window. Was that slim, stylish woman really Violet?

She treated herself to a coffee, still glancing over at a nearby mirror to check her hair. It was fantastic. But her face needed something else. A little bit of fairy dust as well.

So Violet hit Boots and treated herself to some new make-up. One of the wedding magazines had recommended telling the ladies behind the beauty counter that she was a bride-to-be. As promised, they duly offered Violet a huge array of cosmetics to try, along with a few freebies. She stuck to neutral, classic colours that weren't too different from her skin colour. Just enough to highlight and enhance.

She was just walking out of the shop past the perfume counters when she inhaled a familiar smell.

She followed her nose and stared at the display in front of her. It was all the Ralph Lauren perfumes.

She sniffed the top of each bottle until she found the fragrance she was looking for. That was it. That was the perfume her mother must have worn. She glanced at the bottle. Romance was the name. She squirted a little on her wrist and sniffed. Yes, that was definitely the one.

Violet never wore perfume. Yet another piece of femininity that she appeared to have missed out on. But no longer. She squirted a little on her neck from the tester before buying a brand-new bottle.

Then she was on her way once more, weaving her way through the Saturday crowds and continuing to check out her new reflection as she went. By the time she got home it was tea time and Violet knew that Sebastian would be back from his day of golf.

'Hello!' she cried as she pushed open the front door.

Sebastian came out of the kitchen with a scowl on his face. 'Where have you been?'

'Hairdressers,' said Violet, flicking her head to and fro so he could see her new haircut. 'What do you think?'

His eyes popped wide open. 'What the hell have you done?'

'I got a haircut. Like it?'

Sebastian frowned. 'No.'

Violet's smile dropped. 'Really?'

He shrugged his shoulders. 'I liked it the way it was. Anyway, you didn't tell me you had an appointment this afternoon.'

'You were playing golf. What did it matter?'

'You weren't here when I got back.'

'So?'

He was whining like a child, thought Violet. Sometimes he was like a baby that needed constant attention.

Violet drew a deep breath. 'I thought it could do with a change. Anyway, I like it.'

'And that's all that matters, I suppose.'

'What's that supposed to mean?'

Sebastian crossed his arms in front of him. 'Well, it's all about you these days, isn't it? You and your weight loss. You and your new job, which is so great. You and your new friends.'

'You'd have preferred me to stay as I was?' snapped Violet. 'Miserable and fat?'

'At least I knew where I stood.'

'Yes and I knew exactly where I stood,' said Violet. 'At the bottom of the pile, as I recall.'

'What are you talking about?'

'It doesn't matter,' she added quickly. She didn't want to talk about the other woman now.

'I'm sorry if you feel that I'm focusing on myself at the minute but I'm trying to get a life for myself, to get some confidence. Don't you want that for me too?'

'I just want things back as they were.'

Tough, thought Violet, but managed to stop herself saying it just in time. Yet some truths still bubbled to the surface.

'And I'm sick of the fact that I get no support from you whatsoever,' she said. 'After all, I am your fiancée.'

'Then start acting like it,' he retorted. 'This is all to do with those fat freaks you're hanging round with, isn't it? They're putting poison in your head.'

Violet's voice remained calm even though she was simmering with anger. 'They're not freaks. They're my friends. I've never once moaned about your snooty mates who never speak to me, not that it seems to bother you.'

Sebastian went to snap back at her but she held up her hand to stop him.

'And just remember, Sebastian. I was a fat freak too.'

Then she went upstairs and slammed the bedroom door behind her.

Chapter Forty-six

Violet flung herself on her bed and cried until the tears would come no more. She had been so happy that afternoon but now it was all ruined. Her joy in her beautiful haircut, her buoyant mood. All gone. She had ruined it, as usual.

What was wrong with her? She had snapped at Sebastian, pushing him away. He was probably downstairs wondering how he could get the engagement ring back from her. It was the biggest row they had ever had. Why was he irritating her so much at the minute?

She suddenly sat bolt upright and got up, wiping the tears from her cheeks. She cracked open the bedroom door and listened. Her heart thumped loudly in her chest as she strained to hear any movement at all. It was worse than she had feared. He had left. And was probably never coming back.

Suddenly, she heard it. The faint hum of chatter on the television.

Violet crept downstairs and into the lounge. Sebastian was sprawled on the sofa with his feet up.

She cleared her throat to speak but he didn't look at her.

'I'm sorry,' she whispered, unable to find her full voice.

He slowly turned to look up at her as she stood next to him. 'Are you?'

'Yes,' she told him. 'I don't know what came over me.'

He finally turned down the volume on the television. 'I keep telling you. It's these women you're hanging around with. They're giving you ideas. Making you think differently.'

Violet didn't agree with him about that but she stayed quiet. She had already caused enough trouble that evening.

'Friends?' she asked with a tremulous smile.

He rose from the sofa to stand in front of her. 'I hope so,' he told her. 'Now, what about a diet-busting takeaway?'

She was so remorseful about upsetting him that she ate every portion of the Chinese he ordered for them. Later on, Sebastian made love to her. But Violet found it hard to relax after their row and Sebastian never lingered over the foreplay. So she faked an orgasm just so he would finish and go to sleep.

Violet was still feeling low on Monday morning when she walked into work. She had so nearly ruined it. Had so nearly lost him. She had to be more careful. She had to watch what she said. He was all she had, all she would ever have. And she didn't know what she would do without his love.

She flung her handbag under her desk and slumped into her chair, seemingly the first of the department to arrive.

'Hiya,' mumbled Anthony as he came in a few minutes later.

This was as much as anyone would get out of him until at least half past nine. He switched on his monitor and hugged a can of Red Bull close to his chest.

Wendy was next to arrive. 'Oh my God!' she screeched as she stared at Violet. 'Your hair's bloody gorgeous!'

Anthony clutched his head at the shrieking.

'What's all the noise about?' said Julie, taking off her scarf as she approached her desk.

'Look at Violet's hair!' said Wendy.

Julie nodded. 'Looks good, girl.'

Violet blushed at the fuss and wished the hotline would ring so she didn't have to cope with the attention. But, as luck would have it, the phone stayed quiet.

'Where did you have it done?' asked Wendy. 'You've had loads off.'

'Toni and Guy,' mumbled Violet.

She began to print out the report of hotline calls that Mark wanted each Monday morning. The printer sprang into life and she stood next to it whilst it spewed out her report. Then she walked into Mark's office.

As it was so quiet, she had assumed he wasn't in yet. But to her surprise, he was already there, typing on his keyboard.

He glanced up briefly as Violet entered his office and then did a double take. 'Wow,' he said, his eyes wide open. 'You look fantastic.'

Violet blushed and was grateful when she heard the hotline ring. 'The phone's ringing,' she mumbled.

'It's a call centre,' Mark told her. 'The phone's always ringing. Let someone else get it for once.'

Violet hopped from one foot to the other, mortified by the way he was staring at her.

'Smile, for God's sake, will you?' he told her. 'You look great.'

Their hands touched as she handed over the paperwork. Their eyes briefly met before she scuttled out of the office back to the safety of her phone.

The hotline kept her busy all that morning. Mark had been hovering quite a bit so she escaped out into the fresh air at lunchtime, grateful to escape. Her feet led her to the alleyway where Nonna's delicatessen was situated but she walked on. She couldn't face Nonna's friendly face today. She was afraid she would burst into tears.

Instead, she headed towards the Alzheimer's Society shop.

She pushed the door open and went in.

Kathy was on her knees, organising some shoes into their various sizes. She lifted her head to greet the new customer and her face spread into a massive smile.

'Blimey! Look at you!'

'Hi,' said Violet with a small smile.

'Maggie! Come here! Violet's gone all trendy on us!'

Maggie poked her head round the door to the back room and her mouth fell open.

'You look amazing!' she said, coming to stand next to Kathy.

'Toni and Guy?' asked Kathy, getting up.

Violet nodded.

Maggie fumbled in her pocket for her mobile phone. 'I must take a photo for Lucy.' She held up the phone in front of her. 'Give us a smile, then.'

But Violet's face disintegrated into tears. Kathy and Maggie looked at each other for a split second before coming to stand next to Violet and giving her a group hug.

'What's the matter?' asked Kathy.

'Is it Sebastian?' asked Maggie.

Violet nodded between sobs. 'Everything's wrong. He hates my hair. He hates my new look.'

Kathy gave Violet's shoulders a squeeze. 'But you look fantastic.'

'I think he hates me.'

'Of course he doesn't,' said Maggie in a firm tone. 'Besides, you're so much happier now.'

'I know,' said Violet, with a sniff. 'But I'm not really. It's all going wrong.'

'I'm sure it's pre-wedding jitters,' said Kathy. 'Every bride has a minor meltdown before the big day. And you've only a couple of months to go. It's not surprising.'

'She's right,' said Maggie. 'Try not to fret, love.'

Violet wiped her eyes and nodded. They were right. It was just the wedding getting to her.

'Anyway, you think you've got problems,' said Kathy, rolling her eyes. 'I've got this stupid fancy dress party at the weekend.'

'What party?' asked Violet, grateful for the change of subject.

'Edward's cricket club are having a party and he's asked Kathy to go with him,' Maggie told her.

'Just as friends,' added Kathy quickly.

Maggie nudged her in the ribs with her elbow. 'Yeah, right.' She looked at Violet. 'He was in here yesterday, putting the shelves up for us and where was Kathy? At home with some mystery ailment.'

'It was a twenty-four-hour thing' said Kathy. 'I don't know why you don't believe me.'

'What was it my daughter said?' said Maggie, screwing her face up in thought. 'I know! Kathy and Edward sitting in a tree, k-i-s-s-i-n-g.'

'Very funny,' muttered Kathy.

Violet stared at her. She'd been so wrapped up in her own life that she had no idea that Kathy had fallen so hard for Edward.

'My boss called Edward muscly and macho,' said Violet, remembering Edward in the nightclub.

'I'll say,' said Maggie. 'He's so toned and fit now. I don't know how any sane, single woman would be able to resist him.'

Kathy scowled at her. 'Anyway, nothing will happen,' she told them. 'There's no point me even going on Saturday night. He'll be flirting with that tarty barmaid.'

'What are you talking about?' said Maggie.

'Edward's not like that,' Violet told her.

Sebastian was, she thought, surprised at the notion that had popped into her head. But Edward wasn't.

'Humph,' muttered Kathy. 'Besides, what the hell am I going to wear?'

'Actually, Lucy gave me some great ideas about that,' said Maggie.

And then she burst into a wicked grin that made Kathy's knees quake.

Chapter Forty-seven

'I can't do this.'

Kathy turned to face Violet and Maggie, who were sitting on the bed. She had called them half an hour previously to seek reassurance. She wanted them to say that she didn't have to go to the party at the cricket club.

'Course you can,' said Maggie. 'You look great.'

'You're already a size fourteen,' said Violet. 'You look fantastic.'

Kathy turned back to her full-length mirror. She was wearing a short, black, flared dress, tights and high heels. Maggie had pinned a cape on to her dress and Violet was looking for a safety pin to fix on the batgirl logo.

Batgirl. Kathy sighed. Her superhero powers were obviously on the blink.

'I told you both that I wanted to go as Professor McGonagall,' she told them.

'Are you mad?' said Maggie. 'You do want him to fancy you, don't you?. At least this way you'll look sexy.'

'Plus it's the whole play on words thing,' said Violet. 'Batgirl, as in cricket bat. I think it's cute.'

'And your legs are to die for,' added Maggie.

Kathy stared down at them. She supposed she felt a little more confident now that she had lost over four stone. The high heels helped her legs look thinner as well. But she was showing a fair bit of cleavage and her hair had gone fluffy.

She sighed. 'Maybe I should ring Edward and tell him I'm sick.'

'You can't leave the poor guy to show up at a party on his own,' said Maggie. 'It's not fair.'

'Besides,' said Violet, peering out behind the curtain. 'He's here.'

'Oh God!' panicked Kathy. 'I'm not ready.'

'Yes, you are,' said Maggie. 'We'll let ourselves out. So, off you go. And smile! It's a party!'

Kathy took a deep breath but found it didn't calm her nerves at all as she headed down the stairs to meet Edward coming up. They both stared at each other's costumes before bursting into laughter.

'Hello, Batgirl,' said Edward.

'Hello, Batman,' said Kathy.

She was smiling but inwardly she gulped. He wasn't wearing the costume based on the Marvel Comics. This was modern Batman, sexy Batman. Batman in a rubber-looking suit that clung to his muscles. She had to clutch on to the banister to stop herself falling at his feet.

'To the Batmobile,' said Edward, heading down the front path.

Kathy could only stare at the brief glimpse of rubberised bottom as his cape flared behind him. She'd run away if her heels weren't so high.

They made small talk on the way to the cricket club, chatting about her week in the shop and his week at work. As he drove the car into the car park, Kathy spotted the clubhouse all lit up in fairy lights.

'How pretty,' she said.

'The committee kept talking about outdoing themselves this year.'

They got out of the car and walked towards the clubhouse. As they got closer, Kathy could see coloured tealights, which has been lit, as well as more twinkling fairy lights around the windows.

Edward held the door open for Kathy and she walked in. The lights were low enough for the candles to glow but not so low that she couldn't see everyone else's costumes. As they all came over to say hello, Kathy counted at least three witches, two sexy schoolgirls and two men dressed as nuns.

Everyone was very friendly towards Kathy as Edward introduced her. They were all oohing and aahing over their outfits.

'Great idea,' said the captain of the cricket team, who was dressed as Keith Richards.

'Nice for a couple to have his and hers outfits,' said his wife.

Kathy blushed. She and Edward weren't a couple. But he didn't correct them.

Edward asked her if she wanted a drink and they pushed their way through the crowds to get to the bar.

Unfortunately, Kathy's good mood began to disappear at that point. The flirty barmaid was once again stationed nearby and her eyes lit up when she spotted Edward.

'Nice outfit,' she cooed, reaching across the bar to

touch the rubber covering his chest. 'You've gone from chunk to hunk.'

'You're looking good too,' replied Edward with a grin.

And who could blame him for looking so happy, Kathy thought.

The barmaid was wearing a ye olde worlde wench costume which was very low cut at the front. And her boobs were pushed up so high she wouldn't need a pair of earmuffs if the weather turned cold.

'What's your pleasure?' she murmured, winking at him.

Kathy scowled at her as she ordered a gin and slimline. Edward treated himself to a pint of lager.

'My first pint in a long time,' he told Kathy,

As soon as he had handed over his money, Kathy headed away from the bar, desperate to put as much distance between her and the busty barmaid as possible.

The disco had just begun and a few sober souls had started to dance. But at least the music was loud enough that any long minutes of silence were drowned out by the beat.

'You OK?' asked Edward.

'Fine,' said Kathy, taking a big gulp of drink.

'It should be a good night,' he said.

Lord, I hope so, thought Kathy.

'Hungry?'

Kathy nodded so they made their way over to the buffet table. The food was a dieter's nightmare, with most things either encased in pastry or deep fried. But it wouldn't do any harm for one night. Besides, she was past caring. And if she had another of these strong gins, she'd be past feeling her legs as well.

The evening passed slowly. Conversation was a bit

stilted between Kathy and Edward; the easy bonhomie of the early days seemed to have vanished. But between sips of drink and scoffing sausage rolls, there was some dancing as well.

Edward was certainly the life and soul of the party, thought Kathy, as she watched him dance and sing. A very popular member of the team.

Late in the evening, the singing got louder as the drinks continued to flow. Kathy excused herself and headed for the bar with the intention of getting a soft drink. The barmaid was flirting with someone who, for once, wasn't Edward.

Kathy tried hard to get her attention so she could order a drink but the woman was too busy pressing her cleavage together and laughing at some inane joke.

Kathy rolled her eyes and went to turn away but found her route blocked by a man slumped on a stool. It was one of the second eleven team who had obviously hit the beer early as he was now absolutely plastered – and into full drunken sleaze mode.

'Are you Supergirl?' he slurred.

Kathy gave him a small smile and went to sidestep him but he stuck his leg out to prevent her from going.

'So you're the one responsible for getting Ed from lard arse to fit, are you?'

'No,' said Kathy. 'He lost the weight all by himself.'

'I don't blame him,' slurred the man. 'I'd want to look my best if I was with a gorgeous girl like you.'

Kathy gave him a lukewarm smile and looked for an escape route.

'Why don't you give Ed the heave-ho?' he said, suddenly grabbing her around the waist. 'I can tell what you need, cutie.'

'Yes. I need you to piss off,' muttered Kathy, prising off his hand and trying to pull away.

But he was too quick for her and held on tight. Because he was sitting on the stool, his face was very close to Kathy's formidable chest.

'Give us a feel,' he slurred, drawing his face ever closer to her bust.

Suddenly Kathy was free from his sweaty hands and the drunk was lying on the floor with Edward towering over him, his hands clenched into fists.

'You touch her again and I'll be using your balls for batting practice, all right?'

The man scampered away on his hands and knees whilst Edward turned to face Kathy.

'Are you OK? Did he hurt you?'

She shook her head. 'I'm fine.'

'We should have thrown him off the bloody team ages ago,' he snarled, still angry.

Before she could say anything, they were joined by a few of Edward's teammates and wives who all introduced themselves to Kathy and seemed very friendly.

'That Chris is such a lech,' said one of the guys. 'About time someone floored him.'

'And the wife's no better,' said one of the women to Kathy. 'Have you seen her?' She nodded at the busty barmaid.

'She came dressed as a tart tonight,' said someone else. 'Not much of a disguise.'

'She's such a flirt,' said Edward. 'I'm glad she's not my missus.'

Kathy's mind was reeling. Was it possible that she'd been wrong?

Before she had a chance to think, one of the men turned to talk to her.

'It's a good turnout,' he said, with a friendly smile. 'We should raise a lot of money tonight.'

'What's the money going towards?' she asked, thinking it would be new stumps or something similar.

'The Alzheimer's Society,' replied the man.

Kathy turned to him, her mouth dropping.

'Your fella's idea,' he told her. 'Wouldn't take any other suggestions.'

He was about to say something else but 'Rockstar' came on to the speakers and the team hit the dance floor to act out their Nickelback fantasies.

Edward came to stand next to Kathy. 'For the team, it's a night out,' he said into her ear. 'For their carers, it's a night off.' He pointed to where the air guitar solos were in full swing and grinned at his own joke.

But Kathy's mind was elsewhere. 'The money tonight is being raised for the Alzheimer's Society?' she asked him.

He shrugged his shoulders. 'It seemed important to you.'

Kathy's eyes pricked with tears as she stared up into his friendly brown eyes.

'And what's important to you,' he told her, 'is important to me.'

The way Edward was looking at her was making her pulse race.

She was still staring up at him when suddenly everything around them fell black and silent. The music stopped and only the glow of the candles filled the room.

'Power cut,' said someone close by.

'I bet those dodgy disco lights have blown a fuse,' said someone else.

'Stay here,' Edward told Kathy before disappearing into the darkness.

A few people were staggering about drunkenly in the semi-darkness so she flattened herself against the wall out of the way.

It seemed an awful long time before Edward reappeared in front of her.

'Can't see what we're doing to fix it,' he told her. 'The party's over. Shall we go? Thankfully I'm not on the clearing-up committee.'

He put his hand in the middle of her back to steer her in the direction of the door. The cool night air washed over them and Kathy shivered a little.

'There's a taxi rank round the corner,' said Edward. 'We can get a lift from there.'

I'll have frostbite by then, thought Kathy. But it was quite nice walking along in the moonlight, despite the cold.

They were halfway around the cricket field when the clubhouse behind them suddenly sprang into life. Music thumped out and the lights were back on inside.

'They must have fixed it,' said Kathy, stopping to look. 'Did you want to go back?'

Edward shook his head as he looked down at her. 'No. It's actually quite nice to get you on your own for once. There always seems to be someone around these days. Maggie, Violet or the whole of the bloomin' cricket team. It's good to have you all to myself.'

The music in the clubhouse changed from a frantic beat to 'The Power of Love' by Frankie Goes to Hollywood. It was a perfect song for a chilly, moonlit night and there was nobody around. Just Kathy and Edward.

Kathy clutched her cloak around her, causing Edward to frown.

'Are you cold? Sorry, I didn't think.'

'I'm fine,' she told him, her teeth chattering as she spoke.

'Come here,' he said softly, drawing her close to him.

Edward grabbed the sides of his cloak and wrapped them around her, his arms encircling her. But he didn't let go, didn't release her. They were standing close to each other, so close that Kathy could smell his woody-scented aftershave.

Her heart hammering, Kathy forced herself to look up at Edward. He was staring down at her, a soft smile playing on his lips.

'I think I got it all wrong,' she told him. 'I got so muddled.'

'You should have remembered what I once told you,' he said, his arms pulling her even closer. 'Once I set my mind on something, I never waver. I always get what I want.'

'And what do you want?' asked Kathy, now a little breathless.

Edward bent his head down to meet hers, their lips tantalisingly close.

'You,' he said.

Then he kissed her, on and on, until her doubts finally disappeared.

Chapter Forty-eight

Kathy woke up on Sunday morning with a start.

Various snapshots of the evening came flooding into her mind. Edward kissing her in the moonlight. A taxi ride of which she didn't remember very much. Kissing Edward on every step leading up to her flat. Edward peeling his Batman suit off.

Kathy sat bolt upright and stared down at the empty space next to her in the bed. Had he crept off ashamed at having spent the night with her? Was he now bitterly regretting sleeping with her and thinking up excuses never to see her again?

'Good morning,' said Edward from the doorway.

He had a towel wrapped around his waist.

'Hello,' said Kathy, drawing the duvet up to cover her naked body.

'Hope you don't mind but I just grabbed a quick shower. I smelt of that damn rubber suit and wanted to get clean. By the way, is there something you want to confess to me?' he asked with a smirk.

Kathy blushed. She hadn't faked any of her orgasms

361

if that's what he was getting at. Edward drew out a packet of Rolos from behind the door.

Kathy sighed in relief. 'Oh, that! Well, the chocolates are only small.'

Edward handed the tube of chocolates to Kathy who ripped open the packet. She offered him the first one but Edward shook his head.

'That's not what I'm craving this morning,' he said in a husky voice.

He let the towel drop on the floor and suddenly Kathy lost all interest in the chocolate.

Maggie was cooking a healthy breakfast of dry-fried eggs and grilled bacon without the rind when Gordon came into the kitchen.

'Smells good,' he said, giving her bottom a quick squeeze.

'Cheeky,' said Maggie, but she was smiling.

'What are we up to next weekend? We've no plans, have we?'

'Not that I know of,' Maggie told him, flipping the eggs on to the plates.

'Good.'

Maggie suddenly realised he was grinning at her. 'What?'

Please Lord, not his mother coming to stay.

'I'm taking you to Blackpool. There's a special dance on. Thought we could trip the light fantastic in the Empress Ballroom.'

Maggie stared at him in amazement. 'You mean it?' she finally managed to blurt out.

'Of course,' he said, taking her in his arms. 'We'd planned to go, hadn't we? All those years ago. But Lucy came along and that was that.'

Maggie threw her arms around him. 'I can't believe it.'

'You'd better start thinking about what to wear,' said Gordon, pinching her bottom.

Maggie bit her lip. She'd have to start going through her clothes after breakfast. And then go shopping after that, probably.

'Come on,' said Gordon. 'Breakfast is getting cold.'

He added the bacon to their plates and took them over to the small table.

Maggie brought over their mugs of tea and sat down. She was just reaching for the ketchup when she spotted her passport propped up against the salt and pepper.

'What's that doing out of the safe?'

Gordon shrugged his shoulders. 'Thought you might need it.'

'For what? Blackpool?' she giggled.

'Well, you know how strict those American customs chaps are these days.'

Maggie blinked at him. 'American who?'

He reached out and took her hand. 'I thought that if we didn't disgrace ourselves in Blackpool that I should take you to New York.'

'New York!' said Maggie, her voice several octaves higher than normal.

'There's a ballroom just off Broadway where I can show you off to those American fellas. Show them what they're missing.'

Maggie's mouth opened and closed but her brain had shut down.

'I thought we could fly out on the twenty-seventh of this month. Christmas will be over and we can be back in time for Violet's wedding on the thirty-first.

What do you think? We could even try a bit of ice skating in Central Park.'

Maggie finally came back to life. 'I'm wondering who are you and what have you done with my husband?'

Gordon nodded and smiled at her. 'Does that mean you're not against the idea?'

Maggie leapt up and rushed around the table to cover her husband's face in kisses. Gordon grabbed her around the waist and sat her down on his knee, despite her protestations.

'You're as light as a feather these days,' he told her.

'I don't believe it,' she said. 'When did you plan all this?'

'It's been on my mind for a while. The mortgage is nearly paid off and we've scrimped and saved for so long. Besides, I want to have some fun with you before I collect my pension and Zimmer frame.'

Maggie took her husband's face in her hands. 'I love you,' she told him.

'I love you too,' he said, giving her a peck on the lips. 'Now, let me have my breakfast, otherwise I won't take you to Tiffany's.'

Maggie ate her eggs and bacon with a huge smile on her face that morning.

Lucy stopped and drew a deep breath.

'I can't make it,' she said.

Todd held out his hand. 'Come on,' he said. 'You know it's worth it.'

It was the same every Sunday morning. She would be fine going across the flat expanse of Regent's Park but by the time she got halfway up Primrose Hill, she was exhausted.

'I can see Kate Moss,' said Todd, dragging her up the last steep bit of the hill.

'Liar,' she told him, but his words did cause her to speed up a little.

Then they were at the top and, as usual, 'their' bench was free. Lucy sank on to it, grateful for the seat and looked at the view.

'It's always worth it,' said Todd.

And he was right. It was one of the best views in London, from looking down on to London Zoo in Regent's Park and then further out to Canary Wharf, the London Eye and the Post Office Tower.

'You're a hard taskmaster,' she told him, pulling her coat around her.

Lucy couldn't believe it was winter already. Where had the year gone? One minute she had been fat, unhappy and lonely. Now she was slim, happy and having the time of her life in the greatest city in the world. University was incredible and her designs were flowing thick and fast.

And she had made some great new friends. Including Todd. He was only a friend, she knew that much. He had dropped her hand once he had finished dragging her up to the top of the hill. There had been no kisses, no moves made.

But she was sure going to miss him when he went back to Canada for Christmas.

Edward had finally managed to take his hands off Kathy for long enough for them head out for a Sunday roast at the local pub.

'I'm famished,' said Kathy, attacking her roast beef with gusto.

'Must be all the exercise,' he told her with a wide grin.

Edward watched her cheeks redden but she was smiling. She was beautiful when she smiled. He knew this was it for him. He couldn't love anybody else as much as Kathy. The past twenty-four hours had been a revelation and he was hooked for life. People said food was an addiction but as far as he was concerned, Kathy was his drug of choice from now onwards.

'No pudding though,' Kathy said.

'Nope. We've only got a stone and a bit to go.'

'I want to look good for Violet's wedding.'

He put down his knife and reached out for her hand across the table. 'You always look good,' he told her.

She smiled back at him and he knew she had been worth waiting for.

Kathy was a class act. And he was determined to ensure that she knew it too.

Chapter Forty-nine

'War is over,' sang John Lennon over the shop speakers. Not in December it's not, thought Violet as she got bumped and shoved from all directions. The shops were packed with workers desperately trying to get their Christmas shopping done in their lunch hours.

It was a hideous time of year to try to organise a wedding. Sebastian's mother had suddenly become overwrought with the wedding plans and had decided to hand over the organisation to Violet.

'After all, dear,' she had said at the weekend, 'it is your wedding.'

Nice of you to remember, Violet had been close to saying. But she hadn't. She'd kept quiet, becoming ever more cross with herself.

Now she had some huge wedding extravaganza to co-ordinate, as well as the normal Christmas mayhem. She was becoming increasingly snappy, especially with Sebastian who wasn't putting in any effort to either Christmas or the wedding.

'What have you thought to buy my parents for Christmas?' he had asked that morning.

'No idea,' she had replied, slipping on her new winter coat.

'You'll have to get a move on. Time's running out.'

'Well, here's a plan,' she had snapped back. 'Why don't you think of something and buy it yourself? You're quite capable. Besides, I've got far too much to do. Unless you want to make two hundred sodding wedding favours instead?'

He had marched out of the front door, slamming it behind him. Violet knew she would have to apologise later but it would have been nice for him to make a bit of an effort for once.

On top of everything, they appeared to have invited most of Sebastian's family for Christmas dinner and, to add insult to injury, Sebastian had banged on about the Christmas cake and how she'd left it too late. But Violet wasn't planning on baking a heavy fruit cake. She didn't like it and why should she have to make something she wasn't even going to eat?

She made her way out of the crowded shop and found the pavements equally packed. Needing refuge, she made her way up the small alleyway to Gino's delicatessen. But the queue was snaking out of the shop and down the street. Violet decided to head back there after work.

Back at her desk, she found Wendy was also having a nervous breakdown over Christmas.

'I can't believe Steven thought it was a good idea to have his whole family over,' she ranted. 'Doesn't he remember that we have a baby and a toddler to try and take care of?'

'Three wise men,' grunted Julie. 'Hard pushed to find one.'

Violet found herself nodding in agreement.

At five o'clock, Violet put on her coat and was set to go.

'Hot date?' asked Mark, coming out of his office. He was wearing his coat as well. 'I'll walk out with you.'

Violet picked up her lunchtime purchases and walked to the lift with him.

'Christmas presents?' he asked, nodding at the bags.

Violet nodded.

'It's a mad time of year. What are you hoping Father Christmas brings you this year?'

Violet didn't know what to say. She never got what she wanted so she never bothered asking for anything.

Seeing her face, Mark quickly added, 'Not that I'd want him in my house. He sees you when you're sleeping. He knows when you're awake. Sounds like a stalker to me.'

Violet smiled as the lift doors pinged open. They walked through the reception, said their goodnights and then headed exactly the same way.

'Perhaps you're the stalker,' said Mark, raising his eyebrows at her.

Violet shook her head. 'I just need to get one last thing in town.'

'Where are you headed?'

She blushed. 'The delicatessen.'

'Me too,' he told her. 'We can walk together.'

Violet's face turned an even deeper shade of red.

'But you won't find it open,' he added. 'It's the eighth of December so it's early closing.'

Violet frowned. Was it someone's birthday?

'The Day of the Immacolata,' Mark told her. 'It's the day when Italians put up their Christmas trees and then go to a nativity service in church.'

Violet stopped walking. 'I can always pop back tomorrow.'

Mark took her elbow and steered her forward once more. 'Nonna will kill me if you don't come. It'll be my chestnuts roasting on an open fire if she gets wind of it.'

Violet giggled and they walked on towards the delicatessen.

'You should laugh more,' he told her. 'It's a nice sound.'

Violet immediately stopped. Luckily they were at the alleyway. She took a deep intake of breath. The shop was now lit up with cream fairy lights, making it appear magical.

'How lovely,' said Violet as Mark pushed the door open.

'*Buonasera*!' he called as he went in.

The shop appeared to be full of customers. But Mark told her that everyone inside was family or friends.

Violet was quickly met by Nonna who had pushed through the crowd upon seeing them.

'*Buonasera*, Viola,' she said, kissing her on both cheeks.

Nonna had begun to say her name in Italian. She secretly quite liked it.

'*Buonasera*,' replied Violet.

Nonna turned to the crowd and called out Violet's name and everyone greeted her in Italian. Then they went back to their conversations, of which Violet hoped she wasn't the topic.

Nonna rattled off a couple of quick sentences which Violet didn't quite catch.

Mark translated. 'She says she's glad you came to help with *il ceppo*. Looks like you're helping with the tree,' he told her. 'I'd better take your coat.'

So Violet shrugged off her winter coat and went to help Nonna. It turned out *il ceppo* was the 'tree of light' that Italians put up in their homes at Christmas. It was a wooden frame several feet high, designed in a pyramid shape. On each shelf, Violet helped Nonna to place some gilt pine cones, small decorations, sweets and candles.

But one shelf remained empty.

'*Il presepe*,' Nonna told her, before disappearing into the back room.

She returned with a beautiful nativity scene in her hands. All the children oohed and aahed.

'That's been in my family for generations,' Mark told Violet.

'It's lovely,' said Violet as they watched Nonna carefully place it on the shelf.

Mark handed over a packet of candles to Violet. 'As guest of honour, you can light the candles on *il ceppo*.'

So Violet found herself striking a match and carefully lighting each of the many candles on the shelves. She stood back to look at the pretty scene.

'*Bello*,' she told Nonna who had come to stand next to her. Beautiful, she had told her.

'*Va bene*,' Nonna replied, patting her on the arm. 'Prosecco, Marco!'

'*Sì*,' said Mark, and went off to find a bottle.

They spent the next few hours sipping their wine and chatting. Or in Violet's case, listening and watching. There were whole generations sitting around, the noise

371

of their chatter and laughter filling the store. It was a lovely, bubbly sound. A happy sound.

Eventually, and with a heavy heart, Violet knew she had to leave. But before she left, Nonna presented her with a panettone cake, beautifully wrapped in silver paper with a gorgeous red velvet ribbon.

It was exactly what Violet had wanted to purchase at lunchtime: a dome-shaped dessert bread laced with candied fruits and raisins. It was just what she wanted to replace the heavy Christmas cake with. But this was a gift and no money was to be exchanged, she realised.

'*Buonanotte*, Viola,' said Nonna, before giving her a hug.

'*Buonanotte*,' replied Violet, suddenly finding a lump in her throat.

Mark had offered to walk her back to her car. Violet didn't think it necessary but Mark and Nonna were very persuasive.

'Are you OK?' asked Mark.

A small tear ran down Violet's cheek. 'Sorry,' she muttered. 'You must think I'm an idiot. It's just been a really long time since I've felt part of a big family occasion like that. Thanks for taking me.'

'You're welcome. Haven't you got any family?'

'My parents died when I was twelve,' she told him. 'It's been pretty lonely since.'

'What about your fiancé's family?'

Violet pulled a face before she could stop herself.

Mark gave a short laugh.

They carried on walking in a comfortable silence for a while before he spoke.

'They're talking about snow over Christmas,' he said. 'Perhaps you'll have a white wedding.'

Violet didn't reply.

'Are you happy, Violet?' he suddenly asked.

'Why does it matter to you?' she found herself replying, testing him.

'I'm your boss,' he said with a shrug of his shoulders.

'Don't worry,' she snapped back. 'I'll always be here to answer your precious hotline.'

And she ran away into the darkness, leaving him far behind.

Chapter Fifty

'I can't believe it's the last weigh-in before Christmas,' said Kathy, glancing over at Trudie before breaking into a wicked smile.

As usual, it wasn't returned.

'I just wish it was the last time we were going to see her this year,' said Edward, following her gaze.

'Violet had to invite her to the wedding,' said Maggie, whispering to them both.

'She wasn't given much choice,' said Kathy. 'Trudie pretty much invited herself along.'

'At least she's not coming to the hen night,' said Maggie, grinning.

They all looked across at Violet, who was attempting a smile that nobody believed.

'Lucy's coming home on Friday,' said Maggie. 'Said she can't wait for the girls' night out. And she'll see you at the wedding,' she added to Edward.

'Any mention of the boyfriend?' asked Kathy.

'Only to say that he was flying home to Canada on Thursday evening.'

'Do you think she'll be upset?' asked Edward.

'She says not but I don't believe a word of it,' said Maggie. 'But she's keeping busy.'

In particular, Lucy was busy converting Maggie's favourite red dancing dress into a skirt. Maggie had finally admitted that she wouldn't be able to fit into it. Her body had changed with the years and childbirth. That much she couldn't do anything about. But she had a lovely red camisole top to go with her adapted skirt. Lucy had added a new waistband and Maggie had tried it on and spun round and round, the skirt glittering in the winter sunlight. She couldn't wait to surprise Gordon with it in New York.

'Talking of flying, at least I'll be able to fit into an airplane seat now.'

Maggie beamed at them. She was running every day before work, rediscovering her marriage, her hipbones and her husband.

'You're doing great,' said Edward.

'So are you,' Kathy told him, squeezing his arm.

Edward had visited the doctor that week for a check-up on his angina. The doctor had been amazed at his rapid weight loss and had announced him fully fit. No more beta-blockers for his heart. His cholesterol and blood-pressure levels were now perfect for his age. Edward certainly felt great, especially as he was spending nearly all his time with the beautiful woman who was next to him.

'And I'm only eleven stone now,' said Kathy, also grinning. 'Hopefully with a pound or two off tonight.'

'My clever girl,' said Edward, his voice soft with love.

'I've joined his gym,' she told Maggie.

Kathy preferred the swimming pool to the gym

equipment but they had already had a ferocious game of badminton.

'That's great,' said Maggie.

Violet, she presumed, must have also guessed about Kathy and Edward. She glanced across but Violet seemed to have retreated back into her shell.

'We got a lovely Christmas tree from that garden centre at the bottom of my road,' said Kathy.

Maggie noted how quickly Kathy had become a 'we'. They certainly looked very happy.

'One of those non-drop ones.'

'I told her, I don't think they exist,' said Edward with a smile.

Apart from Edward, their Christmas tree was Kathy's favourite thing at the minute. Each night after dinner, they would snuggle up, looking at the lights and candles twinkling. She was so happy she thought she would self-combust.

All year she had been dreading the first Christmas without her mum. But Edward had suggested paying the grave a visit on Christmas Eve, which was a nice idea. They were going to his mum's on Christmas Day for a big family get-together which Kathy was a little nervous about, but Edward kept reassuring her it would be fine. And she felt that, with him beside her, she could do anything.

'Shall we get on with it?' snapped Trudie from the far corner of the hall. She seemed even more scary than usual.

Violet sighed and stood up, wanting to get the weigh-in over with. The others watched as she stood up on the scales and then off again, once it had regis-tered the weight.

'Ten stone exactly,' said Trudie, staring at her.

The others looked at each other before leaping up and running over to Violet.

'That's your goal weight,' said Kathy.

'You've done it,' said Maggie, giving Violet a big hug.

'Well done,' said Edward. 'How does it feel?'

Violet smiled, though Kathy noticed it didn't reach her eyes.

'Never thought I'd do it, to be honest,' she told them.

'You were always going to make it,' said Maggie. 'You've been so dedicated. I bet it's been great to have the wedding as a big goal to aim for.'

Violet nodded. 'I suppose.'

'But you'll keep your weight down after the wedding, won't you?' asked Kathy, suddenly nervous that they might all put the weight back on.

'Oh yes,' said Violet. 'I won't go back to comfort eating.'

'And it's all thanks to New You!' said Trudie.

They others glanced at each other but didn't reply.

Later on, as Violet drove home, she thought that she had never felt so unhappy. Everything in her life felt wrong.

She wished she'd never lost any weight at all.

Chapter Fifty-one

'You look great!' said Maggie, as Violet opened the front door to the girls on Saturday night.

'Thanks,' she told them and stepped out, closing the door behind her.

Violet had been unsure what to wear for her own hen night so had eventually settled for a pale pink, lace-trimmed camisole, black short skirt and killer heels.

It was quite a radical look for her but Sebastian wouldn't see it, as he had headed to Amsterdam early on Friday morning for his stag night. He would be back on Sunday lunchtime, hungover but hopefully not missing any eyebrows.

'Sexy lady,' cooed Lucy as they all got into the taxi.

Lucy was trying to mask how much she was really missing Todd. Should she text him? Or would that seem too desperate when he had only left the previous day?

Violet tugged down the skirt as she sat down, wishing she had worn a pair of safe black trousers.

'I can't believe you've got to goal and I missed it,' carried on Lucy.

Violet nodded and smiled. She really ought to have made an effort to try and enjoy herself, but being the centre of attention had never been her ideal scenario. At least the girls seemed to have avoided the normal hen night trappings, for which she was grateful. Everyone was dressed for a night out on the town, nothing tacky at all.

They got out of the taxi, which had pulled up outside of a busy restaurant in town. The place had been booked by Julie and Wendy, who were meeting them there with a few other girls who were just along for the ride.

It was an Italian restaurant that served great pizzas and pastas relatively cheaply. Violet sighed as she realised that was where they were going. Why did everything seem to come back to Italy?

Maggie told the waiter Violet's name and they were led to the back of the restaurant where a long table had been set up with balloons.

'Hello!' cried Wendy, sitting next to Julie.

They were both wearing pink cowboy hats. Every spare setting at the table was also festooned with a pink hat.

'Excellent,' said Lucy, grabbing a hat.

She shrugged off her black aviator jacket to reveal a white vest, to which she had added some black sequins, and skinny black trousers. She put on her hat and grinned. Lucy looked young, funky and radiant.

Maggie and Kathy exchanged a grimace but said nothing as they sat down at the table and put on their hats. They also silently noted the confetti made of hundreds of silver, sparkly willies that was scattered

379

across the table. Plus the willy straws that were placed next to the wine glasses. So much for being a tackiness-free zone that evening.

Violet had been told to sit at the head of the table. She didn't have a hat in front of her. Instead were a pair of bright pink 'bride-to-be' boppers, trimmed with feathers and diamanté jewels.

'Wait!' cried Wendy, grabbing the headband and flicking a small switch underneath.

The words 'bride-to-be' were now flashing on and off.

'Excellent!' cried Wendy as she plonked it on to Violet's head.

But that wasn't all. There was a matching pink sash, also with flashing lights spelling 'bride-to-be'. Plus a pair of flashing pink angel wings. And a fluffy pink L-plate. Violet knew even she couldn't hide in a dark corner in that outfit. She smiled but wished she were at home.

Everyone ordered their food and then Julie and Wendy began to ask everyone about their weight losses.

'I lost three stone,' Lucy told them. 'Wish I'd done it ages ago.'

'Me too,' said Kathy. 'It's like I've emerged from a dense fog. I bounce around with an energy that I never knew I could have.'

'That could also be down to having found yourself a hunky boyfriend,' Maggie told her, nudging her in the side.

'Oooh!' said Wendy in a loud voice. She had obviously begun hitting the wine early. 'Hunky boyfriend?'

'He was actually one of our weight-loss group,' said

Maggie, smirking at Kathy. 'He's called Edward and he's lovely.'

'He is,' said Lucy, nodding.

'As for me,' said Maggie. 'I wish I'd lost weight years ago too.'

'If only for the sex life, eh?' said Kathy, nudging Maggie in the side.

'No!' screamed Lucy, covering her ears. 'Not my mum and dad!'

Everyone giggled.

'So do you just eat rabbit food?' asked Julie.

'No,' said Kathy. 'It's changing the way I think about food. Every now and then I'll cook steak and chips. But the steak will be grilled and the chips are healthy too. But I always eat well the next day if I have pigged out.'

'Bet you would kill for a McDonald's though.'

'I'm not sure I could eat too much greasy stuff these days,' said Kathy. 'I don't think my stomach could take it.'

Violet watched and listened, enjoying hearing the group sounding so positive.

Wendy drained her glass of wine and reached for the bottle. 'You should start your own weight-loss club,' she said to Violet.

'Humph,' snorted Julie. 'Mark would never let her go. He thinks she's the best thing since sliced bread.'

Maggie took a sip of wine. 'Is that the hunky Italian I saw the other week?'

Wendy nodded as she sloshed the wine into her glass.

'Don't know about hunky,' muttered Julie, her eyes lighting up on the chunky, muscly waiter who was handing out plates of pizza. 'Bit too scrawny for my liking.'

Kathy glanced across at Violet, who was shuffling in her seat, looking uncomfortable. 'How many people work in your office?' she asked.

'About half of them,' replied Julie, deadpan.

Wendy snorted with laughter and took another glug of wine. They all took a mouthful of wine as well, if only to try and keep up with Wendy.

Once the pizzas and desserts had been eaten, Julie brought out a small board game that she had ordered over the internet.

'Truth or Dare,' she told everyone as another two empty bottles of wine were replaced with full ones.

'What's that?' asked Kathy.

'You have to answer the question truthfully or you perform a dare of our choosing.'

'Excellent,' slurred Wendy, who was now feeling no pain. 'Me first.'

Wendy spun the arrow on the wheel in the centre of the board and read out the question it pointed to. 'Have you ever had sex in a theme park?' She burst out giggling.

'Well?' asked Julie.

Everyone leaned forward in their seats. They couldn't help it.

Wendy nodded as she carried on giggling.

'Oh my God!' cried Julie. 'Which one?'

'Disneyland Paris,' sobbed Wendy, now crying with laughter.

'Where?' asked Lucy, her eyes wide.

'Late at night on It's a Small World,' Wendy told them. 'They've banned us from ever going back.'

Everyone was feeling a bit giggly by now. Except Violet, who was dreading any questions.

'My turn,' said Lucy, spinning the dial.

'Have you ever been in love?' read Julie, before looking at Lucy. 'Well?'

Lucy shook her head. 'Nope. Next!'

Maggie and Kathy exchanged a look. Lucy's voice had gone far higher than normal.

Kathy spun the dial. 'Have you ever been unfaithful? No, not me. Some of the lowlifes I've been stuck with over the years but not me. I wouldn't sink that low.' She looked at Violet. 'Your turn.'

Violet flicked the arrow with her finger and watched it spin before stopping at a question.

'Have you ever thought of someone else whilst having sex?' read Julie. 'Probably not, eh?'

Tears pricked Violet's eyes as she shook her head. As Julie begun to spin the wheel, Violet excused herself and went to the ladies'.

She stood in front of the mirror for a long while, watching her accessories blink on and off. Deep in thought, she didn't hear Maggie come in.

'You all right, love?' asked Maggie, coming to stand next to her.

Violet nodded and tried to smile. But it all went wrong and she found herself crying. Maggie swept her into a hug.

'It's the boss, isn't it? Your Italian?'

Violet's sobs began to subside. 'Sorry,' she muttered, wiping the mascara away from under her eyes.

'Nothing to apologise for,' Maggie told her. 'You're in love with this guy, aren't you?'

'I don't know,' sighed Violet. 'He seems to have got under my skin and I can't stop thinking about him.'

Maggie looked at her. 'What about Sebastian? Are you sure he makes you happy? Because I've never seen such an unhappy bride.'

Why did everyone keep saying that? Violet wondered.

'You don't understand,' Violet told her. 'I'm not brave like everyone else. I do the right thing. I keep the peace. It's easier that way, to keep quiet.'

'But what about following your heart?'

'I do love Sebastian,' said Violet.

'Even though he cheated on you?'

Violet nodded. 'That's over now. We'll get married and everything will be OK.'

'Marriage is a two-way street,' Maggie told her. 'There's got to be give and take from both of you. You've got to be equal partners otherwise you'll always be unhappy.'

Violet attempted a smile and grabbed some tissue paper to sort out her mascara.

'I'll be down in a minute,' she told Maggie. 'I just need to sort my face out.'

'Everything all right?' Kathy whispered as Maggie sat back down.

'Not really,' she replied, before looking down the table to where Wendy was swaying in her chair to the background music. 'But I think there's a way it might be.'

Chapter Fifty-two

The girls made their slow journey to the nightclub. The lack of pace was to allow for their high heels and because Wendy could barely walk now that the fresh air had hit home.

'Hello,' she beamed drunkenly at a group of men, peering at the one closest to her.

'Come on,' said Julie, dragging her away. 'Before you're sick and we have to take you home. I want to get a few dances in yet.'

'Thanks for the phone,' said Maggie, giving the phone back to Wendy.

Wendy beamed at Maggie as if she wasn't really taking in what she was saying. So Maggie opened Wendy's bag and put the mobile back in herself.

'What did you need it for?' asked Lucy, with a frown.

'Had to ring your father and I've got no credit,' replied Maggie, keeping her voice casual.

Lucy frowned, wondering why her mother hadn't borrowed her phone.

Violet followed the group, going wherever she was

told to. As per usual, she realised. A fine drizzle began to fall as they reached the nightclub.

They bought more drinks when they got inside and then began to dance. There were two other hen parties already fighting for space on the dance floor but Julie was having none of it and elbowed them all out of the way for Violet and her friends.

The beat thumped around her but Violet was going through the motions, bopping this way and that. She was on cruise control. She hadn't even noticed the compliments and wolf whistles from a group of men as she walked past.

On and on she danced, following the music and letting her mind rest. She was exhausted. She didn't think she'd ever been so tired.

Violet glanced at the other hen parties while she danced. The other brides-to-be were wearing their sashes were grinning and laughing. This was how she was supposed to be feeling that night. Excited and happy.

Her eyes drifted beyond the dance floor to the crowds behind and that was when she saw him, pushing his way through the crowd. She blinked and peered into the darkness, beyond the flashing lights. It was definitely him. It was Mark.

Violet stopped dancing and walked towards him, her eyes held by his. His gaze drew her in until she was standing in front of him.

'What are you doing here?' she said, her voice loud over the music.

He glanced around him. The place was packed and noisy. He gestured with his head to follow him.

Maggie watched Violet disappear into the crowd after Mark.

'Where's she going?' shouted Kathy, also watching.

Maggie smiled. 'She'll be fine.'

The cold air hit Violet as she followed Mark outside. It was still raining.

'How did you know where I was?' she asked as he went past the smokers huddled in the doorway and further down the dark road.

Mark finally stopped walking and spun round to face her.

'You're showing up on the National Grid,' he told her in a wry tone. But his face remained serious.

Violet gave him a small smile. 'I suppose I am a bit bright,' she said, glancing down. Her boppers, sash and angel wings were blinking away in the darkness.

'Why are you here?' she asked him.

He took a deep breath. 'I want you to tell me about Easter.'

'About what?' Perhaps she was more drunk than she had realised.

'I mean, what happened with the cake?' he said gently. 'The one you stole from my hands.'

Violet was amazed. 'Now? But that was a lifetime ago.'

He stayed silent, his green eyes fixed on hers. Watching, waiting. Violet knew he was stubborn enough not to take no for an answer.

'I was upset,' she told him, shrugging her shoulders. 'It used to be my crutch for everything, that chocolate cake.'

'And now?'

'I don't rely on food whenever anything bad happens.'

'What was so bad about that day?'

Violet gulped. 'It's not important.'

'Tell me.' His voice was fierce and low.

But Violet couldn't tell him. She was too ashamed. She dropped her head.

His hand grabbed her chin and brought it up so she had no choice but to look at him.

'He cheated on you, didn't he?'

Violet was stunned. 'How did you know?'

He dropped his fierce hold on her chin and let his hand fall to his side. 'It's not so hard to work out. He hurt you badly and you're still unhappy, aren't you?'

'No,' she said, putting on her brave voice. 'I'm fine.'

'Has he cheated on you since?'

'No. It was just the one time,' she told him.

He snorted a mirthless laugh. 'Are you sure?'

Violet got cross. 'Look, it wasn't easy for either of us. Sebastian loves me. And it was difficult for him, you know. I was fat, gross. Why wouldn't he sleep with someone else?'

Mark was angry. 'Is that your justification?'

'No. Yes. But everything's different now. I'm different.'

'Did you only get thin to stop him cheating?'

Violet took a deep breath. 'Initially, yes. I think I did.'

'Come with me,' he said, taking her hand.

She was shocked at his warm touch, of his hand holding hers, as he dragged her over to a nearby shop window. 'Look at yourself.'

Violet stared at her reflection, flashing dots of light all over her.

'Do you know how beautiful you are?' he told her in the reflection. 'How beautiful I've always thought you were?'

Violet laughed but there was no humour in it. 'Even now?'

Mark shook his head and turned away from the window. 'You can't see it, can you?'

'Of course not,' she told him, turning to face him once more. 'You're only saying that because I'm thin now.'

He frowned at her. 'No, I'm not. I've always thought you were beautiful.'

Violet stared at him, stunned at his words.

But before he could carry on, there were cries from down the road. A group of drunken girls were coming. The rain was beginning to come down a little more heavily now and they were all shrieking.

Mark dragged her away from the shop window and into a small alleyway where they wouldn't be seen.

He grabbed her by the shoulders. 'Let me tell you something, Violet Saunders. You've always taken my breath away, from the first time I saw you.'

'I have?'

'I even went back to that shop to loiter in the cake aisle, hoping you would return,' he told her. 'Why do you think I gave you the job?'

'But I was huge,' she stammered.

He glared at her. 'So? You think I am so shallow that things like that matter to me?'

'Then why did you date all those gorgeous thin women?' Violet shouted at him.

'I'm Italian,' he told her, with a shrug of the shoulders. 'I dated a lot of women, yes. But I only dated them to try and track down the one.'

'The one?'

He reached out and stroked her cheek with his hand. 'You know, the one I want to spend the rest of my life with. The one I can't live without.' His eyes crinkled up at the edges as he smiled at her. 'You.'

Violet drew in a deep breath as he carried on talking.

'The main thing that struck me was how sad you were. And how much I wanted to make you happy. To see those blue eyes of yours shine.'

Violet drew herself up. 'But I am happy now.'

'That's crap,' he told her. 'Why else did your friends ring me? And how can you be happy with him? What if he cheats on you in the future? How can you trust him?'

Violet bit her lip. She didn't know what to think any more.

He took her face in his hands. 'If you were mine, I would never cheat on you. Ever.'

Violet's eyes filled with tears. It was everything she had ever longed to hear. But it was Mark speaking, not Sebastian.

He stared into her eyes, his face closer now.

'If you were mine,' he told her, brushing a tear from her cheek with his thumb. 'I'd take you to Italy and marry you in our local chapel. Just you, me and the priest. I don't need anyone else. Just you. Only you.'

The tears were rolling down her face now as she stared at him, trying to take in his beautiful words.

'*Ti amo*, Viola. Do you know what that means?'

Violet nodded. He loved her. He actually, truly loved her.

Suddenly Mark dropped his hands to his side.

'But you are going to marry him, aren't you? After all that he's done, you're still going ahead with the wedding. Well, I wish you luck, Violet Saunders. I hope you can be happy with him. But you'd be happier with me.'

390

Violet watched him walk away as the rain began to pour down from the sky, soaking his shirt and making it stick to his skin.

It was her hen night. The night when she should have been celebrating her future marriage to Sebastian. But none of it mattered. Sebastian didn't matter. All that mattered to Violet was walking away down the street. And getting further away from her.

And then it struck her. All that mattered was Mark.

Violet began to run down the road, her heels slipping on the rain-soaked pavements.

'Mark!' she cried, running up to him. Stop!'

He spun round upon hearing her shout. She was breathless as she crashed to a halt in front of him. They stared at each other for what seemed a long, long time.

Then Violet spoke the only word she could think of.

'Marco,' she whispered.

He stepped forward and crushed her to him, kissing her hard on the lips. Violet grabbed at him to hold her even closer, kissing him with a passion she never knew was within her.

Finally, she felt truly alive.

Chapter Fifty-three

'I don't think much of this Christmas cake,' said Sebastian's mother, screwing up her face. 'It doesn't taste right.'

'That's because it's panettone,' said Violet, picking up the remaining cake from the coffee table.

She stalked out of the lounge, taking the plate back into the kitchen and closing the door behind her. She'd had enough. Violet surveyed the mess. Serving a dozen people a full Christmas lunch with all the trimmings was exhausting. Not that anyone had offered to help, she had noted.

But actually she wanted to be alone; she craved the solitude. She was content to hide in the kitchen, her Andrea Bocelli folder on constant play on her iPod speakers. Sebastian had whinged about it being 'boring' but Violet had ignored him, playing it at every opportunity. Especially the songs in Italian.

She sliced off a piece of the glorious panettone and took it with her, nibbling at it as she stared out of the kitchen window. She sighed as Andrea Bocelli sung soft words of love to her through the speakers.

Five nights ago, the words hadn't been sung by another gorgeous Italian man. They had been whispered in her ear, tenderly at first and then more fervently. So ardently, in fact, that she had let him take her back to his flat and make passionate love to her.

The lovemaking had been glorious, fantastic, mind-blowing. It was like nothing she had ever experienced, no feelings she had ever known. She only knew of sex through Sebastian but Mark had made her cry out with joy, something she had never done with her fiancé.

Mark had made her feel special, sexy, loved.

Early in the dawn, Violet had awoken and stared across at the man sleeping peacefully next to her. His face was softened in sleep. She reached out her hand to brush his sensuous lips with her fingers but withdrew them quickly.

Careful not to wake him, she got out of bed and quietly picked up her clothes. She got dressed in the lounge and then crept out, clicking the door shut behind her.

Sebastian had returned that lunchtime from his stag do in Amsterdam, bleary-eyed and hungover. He kissed Violet on his return but it wasn't the same. Nothing was the same. He hadn't even noticed that anything was different. That everything was different now.

She had spent the days leading up to Christmas guilt-ridden over her behaviour. She had done to Sebastian exactly what he had done to her all those months ago. She was a cheater, just like him. It occurred to her that now they were even, but the guilt still followed her around like a cloud, hanging over everything, including Christmas.

She bought Sebastian an expensive pair of cufflinks, remorse making her spend three times the normal amount. Sebastian gave her a baking book. 'Hopefully it'll stop you being so skinny,' he told her.

But the worst thing of all had been Sebastian making love to her on Christmas Eve. It was the first time he had attempted to have sex with her since returning from Amsterdam. But Violet knew she wouldn't be able to put him off any longer.

Violet couldn't help but compare the men. Mark had unleashed something primal in her, feelings and urges hidden so deep that she didn't know they existed. She had been able to match his passion with hers, to be his equal, to make him cry out too.

With Sebastian, she found herself unmoved. She just lay there and let him go ahead. Afterwards, he seemed satisfied. But Violet knew she wasn't. Might never be again. Only Mark could make her feel alive.

Not that any of it mattered. She was marrying Sebastian in seven days and that would be the end of the silly crush, if that's all it was. Besides, Mark hadn't called her, or attempted to contact her. He had obviously put it down to a drunken mistake as well, something to forget.

And even if that weren't entirely true, that was how she would remember it. As a mistake. At least, that was what her head was telling her. She wished her heart would listen as well. And the body that ached for his touch just one more time.

'Not this bloody opera stuff again,' said Sebastian.

Violet hadn't even heard him enter the kitchen.

The love song stopped abruptly as Sebastian fiddled

with the iPod. The next minute, Mariah Carey was singing, 'All I Want for Christmas Is You'. Violet sighed and began to tidy up the kitchen.

'Gosh, that music's a bit loud,' said Miriam, coming through the doorway.

Violet rolled her eyes as she bent down to fill the dishwasher. She just wanted Sebastian and his mother to leave her in peace.

'Now, about the wedding cake,' continued Miriam. 'Mrs Henderson has said that, despite the late notice, she could give you one of her leftover Christmas cakes for the bottom tier. That just leaves the madeira ones to sort out.'

Violet straightened up and swung round to face her future mother-in-law.

'But I thought we'd agreed that I would take care of the wedding cake,' she said, hearing the tension in her voice.

But Miriam shook her head. 'You don't need to worry about anything,' she replied.

Violet took a deep breath. 'I'm not worried about it,' she said, trying to remain calm. 'In fact, it's already sorted. One of my friends is bringing a chocolate cake.'

'Chocolate!' Miriam's eyebrows shot up. 'You can't have a chocolate cake, dear! I think—'

But Violet had reached breaking point. 'No!' she said, more sharply than intended. 'I'm sorry but I want a chocolate cake. You have chosen the date, the church, the reception venue, the menu for the wedding break-fast, the evening buffet menu, the florist and the guest list. I am choosing the cake for my wedding and it will be chocolate.'

There was a short silence whilst they glared at each other.

Eventually, Sebastian cleared his throat. 'Why don't you go back into the lounge, Mother. I'll help Violet clear up.'

Miriam considered saying something but appeared to think better of it and left the room.

'That was uncalled for,' hissed Sebastian in a low tone.

Violet felt all the fight seep out of her and turned her back on him, concentrating on filling the dishwasher.

'Mother has been extremely helpful considering how painful this must be for her,' he carried on. 'You know that it breaks her heart not to be able to arrange a wedding for Elizabeth. This is her only chance.'

Violet straightened up and headed to the opposite counter where she poured herself a large glass of limoncello. She took a large gulp before walking over to the iPod station and switched the music back to Andrea Bocelli.

'Christ, you're drunk,' Sebastian muttered before walking out.

Not yet, thought Violet. Give me another hour trapped in the house with your mother and I might just be.

The night before the wedding, Sebastian finally left her to go to his mother's home for the night. Violet was relieved. She was a nervous wreck, hardly eating anything.

'I can't believe you've lost more weight,' moaned Lucy, grabbing another pin. 'Your wedding dress will be too big at this rate.'

Maggie, Kathy and Lucy had come across for the last fitting of the wedding dress and for a girly night in.

'You'll ruin my design,' said Lucy, tutting under her breath.

'Sorry,' said Violet, her voice catching.

'Hey,' said Lucy. 'I'm only kidding. Look at you! You look wonderful!'

She turned Violet around so she could finally see her reflection.

Violet gasped. The dress was beautiful. A classic long sheath of white, with a lace overlay, held up by little spaghetti straps. Both the straps and the lace had been dotted with tiny dots of diamanté to give a subtle sparkle as the dress moved. Around the waist was a wide gold ribbon, to match the gold jewellery Violet had chosen from her mother's collection.

'Just one thing missing,' said Maggie, bringing out a blue garter. 'It's something borrowed and blue. I've had a long and happy marriage, love. I hope it's the same for you.'

Violet burst into tears. And her friends knew they weren't tears of happiness. This was a deep pain.

Maggie and Lucy positioned themselves either side of Violet, each with an arm around her. Meanwhile Kathy went to open the champagne bottle Edward had given her. She poured out a large glass and gave it to Violet.

'Drink this,' Kathy told her.

Violet gulped down the sparkling drink as she tried to steady herself.

'It's him, isn't it?' asked Maggie. 'Mark.'

Violet nodded, still unable to speak.

'Did you go home with him?' asked Kathy.

Violet nodded.

'But you're still getting married?' asked Lucy. 'To Sebastian, I mean.'

Violet finally composed herself. 'I have to,' she told them.

'Why?' said Kathy.

Violet gave her a small smile. 'I've got two hundred guests arriving to watch a wedding tomorrow afternoon. I don't think they're going to be very happy if I call it off.'

'Stuff them!' snapped Lucy. 'You can't get married if you don't want to.'

'But I do,' said Violet. 'I love Sebastian. I've been with him for so many years. He must be the one.'

'But what about Mark?' asked Maggie.

Violet shook her head. 'Call it pre-wedding jitters,' she told her. 'That's all. One final fling.'

Her friends exchanged worried glances but said nothing more about it. Violet had sounded quite firm on the matter, so they let it drop. In the end, it had to be her decision.

Later on, when they had left, Violet walked through the house. The girls had wanted to stay but she was happier being alone. They would be back in the morning to fix her hair and nails. But for now, she didn't want to speak any more.

Violet stared at the suitcases in the hall, packed and ready for the honeymoon. She felt a stab of dread. Two weeks alone with Sebastian. What would they find to talk about? Would he expect them to make love every night?

She sighed. Everything felt false, not right. Thank God it was an all-inclusive resort and all the drinks were free. Perhaps an alcohol-fuelled daze would bring her inner peace.

She shook her head. It wasn't a great start to a marriage, feeling like this.

She wanted to sleep but it seemed out of reach. So Violet wandered from room to room in her dressing gown, trying to think of something to stop her mind racing.

And then she remembered. She reached into the drawer next to the sofa and brought out Isabella's book. There was still one rule to go. Better late than never, Violet told herself, curling up on the sofa.

'Rule Number Six,' she read. 'Be gorgeous.'

Easier said than done, thought Violet.

'Being gorgeous on the outside is easy. But remember there are no ugly faces, only ugly people. People lacking in manners, with no compassion or kindness. This is true ugliness. But you will only ever be as attractive as you think you are. If you think you are ugly, everyone else will think so too.'

Violet sat upright on the sofa but kept reading.

'Tell yourself you are gorgeous and you will be gorgeous. Treat yourself as gorgeous and everyone will treat you as being gorgeous. Think yourself gorgeous and you will become truly gorgeous.'

Violet stood up and began to pace up and down. Her aunt had told her over and over that she was ugly. She had repeated it so often that Violet believed her.

But that was ten years ago. She was free of her aunt now. And Violet no longer believed she was ugly.

She had been through a dreadful experience, losing her parents. Her aunt had given her no love, no hope, no kindness. She had been deprived. So Violet had made herself feel better with the only thing she could find. Food.

She could have lost all the weight in the world and it still wouldn't have been enough. It wasn't the exterior that needed changing so many months ago. It was the mind, the inside, her thoughts.

She had changed.

She knew she wasn't fat any more. And she knew she wasn't ugly. Mark had told her so but she had already begun to think that way, long before sleeping with him.

Violet now knew she needed to be comfortable in her own skin. And she was. She was OK. She liked herself.

She thought of Isabella. She, Violet Saunders, was gorgeous. Of that, she was finally certain. And now she could move on, get married and live the life she had dreamed of.

Chapter Fifty-four

Maggie smoothed down her new blue dress.

'What do you think?' she asked, giving the girls a twirl in Violet's lounge.

'Gorgeous,' said Kathy. 'I presume it's from New York?'

'Of course,' said Maggie with a grin.

She was still recovering from her brief visit to fabulous New York. It really was just like the movies. She and Gordon had wandered the avenues, relishing the crisp winter air and blue skies above the city.

They had gone to the top of the Empire State Building for the views. They had shopped in Bloomingdale's and Macy's. They had eaten salted pretzels whilst walking the paths of Central Park.

But it was the dancing which had been the highlight of the trip. Gordon had waltzed her around a glittering ballroom on the last evening, with a Frank Sinatra soundalike crooning at them from the stage.

She had looked down every time they stopped for a drink, eager to check that her glorious red skirt was still sparkling. Then she sighed and looked back at her husband, ready for the next dance.

Maggie wished she had lost the weight years ago. But perhaps it had to be the right time. Perhaps she needed to be in the right frame of mind with the determination to go through with it. Maybe she needed the help and support of her friends as well.

She only had half a stone left to lose. Maggie would reach her goal, she had no doubt of that. Gordon was talking about a beach holiday the following summer. For once she wouldn't have to worry about swimsuits and revealing the flesh. Her body was more toned than it had ever been. And she was truly happy. Middle-aged spread? Hah!

She and Gordon returned from their romantic break refreshed and rested. And very much in love.

'It's sickening,' said Lucy, with a wink to the others. 'They're always kissing and cuddling. I can't wait to get back to university next week.'

'Aww!' cooed Kathy. 'Can't wait to see your Canadian artist, I'll bet.'

'Don't know what you're talking about,' said Lucy. 'We're just—'

'—friends,' chorused Kathy, Maggie and Violet. 'We know.'

Lucy stuck her tongue out at them and went back to checking the wedding dress one final time.

Truth was, she had missed Todd dreadfully over the Christmas break. She had even rung him, trying to keep her voice casual and friendly. He had seemed surprised that she called him but they had chatted for over an hour. Lucy was hoping not to be anywhere near her father when the home phone bill came through in a month's time.

'What time is it?' asked Lucy.

'Nearly three o'clock,' said Maggie, glancing at her watch.

As she moved her arm, she saw the light glance off her new bracelet from Tiffany's. Maggie admired the platinum bangle as it shone on her wrist.

'Very nice,' said Kathy, glancing over Maggie's shoulder. 'You can always hock it if times get desperate.'

'Never!' said Maggie, clutching the precious bracelet. It wasn't the cost of the gift that made it so dear to her heart. It was the memory of Gordon telling her how much he loved her as he handed it over to her.

She glanced across at Kathy, who was playing with a heart pendant framed perfectly by the purple V-neck of her wrap dress. The necklace was new, a gift from Edward.

She had spent a magical Christmas with him, proudly taking her home-made cake with them to his mother's home. She had shed a tear as she finished decorating the cake with the Christmas figurines but she knew her parents would want her to be happy, to enjoy being in a family again.

Edward had introduced her to his whole family as his girlfriend and she had been warmly welcomed by his mother, sisters and brothers. Edward's family was huge and the atmosphere on Christmas Day had been happy and warm. They had played games with the children and laughter had rung out around the dinner table late into the day.

'We're so pleased to have finally met you,' said

Edward's youngest sister. 'He's gone on and on about you!'

'We thought you were a figment of his imagination,' said the other sister.

'He looks so well,' said Edward's mother. 'It must be love.'

Kathy blushed but secretly revelled in the confirmation that Edward cared for her. This was it, she knew. He was the one. She couldn't wait until they moved in together in the New Year.

Their future was looking so bright. The shop was proving very popular as a find for vintage bargains. She had lots of energy to keep up with Edward, who was getting fitter by the day. But they also found time to sit quietly and she found she could relax and be herself around him. There was no need to be the funny girl any more. She could be quiet and still. It was bliss. She told him about her family and he had let her into his. They welcomed her with open arms.

She still couldn't do without the odd cake or chocolate bar. But everything was in moderation. She felt wonderful. Like a whole new person. She was never going back to the way she felt and looked before. Kathy was going to keep this way for life, for Edward, but mostly for herself.

And now they had a lovely wedding to go to. Hopefully.

Kathy glanced at Violet. She appeared very serene today, as if her doubts and fears had finally been taken away from her. Something seemed to have changed deep within Violet. The hesitancy that was always so close to the surface had disappeared. She was confident and self-assured.

In fact, Violet had had the courage to bin the awful creation of pink carnations that had been delivered from the florist that morning. Instead, she had dispatched Kathy to buy a bouquet of white roses and freesias.

Kathy watched her inhale the scent.

'Wonderful,' said Violet, twirling the bouquet around in her hands.

Her hair and make-up were done. Violet had also dismissed Miriam's expensive make-up artist and done her own. All that was needed was for the bride to get dressed.

There was a knock on the door and they all stopped chatting.

'Who's that?' asked Kathy.

Violet shook her head, suddenly looking a little less sure of herself.

'I'll get it,' said Maggie, taking charge.

She went into the hallway and drew herself to full height in her heels. If it were Sebastian backing out, she was ready for a fight. If it were Mark, she was going to drag him inside and not let him or Violet out of the house.

But it was the last person Maggie had expected to find on Violet's front doorstep. It was her husband.

'Hello,' said Gordon, with a smile.

'Everything all right?' asked Maggie, suddenly fearful.

They had arranged to meet at the church and this wasn't part of the plan. Perhaps it was her mother. Or his. Or any number of awful scenarios conjured up in her mind.

'Sorry to interrupt your preparations but I need to see Lucy.'

'What's happened?'

'Go get our daughter and I'll show you.'

Maggie went back into the lounge. 'It's your dad,' she said to Lucy, trying to keep her voice calm. 'He wants a word with you.'

Lucy frowned. 'Now?'

She followed her mother to the front door.

'Hello, love,' said Gordon. 'I was just getting ready when there was a knock on the front door about half an hour ago. Thought I'd better tell you about it. It seemed quite important.'

'Who was it?' asked Lucy.

'Him.'

Gordon moved aside to reveal a tall, dark stranger walking up the front path.

'Hello, Lucy Walsh,' said Todd.

'Todd!' squealed Lucy, stepping towards him. 'What are you doing here? You're not due back for another week.'

He broke into a huge smile. 'Can't a fella miss his girl so much that he gets an earlier flight?'

Lucy smiled back and then glanced at her parents.

'We'll give you two a bit of privacy,' said Maggie, leading Gordon indoors.

'Since when did you decide that I was your girl?' said Lucy, hands on hips.

He reached out and grabbed her round the waist, pulling her to him. 'When I heard your voice and then couldn't think of anything else for the rest of the holidays. You've ruined Christmas for me.'

Lucy snaked her hands up around his neck. 'Then I'd better give you a bloody good New Year, hadn't I?'

And she pulled his head down to kiss her.

'He's lovely,' whispered Kathy, peeking out of the window.

'Come away,' hissed Maggie. 'I'll be in that much trouble if she thinks we're spying on her.'

'She won't care,' said Kathy. 'The girl's in love.'

'Seems a decent enough fella,' said Gordon. 'For a foreigner.'

'He's Canadian,' said Maggie, nudging him playfully. 'At least it's still in the Commonwealth.'

'They're coming!' said Kathy, flinging herself away from the window.

Everyone tried to look busy but failed. However, Lucy didn't care.

'Hi, everyone,' she said, beaming from ear to ear. 'This is Todd.'

'Hi, Todd,' chorused everyone back, grinning at them.

'Hello,' he said, before looking at Violet. 'Sorry to crash your big day.'

'That's fine,' said Violet, smiling. 'Do you want to be Lucy's guest? You'd be more than welcome.'

'Thanks,' replied Todd. 'That would be cool.'

So the young lovebirds went with Gordon to the church, leaving Kathy and Maggie to finish dressing the bride.

They held the dress open for Violet to step into and then Kathy gently pulled the zip up whilst Maggie fiddled with the shoulder straps.

They stepped backwards and smiled.

'You look beautiful,' said Maggie, with a tear in her eye.

'You really do,' said Kathy, also a bit sniffly. 'Such a beautiful bride.'

Violet turned to look at her reflection and sighed with contentment. Yes, she did look beautiful. Lucy had done an amazing job with the dress. And there wasn't a trace of fat bride about her. She had done it. She was looking and feeling gorgeous.

She turned back to her friends with a smile.

'I'm ready,' she told them. 'Let's go find my groom.'

Chapter Fifty-five

The bridal party pulled up to the church car park with five minutes to spare.

'There're still a few people milling about,' said Kathy, opening the car door for Violet. 'Do you want to stay in the car?'

'No,' said Violet, getting out. 'As long as Sebastian isn't about, I don't mind seeing anyone else.'

Maggie glanced up at the entrance to the church. 'I think he's gone in already.'

Kathy checked her reflection in the car window.

But Violet didn't feel she needed to see herself again. She knew how good she looked. She remained calm, even when she spotted Sebastian's mother heading towards her.

'Violet?' barked Miriam. 'What are you wearing?'

'My wedding dress,' said Violet, twirling around. 'Do you like it?'

'What about Sebastian's cousin's dress?'

'This is it.'

'You've ripped it apart?'

Violet shrugged her shoulders. 'It was huge. Plus I didn't like the original design. And seeing as I'm the one who has to wear it, I think I should actually decide, don't you?'

Miriam pursed her lips together. 'I don't know what I shall say to my sister.'

'Tell her it was a horrible dress that now looks a million times better, thanks to my designer friend.'

Sebastian's mother was glaring at but Violet didn't care. She finally felt in control.

'Hello, Miriam!' said a female guest in a rather ugly hat, coming to join them. 'Is this the bride?'

'Hello, Daphne,' said Miriam, fixing a smile on her face. 'Yes, this is Violet.'

The complete stranger looked Violet up and down. 'Dumped the fat one, did he? Thank goodness. This one looks a much better prospect.'

'Thank you,' said Violet, with a warm smile. She leant forward. 'By the way, the fat one was me. I've lost five stone.'

The woman looked horrified and scurried away.

Miriam was looking around, as if desperate to get away from Violet as well. Thankfully, the arrival of a couple of bridesmaids gave her the perfect excuse.

Violet had met the bridesmaids only once; they were cousins or something. She didn't know and found she didn't really care either. If there had been a choice, she would have had Maggie, Lucy and Kathy. But it was too late now.

'You look nice,' said one of the bridesmaids, breaking away from the pack to stand next to Violet. She was in her early twenties and obviously quite nervous.

'Thank you,' said Violet. 'So do you.'

The bridesmaids were in some hideous peach

confection that Violet wouldn't have chosen in a million years. But as long as she didn't have to wear it, she didn't care.

'Can I have a quiet word?' whispered the girl.

Violet was nonplussed. 'Now?'

The girl nodded and, taking Violet's arm, led her away a small distance.

'I have to tell you something,' she said.

'What is it?'

The girl glanced around her before turning back to look at Violet. She looked upset.

'Are you OK?' asked Violet.

The girl shook her head but still didn't speak.

'It's all right,' said Violet with a wry smile. 'I've only got a church full of two hundred guests waiting for me. Take your time.'

'Sorry,' said the girl quickly. 'It's just hard to say, that's all.'

Violet didn't reply and waited for the girl to speak again.

The girl took a deep breath. 'I slept with Sebastian last month.'

Violet gazed at the girl, who was now looking downcast. She was obviously telling the truth.

'I'm so sorry,' carried on the girl. 'I don't know what I was thinking. We bumped into each other one night at a bar. I was drunk and so was he. It's no excuse, I know. I feel just terrible.'

Violet stared at her for a while longer and then burst out laughing.

The girl looked shocked, as if this were the last reaction she had been expecting.

Violet laughed and laughed until she felt the tears sting her eyes.

'Was he any good?' Violet asked, between guffaws.

The girl was still staring at her goggle-eyed when Sebastian's mother came over to them.

'What is it?' she snapped. 'What's going on?'

'Private joke,' said Violet, still giggling. What an unholy mess.

'She's hysterical,' said Miriam, frowning.

She whipped up her hand as if she were going to slap Violet. But Violet suddenly sobered up and grabbed Miriam's wrist.

'There'll be no slapping of the bride today,' said Violet in a firm tone. 'Or any day, come to think of it.'

Miriam quickly withdrew her hand. Violet stared at her until she backed away.

'It's OK,' Violet told the girl. 'Don't worry about it. You can go back to the other bridesmaids now.'

The girl started to say something but thought better of it and went back to the main group, glancing nervously at her every minute or so.

Kathy and Maggie came to stand with Violet.

'Everything OK?' asked Maggie.

'What was that all about?' said Kathy.

'Nothing,' she told them, shaking her head. She was still too shocked to tell them.

'We'd better go in,' said Kathy, giving her a hug. 'Good luck.'

'Be happy,' said Maggie, also hugging Violet.

Then they went inside the church, leaving Violet alone.

Well, that was unexpected, she thought. Or maybe not.

Violet had given so much time and thought to her own personal changes that she hadn't considered that Sebastian needed to change as well. But perhaps she had to accept that he wouldn't change, that he

412

didn't want to. That he would always lie and cheat on her.

'It's time,' called out one of the bridesmaids.

Violet glanced at the church door and there was the vicar. Time to get married.

Miriam went ahead into the church whilst Violet and the bridesmaids organised themselves. Violet had no one to give her away so she would walk down the aisle on her own.

The bridesmaids began their slow walk up the long aisle. Violet stood waiting until she saw her cue and then began to follow. The church appeared to be filled with at least twenty pedestal flower arrangements of carnations, in various shades of pink and peach.

Something drew her glance away from the altar. She looked over and saw Mark. They locked eyes as she walked past, his green eyes burning into hers.

Violet turned her attention back to Sebastian waiting for her at the altar. Why was she waiting for him to change? What if he didn't? Why was she so afraid of life without him? She knew she was frightened of being alone again, just like when she lost her parents. But she had been alone for a long time anyway, it felt. Even when she was with Sebastian.

Until this year. Now she had friends, true friends. And Mark.

Except she didn't have him. They had had one glorious, unforgettable night together. And that was it. That was all Violet had to hold dear to her for the rest of her married life. Her memory of another man.

By now, she had reached Sebastian at the altar. He smiled warmly at her, acting the part of the loving groom.

The vicar began to speak but Violet heard none of

his words. Marriage would be wonderful if you loved your husband, like Maggie and Gordon. There was a marriage built on trust and friendship.

Sebastian had never really been her friend. Not fighting her cause and battling her corner, as Edward had done with Kathy. Edward adored Kathy, any fool could see that. Sebastian had never adored her. He almost seemed to hold her in contempt sometimes.

'Lord of all Hopefulness' was the first hymn. Hopeful, thought Violet. Was that all she was hanging on to regarding her impending marriage? Hope?

She glanced across at Sebastian as he sang. Did he even like her? It was great to love someone but it was equally important to like them as well.

Then Violet remembered something. Herself. Violet. Forget about Sebastian, what about her own feelings? What did she really want?

The hymn was over and the vicar was speaking of love and marriage. Violet stood in a daze, the words drifting over her.

'Marriage is a solemn vow, therefore if any person can show any just cause or impediment why this man and this women may not lawfully be joined together, let him speak now or forever hold his peace.'

Suddenly Violet found herself holding her breath. Would Mark speak up?

But the church remained silent.

The vicar smiled. 'Excellent. Now, if you could turn to—'

'Wait!' Violet found herself blurting out. 'I do.'

'Not yet, dear,' said the vicar with a smile. 'That bit comes later.'

'I meant me,' said Violet. 'I object to this marriage.'

Sebastian spun round to glare at her. 'What are you talking about?' he hissed. 'Don't be ridiculous.'

Violet was quite calm as she turned to face him. 'Do you love me?' she asked him.

'What are you talking about?' Sebastian glanced at the congregation who were staring at them agog. 'Don't be so stupid.'

Violet shook her head. 'I'm not stupid,' she told him, her voice clear and loud as it echoed around the church. 'I would be if I spent the rest of my life being perfectly miserable with you. And I'm worth more than that. I'm worth more than you will ever be.'

He was staring at her in shock.

'You're not worth all the tears and the pain,' she carried on. 'And, I'm afraid, the sex isn't worth it either. Seriously, read a manual or something.'

Sebastian tried to speak but couldn't.

Violet slipped off her engagement ring and placed it in his hand.

'Thanks for the offer,' she told him. 'But I think I'll pass.'

She turned from the altar and began to walk back down the aisle alone.

Sebastian's mother leapt up from the pews to block her path.

'Where do you think you're going?' she snapped. 'Get back there and marry my son!'

Violet's eyes glittered as she stared at Miriam.

'Your son is a cheat,' she said. 'A lying, cheating idiot who was only marrying me for my money, I think. He doesn't love me. And I don't love him, I've realised. The truth is, I'm too good for him. And you know it.'

Violet brushed past her and continued to walk all the way out of the church, her head held high.

Chapter Fifty-six

Violet stood outside the church, breathing in the sweet air of freedom. Well, she'd done it. She'd finally spoken her mind. And it felt good. Really good.

Kathy and Maggie came to stand either side of her.

'Well,' said Maggie, still in shock but grabbing hold of Violet's hand. 'That was unusual.'

'Best wedding I've ever been to,' said Kathy with a grin as she clasped hold of Violet's other hand.

They both looked at Violet, who was standing still but looking serene.

'So? What happens now?' asked Maggie.

Violet looked at them both before breaking into a lovely smile. 'I have no idea.'

Edward joined them. 'How about a large drink?'

'Good idea,' said Violet, still smiling.

'Do you want to go to the reception?' asked Kathy.

Violet shook her head. 'I think I'll leave that for Sebastian's family to sort out. After all, it is their country club.'

'What about the wedding cake?' asked Maggie. A

three-tiered chocolate cake was in the back of Kathy's car.

'There's always room for chocolate,' said Violet with a small smile.

'I agree,' said Edward. 'Pub?'

'Pub,' said Violet.

An hour later, they were settled around a couple of large tables in the pub where they had ended up after Trudie had walked out on them many months ago. It was New Year's Eve and the place was gearing up for party night.

There weren't many of them around the table but Violet didn't mind. Most of the congregation had been complete strangers. The people who were with her now were friends, good friends.

She glanced across at Maggie and Gordon, who were telling Julie about New York and their plans for a trip to Greece the following year. Wendy was feeding her baby with a bottle whilst she talked to Kathy and Edward, who were holding hands under the table. Wendy's husband and Julie's boyfriend were chatting and keeping an eye on Wendy's toddler.

Lucy and Todd were deep in conversation with Anthony and his girlfriend about webcams and long-distance communication. That was a romance that was destined to run a long time, thought Violet with a smile.

The surprise guest was Trudie, who had quickly followed them down the road as they had escaped. She was currently outside, calling Trevor on her phone. Nobody quite knew why she was there but everybody was accommodating her. Sort of. Besides, they were desperate to find out what kind of man would marry Trudie.

Somebody had ordered some bottles of champagne and everybody was enjoying themselves as if it were the most normal thing in the world to walk out of your own wedding. Nobody questioned Violet about it. Perhaps they already knew, she thought. Perhaps she was the last one to realise that the marriage would have been a disaster.

Sebastian had texted her a few times. The texts had gone from irritation to panic. But they didn't affect Violet. In the end, she didn't bother reading any more from him. She knew she wouldn't see him ever again.

There was only one person missing and that was Mark. Perhaps he felt guilty, having witnessed her bridal meltdown. Perhaps he didn't really care that much. Violet felt a little sad, but ultimately she would survive. The wedding had shown her that. She had finally come out of her shell and she wouldn't be going back in there now. There was a big, wide world out there just waiting to be enjoyed.

Violet went to the ladies' and stared at her reflection. Had she really just done that? Walked out on Sebastian in front of all those people? She found she couldn't stop herself breaking into a grin. Yes, she really had.

What would her parents have said? She knew they would have supported her, wanted her to be happy. Of that, she was certain.

Violet suddenly realised somebody was sobbing inside one of the cubicles.

'Are you OK in there?' she asked, knocking gently on the door.

The door slowly opened to reveal a large woman in her mid-twenties with mascara running down her face.

'Sorry,' she muttered. 'I've just been dumped.'

'Poor you,' said Violet, grabbing some tissue for the girl.

'He said I was too fat,' said the girl with a sob. 'Left me for some stick insect called Mandy.'

Violet let her cry for a little while before saying, 'He's obviously not worth it if he dumped you because of your size.'

The girl sniffed. 'Easy for you to say. I don't suppose a skinny minnie like you would understand.'

Violet broke into a smile. 'Actually, I lost five stone this year through healthy eating and exercise. No fads. No extreme diets. No food off limits. Just good old-fashioned willpower and group help. You can join us, if you want. We're a small group but extremely friendly. We've all been there.'

'You were fat like me?' said the girl, shocked. 'But you look like you've always been slim.'

Violet smiled and gave the girl her number. 'Call me,' she told the woman. 'Don't struggle on your own.'

She walked back to the party; the pub was now beginning to fill up with people coming out for the evening festivities. The atmosphere was getting more lively as the New Year's Eve celebrations began. A few people glanced at Violet but nobody said anything. Perhaps they thought it was fancy dress.

Maggie and Kathy came rushing up to Violet with distressed looks on their faces.

'It's about the cake,' said Maggie.

'What's happened?' asked Violet.

'That!' Kathy told her, turning to point at the table where the cake had been set up.

Violet couldn't believe what she was seeing. Trudie was grabbing handfuls of chocolate cake and shoving them in her mouth. There was chocolate in her hair, across her face and down her pale pink dress.

They went over to stand with Lucy, who was staring down at Trudie.

'What are you doing?' asked Kathy. 'That's Violet's wedding cake.'

'I don't care!' wailed Trudie. 'I just want to die.'

'It would probably take a wooden stake to finish you off,' snapped Kathy.

'He's left me,' whined Trudie.

'Who?' asked Lucy, leaning down into her face. 'Your conscience? Your compassion?'

'Trevor,' said Trudie, grabbing another lump of cake and stuffing it into her mouth.

'Let's move you here,' said Kathy, pulling Lucy back. 'Just in case she swallows you whole.'

'My husband's left me for a huge fattie,' shouted Trudie, causing a few heads to turn. 'You know, like you lot used to be. Can you imagine anything more disgusting?'

'Oh dear,' said Violet trying to be sympathetic. 'What's her name?'

Trudie swallowed hard before muttering, 'Gareth.'

The four woman looked at each other.

'He left you for a man,' said Lucy, trying not to smirk and failing.

'A fat man,' replied Trudie, emphasising that the fat was worse than the man part.

'Oh dear,' said Maggie, her shoulders beginning to shake.

'Maybe you could give him some of those horrible shakes,' said Kathy, grinning.

'Or those disgusting cereal bars that we threw away,' said Violet.

'You can't have thrown them away,' snapped Trudie. 'Otherwise you wouldn't have been able to lose all that weight.'

'Actually, you're wrong,' said Edward, coming to stand with them. 'We've started our own weight-loss club without you. Violet had some great ideas and put us all on the right path.'

'Her?' stammered Trudie, staring at Violet.

'We helped each other,' said Maggie.

'With no snide comments,' added Lucy.

'And no bitchy asides,' said Kathy.

'So we won't be returning to your class in the new year,' said Maggie.

'Maybe you should take this opportunity to do some soul searching,' Edward told Trudie, who was looking up at them all.

'Yeah,' said Kathy. 'If you can find one.'

They stared at Trudie until she slowly stood up and walked out of the pub.

'Now I need a drink,' said Violet.

But she was smiling. The last negative person was out of her life.

As she returned to the table, the champagne glasses had all been topped up in her absence. Violet picked up one of the full glasses as everybody sat down once more.

'Speech!' called Kathy.

Violet shook her head but then the whole group began to call for a speech.

She took a long breath and looked down at her friends gathered around the table.

'Well,' she told them, hugging the glass to her. 'I don't know what to say. I don't know what the future holds for me now. But I'm just grateful to have friends around me that care and want to see me happy. Despite everything that happened today, I can honestly say it's been the most amazing year.' She held the glass out in front of her to toast. 'I can't wait to see what next year holds for us all. Cheers!'

'Cheers!' they all chorused and chinked their glasses together.

Violet took a large gulp of champagne before smiling down at them all.

'Doesn't the first dance normally come next?' asked someone behind her.

She suddenly felt goosebumps all over, her heart thumping hard as she turned around. It was him.

'Shall we?' Mark asked, holding out his hands.

She turned to put down the champagne glass before taking his hands, letting him guide her away from the table and into his arms. A slow song came over the speakers just as they began to sway in time to the music.

'So . . . ?' began Violet.

But Mark shook his head. 'Not yet,' he told her with a soft smile. 'Just let me hold you.'

He drew her back into his arms where he held her until the song was finished. They rocked together, oblivious to the stares and nudges from the crowd. There was nothing except each other. Violet relaxed and let him lead her, joyful to be back in his arms again. She knew it was where she belonged.

Eventually the song finished and the music changed back to the party music. As the beat thumped out, Violet finally pulled away to look up at him.

'You're sacked,' said Mark, still holding her.

Violet stared up at him. 'What?'

'I don't think you should work for me any longer.'

She couldn't believe it. After everything that had happened, she had always had her job to rely on.

'But why?' she stammered, suddenly a little unsure of herself.

'Because if we keep working together, I'm going to end up getting the sack too.' He stroked her face with his long fingers. 'I can't concentrate on work whilst you're around. I had enough trouble keeping my hands off you before you had your wicked way with me.'

Violet blushed in his arms but had relaxed again.

'What will I do?' she wondered aloud.

And then she knew. She would start her own weight-loss club, using the money from her inheritance to start the business. She would help women like her find a happier side of themselves. But not using dreadful shakes and bars. With proper advice and maybe an exercise class.

Mark watched her break into a smile.

'You're the most beautiful bride I've ever seen,' he told her.

'Even though there wasn't a wedding.'

He shrugged his shoulders. 'He didn't deserve you.'

'And you do, I suppose?' she said, grinning up at him.

'Absolutely,' he replied, drawing her close once more. 'I'm going to take you to Italy with me. I want to show you the colour of the sea, the sky and the wonderful food. I want to watch your beautiful face glow in the evening sun and make love to you all night.'

He smiled at her blushes and moved his mouth next to her ear. Then he whispered words of endearment in Italian to her. Words of love, of their future together. Promises she knew he would keep.

As he drew away, she stared up at him, taking in his beautiful face.

'*Ti amo*, Marco,' she told him. 'I always have. It just took me a while to realise it.'

He smiled down at her. 'I'm going to spend the rest of my life loving you.'

They stood together in each other's arms.

'It's a bit premature,' Mark told Violet. 'But Happy New Year.'

'It will be,' she said. 'And all the years after that.'

Then she reached up and kissed him once more.

Chapter Fifty-seven

Violet smoothed the dress down and smiled. It fitted her beautifully. She hadn't put on any weight since the New Year. Nor had she lost any. She was finally happy with her body and finally happy within herself.

The July sunshine was beckoning her. Violet stepped outside. It was the best of days. The sun was still warm as it set on the horizon, streaking the blue sky with deep orange.

Violet thought it wonderful how she wasn't afraid any more. No longer afraid of walking into a place alone. Of trusting her own opinion. Of daring to love life.

She smiled at her friends, so grateful that they were with her.

Maggie and Gordon were standing next to each other, closer than ever before. Lucy and Todd were smiling and holding hands. Edward had his arm around Kathy. She had her hand on the small bump that was now beginning to show through her dress. Kathy was already blooming at four months pregnant.

Violet's new assistant was holding the fort back at home. Her weight-loss club was full to capacity three mornings and two evenings a week. Violet was going to open another class when she returned. But that was a month away yet.

Nonna gave her a watery smile as she walked past, already mopping up her tears with a lace handkerchief. Violet reached out and gave her hand a quick squeeze before carrying on.

The village was perched high above the coast, the azure Mediterranean glittering at the bottom of the dramatic cliffs. The small square was edged with bougainvillea and dotted with lemon trees giving off a heady scent. Italy was as bewitching as she had always imagined it to be.

Mark took Violet's hand in his as she reached him. They smiled at each other and then turned to face the priest.

It was a perfect wedding day of simple, Italian elegance and wonderful food.

Isabella would have heartily approved.

Turn the page for a sneak preview of

A RECIPE FOR FRIENDSHIP

Coming soon from Alison Sherlock

Chapter 1

Charley Summer's hair was completely straight and that made it a perfect day. She glanced at her reflection in the salon window. The wild tangle of dark hair that she had been blessed with now hung in a smooth sheet around her face. Thank heavens for professional blowdries.

With a satisfied sigh, Charley waited for the credit card machine to be placed in front of her.

'I'm sorry, Madam,' said the receptionist. 'There appears to be a problem with your credit card.'

The receptionist placed the gold plastic card onto the counter between them. Charley stared at it to make sure she hadn't accidentally picked up someone else's by mistake. But no, it was definitely hers.

'Are you sure?' she asked, frowning.

She received a sympathetic smile in return. 'I'm afraid so.'

'I see.' Charley fumbled around in her handbag, her cheeks beginning to grow pink. She finally found her purse and handed over the cash. 'Sorry about the card.'

'Not at all, Madam,' cooed the receptionist, counting out the change.

'Thank you. Sorry, again.'

She scurried out of the salon and took a deep breath of spring air to calm down her racing pulse. How embarrassing. Something had obviously gone wrong with the bank.

She whipped out her iPhone and rang Steve. It went straight to voicemail but she didn't leave a message. She'd talk to him later about the problem. After all, he was the one in charge of all their finances. She was far too busy to get involved in all that boring paperwork these days.

Charley decided she wouldn't let the small matter of the credit card ruin her afternoon. She flicked a smooth lock behind her shoulder and began to walk down the road. One small blip in a glorious spring day in the English countryside. The sun shone down onto Grove high street where the tulips and daffodils were in full bloom along the pavement.

Every shop had at least two plant pots and a couple of hanging baskets. Grove village was making yet another bid for 'Best Blooming Village'. It was going to make the place a no-go zone for anyone suffering with hayfever this summer.

The high street ran through the centre of the village, the second largest in the country. Only one hundred yards of farmland prevented them from snatching the number one slot from a village in Devon. Hence the struggle to win the horticultural prize instead.

Charley strolled past the numerous coffee shops, florist, organic greengrocers and chemist. All the basics required for country life, plus a few trinket shops where you paid over the odds for a smelly candle.

She stopped in front of the designer lingerie shop at the end of the parade. They must have changed their window that week to reflect the oncoming holiday season as the mannequin was now wearing the most beautiful purple bikini. Instead of ties, it had big gold buckles on each thigh. The price tag read £85.

Out of loyalty, Charley knew she should buy her beachwear from one of Steve's clothes shops. However, as up-to-the-minute as the fashions were, they were cheap and cheerful clothes. Not quite in keeping with the St Kitts crowd they would be mixing with on holiday in few weeks' time.

Charley was tempted to try on the bikini but a quick glance at her reflection stopped her from going in. She knew she wasn't fat but she had gone up a whole dress size in the past year. She really would have to do something about all the extra weight that had piled on. There was a new weight loss club in the area, run by a lady called Violet. Charley had seen the advertisement in the local paper but didn't have time before the holiday to only lose a pound or so a week in a sensible fashion.

Charley wondered whether she should hire a personal trainer instead or attend one of those boot camps that helped you lose weight fast. In any case, perhaps it wasn't the best time to be trying on swimwear. She'd have a think and decide what to do later. Maybe talking to a nutritionist would help.

As she walked on, she spotted a few schoolchildren at the other end of the high street. Glancing at her watch, Charley realised time was getting on. Her best friends were coming over that evening and she wanted everything to be perfect for when they arrived.

She turned the corner and walked up the small

alleyway to Gino's delicatessen. It was her favourite shop in the whole universe and that included Selfridges. Where else could she buy truffle salt for her steaks? Authentic balsamic jelly to be served with her cheese board? Pistachio cream to be swirled into her ice cream? These were hardly ingredients she could buy from just a normal supermarket.

The aroma as she entered the shop was Charley's drug of choice. It was a heady mix of oils, spices and herbs, mixed with fresh coffee which was served to the small number of tables and chairs tucked away in the front corner.

Charley chose her purchases carefully. She decided on handmade grissini to start, picking up some black olive paté to dip the breadsticks into. She had already bought a beautiful piece of salmon from the fish-monger but it needed the expensive green pesto alla genovese to give it extra flavour. She picked up two bottles of Chablis and then headed to the till.

Charley opened her purse and remembered just in time not to hand over the gold credit card which had already failed. Instead, she handed over her bank card with a smile.

The wizened old Italian woman behind the counter put her purchases in a bag and then glanced at the credit card machine. She muttered to herself in Italian and then fixed a stare upon Charley whose stomach dropped.

The woman was shaking her head and handing back her card. Charley couldn't believe it. The bank card didn't work either?

This time she didn't question the error, merely fiddling about in her purse, trying to come up with the correct amount. When the money came up short, she had to choose what to leave behind. In the end, Charley handed back the bottles of wine. She knew they already had enough at home.

She quickly left the shop with her purchases. Charley considered that it was possible that they had reached their credit limit. Steve had been making ominous rumblings over the last couple of weeks about pulling in belts on the spending front. Charley knew he was just stressed about the opening of their fourth shop but that didn't mean he should let their accounts lapse into the red. She would have to talk to him later about transferring some money into the account.

The high street divided the village into Upper Grove and Lower Grove. She lived in Upper Grove which was posh and privileged. Lower Grove was grim and gloomy – a place to have your hubcaps stolen and to pick a fight with someone. Charley never went there. Didn't dare. The high street was their Berlin Wall and they were grateful it was still standing.

Upper Grove had houses that were big, roads that were wide and neighbours who ignored each other. The only person Charley had ever spoken to in the road was Judy who lived next door.

Judy was one of a group of five friends who met up once a fortnight. Every other Wednesday night, for the past two years, they had dinner at someone's house. More often than not the girls demanded Charley make ice cream for pudding and it had become a sort of ritual.

Charley swung her car into the gravel driveway and allowed herself a small smile. It was still the prettiest house she had ever seen. Charley had fallen in love with this house four years ago as soon as she had seen it. The timber beams set against the white paintwork stole her heart. Once she had ventured inside and had seen the open fireplaces, the exposed beams, the leaded windows and the south-facing garden she knew they had to live there.

It was their first proper home, bought with the ever-increasing profits that they were making from Steve's business empire. And she had enjoyed turning it into their dream home ever since.

Charley headed into the kitchen to unpack the food shopping. The kitchen was her favourite part of the house. It had been a poky, dark room when they had moved in and she hadn't imagined there was a worse place to dabble with her cooking. But knocking through into the utility room and adding pale, shiny tiled flooring and walnut cabinets had made all the difference. The cream marble work surfaces held metallic flecks of silver which gave the whole look just enough bling without being tacky.

Charley switched on her Gaggia Gelatiera ice-cream maker. For years she had made her ice-cream by hand but, as soon as the business had begun to make a profit, she had placed an order for the sleek, silver appliance. Loved by cooks everywhere, the paddles churned the ice-cream so well that it always turned out velvety smooth.

Charley began to break up a bar of Venezualan Black chocolate into chunks so that it would melt easily before pouring it into the ice-cream maker. She already had a box of home-made strawberry sorbet in the freezer but there would be hell to pay later from the girls if there wasn't any chocolate on the menu.

Chapter 2

Maddie Hayes opened the cupboard and stared at the bottle of wine. She blew out a long sigh before shutting the door and switching on the kettle. It was only three o'clock in the afternoon. Too early to pretend it was time for her tea-time tipple.

Plus she was driving to Charley's house that evening so there was no chance of any alcohol before then to dull the boredom of her day.

She and Charley had become close when they had arrived at college together and Maddie didn't appear to look much older than she had at seventeen. Thirteen years later, her hair was still blonde and her body slim. Only the dark circles under her eyes belied the youthful appearance.

Whilst the kettle boiled, Maddie wandered into the lounge to make sure her toddler wasn't killing the baby. But all was quiet and calm. CBeebies was playing on the widescreen television. Her three-year-old son Jack stared at the screen, mesmerised. Six-month-old Ruby slept.

'Eh-oh!' said the *Teletubbies* from the television.

Bloody speech therapy is what that bunch need, thought Maddie as she went back into the kitchen. She poured herself a cup of tea and sank down on to a chair, relishing the peace. She nibbled on a Farley's rusk whilst staring into space.

Maddie knew she should have been doing some dusting or hoovering. The tumble drier needed emptying and the dishwasher needed loading. There was a pile of paperwork and bills on the table that needed sorting and filing. That mountain of ironing was getting so high it was soon going to require a planning application. Plus her hair needed washing before going out in public later.

But Maddie didn't move. She just sat in her kitchen, listening to the clock tick and tock the minutes away. Because any minute now the *Teletubbies* programme would end and Jack would be requiring some kind of attention. Shapes would need sorting. Blocks would require stacking. Jigsaws needed to be solved. Story books waited to be read. Then Ruby would wake up and require attention in the form of feeding and cuddles, in between nappy changes and rolling around on the carpet.

Hearing the music to signify the end of the programme, Maddie finished her cup of tea in one swig and went back into the lounge. *Wibbly Pig* had come on but Jack wasn't interested. He was up and on to his tricycle – it had recently been brought inside due to the April showers and Maddie hadn't bothered to take it back outside once the sunshine had arrived. Also she couldn't handle yet another toddler tantrum in response to saying 'no' to him.

But Jack was on full speed and rammed the armchair where Ruby had fallen asleep. Ruby woke up with a start and a scream. Jack screamed back at his baby sister before racing off around the house on three wheels, knocking over the pile of ironing that had been perched on the end of the sofa. Both children were now shrieking at the top of their voices.

Maddie ran a hand through her hair and encountered something sticky. It felt like Play-Doh. She tugged at it for a while before giving up. Perhaps she could get Neal to cut it out of her hair later before she went out.

But the problem wasn't how she looked. The problem was how she felt. Maddie was bored senseless with a side order of guilt for feeling that way.

Sighing, Maddie picked up the crying baby. Everything looked a mess, including herself. She wasn't even slummy mummy, let alone a yummy one.

She knew she was failing miserably in her attempts to be a perfect mum to her children. She was Mother Inferior.

Caroline Jones didn't have time to be bored with her life as a stay-at-home mother.

She logged into her email on her laptop whilst cradling her mobile between her ear and neck.

'We have one place left on the Tuesday class,' said the lady on the other end of the line. 'Would you like me to reserve it for you?'

'Yes, please,' said Caroline, relief flooding her voice. 'It's just such a rush on a Wednesday when Flora does her ballet class as well.'

'I understand. We'll transfer all of the future classes to Tuesday at 2 p.m. and cancel the Wednesday lessons.'

'Thank you so much,' said Caroline, as she grabbed her desk diary and placed it on the kitchen worktop.

She flipped over the page to the following week and scribbled 'Mandarin class, 2 p.m.' under Tuesday's heading.

She was so pleased she had been able to transfer the class to a different day of the week. Flora would continue to benefit from learning Mandarin and that was so important. It was such a good investment for her future with China becoming an international player in the world markets.

But Caroline also knew how much Flora's ballet classes should be valued as well. After all, health and fitness awareness could never be started too early. Plus correct deportment was so much better for her bone structure.

Flora might have enjoyed her disco classes when she was a younger but Caroline had found the hour unstructured at best. What was the point of taking Flora to a class where the benefits were minimal? As soon as she was over the age of two, Caroline had moved Flora into ballet classes and dropped the disco.

Caroline glanced at the clock. Four o'clock and she still had so much to do before going to Charley's house that evening. She didn't really want to go, reluctant to let Jeff take over the bedtime routine. It was so important, in these last precious months before Flora started school, that every effort was made to ensure her reading skills were up to scratch. Jeff was always a little too lax, always willing to succumb to his daughter's pleas to be read that dreadful *Maisie Mouse* book that his sister had bought Flora for her birthday. Caroline's choice was from the Oxford Reading Tree. Flora was already over halfway through level one.

But Caroline had known Charley since they had worked together and didn't want to let her down.

Besides, she always ended up enjoying the evenings with the girls. After college, she had been a top PA for six years at a blue chip manufacturing firm where Charley had been a secretary. They had bonded over their mutual loathing for the personnel department and had remained friends ever since.

Engaged at twenty-five to Jeff, Caroline was married at twenty-seven and pregnant at twenty-nine. Her life was orderly, planned, smooth. Even her titian hair was perfect and straight.

Caroline skimmed her emails. A couple of party invites which would have to be carefully dealt with. All of Caroline's diplomatic skills learnt from her career had been used to the full in weeding out any 'friends' from the playgroup whose parents might not share the ambitions for their children that Caroline had. It was all very well now but as soon as school began, so did the real work. Every attention needed to be paid to Flora's education. She and Jeff had scrimped together enough money for Flora to attend the private school for girls on the edge of the village.

Flora was still in her ballet outfit from that afternoon's class and Caroline's heart warmed as she watched her four-year-old daughter reading her *Angelina Ballerina* book. Dressed in her pale pink ballet outfit, her dark red hair swept back into a tidy bun, she was the splitting image of Caroline but thirty years younger.

Except Caroline hadn't been allowed to take ballet classes when she was a child. Or any other extra-curricular activities, come to that. No Brownies, no dancing. No extra tutoring when she fell behind with her maths. Everything that Caroline had achieved in her life had come from her own determination to make the best possible life for herself and, these past five years, her family.

Flora would have every benefit that Caroline hadn't been given. For her daughter's sake, she had to be a super mummy, an alpha mum. It was exhausting but it would be worth it. Of that she was certain.

Judy Gordon unpinned the butterfly brooch from the lapel of her black jacket and stared down at the gold detail. It had been on her mother's dressing table for most of her childhood. Not worn very often, of course. Perhaps at her grandmother's funeral. Judy wasn't sure. It had felt the right thing to wear it that afternoon.

There hadn't been many people at the funeral which saddened Judy but she wasn't entirely surprised. Her mother's social circle had diminished significantly once her husband had been sent to prison all those years ago. Nobody trusted a thief at a party. Or the wife of one either.

There had been a few close friends, some of whom were still alive and had been at the crematorium that afternoon. Dear old Sheila and Daphne, muttering under their breaths about how Judy's father had been scum and undeserving of his wife.

Judy didn't offer any defence of her father. Why should she? His infrequent visits between stays in prison had stopped sometime around her fifth birthday. From then on, it was just her and her mother.

Until Judy had fallen for Clive Gordon at the age of seventeen, that is. He had managed to stick around long enough to see their son Nick's sixth birthday. But then he too had left, deciding life would be much better spent in Spain with Tracy, the barmaid from their local pub.

Clive left behind a large mortgage for Judy to try and cope with and a son to bring up. She had never wanted the four-bedroom house in fancy Upper Grove. But her husband had made a deal with the landowner just after they were married. Another dodgy contract whose details Judy didn't want to know.

The house had never interested her enough for her to try and make it into a home. It was far too big for them, even after Nick came along.

Nick. Her twenty-year-old son. A chip off Clive's block. Another lazy, cheating, lying man in her life. But she had given birth to him so surely it was her fault that he had turned out so badly? He hadn't even bothered to finish school before leaving home at sixteen. Nick had turned up at infrequent periods ever since. He hadn't come to his grandmother's funeral, despite the promises that he would.

Judy looked out of the kitchen window and, as always, felt a little more optimistic as she stared out to the garden beyond. It was a riot of colour in the early May sunshine. Judy loved the chaotic nature of her country garden. Not for her the neat and tidy borders, everything clipped and restrained. Her garden was left to grow in wild abandon. And any place where a gap appeared, she would cram in a new plant or throw down some seeds.

Judy loved May, heralding the beginning of summer. Most of the plants weren't in bloom yet but the rhodendrons near the back were covered in bright pink and purple flowers. The fresh new leaves on the trees and plants were bright green, contrasting with the purple agapanthus and deep red tulips. The roses were in bud, just needing a little more rain and sunshine before revealing their true glory.

The garden had become Judy's refuge from the loud arguments and painful bruises that had been a staple of her marriage. After Clive had left, Judy had fled to the garden to escape the quiet house whilst Nick was at school. It had become her sanctuary, her favourite place in the world. It was her work of art and she loved it.

The garden was the only reason that Judy had continued to live in Upper Grove. She had no friends there. Nobody until Charley had moved in next door four years previously.

Judy had popped round as soon as the removal vans had left, desperate to size up the new neighbours, she had told Charley later. She was grateful to find Charley wasn't the sort of rich bitch who now inhabited their leafy avenue. Of course, Charley had become more affluent over the past couple of years thanks to Steve's business.

But at least Charley wasn't stuck-up like the other women down the road. She was easy to talk to and get along with. A bit of a lifesaver when the house felt too big and empty like it did that afternoon.

At this time of year there were lots of jobs that needed doing in the garden but she was glad she was heading over to Charley's place that evening. The other girls were nice and it was lucky they all got along so well, even though the only common factor amongst them was Charley.

Judy stared down at her mother's brooch in her hands. In any case, she didn't want to be alone that evening.